Stow Away Zone

The Sunrise Trilogy book 3

·Chris Towndrow

Valericain Press

Praise for Tow Away Zone (Sunrise Trilogy book 1)

"A gripping yarn - quirky characters, a pacy plot and a setting like you've never read before. A fun ol' read."
Paul Kerensa, Comedian & British Comedy Award-winning TV co-writer BBC's Miranda, Not Going Out, Top Gear

"Very enjoyable and easy to read with an unusual plot that keeps you guessing throughout. Highly recommended." ★★★★★
Amazon review

"This is a brilliant story. Clever, laugh-out-loud funny, and mysterious all at the same time. Heartily recommended." ★★★★★
Amazon review

"Really good fun to read with more than a touch of darkness, so much neon, a very odd pet and the best breakdown service on the planet. Very enjoyable and highly recommended!" ★★★★★
Amazon review

"An original, inventive storyline and a variety of three-dimensional characters that you will genuinely care about. Dialogue sharp enough to shave with, well-paced and bubbling with humour." ★★★★★
Amazon review

"In a surprising town a salesman finds everything he ever wanted. This is such an incredibly interesting story. I couldn't put it down. And I could never decide if the town was real or not. But the characters could have lived next door!" ★★★★★
Amazon review

"This is one of those books that will leave you with a smile on your face. Funny, relatable perfect characters, a story that kept me turning the pages and an ending that did not disappoint. This is a great book to take on holiday because it is light-hearted and fun." ★★★★★
Amazon review

"I struggle to compare this book with others. The words 'unique' and 'inventive' come to mind. The dialogue is well-crafted and funny, the characters are wonderfully individual, and the narrative is a kaleidoscope of colourful drama.
This book will stick with you." ★★★★★
Maddie – Professional editor

Valericain
Press

Valericain Press
Richmond, UK
www.christowndrow.co.uk

Publisher's Note: This is a work of fiction. Names, characters, places, and incidents are a product of the author's imagination. Locales and public names are sometimes used for atmospheric purposes. Any resemblance to actual people, living or dead, or to businesses, companies, events, institutions, or locales is completely coincidental.

Stow Away Zone / Chris Towndrow. -- 2021 ed.
978-1-9168916-4-7

For my family.

Chapter 1

It was only the third time he'd seen her cry.

No. Strike that.

It was only the third *thing* that had made her cry. She'd cried more than once about this—which was surprising. He'd expected it to shake her, perhaps cause a period of reflection, but tears? Not really.

After all, everybody dies. Often unexpectedly. Especially parents.

Even parents you weren't especially fond of.

Still, Beckman preferred it this way. It would have been odd if Lolita had brushed off Jack's passing— which, not six months earlier, she might have done. The reconciliation had come late, but thankfully not too late.

He felt blessed that he and dad were again on speaking terms.

You and Jack were both asses, dad, but I know I'll cry when the day comes.

Just don't make it too soon, huh?

He felt Lolita squeeze his hand and snapped out of the reverie.

'Okay?' she murmured.

'Isn't that my line?'

'Yeah, I'm fine. Well, as fine as I can be—you know, at a funeral. You daydreaming again?'

'Inner monologue is no respecter of circumstance.' He pulled a sheepish face. 'Sorry.'

She smoothed the lapel of his monochrome ensemble. 'At least you're here in body, if not in spirit.' She winked, and he felt blessed—for about the trillionth time in barely nine months—that she knew him inside out.

The funeral—this emotional dagger—was merely another boulder that Fate had cast in their path, testing that their relationship and fledgling marriage was up to the task. Well, Fate had come up short. Again.

Up your ass, Fate. We're stronger than that.

You tried bullets, flames, jealous rivals, high-stakes business high jinks, and even an interdimensional gateway.

Losing a diminutive and problematic paternal personage to Nature's inevitable exit door?

Lolita and I will cope.

You watch us.

For a second time in barely five seconds, he returned to the here-and-now. His life's anchor was displaying The Eyebrow—surely at his latest introspection.

He smiled. The temptation to compliment her resurfaced, but he suppressed it again. Yes, she did look great in black, though this was one hundred percent neither time nor place for such aesthetic levity. He'd get more than The Eyebrow for a mistimed inference of shenanigans—probably a slap on the ass… and this was one hundred percent not the time for intramarital cheek-whackery.

Instead, he gazed around.

People were starting to drift away from the wake—and there were *plenty* of people to be drifting.

It felt like half the town were there. Almost all the employees of Milan Lighting had attended. Reba and Randall had offered condolences and then kept a respectful distance. Tyler and Amaryllis had driven over from Pegasus' head office specially. Even longtime business rival Walter Whack had conjured a few friendly words.

If anything had *specifically* caught his eye, it was the proximity of sometime thorn-in-the-side Wanda Whack and Milan's own Mack Hood, head of Warehousing. Despite Mack's 58 years shading Wanda's age by a clear two decades, the closeness was undoubtedly rooted in more than event-based conversation.

'Mack and Wanda?' he asked out of the corner of his mouth, hoping this classed as acceptable small-talk.

'It would be a damn interesting rebound after Carlton,' Lolita replied.

'Mack once told me he'd crashed more than his fair share of forklifts.'

'Well, nothing wrong with his eyesight. Wanda looks… good in black, I have to say.'

Huh? So she gets away with that kind of comment?

Just don't speak your mind, i.e. don't agree. (Although she's not wrong).

'I hope his inability to judge speed and apertures doesn't carry into his home life.'

Lolita fixed him a glare of mock disbelief, then shook her head. 'I know you're trying to lighten the tone on a dark day, honey, but I'm fine. Really.'

Except, she hadn't looked fine. Perplexed, if he had to pick a word. Maybe even disappointed. Pissed off, at a push. Sadness was to be expected; being rankled—no.

He opened his mouth to enquire about it, but the answer was stayed by the appearance of a short, middle-aged woman whose blonde hair was swept dramatically back at the sides.

Lolita visibly backed off. 'Mary-Ann,' she said, deferentially—maybe warily.

'Lolita, thank you for letting me come and pay my respects.'

'I try to rise above most things—especially for an occasion like this.'

Another enemy at the gates? Skeleton from the closet?

Mary-Ann sighed sadly. 'Look, I said it before, but this will be the last time.' She looked Lolita in the eye. 'There was never anything between Jack and me. You two weren't close, but I knew him well—just not *that* well.'

Lolita made a throaty noise. 'Hmm. I guess he and I made up.'

'Good. I didn't ever bury the hatchet with my father. So I know that holding grudges is dumb.' She reached out and, after hesitation, touched Lolita's sleeve. 'Especially for things which aren't true. There was no affair. You have my word. I worked for him. That was it. Period.'

Beckman's gaze explored Lolita's face. She didn't seem convinced. He was. To a student of human behaviour, Mary-Ann's honesty was plain as day. The problem was, his view didn't matter a fig.

'A lot of after-hours overtime, Mary-Ann—you have to admit. A lot of weekends away.'

'Jack worked hard—you know that. And it didn't do a whole lot of good. I tried to tell him, but we both know he was a workaholic.' She looked at her feet, then put her shoulders back for the final word. 'Don't think bad of him for a lie. I only wish Ginetta hadn't created the lie—or at least believed it.'

Lolita shrugged. 'Hindsight is twenty-twenty, huh?'

'He was a good man.'

'He was an ass.'

Mary-Ann simply gazed around the scene. 'Maybe. But a popular one.' She nodded solemnly. 'I'm sorry for your loss.'

Lolita gathered a sigh, let it out, then gathered civility and dissipated that too. 'Thank you, Mary-Ann.'

The woman, who Beckman now gathered, was departed Jack's departed PA, departed.

A waiter appeared, bearing a drinks tray.

Lolita waved him away.

Well, I was thirsty, but I guess I'm not now.

Don't be an ass, Beckman. Just because one has left this world, it doesn't open a defacto vacancy.

Let your wife deal.

The breeze around the outdoor area had keened, so he buttoned his jacket.

She faced him. 'I think I'm about done now, Beckman.'

'Whatever you say.'

She forced a smile. 'However long I stand here, he'll still be dead.' Yet, she again glanced around the thinning throng, and that expression of perturbation returned.

'Is everything okay? I mean, apart from—'

'It's nothing.'

'You can't kid me, baby. It's not nothing. Is it... Mary-Ann?'

She clasped his arm and turned them away from prying eyes and ears. 'It's Buck, okay?' she hissed.

He swallowed. He'd noticed it too—if an absence of something was technically a noticeable 'it'.

'There'll be an explanation,' he said, as mollifying as possible.

'There better damn well be.'

'Maybe he couldn't get staff cover to be able to leave the café.'

'He should have closed it. It's like he doesn't care— today of all days.' She shook her head in disbelief.

'Maybe he's away. Out of town.'

'He's never left Sunrise. Makes me look like a goddamn globetrotter.'

Beckman bit his lip. 'He could be sick.'

'I've never heard him be sick a day in his life.'

He gently cupped her waist. 'Look, Dixon isn't here either. Think positively—maybe they eloped.'

He flashed a cheesy grin, hoping for at least a straight-line mouth to replace her downward curve. Even The Eyebrow would have been a break from vexed indignation.

'I know you're trying, Beckman. But maybe don't. He's the closest friend I have in the world, and it's days like this he proves his worth. And he's not here. Sad—I can do that. Pissed off should not be on the radar.'

As he prepared to dredge up an appropriate response, he was saved again by the bell.

'Miss Milan?' came a male voice.

Lolita's eyes flared, then the muscles in her face pulled the eyes back to normal and painted a half-decent sweet smile on her tactfully-lipsticked lips.

Will she correct this guy's Miss misstep? At the moment, he'd be lucky to get away without a swift right hook.

'Yes?' she enquired.

The owner of the voice sported a shabby navy suit, badly-tied burgundy tie, and a haircut seemingly delivered by a barber on PCP.

He extended a hand. 'Clarke Brollock. We haven't met.'

Not sure that meeting now is a stellar idea, buddy.

She nodded tersely. He retracted his hand.

'Mr Brollock.'

'Firstly, my condolences.'

'Thank you.'

'I never truly knew your father, but I heard many good things.'

Where from? Your barber?

'Jack had… his strengths. And his moments.'

Brollock nodded, apparently sagely. Beckman wasn't buying it—whatever the guy was selling.

'And was very successful, by all accounts,' the visitor said.

'Uh-huh.'

'I'm proud of my cousin.'

Lolita's head cocked. 'Cousin?'

'Distant.'

'Uh-huh.'

'How distant?' she asked.

Beckman recognised that tone. It was a Here's-A-Spade-How-Deep-Can-I-Help-You-Dig special.

'We were… estranged—let's say that. But still related. Oh yes, most definitely so.'

'Oh. Excellent. Well, it's good to meet you, Mr Bollock—'

'Brollock.'

'—yes. So, your appearance here today would be by way of enquiring about the date of the Will reading. The division of inheritances—things like that.'

Crazy Hair bowed somewhat graciously. 'I can't deny that's a factor. That, and paying my respects, of course.'

'Of course.' Lolita smiled thinly.

'Jack didn't have much family, so…' Brollock ran a fat hand through his unkempt follicular disaster area. 'So it's important that I be in town at this time. For support, and such.'

'And such.'

'Indeed.'

Beckman sensed the boiling blood and fake charm rise up through Lolita's body as if they were the waters of Old Faithful.

She beamed. 'Here's the thing, Mr Bollock—'

'Brollock.'

'—yes. Whilst Jack and I didn't see eye to eye, and his days as a family man... tailed off somewhat, there was always this. He happily talked about his modest crop of relatives, and damn sure as mustard, you're not one of them.' She leant in. 'What you are is a piece of ambulance-chasing pond life. An opportunistic scum-sucking mollusc. I may not be the most widely-travelled woman in the neighbourhood, but I think I'd know if I had any long-lost relatives! So, seeing as my Head of Security is also here, offering their condolences, I suggest you make yourself lost—and remain lost, before you get dragged out on your dime-store-suited ass.'

Lolita beckoned to the aforementioned staff member, and Clarke Brollock's gaze followed the direction of his intended con victim's arm.

Upon seeing the person, Clarke sneered.

Lolita leant in. 'Iolanda can bench-press one fifty. She's also a seventh dan Taekwondo-do master. But, go ahead, pick a fight in the middle of my father's wake.' She rolled up her right sleeve. 'I dare you.'

Chapter 2

Beckman lazily steered the Mustang across town.

The March afternoon was clear, cool and bright, but the atmosphere within the car was sombre and frosty.

He loosened his black tie.

She looked across, and a sad smile caressed her lips.

'What?' he asked. 'What'd I do?'

'Nothing. Just thinking how ironic it is that after being Mr Monochrome for most of your life, then finally getting a release into a world of colour, you actually rock that look.'

'Yeah—I'm the life and soul, huh? Give me a black suit and a crying wife, and I'm in my element.' He blew out a sigh.

'I didn't mean anything by it.'

'I know. And I'd much rather not to have to wear this get-up.'

Her hand clasped his, where it rested on the quinquagenarian gear shift. 'People die, Beckman.'

'And assholes crawl out of the woodwork and try to take advantage, it seems.'

She chuckled. 'The nerve of the guy. A secret relative? Jeez, that's lame.'

'Well, if Brollock doesn't get the message, we can always ask Randall to pay him a visit. I'm sure he'd come out of retirement for a... quiet word, even if not a full-on hit.'

She waved it away. 'Randall's done plenty for me—us. Everyone has. Look at today. Part of me feels bad for not believing that dad was… I don't know… *liked.*'

'Ever think that everyone turned up for you, not him?'

'I don't deserve that much love.'

'You seemed pretty keen on Buck being there to show you some.'

She pounded a fist into her leg. 'Dammit, yes! I know I have you, honey—I know that. Even so, a little damn support would have been nice. You've had that bear hug of his—you know what it's like.'

He recalled such supportive embraces during the past year's travails and couldn't deny their efficacy. To Lolita, who'd regarded Buck as a father figure for almost two decades, those hugs were as close to a comfort blanket as she had.

Beckman's own embraces were a different animal; his presence and words vital, but not comparable to those of a longtime friend who knew Lolita better than Beckman did—and maybe ever would. They hadn't seen him for a few days—that was true; other things had commanded their attention. Lolita had shuttled between home, the office and the funeral directors, often sullen.

The man's absence was indeed a mystery. Beckman hoped for a non-serious and straightforward explanation. After Brollock's unwitting stoking of Lolita's fire on such an emotional day, Buck had better watch his step, or Lolita might roll up both sleeves this time.

The cheerful neons in the window of Our Buck's café counterpointed the invisible grouchy fug hanging over Beckman and Lolita as he led her to the door.

He'd eschewed the coffee available at the wake—they seldom caffeinated themselves at anywhere other than Buck's or at home—so his bloodstream needed topping up. Hopefully, it would elevate their moods as well as their heart rates.

The café was sparsely populated. Buck was at the counter, busy with Bessie, the brewing behemoth. The bear-sized proprietor glanced up, then continued his travails.

Was the man remaining cordially distant, avoiding cheery greetings on a day which didn't warrant them?

Lolita strode to the counter. Beckman swallowed hard.

'What did I do?'

Buck calmly set down the cloth. 'Pardon me?'

'What did I do—to be abandoned today?'

'*You* abandoned?'

'Yeah, me. I mean, you're the guy in town who knows everything that's going on. Did a little wake sneak under your radar?'

After a brief staring match, Buck scooped up the cloth and resumed wiping down the counter.

'What did I miss?' She shrugged theatrically. 'Something more important than a huge event in my life? Huh? *Buddy*?'

'Take a seat. I'll bring your order.' Buck didn't look up.

Lolita audibly took a deep breath. 'If it's a medical thing, I wish you'd tell me because you and I don't do secrets, and I'll give you all the rope on this, and I can't have any more heartache right now than worrying if—'

Buck slapped the cloth down. 'Dixon left. Okay?' He locked Lolita in a stare tinged with despair.

'What?'

'She left. Gone. But what do you care, huh?'

'Pardon me?'

Beckman's arms tingled in the electric air.

'She dumped me. She's gone. And where were you? Nowhere.' Buck picked up the cloth and wiped, furiously, redundantly, on the clean wooden surface.

Beckman glanced around the room; evidently, the voices hadn't carried to the light-hearted drinkers and diners.

Lolita's face set hard. 'In case you weren't aware, I've had other things on my mind.'

'Yeah—making me superfluous, it seems. Some friend.'

'I've been running a hundred-million-dollar business and burying my damn father. Sorry if that's too inconvenient for you.'

'And you have the nerve to come in here and try to chew me out about missing a *wake*? When it's all I can do to hold my own heart together.'

'It's a breakup, Buck. Get over it.'

Buck's teeth set on edge. 'It's a funeral, Lolita. Get over it.'

Her eyes flared. Beckman reached for her hand, trying to steady her temper. She swatted it away. 'I thought friends supported each other.'

'I thought you cared about my relationship—certainly a damn sight more than your asshole father.'

She leant in. 'Pardon me?!'

'You hated the guy. What's the big issue?'

'Hated, past tense. He's still my father.'

'And she was my girl. And I loved her.'

Lolita shook her head vehemently. 'Uh-huh. Death beats love. Relationships come and go. Lives don't. Parents don't.'

Buck jabbed a finger at Beckman, who wondered what he'd done.

Existed, it seemed.

'You've got *him* now. So wound up in your own love, and money-making, and giving a lot of thought to a person like Jack—who played second fiddle to me in your life for years—and you don't care I got my heart broken this week.'

'It's not that I don't care, it's that—'

'Well, that's what it looks like. I needed you, Lolita, and you were nowhere.'

'I. Was. Busy,' she hissed.

'And I was grieving too. So get off your damn high horse.'

'Grieving, my ass.'

Buck thumped the counter. 'She was the one. My last shot at happiness. Gone. Back to the big city.' He bowled the dirty cloth into the trash can beside him. 'I wish I'd let her drive into that damn Portal.'

'What?' Lolita exclaimed.

'I shouldn't have bothered.' He eyed her straight. 'Looks like I'm not worth any woman's time. Even yours.'

'You wish she'd *died*?' Her mouth hung open.

'We don't know it's fatal going in there. Hell—you survived.'

'Even so, that's unbelievable spite. It's burning your bridges. Who knows—maybe she'll come back.'

Buck shook his head. 'Not in a million years.'

'People change.'

'Damn right they do.' He looked her up and down in disdain.

Lolita's lip curled. 'So maybe they won't come back. Ever.'

She grabbed Beckman's hand, tugged hard, and strode out like she'd tossed a match onto a pool of gasoline.

Chapter 3

Beckman clamped his mouth shut and left it closed all the way home. If finding something appropriate to say at Jack's funeral was like traversing a tightrope, it was a cakewalk compared to his current position.

Mercifully, Lolita didn't say anything, or look like she expected him to either.

He pulled onto the sloping drive at 1002 Edison Avenue, double-checked the parking brake was on tight, and followed her into the house.

Try not to say something dumb like, "We didn't even get to have coffee."

She must have heard those silent words because she went straight to the espresso maker and fired it up.

He tried to discern her demeanour and formulate what might be a good opening gambit. He knew it wasn't him that she was angry at, but he was still within the detonation radius.

Had she really lashed out at Buck because of what he did, or was it Brollock's fault, or merely her own pervading sadness and emptiness? Or was there another unexplored layer beneath?

Her attention was locked on the coffee machine, trance-like, so he gathered the cups and creamer together and brought them over.

'I used to have a real dad, and a fake one—a stand-in. Now I've got neither.' She hadn't looked up.

'You have a husband, if that's any consolation. I give pretty good hugs, and I can be an ass sometimes, so maybe that's a twofer.'

She glanced around, and he was sure he saw a gust of despondency leave her lips. That was good—it was better let out than kept inside.

He opened his arms.

She gingerly came closer, took his embrace gently, then pressed in tight.

Hugs are hard to screw up. Words, not so much.

He let her just be, while the espresso maker whirred and his heart clattered. Her breath was warm and noisy on his neck.

Not for the first time in their relationship, he wanted to suck all her pain away. The grief would pass. The nuclear detonation at Buck's? It felt like a fallout that would outlive them both. Yet, the friendship would only remain broken if he allowed it to be. The least he could do was—however slowly or tactfully—to engineer a peace.

'If you know what's good for you—for us,' she said quietly, 'You won't go back into that… place and try some dumb, misplaced, secret reconciliation stunt. This was my argument, not yours.' She drew back and looked at him squarely, arms around his neck. 'Promise me you won't go back.'

He raised a palm. 'Agreed. I like my balls, and I get the feeling either you or Buck would rip them off.'

She cupped his cheek. 'It's not the end of the world, okay? It just damn well feels like it.'

'At the risk of losing the ol' Spiers *cojones* without trying to surreptitiously step out for world-class root beer, is there something else chewing at your gut? I'm not an expert on losing a loved one, but I'd swear that big heart of yours is leaking a few drops about something else.' He unwrapped her arms. 'Or, you know, I could butt out?'

She examined his face, clearly cogitating, so he submitted to the interrogation whilst also enjoying the view of her eyes and everything that surrounded it. The painted, pursed lips; the tumbling chocolate curls; the button nose.

'I basically forced Jack to retire. The company was his life. He had nothing to do. Retirement kills people—it's a fact.' She sighed. 'So maybe I was responsible.'

She silently gathered the coffee things together and brewed their long-delayed drinks.

Beckman spent the time musing.

He took her hand and led her into the sitting room. They plonked into the comfortable sofa.

He sipped. 'Here's another angle. His company was soaring—under your guidance. You two made peace after a long war. He saw that you finally snagged the awesome husband you deserved all along—'

She flashed The Eyebrow (Amused version).

'—and all that happiness caused his heart to overflow, and it couldn't cope anymore.'

'Hmm.'

'Just an idea.'

'Better than my idea, though.'

'Much better.'

She toyed with her cup. 'Maybe I'll go with yours. I don't need any more shit in my head at the moment.'

'Amen to that.'

She drained her cup, set it down, sank back into the cushion and stared at the ceiling.

'Awesome husband?' she queried after a minute.

'Yeah?'

'Mary-Ann—did you buy it? Mr People Watcher. Mr… Student Of Behaviours And Motives.'

'One hundred percent. She's either studied Stanislavski and is chillier than a shipping container of cucumbers at the South Pole, or she's on the level, and Jack never had an affair.'

Lolita took Beckman's hand and fingered the wedding band. 'It hurts me to say, but I agree.'

'Why "hurts"?'

'Because it means mum and I wasted a lot of years resenting the man. It was one of the reasons she left town. It's a hell of a come-down to be wrong about that. I'd already re-evaluated his Ass Quotient. Seems I need to go further.'

'It cuts both ways, baby. When Carlton was two-timing you, that seemed pretty plain as day. Yet Jack did nothing. Even you didn't know the truth. Sometimes we only see what we want to see—what suits our purposes.'

'Hmm. Am I that self-serving?'

'You're fallible. Like us mortals.'

'Now I know you're *deliberately* being an ass.' She playfully slapped his hand.

'Well, it made you smile, and after a day like today, I'll willingly accept that role.' He brushed hair from her cheek. 'Now, go take a long bath, and I'll try and make a half-decent dinner.'

The sun wasn't over the yardarm, but he felt she deserved something less innocent than a coffee to go with her ablutions. Hence, a few minutes later, he took a beer up to the ensuite.

Now, we both know that part of you—a specific part—is maybe hoping to get a flash of something appealing during the course of this gesture. The main thing is not to take advantage of it, okay?

Lolita was in underwear, sitting on the (closed) toilet seat. Something familiar was in her hands. She caught wind of his arrival and hastily threw the cassette in the small wastebasket.

The whole Lolita-in-underwear spectacle was instantly brushed aside by another thought belting through his mind.

She closed her eyes in tell-tale guilt.

He pressed the beer into her hand. 'Might this be a sharing thing too?' he asked as comfortingly as he could muster, even as his spirits yoyoed with the possible outcomes of what she'd just done.

'It's okay. Test was negative. I was late, again.'

'You sound relieved.'

'I am.'

His shoulders fell. 'Oh. Okay.'

'What?'

'Would it be so bad? Having a child with me? Look at it this way—if they have your brains *and* your looks, it wouldn't be terrible.'

'No, Beckman, it's not that. It's…' She sank onto the edge of the bath.

'What it would do to your work life?'

'Just… life in general.'

He perched beside her, backside inches from the foamy dip she'd prepared. 'I suppose we never had that important conversation.'

'Not now, honey. I don't want another fight.'

'Would we fight?'

'I hope not. Look, the timing is way off—that's all. You have to admit, it's been a crazy few months. Carlton, the merger, the fire, the wedding, Jack…. It's just that I could do with a break, not another thing to worry about.'

'For how long?'

She held up a finger. 'If the words "clock" and "ticking" pass your lips, a dunking will be the least of your problems.'

He plucked that finger from the air and caressed it. 'Okay.'

'I just lost my dad and best friend on the same day. If you're that desperate to nest, get a pet.'

'"Desperate" makes me sound… desperate.'

'Okay—disappointed. I'm not. It's a small blessing at the end of a bad day. There's plenty of time for a mini-me. Or, if we get unlucky, a mini-you.' She smiled.

He kissed her. He loved it when she was as irreverent and cheeky as he was.

'You're right. You mostly always are. It's been a hell of a year for me too. Lot of upheaval. Some calm, some space—some *us* time would be good.'

'No traumas, no surprises. You, me, and our new life.'

He kissed her again, which was no chore.

Don't ask if she wants help scrubbing her back. We're not off the emotional teeter-totter yet.

She rose. 'Let's just get the Will done tomorrow, wrap up Jack's affairs and get on with our lives. Maybe if we get lucky, there'll be a secret bank account, and we can open our own coffee place, so I don't have to see that so-called friend of mine again.'

Chapter 4

It was an auspicious day, Tyler Quittle mused as he piloted the Porsche from Jack's wake towards Sunrise's Main Street. Unfortunate that it clashed with a solemn occasion, but those were the breaks.

Besides, the event hadn't been a total maudlin-fest. He was proud as a peacock on the arm of Amaryllis, who looked damn fine, and they'd met some interesting folks. Except, of course, a douche by the name of Ballsack or similar. It was a refreshing change for Tyler *not* to be the person at any gathering who was the monumental jerk.

The flag-bearer for the scope of his rebirth was the significance of the date: their six-month anniversary. He didn't recall having a relationship that lasted six months. Six weeks was a pretty stellar achievement.

Now? There were plenty of new female faces at the funeral, and he hadn't given one a second look.

Life was rosy: the investment in Milan Lighting was looking like a sure-fire winner; his nine-month tenure at the helm of Pegasus had yielded good results; he had a classy and desirable woman on his arm, and they had spent many happy days getting to know Sunrise and its inhabitants.

He had friends. Proper friends.

All it had taken for this to happen had been a near-death experience. Based on today, not dying was a great result. He wondered how many would be at his wake, years from now. Hopefully, *many* years from now. More than there could have been.

'Penny for your thoughts.' Amaryllis gently squeezed his thigh.

He focussed on her, then the road ahead. 'Nothing important.'

'Mortality? Blessings? Regrets?'

'Nothing so deep. I was wondering if it's appropriate to go for a fancy dinner tonight.'

Granted, he didn't *technically* think that, but it was in the ballpark.

'Because of the date?' she asked, with a knowing smile.

'A good boyfriend would have booked something and kept it secret, huh?'

She laughed. '"Boyfriend"? At forty-three? Me, I mean, you young whippersnapper. From what I know, you've never stayed the course long enough to qualify for the term.'

He held up a hand. 'Busted, okay? So—do you think it's… disrespectful?'

'For you to wine and dine me?'

'And check-in to The Sunset to avoid a late drive home?'

She looked over the top of her glasses. 'I know what *that* is code for.'

He held up both hands. 'Very busted.'

'Yes, lover boy—take me out for our anniversary, and then find a nice big bed for us to *not* rest our bodies at the end of a long day.'

'Amaryllis, you're the best *girlfriend* ever.'

'By a long way, I'm sure I am, Tyler darling.'

Main Street was oddly quiet—he guessed many folks from the wake had gone home to consider the self-same mortality/blessings/regrets that Amaryllis had propounded.

He slid the car into a space near Our Buck's, loosened his tie, gestured her ahead, and watched her locomote towards the door. It was allowed, he comforted himself, because he was still getting used to the novelty of *legitimately* eyeing up an unavailable woman—unavailable to everyone else.

Buck greeted them with an unusually terse nod. Tyler put it down to the subdued nature of the day—Buck was probably feeling grief by osmosis from Lolita.

They found a table and awaited the proprietor's attention.

After a longer wait than usual, Buck attended.

Tyler had only known the man six months, but even so, he'd never seen the big bear appear to be carrying the weight of the world on his broad shoulders.

'Bad day? We can hold the fort if you want to close early.'

Buck eyed him suspiciously. 'What do you care?'

'I thought we were friends.'

'Friends come and go,' Buck proclaimed.

Tyler was bemused. 'We never went anywhere.'

Amaryllis touched Buck's shoulder. 'What is it? Pretty serious if you missed the funeral.'

Again, Buck weighed this, as if assessing whether this was a trap.

Amaryllis pulled out a chair and gestured.

Tyler glowed inside. For a woman who'd been terse and distant for so many years, it masked a big heart and a kindly, almost matronly quality at times. Plus, she had a streak of wicked humour. Oh, and he enjoyed the not-sleeping part of sleeping together.

Buck caved in and sat heavily down. 'Dixon left. Permanently.'

'Shit,' Tyler breathed.

'Oh heavens,' Amaryllis said. Swearing, Tyler knew, was rarely on the menu.

'Why?' he asked.

Buck blew a hurricane from his lungs and rested huge paws on the table. 'She didn't feel at home here.'

'What's not to like?'

'Not enough cut and thrust—that's what she said.'

'So it wasn't you, or her, or a bust-up?'

Buck shook his head. 'Big fish, used to swimming in a deep ocean. Ran out of air in this little pond.' he gestured around disconsolately.

Amaryllis rose. 'I'll get drinks.' She pressed Buck into his seat—no mean feat. 'You stay.'

Buck looked nervous, then nodded.

Tyler watched his girlfriend/lover/PA/gal walk to the counter, and hoped she wouldn't try anything too complex, break something, and make Buck's lousy day worse.

'So the pull of the big man didn't beat the gravity of the big city.'

'It's just too slow here, she said.'

'She didn't even start at Milan yet. Was that it—bailing before her garden leave was up?'

Buck shrugged. 'I dunno. She was honest—I give her that. She felt she *owed* it to me to stay, after what we did for her, but the love wasn't strong enough.'

'But she never gave it a real chance.'

'Don't lecture me. With all due respect, you never had your heart broken like this. One-night stands don't do that, huh?'

Tyler hung his head. 'I guess not.'

Buck stroked the tabletop. 'So, a second time, I've been left for a city type who wants what I—and

Sunrise—can't give. So that's it. I'm done. My heart's not getting any younger. It's closing time for this Romeo.'

'You can't do that.'

'Like I say, you're a nice guy, Tyler, but you were never engaged like I was years ago. Or had something real. Probably never even been in love.'

That cut Tyler a little. 'True. I never was in love—not before now.'

At that moment, Amaryllis appeared, drinks in her hand and wide-eyed delight on her face.

He knew she'd heard. He smiled, coughed, composed himself, and pulled out the chair for her.

Inside, a part of him cursed Buck for making him say that aloud. Yet, he didn't regret it. Or deny it. He didn't know how he felt about it. It was just so alien.

Chapter 5

Beckman carefully studied Lolita at breakfast, seeking clues to her state of mind.

Luckily, she'd provided a clue with her attire. She sported a mustard yellow swing dress and matching hair bow. A massive change from yesterday's sobriety, sure, but also a barometer of mood: she'd picked out something to instil an upbeat, carefree demeanour.

He recalled the morning after their first night together, when she'd revealed her extensive wardrobe of swing dresses: it seemed to be all she ever wore. It had been the clothing of choice for two reasons, (1) she looked terrific, and (2) it pissed off Jack, who considered it chintzy and beneath her.

Since she'd reconciled with Jack, her desire to rankle him had waned, and she'd thinned out her collection. Now, with no agenda behind the decision, she wore it to give herself a lift. Maybe even to remind herself of happier days.

What he saw was the girl he'd spotted across a certain café and, pretty quickly, fallen hard for.

'I see you watching me, Beckman Spiers.'

Busted.

'Planning how not to put my foot in my mouth—or a bear trap. That's all.'

She stroked his arm. 'It's fine. My 101 is not to snap at you—for anything. I lost too much already, and I don't want to piss you off when you did nothing.'

'Okay.'

'Except sometimes be a bit of an idiot.'

He shrugged. 'Comes with the territory. And the marriage license.'

'I'm not perfect either.'

'I'll take the Fifth on that.'

'Hmm.' She plonked onto the breakfast bar stool and chewed on a bagel. 'Do you think I was out of line with Buck yesterday?'

Time for a politically correct, manhood-retaining answer.

'I think, even in his obvious heartbreak at losing Dixon, he could have spared a couple of hours to offer you his shoulder to lean on. Hell—maybe it would have been good for you both to share your woes.'

'Yeah, I thought so.'

'All the same—and noting where you're coming from—I know you loved him, but I'd hope I was sufficient sounding board now. If not, what's marriage for?'

'Is it wrong to want both a longtime soulmate *and* a new husband on my side in times of crisis? Am I just greedy?'

He pondered. 'Buck has done a lot for you before, so I don't know why the blind spot now. He's not himself. Maybe *he* thinks I'm sufficient for you now. Maybe he thinks you don't care, because you weren't there to be a shoulder for *him* to cry on.'

'He's big and ugly enough to take care of himself.'

'He'll have to be now, won't he?'

Her eyes narrowed. 'Let's move on, shall we?'

Nearly, buddy. Almost stepped over the edge there.

Because her dress would occupy most of the Miata's cabin, they took the pony car for the ride across town to the executor's office.

He debated avoiding Main Street—as it contained a certain verboten premises—but as they couldn't do that forever, he chanced that the sight of Our Buck's wouldn't raise her hackles.

As they passed, his mind turned to the problem of sourcing the best available coffee and root beer until this episode was over (he hoped it would be finite and not eternal). For now, they'd have to get their repasts at either Jen & Berry's diner or Winston's Coffee. Alternatively, they could source beverages for use at home.

Was it feasible to find out where Buck procured his beans and root beer? The man guarded that secret like it was the Holy Grail, but surely he didn't have a monopoly with the supplier?

Maybe if I secretly meet Esme, Buck's go-to barista, she'd spill the beans about the beans?

Hmm. Risky, but possible. I'll need to get on her good side first. Wonder if she gets headaches? Pegasus' little brown box miracle cure is a great way to win hearts and minds.

Patience, young caffeine detective. One day at a time.

'I hope this isn't too tedious. I could do with throwing myself back into work.'

'Absolutely,' he replied.

'What do you think the old gnome has in store for me? I have his company. Apart from the house, what else could there be? A dirty secret? A way to screw me from beyond the grave? A secret brother I never knew I had? We turn up, and some mystery guy is sitting there, and he gets all the stuff?' She peered over the top of her sunglasses.

Clearly, yesterday's disquiet was still causing gentle aftershocks. Still, sarcasm was a significant improvement on ire.

'But you don't want *stuff*, honey. You're not that shallow. And you've already met one non-existent secret relative.'

'I should let it go, huh?'

'Ideally. I thought you were re-evaluating Jack.'

'I was. But if this Will is a screw-over, it'll prove his recent behaviour was a front, and the leopard was only wearing a thin jacket.'

Beckman dearly hoped this meeting was duller than dull, because they didn't need any more dragons to slay.

Chapter 6

The offices of Spodge & Sons stood out on the street like a wonky tooth. Photon Avenue was a short side-turning off the main thoroughfare. Still, this office predated the other buildings by decades, if not a century. Perhaps this was where the original, one-horse town of Sunrise was centred... if such a thing ever existed?

Wonder if it's now populated by Spodge's great-great-great-grandchildren?

Always demand for lawyers, though. Wonder if this one's a sharp-suited, overpaid, wordy nimrod?

Let's go see.

The receptionist (young, bright, quite the antithesis of the pre-watershed Miss Broomhead) directed them to a door on the short, dark, narrow corridor. Lolita's dress lit up the place like the sun.

The door was shut. Beckman leant an ear towards it. Was that... heavy metal music?

He and Lolita shared an amused glance, then he knocked. The music ceased.

The door was opened by a wiry man of about sixty. Bald at the front, white hair started halfway back on his head and was almost as long as Lolita's.

Don't stare.

A bony hand extended. 'Jeremiah Spodge. Mrs Milan?'

'Yes.' She shook, then Beckman followed.

It felt like meeting Death.

Appropriate, huh?

Spodge (generation as yet indeterminate) showed them into his office. It was piled high with papers and had bookcases on every side except the window.

'Will thee sit?'

Yes, thee will.

Lolita flashed him The Eyebrow (Curious version).

Spodge shuffled papers on his desk as Beckman shuffled his buttocks on the worn cloth seat.

'The representatives of the estate here assembled are the sum total of attendees?'

Lolita glanced around. 'Yes. There's just us. Were you expecting more?'

'There is one more name in the document, Mrs Milan, however one was unable to make communique with thy maternal parent.'

(Beckman has finally gotten used to his belle being addressed in this way. As the Milan name carried such weight in Sunrise, he hadn't really expected her to take on the Spiers moniker.)

'I'm not sure mom would care to be here anyway. Being within ten miles of Jack, even in a coffin, would probably still be too much.' She sighed.

Beckman surmised that Lolita's exhale was less about the estrangement and more about her realisation that it had been misplaced. It showed that she considered forgiving Jack some of his antics. Whether her mother would was much less certain... if they ever saw her again (or even met her, in Beckman's case).

'As a lifelong resident of this conurbation, one has gleaned that not all was well in the household.' Spodge shuffled papers. 'Then let us commence.'

The opening few minutes were procedural legalese, made more lengthy and impenetrable by Spodge's rather *individual* phrasing.

Next came confirmation that only Lolita and her mother were named in the Will, and her shoulders relaxed.

Then came the short list of bequests: the house (not a surprise), effects and 'automobiles' (ditto), shares in a company Beckman hadn't heard of (reaction TBC, dependent on windfall), and debts ($279 in late fees on a library book Jack had clearly forgotten he'd borrowed).

'There is one final item,' Spodge intoned, 'Which one shall outline in a moment. In the meantime, there is the question of the bequest to Mrs Ginetta Milan.'

'What is it?' Lolita asked.

The executor thumbed through the sheaf of papers and pulled out a sealed envelope. On the front was handwritten, "Ginny".

Lolita peered at it. 'I take it that this is personal, addressee only.'

'It would seem so, from the cartography in thy father's hand.'

'Could you post it?'

'One has not been able to locate Mrs Milan *senior*'s address at this juncture.'

'Can... we take it? And pass it on to her? If I promise not to open it, cross my heart and hope to die?'

'Are thee availed of the address of the aforesaid individual?'

'No. I mean, not at the moment. But, we do have a Private Eye or two in town, if you get my drift.'

Jeremiah Spodge raised a single, thin, grey eyebrow.

Anything you can do, honey, he can do... older?

Beckman cleared his throat. 'I think what Mrs Milan *junior* means is that we'll move heaven and earth to get that important *missive* into the hands of the addressee. Unless, of course, Mr Milan—*deceased*—indicated that it was to be delivered directly, i.e. to whit without an intermediary.'

Spodge raised the second eyebrow in line with the first.

Beckman glanced at his consort.

Aha! You can't do that trick, baby. Old Spodge is one hundred percent more Eyebrow articulate than you.

On the flip side, you look a damn sight better in that dress than he would.

Spodge looked at Lolita. 'That will be… acceptable.' He tendered the envelope.

She took it and unsubtly checked her wristwatch (a genuine 1950s example, oval, in white gold, which he'd bought as a wedding gift).

In the absence of a third eyebrow to raise, Spodge coughed a reedy cough and cast his gaze down at the papers.

'The final item. The most important, critical item.'

'Okay,' Lolita said nervously.

Spodge rose glacially and went to one of the bookcases. He pressed on one spine and an entire panel of books, maybe two feet square, sunk back and slid aside.

Ah. The old safe-behind-a-bookcase trick. Very intriguing. And cool, obviously.

Just don't let on that you think it's cool. That would not be cool.

The spindly administrator dialled the combination with practised efficiency, swung the door open and withdrew something. Then he reversed the procedure, shutting away other secrets and valuables, and retook his seat.

He placed the item on the table. It was a wooden box, nine inches long and at least a century in age. It was weathered, bore a sliver of carving on its lid, and had a single rusty clasp holding the lid closed.

'Indiana Jones leave this?' Beckman asked, unfortunately, before gaining the wisdom *not* to ask it.

Both silver tufts of hair wrinkled up the man's forehead.

'Sorry for… that,' Lolita said, eschewing The Eyebrow for a firm pat on Beckman's knee. 'Do go on.'

'This is the last item in Mr Milan's estate. Thee must listen with due diligence, for this is a matter of some gravity.'

'We will.'

'This box is now in thy possession. It is not to be sold. It is not to be pawned. It is not to be lost. Most, *most* vitally, it is not to be opened unless—and one cannot over-stress the criticality of the following verbiage— unless this town is in existential danger. Is one being, explicitly, crystal clear?'

'Yes,' she replied gravely.

'On no account is this box to be opened, and its contents revealed, by anyone other than thee, unless and until the survival or singularity of Sunrise—and its inhabitants—is explicitly threatened by forces known or unknown.'

She nodded. 'Don't open the box unless things get *very* serious around here.'

'Something, some person, or some event that would threaten all that we know and love about this most special conurbation.'

'Okay.'

Spodge leant forwards and clasped ageing hands together. 'Further, in the felicitous event that this box remains closed, thee are obliged to bequeath it to thine own heir under the same instruction. Such instruction must and will be carried out by an individual at this place of business, a successor to myself no doubt, who will be wholly versed in the peculiarities of this imperative inheritance.'

'I understand.'

Spodge leant back. 'Exemplary. One is informed that thee are a citizen of good character who will treat these longstanding instructions with due respect and diligence.'

'Most kind.'

'Do thee have any questions?'

Beckman watched Lolita finger her wedding ring. 'And if an heir is… not forthcoming?'

'Such an eventuality—unusual as it would be in the history of this artefact—would need to be considered by this firm at an appropriate time.'

Beckman raised a finger. 'Just to get this straight—this box has been handed down through Jack's family for, what, generations?'

'That is an accurate assumption.'

'Okay, forgive me, Mr Spodge, I have to ask—what's in the box?'

A thin smile appeared. 'Mr… Spiers, isn't it? One is not in possession of that information. One imagines that thee would have gleaned such a fact from my specificity regarding the non-opening of said box. Opening it without due cause would be a grave matter, especially for someone charged with ensuring that its lineage is maintained, and the instruction carried forwards.'

'How will we know what due cause *is*?'

'Mrs Milan—the rightful heir—and thee will surely know, when the time comes. It is our prayer every year, here at Spodge and Sons, that the time does not come. One has outlined the decree, such as has been honoured for generations. It is now thy duty, Mrs Milan, to uphold the wishes of thy father and his ancestors, and help protect this town.'

She gently reached out. Spodge gave a gentle nod, and she gingerly picked up the casket.

Great.

Thanks, Jack. Thanks for the opportunity to screw up something even more important than looking after both your daughter and your business.

You carry on sleeping forever. I doubt I'll sleep at all.

Chapter 7

Beckman closed the office door behind them. His mind raced with questions.

He took one step down the corridor.

Faint heavy metal music began. He paused, mid-stride, and craned an ear.

Nah. Can't be.

Although… Yes, I think it is.

Anyhow, bigger fish to fry.

They reached the Mustang, climbed in, and he slotted the key in the ignition. Lolita put the box and the envelope in her lap and tugged on her seatbelt.

His hand hovered over the key. 'I wonder what "existential" means?'

'In this context? The end of Sunrise as we know it—that's my interpretation.'

'It wouldn't mean running out of root beer? Carlton Cooper re-emerging from The Portal?'

'Only you could belittle something like this.'

'Yep. You scored a bullseye with that wedding ring, huh?'

They exchanged a look of mutual good humour, then eyed the box. Before the silence became too deafening, he turned the key and pierced the air with beautiful V8 song.

The box and the envelope sat on Lolita's dining room table.

She and Beckman sat in two chairs, staring at the objects, and drinking coffee. He knew it wasn't on a par with Buck's. He knew that she also knew it wasn't. He also knew that he shouldn't say it wasn't.

Bigger fish to fry.

'Are you thinking what I am?' he asked.

'Open it?'

'The box?'

'The letter!' She plucked the envelope from the table and ran a finger down one edge.

'Best not.'

Lolita shook her head. 'I can't believe this is all he left her, even with… what happened.'

'You have an address for her?'

'A town.'

An alarming thought struck him. 'So… you didn't even tell her he died?'

She met his gaze, and her shoulders fell. 'Well, of course, I feel bad *now*. Last week? I didn't want to organise a nice, fancy, big crowd wake for him and have it ruined by her rocking up to do a soft shoe shuffle on his grave.'

'Hmm. Figures.'

'Feeling bad is good, though?'

He nodded.

She bowed her head sadly. 'A letter. Years of marriage and just a letter.'

'If it even is a letter. Maybe it's more than that. Much more.'

'I don't see there's much more left. I got everything.'

'But you *wanted* everything. Especially the business.'

'I wanted it because I was told I couldn't have it.'

He glowered at the old wooden casket. 'And now there's something else I bet you want but can't have.'

'What?'

'Come on—can't we just admit we're dying to open it?'

She gently slapped his hand. 'How *can* you?'

'Curiosity. It makes me tick.'

'Much as I love you, Beckman, you have to admit, you're not even *from* Sunrise. This is my deal.'

'What happened to "what's yours is mine", and "a problem shared is a problem halved"? Not to mention the whole handing-it-down-to-your-heir part. I'm pretty involved in that particular… element of our future.'

She toyed with her empty mug. Then she got up and paced.

'What if the box doesn't have to go to a blood heir? What if… a nominated person would do? Maybe we can ask old Spodge that?'

Beckman's spirits sank.

This sounds like she doesn't want your genes, buddy.

'That sounds a lot like your beauty and brains don't get to go into some other lucky little guy or gal.'

She fixed him in a pensive, uneasy look. He went over to her and took both hands.

'I don't like the pressure, that's all. I'll admit I was ambivalent about kids before, but now….' She sighed.

'Because they'd have no grandparents to run circles around? Now, you only have your mom, and not even her. I guess Marlon would be delighted, but mom's in Australia, and—'

She squeezed his hands. 'It wasn't about what other people think or want. But, I guess now I'd be letting Jack down.'

'And maybe the whole town. There isn't anyone else for the box to go to. We're only children. If you had a potential nominee before, then you just….' He caught a cautioning look in her eye. 'Had a disagreement with him. But, you know what, you *are* right. To have a kid just because some chunk of wood and an overly loquacious headbanger says we should is not the right reason. Only do it if you want to.'

'You mean, "Only do it if you love me".'

'No, I know you love me. Heck knows why. Sure, it seems history expects, this crazy town expects, but we should do it because it will make you happy.'

She nodded gently, released his hands, and padded into the kitchen, where she fussed around.

He sank into the chair and watched the yellow orb of delightfulness try to put her worktop, and her mind, in order.

She leaned against the kitchen island and smiled at him.

'This is not a five-minute decision. But something else is. Mom needs to have that envelope. Hell—she needs to know that her hateful ex- is no longer around… and perhaps not quite so hateful.'

'But you haven't spoken in, what, fifteen years?'

She shrugged. 'I think the world is sending me a sign. I don't *want* to, but I think I *need* to.'

'You have her address?'

'She deigned to tell me the town—when she left Sunrise. That's it.'

'You have her cell?'

Lolita drummed her fingers on the worktop. 'Where did I put it?' she murmured. She pulled open all the kitchen drawers, then went to the living room shelves and drawers, and finally disappeared into the dining room.

She returned with a scrag of paper between her fingers.

Sheesh, nothing says "I don't wanna talk to you, daughter" like a five-minute treasure hunt.

She pulled out her cellphone and, with a surprising lack of hesitation, dialled.

He went to her for support. She pulled a fake grimace as she listened for the dial tone.

She hung up. He shot a query.

'Number out of service.'

'Ah, snap. She's gone properly dark. Try the directory?'

Lolita shook her head. 'She'd never be listed. Always afraid Jack would find a way to get in touch.'

'So?'

She bit her lip. 'I—we—went to the end of the world to save our relationship and our business last year. If I give up on my own mother—granted, I have no desire to throw her hugs of forgiveness—just because her cell won't connect, that gives me no leg to stand on. No high horse to ride. I'm not sure my conscience will sit well with, "Never mind, you tried" if I didn't *really* try. Dad wanted me to have all his stuff. She only got that letter. Even if I disagree with his logic, I should at least do what he expects.'

'Absolutely.'

She cupped his cheek. 'Sorry, honey. One more hurdle. *Then* we can get on with our lives.'

Chapter 8

Mystery heirlooms and missing parents are no respecter of the need for the human digestive system to be topped up, so he suggested that they spring for something unhealthy at Jen & Berry's.

She acceded, so they walked—hand in hand—to the neon-bedecked diner/ice cream parlour, which lay at the near end of town.

At the door, she pointed subtly to one of the tables beyond the expansive front window.

Reba and Randall were seated there.

'Jeremiah didn't say so, but I'd bet the value of Jack's old mansion that us having that box is supposed to be a family-only secret. So, much as you can be nosy, curious, prone to over-sharing and sometimes downright idiotic— in a very loveable way—let's keep this between us, okay?' She gave him the Do We Understand Each Other? version of The Eyebrow.

He drew an invisible zip across his lips.

'Good, now let's get some empty calories.'

After embraces all round, then lightning-quick ordering from Jen—who was passing by on her pink roller-skates—they pulled up chairs to join Sunrise's diminutive P.I. and her ex-hitman beau.

Reba wore a sober expression. 'We heard about you and Buck. Sorry.'

Lolita held up a soft hand. 'Nothing is forever—'

Excluding that old no-lookie-insidie box, it seems.

'—much as we may wish it was.'

'It's a bummer,' Randall agreed.

'And I don't want you two trying to broker a peace, okay? He and I made this, and either he'll wake up and smell a whole pallet of his own coffee, and make his apologies, or we'll just go on with things. After all, it's not like I don't have other lovely folks like you to chat to.'

Reba nodded. 'Agreed. So, did you see the lawyer?'

'Jeremiah? Strange fish.'

'Did you get the house?'

'We got everything, honey. After all—who else is there?'

'You gonna move in?'

Beckman was startled—though he didn't know why. Reba was a *direct* kinda gal. It probably came from sporting a glass eye, a failed marriage, a girl to raise, and a line of work that could get interesting at times. If she didn't have her Sig Sauer in your face, anything less direct was almost friendly. Still, he adored her in an entirely platonic way.

Lolita shot him a query.

He held both hands up. 'We're barely an hour into this, Reba. Other priorities to work on.'

'Like what?'

The drinks arrived. Lolita stirred in her creamer, Beckman sipped his black coffee. Reba and Randall put on expressions of forced patience.

She's a P.I. Never takes an hour off from digging, it seems.

'Jack left something for mom,' Lolita said.

'I'd damn well hope so, the amount of crap she put you through by walking out.'

'Be fair—Jack kinda precipitated that.'

Beckman assumed Lolita wasn't going to regurgitate Mary-Ann's denial of the affair: (1) it wasn't really anyone else's business, and (2) the last person you'd tell is someone always itching for a story or the chance to delve into reports of marital disharmony.

'Well, I guess she gets the last laugh by not being dead.' Lolita forced a laugh, then fell sober and buried her face in her latte.

'What was it?' Randall asked quietly. 'You know, if—'

'Just a letter,' Beckman replied. 'Technically, envelope. Who knows what's inside. When we see her—if we see her—maybe we get to find out. If it's any of our beeswax. If not,' he shrugged, 'We've our own rows to hoe.'

'That's the truth.'

Lolita surfaced. 'So I'm gonna grow a pair of balls and reach out to the old town-skipping, backbone-less quitter.'

Reba patted the table. 'I, for one, applaud you. I wish I'd had the balls to make up with my old man.'

'You're hardly short of balls, honey,' Randall whispered, giving her a soft chuck on the shoulder.

'Jack was an ass, mine was an ass—what was yours?' Beckman asked.

'Oh—ass. He disapproved of me marrying Elmer. Thought he wasn't good enough for me. Couldn't be trusted.'

'But… I thought…'

'Yeah, yeah, so dad was right. You think that makes me *more* likely to rush over for afternoon tea?'

'Elmer's loss is my gain.' Randall squeezed Reba's hand.

'And Jack's gains are now our gains,' Lolita added. 'Which we will make decisions about—for the benefit of the endlessly nosy souls at this table—as soon as I get rid of this envelope.'

'You call her up?' Reba asked.

'Line was dead. Out of service.'

'So, write her.'

'I don't have the address. She always boasted, "Call me any time, honey, my cell's always on", but she didn't think to back that up with saying exactly where she was. That's code for "I'll make myself just available enough, so it doesn't look like I'm turning my back on you too, but I'm not putting out the Welcome mat".'

'And she's not in the directory,' Beckman added.

'So, how will you find her?' Reba asked.

Lolita sighed, burbling her lips. 'Call up the County authorities, see if they can help out. Google her? I don't know. Worse case—maybe there *will* be a sleuthing job for you.'

'You know I'm always there for you two. Which County?'

'I'd have to check. But it's Garden City, Kansas.'

Reba's eyes widened. 'Shoot. I hope she's okay.'

'Okay? Why?'

'They had a big twister blow through there last week. Flattened half the place.'

Beckman felt Lolita's hand grip his. For a woman with apparently scant care for her mom, she looked more than a little terrified.

Chapter 9

Romeo gingerly set the cardboard box on the floor. It was marked "crockery" in thick black pen.

He stood aside as his able assistant plonked a small, transparent plastic carry box on top. She pushed up one of the rolled sleeves which had slipped down.

He wrapped his arms around her waist. 'I love you, Mrs True.'

'I love you, Mr True.'

He gazed around the box-strewn living room. 'It really begins now. The marital house.'

She kissed him. 'It certainly does. After I've, you know, vetted all your stuff and thrown half of it out.' She winked.

'If I get to do the same to yours, sure.' He winked back.

'Mutual desecration of property, now that's true love.'

'With us, everything is True love.'

'That *will* get wearing, I hope you know.'

'True love is putting up with my baloney, I hope you know,' he replied.

She shook her head. 'True love is you finding which of these million crates has beer inside it that we can stick in the fridge.'

He looked askew at the plastic box. 'Well, it ain't this one. Hey—this isn't even marked. What happened to the system?'

'It's for the attic.'

'You mean—miscellaneous junk.'

She pulled the box to her waist. 'No, not *all* junk.'

'Ah.' He cupped her cheeks. 'Secrets, Mrs True?'

'Not secrets like *that*.'

'Secrets like what? Anyway, we agreed we wouldn't do "secrets". Especially when you married a cop. We find stuff out—didn't you get the memo?'

'There's nothing bad, I promise,' Julie said.

'Okay—I believe you. But we agreed to throw out all the junk from our single lives, rather than just move it to the new place.' He unlatched the crate's lid.

'Romeo, no!'

Now he was beyond intrigued. He was worried. Would the fledgling marriage come crashing down already?

'What are you afraid of? You've really got me spooked here. I'm opening the crate, okay?'

She swallowed. 'Okay.'

He removed the translucent plastic lid.

His heart thumped, and his mind did a backflip. This didn't compute.

'How did my casket get in here?' he growled.

She frowned. 'Yours?'

'Yes, mine.'

'No—mine.'

'Baby, I know that marriage is about sharing what we have, but—'

She gently clasped his arm. 'You don't understand. This is my box. I packed it. I've had it for years—since before we met. You can't know I had it.' She sought his eyes. 'It can't be yours.'

'So what you're saying is… it's a secret.'

She nodded.

He sought out a chair, tugged a dust sheet off it, and sat down hard.

She perched on the arm, grabbed his hand and squeezed it. 'I didn't mean to…'. She sighed. 'The thing is… .'

He looked at her very directly and shook his head. 'You don't understand.'

'Don't understand what?'

'Stay there.'

He sprang up and went to the end of the living room, where French doors were partially obscured by stacks of removal boxes. He moved a couple aside and then, with the toned arms of his six-foot frame, picked up a portable safe.

The sturdy, two-foot cube bumped to the carpet near Julie.

He crouched down, tapped in the digital code, and opened the door.

He cast a glance to his wife, whose hand was at her mouth in concerned expectation.

He carefully pulled out the casket and set it on the floor between them.

She inhaled sharply, audibly.

'This one is *definitely* mine, he said.

Almost robotically, she went to the crate, removed the second casket, set it down on the floor and sat cross-legged beside him.

They eyed each other with unusual wariness. The facts were plain—he'd put those together quickly. Then he shook away his disbelief because he'd kept the secret from her as much as she'd kept it from him. Plus, the instruction was explicit—possession of the casket was not to be broadcast.

'Did you get that when your folks died?' she asked.

'Mm-hmm.'

'At the Will reading—that old guy?'

'Yeah.'

'Me too. Sponge or Splodge or whatever.'

'Yeah. He talk about a… grave threat?'

'Emergency use only. That was the headline. Oh, and don't tell anyone.'

Romeo sighed with deliberate relief. 'I guess the secret's out now. If it has to go to our heir, we'd both have to know, huh?'

'Yeah, we would.' He pondered. 'Two boxes to one person, though? You think that's even allowed?'

'Honey, two boxes in the same house has got to be a million-to-one shot.'

He stood, and helped her up. 'Baby, I think this means something.'

'Means what? Don't tell me you feel luckier, having *more* responsibility for those things?'

'No. It either means we're the final backstop for this whole ancestral hand-me-down, or….'

'Or?'

'There are more boxes.'

Her eyes darted. 'Either way, we need to take good care.' She knelt, gathered both boxes and pushed them into the safe.

When she stood, he clasped her arm. 'I think it means something else.'

'What?'

'*All* the boxes—even if there's just these two—need to be opened if things get serious.'

'Why? Why not just one box? Surely only one person needs to raise the alarm or do whatever is demanded by opening the box.'

He shook his head. 'Doesn't make sense. Why doesn't the old lawyer guy just keep one box, and do the deed when the shit goes down?'

'He couldn't be trusted?'

'That can't be it. He's the one telling *us* to be so damn careful and trustworthy with this secret, this Get Out Of Jail Free card—whatever it is.'

'Romeo, I don't follow. And frankly, you're scaring me a little.'

He laid a hand on her shoulder. 'Scary is what we're trying to *avoid*. Something which would endanger the town—its security, its safety. Don't you see? Those two caskets, winding up under one roof, it's a sign.'

She frowned. 'A sign of what?'

'I'm a cop. I'm charged with keeping the citizens and the town safe. I need everything at my disposal to do that. When something bad happens—this holocaust event or whatever—I need to be front and centre. We can't be waiting for some old shuffler to try and remember what cupboard he hid his box in, or where in the garden someone buried it! Time is *everything*. As a cop, as a public servant, I need to be ready.' He took her in an embrace. '*We* need to be ready. I need to save the woman I love.'

'I don't like this, baby. What are you saying?'

'I really think we need to open the boxes.'

Chapter 10

Beckman's insatiably curious mind woke him before seven.

He lay there, staring at the ceiling, myriad questions tumbling through his frontal lobe.

After a while, he felt Lolita stir and watched her breathing change, her facial muscles tic, until her eyes opened. The corners of her mouth turned up, her shoulders wiggled, and she draped an arm across his bare chest.

Outside of coffee, morning may be my new favourite thing.

Come to think of it, with Buck's coffee now off-limits, I think mornings have just hit the Number One spot.

'Hey,' she purred.

'Hey. You sleep?'

'Damn well. Considering.'

'Any conclusions?'

'The decent thing is to go and see her.'

'Absolutely. Unless it risks more heartache than it's worth.' He lifted her hand and kissed each finger in turn.

'She has to know. About the envelope. About dad. About what Mary-Ann said.'

'You do realise that means leaving the State?'

'I won't say I'm not nervous.'

'I thought you'd say that. I also realised something. Carlton's affair, the fire, the GigantiCorp approach—they all happened right here. If you think this place is a safe haven you don't wanna ever leave, I might beg to differ.'

She made a throaty noise, pulled herself across and lay her head on his chest. 'I guess I wouldn't be going alone.'

'The flights are like four hours. I'll hold your hand every single second.'

She sat bolt upright, eyes dancing. 'Now you made it *very* real, and I don't know.'

'Every day's an adventure. Besides—you're trying to do the right thing. Isn't that worth some nerves?'

'I never flew. I'm *just not sure*, baby. I know I'm a grown-ass woman, but all the same, I've got visions of getting paralysed with nerves, or drinking too many beers to calm those nerves and getting thrown off the plane.'

'Relax. It'll be fine.'

She pulled up a pillow and leant back against the headboard. 'Jesus, Jack. Jesus, mom. You don't make it easy.'

He threw back the covers. 'Wait there a while.'

He set the breakfast tray on her lap and slid under the duvet.

'You're the best,' she said.

'I thought of another way. A better way—because it's right in my wheelhouse.'

She drank. 'Go on.'

'We drive. I reckon it's about fourteen hours. Get a motel on the way. My whole life has been on the road. If you want a comfort blanket, I'm the guy. Wind in our hair, time away from this nonsense.'

She bit her lip. 'Feels awfully slow. What if she's in trouble?'

'They have FEMA, you know. It's not our job to be racing over there. This is a courtesy. What—you worried her house has been sucked up to Oz?'

'If she has, the Wicked Witch is in for some competition.'

'I don't get it. If you hate her that much, why even go?'

'She has no family anywhere—definitely not in Kansas. If I'd been there when Jack had his heart attack, you think I wouldn't have given him CPR just because he was a sexist ass? I'm not denying I'm conflicted about being the one to hold out the olive branch to her. Maybe it's banking some karma—if I help her now, if she's got a decent bone in her body, she'll help us later if we ever need it.'

She drank, and set the mug firmly down on the tray. 'Especially as Buck's white knight status is on permanent hold.'

'So it's a Yes to the road trip?'

Lolita sighed. 'Okay. We tell her the news, check she's okay, and come home. Don't worry; it won't be a love-in. If she gets away without a half-dozen eye rolls, it'll be a major result for entente cordiale.'

'Even three days away would be a break.'

'Think of it as the honeymoon we never had.'

'Every day with you is a honeymoon,' he replied.

'Bleurgh.'

In the afternoon, they packed a case and made the necessary arrangements. Randall would hold the fort at the office, and Reba would be on the end of her cell if they needed assistance.

They told Tyler and Amaryllis they could house-sit if they wanted to save on hotel bills for a couple of nights.

Beckman wondered how long Jack's old house would lay empty—it would be a more spacious hangout for the Pegasus twosome—but decided not to broach the subject: one item at a time on the To-Do list.

As darkness fell, Lolita was still apprehensive. It would undoubtedly be an emotional journey as well as a logistical one.

He pulled her closer on the sofa. 'What can I say to set your mind at rest?'

'That you'll butt out when you need to, and at the same time come up with the magic words if I need them. To make this trip—this errand, gesture, whatever—not a blowout.'

'I'll do my best. At least you'll know we tried. At worst, if we find Ginetta, I'll push the envelope into her hand, and then we run. Jack's request will be fulfilled.'

'And you're sure a fifty-year-old car is up to the trip?'

'Positive. What I'm worried about is how to find decent coffee or root beer at every stop.'

She gazed into his eyes. 'Sunrise has really spoiled you, huh?'

'It has its upsides.'

'So you're prepared to uphold some strange ancient directive to keep those upsides?'

'When I married you, I took on much more than a one-woman force of nature; that much seems clear.'

'If mom approves of you—about six months too late—I'll have chosen well.'

'And if she doesn't approve?' he wondered.

'Then she'll have one less person taking drinks at *her* wake.'

The morning dawned warm and bright: perfect for a road trip in a beautiful convertible with a beautiful woman.

He fired up the Mustang and let it warm through while he packed the trunk.

He was checking the tire pressures when Lolita came out, locked up and slid into the passenger seat. She sported a navy skirt, white blouse and a scarf.

Very… road trip.

'You look like Louise. Or Thelma. I forget.'

'As long as we don't shoot anybody and wind up off a cliff, meeting my mother will be a cakewalk.'

He slid behind the wheel and buckled up.

'You had Saul service this, right?' she asked. 'It's nearly a thousand miles.'

'Carlton treated it like royalty when he had it. Better than he treated you, by all accounts.'

'I thought we'd stopped talking about all that.'

'Sorry. Point is, he rebuilt the engine, upgraded some parts, kept the hood serviced.' He took her hand. 'We'll be fine.'

Chapter 11

They broke down after an hour.

Beckman girded himself for a small detonation from the passenger seat, but all that transpired was a particularly extended deployment of The Eyebrow.

Telling her that I haven't broken down in three years is probably not a good idea at this point.

He forewent any words of disappointment, apology, regret, disbelief, bemusement, sarcasm or mollification, and climbed out. He levered up the pristine red hood and locked the metal strut in place. Then he carefully cast his eye over every nook and cranny, poked and prodded. He even checked the oil level and said 'Hmm' a few times for good measure.

Lolita appeared beside him.

'It's what I thought,' he said.

'What?'

'We've broken down.'

'You know, at the wedding,' she said, 'Marlon privately told me you were an annoying little shit when you were young.'

'I think I know where this is going.'

'*That* was going.' She pointed at the car. 'This is not.'

'I'll get right on that.' He pulled out his cellphone, then flashed a sheepish grin. 'Do *you* have any signal?'

She took out her phone, then quickly replaced it. She looked up and down the road. All was quiet.

He sighed. 'I'm guessing Saul doesn't come out this far?'

'He'd be here by now.'

She returned to the passenger seat. He took his own leather pew. The sun beat down.

'Do you think this is Carlton's revenge for us putting him in the Portal?'

'Or Wanda's for the same.'

She gave a chuckle of gallows humour. 'She's better off now, though. Dating again. Quick, huh?'

'Yeah, because of course, you waited what, five, ten minutes after dumping him before dating me.'

She looked over the top of her sunglasses. 'Would you rather I'd teased you along, let you suffer unrequited love?'

'I think it all worked out beautifully, thank you, darling.'

'Snake.' She flipped down the visor and checked her reflection in the vanity mirror. 'It certainly worked out better than this little vacation, huh?'

'It's a nice enough spot for a break.'

'All the same,' she swung open the door and hopped out. 'We need a ride. Would you rather I flashed thigh or cleavage?'

'Let me try it one more time.' He turned the key.

Nothing happened.

He thumped the steering wheel.

'You checked the battery connections, right?' she asked.

Ah.

He got out and peered under the hood. She joined him, hands on hips.

He located the offending wires and checked them. 'Yeah—see?'

She made a disbelieving throaty noise. 'Thigh it is.'

Well—here's the good news. I'd stop for Lolita's thigh. Let's hope someone else on this remote ribbon of asphalt has the same amount of taste.

And ideally is the local root beer distributor.

They stepped around towards the cabin.

A tow truck was sitting there.

Chapter 12

At Spodge & Sons, they'd shared a look of disbelief and intrigue.

This time, it was mutual stupefaction.

The tow truck was very different to Saul's; modern, silver and sleek. The driver was very different to Saul; about Beckman's height, black hair in a ponytail, regular dress code, fancy wristwatch.

But did he have similar powers of foresight?

'Sorry. Did I startle you?'

'Er… no?' Beckman replied.

'You can kinda creep up on people, even when you don't want to.' The tow-trucker thumbed over his shoulder. 'Electric. Built it myself.'

'Very… impressive.'

'I'm guessing you need a hand?'

Beckman was watching like a hawk for any unnecessarily long gazes at his belle. Being rescued was unarguably terrific—just not by a douche.

Lolita waved towards the hood. 'We just… broke down—right, honey?'

Beckman nodded. 'Run like a peach for years. One mercy dash—boom. Some luck, huh…?'

'Xavier.'

'Good thing you happened along. Be our guest.'

They huddled together while Electric Xavier rootled around in the engine bay.

Lolita pressed her lips to Beckman's ear. 'You got lucky. Mister.'

'You've left me with the tools to provide an heir. I guessed that I'm lucky.'

Electric Xavier folded his arms.

Ah. This looks expensive. Or time-consuming. Or both.

'Bad news and good news.'

'We'll take the bad,' Lolita replied.

'You know this is not a regular set of wheels.'

'We do.' She flashed Beckman The Eyebrow (Told-You-So version).

'You need a new part. Pretty rare one.' Xavier rubbed his neck and waggled his head.

Beckman deflated. 'Okay. The good news?'

It's under a thousand bucks? They have one just two days mailing from here? You have a coffee machine in the cab?

'I have one in the truck.'

Beckman waited for the guy to say "Gotcha!" (because there's no way Xavier could be on the level), then wondered whether he had to appear to *accept* the fake offer for the Gotcha to be forthcoming, then pondered how he might style out the Gotcha and pretend he'd seen it all along—or at least appear not to be disappointed at the inevitable absence of the spare part, and then moved on to consider the possibility that it was a genuine statement that he should simply take at face value. Because what could be more sensible than unnecessarily prolonging a conversation beside a remote highway on a warm March morning while your wife stands beside you with her arms folded, probably inwardly chastising you for your idiocy or at least the full-term nature of the pregnant pause you were precipitating?

'Really?'

Xavier cracked his knuckles. 'Yeah. Your lucky day, I guess. I got a pony just like this. Blue. Bought the part a few months back—then wound up repairing the old one. So—is that okay?'

Beckman had visions of Lolita dropping to her knees and showing Electric White Knight exactly how 'okay' it was.

'Thanks, thanks a million,' Beckman said.

'Road trip?'

'Yeah. Kansas.'

'If you have a bagel or whatever, there's time while I change the thing over.'

'I brought some things.' Lolita leant on the trunk, allowing a glimpse of cleavage to cement the deal.

Xavier nodded. 'Great. It'll take about a half-hour. Take out your picnic or whatever.'

Lolita popped the trunk.

'I have coffee in the cab too, if you're thirsty,' Xavier added.

Beckman's head exploded.

Xavier closed the hood, slid into the driving seat and turned the Mustang's V8 over.

'Who needs Saul?' Beckman murmured to Lolita.

'You did. More than once. Now—I hope you brought cash.'

'What do I owe you?' he called to their automotive saviour.

'Call it two-fifty.'

To save the day? Priceless.

He fished out the notes, and also dug something out of his shoulder bag.

'What's this?' Xavier asked.

'For your headache.'

'How did you…?'

'There are more things in heaven and earth, Horatio, than are dreamt of in your philosophy.' He handed over the small brown box.

Now it was the mechanic's turn to be nonplussed. 'O-kay.'

Lolita laid a hand on his shoulder. 'Take it from a past customer. It works like you wouldn't believe. Hell—it can create marriages, if that's your thing.'

'Then—great.' He offered his hand, and they all shook. 'Good luck in Kansas. Hope you don't wind up with Dorothy, this time of year.'

Lolita brushed back her hair. 'Well, if mom is okay, that's the blessing.'

'Visiting your mom? Did she catch a twister?'

'That's the problem—we don't know. Phone lines down.'

'Whereabouts?'

'Garden City.'

Xavier rubbed his stubbled chin. 'Heard about that.' He tutted. 'Not pretty. My brother's up there.'

'Helping out?' Beckman asked.

'He's a cop. Hey—if you need a hand finding what's what, give him a call.'

Lolita waved it away. 'We couldn't.'

Xavier shrugged. 'You're doing her a favour going all that way. You did me a favour with this box; find Wilder when you get into town.'

She darted in and pecked him on the cheek.

He coughed self-consciously. 'Well, I'd best leave you to get on your way. Look after these beautiful ladies, won't you, sir.'

'Beckman,' Beckman said.

'Ah. Your parents got a sense of humour too. I feel your pain. Have a nice day.'

With that, Electric Xavier, brother to Wilder (surname unknown), climbed into his homemade futuristic transportation and whirred away down the long road.

'So?'

She ruffled his hair. 'Saul is still number one. Let's go.'

'You want to drive?'

She looked at him like he'd never offered her the wheel before—because he hadn't. 'Sure?'

'I already broke it once today. Hard for you to do worse.'

'Fair.'

They climbed in. His nerves jangled.

She couldn't break it? Could she? My dream car spoiled by my dream woman?

Lolita tickled the throttle and gingerly steered them back onto the blacktop.

He eased back into his seat and let the tension ebb.

She jammed the throttle to the stop.

Chapter 13

It was smooth sailing after that, sliding into New Mexico and stopping for the night at a motel north of Santa Fe.

The high point was reacquainting himself with the delights of Coffee Planet. The barista asked if sir would like to join the Loyalty Card scheme. Beckman didn't bother checking Lolita's facial expression, and summarily declined.

It was odd being back in a motel room. For twelve years, they'd been a home from home; now, he couldn't imagine being in any bed other than Lolita's... although, so long as she was beside him, any bed couldn't suck too much.

The motel sign didn't flicker crimson or imperial.

They slept well.

Early next morning, they struck out North-Eastwards.

Soon, the barren flats of Oklahoma were passing beneath the Mustang's radials.

'How come your parents never took you to see the country?' he asked.

'There was plenty to see in the State. Plus, you know, dad was too busy for long trips away.'

'What did you do with your vacation time?

She shrugged. 'Dated boys.'

'Hmm.' He adjusted the visor against the sun. 'How many?'

She peered over the top of her shades. 'Wouldn't you like to know?'

'That was the general idea.'

'How will it help you to know? If I say "a hundred", will you regret marrying me?'

'Give me a clue. Is it between fifty and a hundred?'

She jabbed his thigh. 'What about you?'

'It's between five and seven.'

'Well, okay,' she said sheepishly. 'At least I made double figures.'

'*High* double figures?'

'Look—it's only the last one that counts, right? The one after which there's no more.'

'I know.' He squeezed her thigh. 'So you didn't do family holidays?'

'When I was younger, yeah.' She sighed reflectively. 'Mom and dad were inseparable. There was a lot of love. I suppose I should hang onto that.'

'This is why we're here.' He gestured to the blue canvas above the open cabin. 'You did hang onto that, deep down.'

'Walking out broke the closeness and respect, but it didn't break my heart. And she was as disappointed in me for staying as I was with her for leaving.'

'You're stronger than she is, that's all.'

'She gave up too easily. She snapped like a twig. Always living under his shadow, yet needing him around to cast that shadow. She *let* him never be there. Until she didn't. She begged me to come with her.' Lolita played with the folds in her skirt. 'I wanted her to stand up to him. He'd never listen to me. I was just another girl, designed to be a homemaker, to make do with whatever attention he could spare. Mom was too subservient for too long. She'd rather leave than have a blazing row with Jack.'

'The affair was the straw that broke the camel's back.'

She nodded. 'At least Carlton *tried* to treat me right. I wonder if mom would have approved of him.'

Beckman shook his head. 'He was part of Jack's disdain for you, a side-effect of holding you back, keeping you out of the boys' business club.'

She smirked. 'It's funny. She was the one I learned from—how not to be a subservient little lady in the kitchen. How to show two fingers to Jack—wearing the swing dresses, starting my own business. Hell, even finding a surrogate father….' She hung her head.

'Nature and nurture are what make us. I think you have Jack's genes. And the nurture? Maybe when you don't have enough of it, it defines your path as much as it does to someone who is smothered. You had enough of it—you're no tearaway. No years in juvenile hall. You just wish your parents had done things better… in *your* eyes. You're not alone in that.'

'But I couldn't change Jack's need to work hard to make money and a better life, no more than you could tell Marlon to stop shifting Army bases every two years, trying to get a promotion.'

'No, but he could have been less of a disapproving ass.'

'He seemed to approve of *me*,' she said.

He smiled. 'How could anyone not?'

'Ask me again later.'

'You think she'll speak to you?'

'So long as she listens, that's all that counts. You can lead a horse to water, and all that. Her choice whether to open the envelope. Her choice whether to forgive Jack or not.'

'Have you—forgiven him?'

She studied her lap. 'I'm working on it.'

'Why didn't Jack work harder to set the record straight? Even in the last few months when you'd give him the time of day?'

'The damage was done years ago. You can't un-ring that bell.'

'Does it really matter whether mom believes Mary-Ann?'

'I don't know. I'm only trying to be a decent daughter.' She laid her hand on top of his, where it rested on the gearshift. 'I stopped at boyfriend number twenty-three because you're the most decent man I know. And I want you to stop at number seven.'

They rolled into Garden City just after two in the afternoon.

It wasn't pretty.

Lolita's mood fell flatter than the rows of destroyed houses.

'I can't see how opening a box would stop something like this, if it came to us.'

Beckman surmised that this wasn't due an answer, so he remained mute and trundled the car through the detritus which littered the roads. He'd spent a few years of his youth in the Midwest but never seen destruction up close and personal.

Dogs wandered the streets. Owners picked through their shattered homes.

Air is funny.

We rely on it to live, and then it does this.

Lolita pulled out her cellphone and dialled, then hung up.

'No service?'

'Maybe mom disconnected the number.'

'Head for the Sheriff's office?'

'Yeah. I'll Google it.'

As Lolita tapped away on her phone, Beckman spied a police car heading towards them.

In an uncharacteristic act of hopeful desperation, he yanked on the fifty-year-old handbrake and slewed the car across the road.

Blue lights flicked on, and the police car braked sharply to a stop.

'Decent people get arrested for dumb stunts too, you know?' she said.

'I'll say the handbrake was faulty.'

He raised both hands out of the cabin, popped the door and climbed out.

A cop emerged from his patrol car, hand at his waist.

'Can I help you, sir?'

Beckman moved closer. 'This is a dumb question, but is there a Wilder on your force?'

The cop cocked his head. 'Maybe. Why?'

'Xavier told us to ask for him.'

'Uh-huh.'

'And if his brother's as much of a stand-up guy, we're in luck.'

'For how?'

'We're searching for a missing woman.'

'Missing?'

'She's not answering her phone,' Lolita said.

She'd not only exited the car, but she'd also loosened a button on her blouse.

Not as overt as my act of hopeful desperation, perhaps, but more likely to win hearts and minds. No wonder she never got a speeding ticket.

The cop's gaze flicked between them. 'I'm Wilder.'

'Well, that's a break, officer,' Lolita said.

'Not answering a phone doesn't make someone missing.'

'We've driven up for two days to find my mom. Her husband died. I've an important message for her. All we're looking for is an address, then we'll get out of your hair.'

'She live in town?'

'The last I heard, yeah.'

'Some parts are fine. Some parts…,' the cop gestured around, 'got hit bad.'

'Can you look her up?'

The cop stroked his chin. 'Bumped into Xavier, huh?'

'He sends his best,' Beckman said. 'Got us out of a real spot.'

Wilder eyed the Mustang. 'Shares your taste in metal too, I see.'

'Happy to help us on our… mercy mission.'

'Sure. Let me check our database.'

They followed Wilder (surname probably Vespers, based on his chest badge) to his car, where he perched on the edge of the driver's seat and fired up the mooted police systems.

'What name?'

'Milan. Ginetta Milan.'

Wilder tapped and scrolled for a few moments.

'Sorry, sir, ma'am. Nobody of that name resides in town.'

Chapter 14

Tyler had grown worried about Amaryllis over the last day or so. She'd been unusually quiet. He wondered what he'd done wrong. In his previous incarnation, it was likely that he'd done something wrong where women were concerned. Now, though, he believed he'd buried that rascal. Perhaps all that remained was merely every man's genetic inability to understand what he'd done wrong or to know what a woman was thinking?

On the outskirts of Sunrise, there was a hiking trail that offered good views of the town. It constantly piqued his curiosity that the town was apparently set in a vast crater—an island of civilisation in a desolate landscape. At the start of the trail was a café-diner with a terrace, and that's where he'd brought her for an early evening drink, to watch the sunset and try to winkle out the reason for the temporary frostiness in her demeanour.

'Is it something I said or something I did?'

Amaryllis carefully set down her glass; a white wine spritzer was her poison. 'What you said to Buck about being in love—were you serious?'

Tyler opened his mouth, but no words came out.

'I mean, things like bringing me here, the general chivalry, heck—even being a more than decent boss— these are all good signs, but I don't hear a lot of real *words*.'

'Is this the "What are we doing?" conversation?'

'I know you never had it before.'

'That's the understatement of the century.'

'So, were you just trying to get on Buck's side—talk sense into him or whatever, or was it genuine?'

He wiped a bead of condensation from the side of his beer bottle. 'If you left, I think I'd feel the way Buck does now.'

Her gaze probed his face. 'You could just say, "I love you".'

He swallowed. 'I could. Sure, I could do it because you want me to. You expect it.'

She shook her head. 'No. Say it because you mean it.'

'I want to say it because it is the whole truth. Neither of us is under any illusion that this is new ground for me. Every day I pinch myself—for one because you're with me; for two, because you trust that I am who I appear to be.'

'Do you not think you are?'

'This last six months has been crazy. At the start, anyhow. Malvolio, the money, this place. Us…'

'Your point being?'

'I need to know that it's an irreversible change. That this is the new world. That my roving eye has truly gone. Because you don't deserve to be jerked around.'

'I'm not getting any younger, that's true.'

'And I need to figure out what I want.' He took in the view. 'On days like this, it's pretty easy. Other days, I doubt myself.' He shrugged. 'That's all.'

She stroked his hand and picked up her glass. 'Okay. I don't mind treading water in a place like Sunrise.'

'On and off.'

'I can't imagine you'd move the whole of Pegasus to here, simply because it suits the boss. That feels very selfish. Very… Malvolio.'

'No. High days, holidays and visits are fine.'

Two uniformed cops passed the table. Tyler nodded a greeting, which was returned. Their voices died away.

'Are you sure you locked the door, Romeo?'

'Hey, Emory, I think I'd know a break-in when I saw it. I can't believe they had the nerve to hit a cop's house.'

'Saw you move in, I guess. Probably assumed you wouldn't have security fixed up.'

'Well, we got away lightly….'

Amaryllis tapped the table to get Tyler's attention.

'I thought Lolita said there was almost no crime here.'

Tyler slugged his beer. 'Nowhere's perfect.'

'More perfect since they ran that asshole ex- of hers out of town. What a prick.'

He beamed. 'Amaryllis, I love it when you curse and stoop to the level of us mere mortals.'

'"Love *it*?" That's as close as you'll give me for now, is that right, Tyler?'

He winked. 'It's halfway there, isn't it?'

Chapter 15

Lolita kicked the ground. Beckman reached for her hand and squeezed it.

'Is it possible she moved?' Wilder asked.

Lolita threw her hand up in despair. 'Absolutely.'

'Trying not to be found—is that it?'

'As likely as anything. She'd change her name if….' Lolita's back jolted straight up. 'Can you look for a Ginetta *Thornton*?'

The cop tapped through the computer. 'Got her. 1138 Gale Street.'

'Officer, I could kiss you.'

Well, why stop at one brother, eh honey?

'That won't be necessary, ma'am.'

'Is that part of town…?'

Wilder nodded sombrely. 'Lot of cleaning up over there. We had a few minutes warning. Only lost a couple of people. Everyone in town is accounted for. She's probably in a shelter. Try the church on Toto Street.'

Lolita bypassed the smooching for a firm handshake, Beckman did likewise, then they fairly leapt into the Mustang and burbled away.

'Maybe she'll be injured and high on morphine,' she said hopefully.

'Maybe she's had had a bump on the head and turned into Snow White.'

They parked as close as possible to the sturdy, ugly, religious edifice. He raised the soft top, locked the car, nervously checked the neighbourhood, then followed Lolita, who'd set off with commendable enthusiasm.

This is certainly one way to meet your mother-in-law. At least I know in advance that she's likely to be objectionable. Plus, if she has any reservations about Lolita creating the "in-law" part, she's missed the boat. Ginetta may not have been whirled up to Oz, but Lolita's what transported me from monochrome to colour—and that trumps twenty years of familial sour grapes.

At the wide double doors, Lolita asked, 'Is Ginetta Thornton here?'

The well-meaning woman looked Lolita up and down. 'Gee? Yes, she's here. Are you…?'

'A relative. Is she okay?'

'She's fine. Come on in.'

They entered the capacious hall. The place looked like an indoor festival, with groups of seats, blankets, sleeping bags, even a few tents. At one end was a makeshift soup kitchen. A baby cried. Two young children chased around between the tightly packed encampments. It smelled of bodies and petrichor and despair.

Lolita stopped dead. He did too.

He saw Ginetta. Mrs Milan *senior*. The maternal parent.

He didn't know it was her: he'd never seen any pictures. But it was her.

She was chatting to another middle-aged lady, until she wasn't. She swivelled slightly on the spot. The cheer of her unexpectedly good-natured conversation (given the general situation) vanished from her face.

She took a long look in their direction.

Then she pointed at the door.

'Oh, mom, no,' Lolita breathed.

Ginetta continued pointing.

'It's that or a scene,' he suggested. 'We can leave the letter at the door.'

'We came all this way.'

'I know,' he murmured. 'And she's alive and okay. In fact, given what's she's doing, I think it's fair to say she's not changed a bit, huh?'

Lolita scowled, then softened.

He put his arm around her. 'We came. You were a decent daughter.'

She let out a sigh that might have passed for its own twister. 'Yeah.'

The children scampered past. Ginetta was still pointing at the door behind them, so they turned and walked disconsolately out.

Chapter 16

The air felt much colder than it had three minutes earlier. The sky greyer.

If you're looking for any witticisms up here, you're out of luck, buddy.

They walked silently back to the car.

'I'll take the envelope back,' he offered. 'I'm sure the woman on the door will pass it on.'

'Hmm.'

His hand closed on the door lever.

'Lolita?' came a female voice.

Every part of him froze. Except his eyeballs, which swivelled to look at Lolita. She turned her entire head.

Ginetta Milan/Thornton* (*delete depending on point of view) stood five yards away.

He watched the silence like a tennis match: one moment, a striking brunette with a worried expression; the next moment, a not un-aesthetic late-fiftysomething wearing shabby dungarees and a look of circumspection. And back. And forth.

Who would crack first: the mountain or Mohammed?

'I. I… didn't want a scene. Not in there.'

Lolita folded her arms. 'Do you want one out here?'

'Do *you*?'

'Is it serious? The reason you came?'

'I suppose. But you're okay?'

'I have what I could carry.' Ginetta mirrored her daughter's pose. 'Is that what you wanted to know?'

'Kind of.'

Silence fell. The crackle of electricity was only in Beckman's mind.

Ginetta moved closer, like a lioness in the long grass. 'Who's this?'

Lolita looked at him, which he took as a cue to respond.

'Beckman.'

Ginetta frowned in amusement. 'No, seriously. What's your name?'

'Still Beckman.'

'Mm-hmm. A friend?'

'At the very least.'

'Your car?'

'Yep.'

'What do you do?'

'Salesman.'

Ginetta's shoulders fell. 'Travelling?'

'Not so much now, but I came out of retirement to drive your daughter all the way here.'

Boom. Try that for size.

Ginetta turned away, as if lamely shielding her words. 'I thought you learned your lesson?'

Lolita took a step forwards. 'The lesson I learned was not to carry a grudge. I mean, I'm here, aren't I?'

Ginetta looked at Beckman and wrinkled her nose. She eyed Lolita's left hand, then his. She had heterochromia, which was interesting, but it didn't make her any less standoffish.

'I guess you want me to be happy about this?'

'Mom, honestly—I don't care. I am. That's enough.'

Ginetta looked at Lolita's hand again, then angled back to Beckman. 'You steal that ring, or get it on the black market?'

'I bought it. My boss paid a hitman to kill me, so I paid the hitman to blackmail my boss into handing over half his fortune in exchange for his life. He died anyway, but he was blacker than the heart of the twister that took your house. Then I took the money, gave most of it to your daughter because I was in love with her, and we kicked your ex-husband out of the business he'd denied her. And then I bought the ring. Oh, and we blackmailed your daughter's ex-fiancé's fiancée into giving us this car. And we got married.' He pondered for a second. 'I think we're all caught up now, Mrs Milan or Thornton.'

The woman looked like an errant breath of wind would knock her clean over.

She inspected Beckman. Her eyes narrowed.

Well, go big or go home, eh, buddy?

'I think I'm going to like you… *Beckman.*'

'Mom-in-law, honestly—I don't care. I like Lolita. That's enough.'

A faint smile crept onto Ginetta's lips.

Dropping down to DefCon 2 now.

'Do you want to come inside?' Ginetta gestured to the warehouse of misery.

'If it's all the same, mom—no,' Lolita replied.

'Oh.'

'Is your house really all gone?'

'We could sit on the roof without needing a ladder, if that's what you mean.'

'Are you *allowed* to go back?'

'Sure. But why?'

Lolita shrugged. 'We could stand on the street. Or I could go back to Sunrise. Or…,' she took a deep breath, 'We could hang out for a few minutes.'

'Why?'

'Because you didn't already tell me to get lost and leave you alone.'

Ginetta cocked her head, looked at them both yet again, and pondered. 'Alright.'

Lolita graciously slid into the Mustang's back seat and let mom take the front pew. No physical contact was evident.

Beckman followed Ginetta's brief turn-by-turn directions until they reached a debris-strewn suburban street. Two guys were loading a pickup with remnants of their belongings.

He brought the car to a halt outside what used to be 1138 Gale Street. It was the obliterated mess he'd expected.

If you wanted to swing the balance of pity in your favour, Mrs M/T, this'd do it.

They clambered out, Lolita went into the trunk and lifted out the remains of their picnic comestibles, then they picked their way onto the lot.

It had been a decent-sized place, evidence of porches front and rear, and a double garage which was now half a garage wide.

'Shall we sit in the kitchen or the living room?' Ginetta asked despondently.

He spied a swing set upside down on the rutted turf, went over, and with Lolita's help, they righted it. She pulled a napkin from the picnic basket and wiped the seat down. Meanwhile, he located a plastic chair—probably from the garage or loft—and brought it over.

En route that morning, they'd topped up their flask at Coffee Planet. Lolita wordlessly handed the first plastic tumbler to her mother. They sat, widely spaced, on the forlorn bench seat.

The sky was milky white, and a breeze tickled the leaves of a horizontal tree nearby. In the distance, a chainsaw buzzed.

Beckman sensed the fighters circling each other at the start of Round Two.

'How is your father?' Ginetta asked her coffee.

Lolita exhaled heavily. 'That's the reason we're here.'

Ginetta looked up, saw the truth in her daughter's face, and her shoulders collapsed.

'I thought you'd be happy, or at least ambivalent.'

Ginetta shook her head. 'Am I that bad of a person?'

'I'll take the Fifth.'

'I didn't want him *dead*.'

Lolita hung her head. 'Me either.'

Eyeing the coffee cup, awaiting your turn, is bang out of order.

'Was he living with Mary-Ann?' Ginetta asked eventually.

'No. Alone. There was nobody else. There never was.'

'Apart from her.'

'No, mom. Not even her. We joined dots that weren't there.'

'You mean *I* joined dots.' Ginetta glowered at her daughter. 'Is that what this is? A road trip to tell me I was wrong? That I should never have left? That I should have put up with his absence and sexist bullshit?'

'You seemed pretty happy to.'

'Well—that was my mistake,' she sniped.

Lolita stood. She pulled the envelope out of her pocket and tossed it on the seat. 'He left you this. See you, mom.'

She spun on her heels and strode back to the car.

Chapter 17

Beckman scooped up the picnic basket and gave chase.

We did our good deed—can't deny that. Anything more was always going to be a bonus.

'Why didn't you post it?'

Lolita slowed to a halt. Beckman experienced déjà vu.

She turned. 'We didn't know your address, mom. You never gave it to me. You were gone.'

'You can find it through the Sheriff's office.' Ginetta was halfway across the house-littered lawn. The envelope was in her hand.

'I wanted to do the right thing. No—scratch that. I needed to. Life's too short. Jack just proved that.'

That awkward pause came again. Beckman didn't know whether to lob a grenade or a food parcel into the war zone.

'Did you get everything else?' Ginetta asked.

'Who else is there?'

'I guess.'

'So, I hope you get a decent insurance pay-out from that.' She gestured to the envelope. 'Because I know you won't take my charity.'

'But you'll take Jack's? You'll throw away your principles and move into the fancy house he left you?'

'I'm… re-evaluating him. And you should too. He didn't cheat on you.'

'He was a sexist, workaholic ass.'

'Yeah, he was. He worked hard for us. And now I know what it's like to run that company and work hard. Only, maybe I'll try to be less of an ass. Anyway, you got your alimony, you got your new life. What happened to Lowell anyhow?'

Oh, yeah. The rebound marriage. Conspicuous by your absence, Lowell. Unless…

He looked at the squished house.

Oh no. Now, how bad would I feel if…

'He left about five years ago. He found someone half his age,' Ginetta said.

'Oh.'

'Yes. It put me right off men for a while.' Ginetta looked at the wrecked property. 'And then Jo left a couple of days ago. Turns out I wasn't insured after all. It seems an old divorcee *without* a house or a pile of cash is not such hot property after all.'

'Well, this Joe is clearly an ass. Dating you for your money? You're better off without, mom.'

Ginetta shrugged in resignation. 'Yes. It's put me off women too.'

'Why?'

'Because clearly, she was a gold digger.'

'Who?'

Ginetta frowned. 'Jo.'

'Joe?'

'Jo. She walked out on me—well, walked out of the church shelter—when I found the house insurance had lapsed.'

Beckman watched Lolita's mouth try to form some words. Redness coloured her cheeks. His insides were doing odd things.

'Mom—you dated a woman?'

'More than dated, honey. It was going well.'

'Was…? Did…?'

Ginetta approached. Her voice fell plaintive, almost friendly. 'I was happy. Is that okay?'

Lolita searched her mother's face. 'Of course it is. I never wished *ill* of you. I just never expected… you know.'

Ginetta flashed a crease-lined version of The Eyebrow.

Ah. So it does run in the family.

'And I never expected you to marry a travelling salesman.'

'Looks like we both… changed.'

Ginetta nodded.

Mother and daughter were the closest yet to actual contact. Maybe not something as wild as a hug, although it had been a few minutes laden with *surprises*.

Lolita indicated the envelope. 'Are you going to open it?'

Ginetta looked down at it. 'I don't know.'

'Well, at least you have it. Not sure what it can be, but maybe it's none of my business.'

'I could really do with a million bucks.'

'I doubt it's that.'

'Me either.'

Lolita flashed Beckman an unknown query, as if seeking permission. He could only smile, not being on her wavelength.

She put her shoulders back and looked squarely at Ginetta. 'If you want the house, it's yours.'

The response was a half-smile. 'That's… a big step towards forgiving him. Huge. At a few minutes notice?' Ginetta shook her head. 'The asshole would be laughing in his grave. Thanks, Lolita, but no.'

'You can't live here.'

'You were always smart like that.' For the first time, Ginetta properly smiled.

'Don't do it for Jack; do it for me.'

Ginetta tentatively touched her daughter's shoulder. 'It was good you came. Maybe in different circumstances, I'd offer you the basement den. You know—if we were talking.'

'We *are* talking, mom.'

'And who's more surprised about that—you or me?'

'Me.'

'I'll work something out here. I did alright for enough years. Thanks for checking up on me. I'm pleased, after everything Jack did to shut you out of his inheritance, he saw sense at the end. No nasty surprises.' Her brow creased fondly. 'You deserve to be happy. I didn't approve of you staying, but you had to do what was right for you. If it meant you two made up, then… good. Just look after this man of yours—better than Jack looked after us. Call me up, okay? Especially if… Especially if a ballsy little granddaughter comes along.'

Lolita's cheeks coloured. She took a step back, then regained her composure. 'Sure. I will.'

'We always… hoped, you know? To continue the line.'

An echo of something recent—something curious—blew through Beckman's frame, like a ghost. From Lolita's expression, it caught her too.

'Mom. Is this….' Lolita lowered her voice—although there was nobody else in earshot. 'Is this about the box?'

'Box?'

'Wooden casket. From the Will.'

'Casket? What…?' A sudden sternness arrived on Ginetta's face. She shook her head as if in disbelief. 'So she handed it back to Jack. I might have known. The cow. Currying favour. About five minutes after I left Sunrise, I'll be bound.' Ginetta scrunched her hair in annoyance.

'Mom, what? Who handed it back?'

'Small box? About yay big?'

Lolita nodded. 'That's right.'

'She couldn't even do me that simple favour. I mean, sure, you'd get it anyway, but—'

Lolita took hold of her mother's agitated hands. 'Mom, mom. Who? Mary-Ann?'

'Mary-Ann? No! Why would I…? No. Sandy. I gave the box to Sandy to look after.'

'Sandy? Who the hell is Sandy?'

Ginetta pulled her hands away and stepped back. 'O, Lord. Look, honey, promise you won't be angry?'

'How can I get angry when I don't have the slightest clue what you're talking about? Who is Sandy?'

Ginetta took a deep breath, glanced at Beckman—who remained equally at sea about the whole business—and then looked at Lolita as if she were a child apologising for breaking a vase.

'Sandy is my sister.'

Chapter 18

'But you don't *have* a sister.'

'Half-sister.'

'But you don't have a….' Lolita shook her head vigorously, grabbed her mother's hand—as if it belonged to that errant child, and marched her back to their impromptu outdoor seating area.

'This beats any damn tornado, and you're giving me the full works, or your own eulogy will suddenly be a whole lot briefer and less complimentary.'

Beckman, puppy for the day, followed.

This box is only supposed to be relevant to existential crises in Sunrise—not precipitate a swift end to an unexpectedly positive reconnection of its inhabitants.

They retook their seats.

'Start at the beginning, mom.'

Ginetta laid her hands in her lap, gathered a deep breath, and dredged up the past. 'You know my mom divorced. Well, pretty soon, she had a fling and out popped Sandra. She and I are… different, and it wasn't a lot of fun sharing a house. Then when we grew up, she was always ahead of me when it came to men. And that included trying to steal whatever boy I was dating.' She shook her head sadly. 'When Jack and I got together, and it got serious, that pissed her off. She was taller, thought she was prettier, and got jealous. She tried to sink Jack and me more than once.'

'Taller? Hell, you were already taller than he was. I remember he used to snap if you went out together with heels too big.'

That made Ginetta smile momentarily. 'But she didn't steal Jack, and I made damn sure she didn't get invited to the wedding. We'd long passed the not-talking stage. So, when you came along, honey, I had no reason in the world to tell you about her. Because if you think *I'm* not worthy of your Christmas list, she sure isn't.'

'What about the box? What's up with that?'

'When I left town, I put on a brave face and asked Sandy to look after the box for me. I got it when my dad passed, when I was about ten. I was his only child. At that stage, there was no way Sandy deserved anything he left—because she wasn't his kid.'

'Why ask Sandy, then?'

'Because the box is a Sunrise heirloom. I'll bet the executor said to you what he said to us—it's about protecting the town. I couldn't do that if I'd left, could I? So I left it with Sandy as the next best thing. It had to stay in town, for safekeeping.'

'Sandy lives in town?' Lolita asked in disbelief. 'I've been walking the streets, maybe bumping into an aunt I never knew I had?'

Ginetta rubbed her forehead. 'I'm sorry. But what difference does it make? Doesn't affect your inheritance. Besides, it's not like you've gotten along famously with Jack or me these last few years—why would you want another dose of family angst?'

'So why would she hand it to Jack? It's crazy. And why would Jack pass it off as his possession to leave to me? It's not a Milan heirloom; it's a Thornton one.'

'That's true. Maybe it was her way of wheedling herself back into his affections. Better late than never. Trying to get hold of his millions before he popped off.'

Ginetta sighed. 'That's Sandy, always wanting what she couldn't have.'

'Well, I know he and I didn't break bread together, but I didn't even get a sniff of him with someone else.'

'Maybe it was just the box. I mean, I got rid of it because I didn't want the responsibility. She was happy to take it at first. Intrigued by the history and mystery, no doubt. That's the bookish librarian for you.'

'She works in the library?'

Ginetta nodded. 'You go there a lot?'

Lolita chuckled. 'Not once.'

'You still have all your Egyptian history stuff at home, I suppose.'

'Not so much now. I dumped most of it when I took over the business.'

'Anyway, maybe Sandy got fed up of having the box on her shelf, or under the bed or whatever, and gave it to Jack. She must have thought it should go back to the real family—a rare spark of honesty and good grace.'

'We're certainly not keeping it on the shelf or under the bed. Too likely to get lost or damaged.'

'Good. That thing is like a hundred years old.' Ginetta wrung her hands gently. 'Even I was messing around one day, soon after I had it, and chipped the corner off. I never looked inside, though.'

'Chipped the corner off?'

'Yes. I felt terrible.'

'Did you get it repaired?'

'I didn't see any point. Spodge didn't say it had to be pristine, only handed down, not spoken about—all the cloak-and-dagger warnings he probably gave you.'

Beckman hadn't had much to say, and certainly didn't want to butt into an unfolding air of familial harmony. Now, though, something rapped at the inside of his skull.

'Ginetta,' he asked, still unsure whether to address her as Milan or Thornton. 'Just for completeness, you know, to make sure we're all on the same wavelength here, this box of yours—it has what looks like a raised pentagon motif on the lid? Plus the chip, maybe—if Sandra or Jack didn't get an artisan to repair it.'

The woman frowned. 'Pentagon? No. It has… like a Roman 'one' on it. An 'I'.'

'No, that can't be right,' Lolita said. 'It must have got damaged again. Or that damn sister of yours played My First Carpentry Set with it.'

'I wouldn't put anything past her.'

A foghorn went off in Beckman's brain. 'There is another explanation, isn't there?' Both Mrs Milans, senior and junior, looked at him. 'It's not the same box.'

Chapter 19

Tyler glanced at the huge iron clock on the wall in Our Buck's.

Some days, he wondered which was more out of place—the carefully constructed, antique-looking timepiece, or the dozens of garish neon lights which festooned the room in all colours of the rainbow.

Perhaps it was just a microcosm of the town's quirkiness.

The clock showed ten minutes since Buck had disappeared into the back room.

Tyler eyed the door to the small adjunct, where Buck kept various supplies and unwanted items.

He wasn't cursing that the man hadn't yet reappeared with the new sack of beans to make Tyler his long-overdue coffee. He was growing concerned that bulky men are prone to heart attacks, and also wishing he knew CPR.

He considered Buck a friend—whether or not the feeling was reciprocated—and felt a civic duty to investigate. The barista had been maudlin for a few days, and people do crazy things when they're at a low ebb.

Tyler crossed the room and gingerly opened the door.

Buck was perched on a chair, head in hands.

He looked up. 'Oh, yeah. Sorry, Tyler.'

'Whoah. What gives, buddy?'

Buck waved it away. 'Nothing.'

Tyler tugged over a dusty bar stool. 'You just lost the two favourite women in your life. You may be a great barista, Buck, but you suck at lying.'

'Not a lot of people can talk to me like that.'

'I'm not sure anyone feels much like talking to you right now.'

'That's fine. It's mutual.'

'In that case, I'll close the door and go work out how to make Bessie sing, before you lose more customers.'

'Touch her, and you die.'

'You should talk to someone.'

'What do you call this?' Buck spread his enormous arms wide.

'Hiding.'

'And I should talk to *you*?'

'Seems you lost your number one sounding board.'

'And you're calling yourself number two?'

Tyler shook his head. 'No. I'll guess Saul is number two.'

'He's out of town. First vacation in ten years.'

'Wow. Lucky guy.' Tyler frowned. 'Hang on. What if people break down?'

Buck waved it away. 'Not our problem. Besides, he chose the quietest time.'

'There's a *quietest time* for breakdowns?'

Buck leant back. The creaky old chair held his weight. 'Sure. Saul analysed it, went back over his last ten year's bookings. Put it all in a spreadsheet.'

'A spreadsheet? Our Saul?'

'"Our"? Isn't that kinda presumptuous?'

'Maybe I feel part of town now.'

'You thinking of staying?'

'I dunno.'

'Well, here's a free tip—don't convince someone you love that you're happy to stay, and then up sticks at five minutes notice.' Buck slumped forwards.

'I'm not sure if Amaryllis wants to stay here long term.'

'Is your future dependent on her?'

'I haven't decided.'

'You better had.'

'Why, you want to jump in?' Even as he said it, he wished he hadn't. He didn't want Buck taking Amaryllis away from him.

'No, of course not. But recent experience shows things can end quickly.'

Buck rose and pushed open the Fire Door. Light flooded in, making Tyler wince.

Buck considered the outside world. 'Maybe I should have asked Dixon to marry me.'

'Only if you meant it.'

Buck leant on the door frame. 'I dunno. Grasping at straws right now.'

'What's done is done.'

'You try and speak real wise for a guy who told me he was never in love.'

'I'm only trying to help, buddy. You're right—I don't understand you losing Dixon any more than you losing Lolita. Lolita's probably the thing I've got even less experience of—having a female friend I didn't either *want* to sleep with or actually *did* sleep with.'

'You've got about as much in common with me as the types of business we run.' Buck turned. 'And I'd rather have one Dixon—even one Lolita—than a chain of flings.'

'Hey—don't knock it 'til you've tried it.'

'I have no intention.'

'Why not? Might help you forget Dixon.'

'Lolita would be disappointed as hell.'

'You make it sound like she's your mother.'

Buck stepped close. 'She cares—cared—that's all.'

Tyler threw his arms up. 'Sorry for trying to help.'

'Screwing around isn't the answer.'

'Maybe you're just waiting for me to give you the answer you *do* want to hear.'

'Which is?'

'Run to the big city, scoop Dixon up, say sorry, and get the big hearts and flowers ending.'

'I don't think so.' Buck pulled a sack of coffee beans off the shelf.

'Okay, well, how about I give you all the options and let you pick the one you want?'

'Now you're being an ass.'

'Out of the two of us, I don't think the ass is me,' Tyler suggested.

'I sure as hell wasn't the ass to her. I don't know.' He sighed. 'Anyway, I gotta get back to it.'

Buck pulled the external door closed. Tyler didn't mind—because Buck was no longer brewing his own solitary misery. It looked like he was about to brew up something better.

Tyler pointed at the sack. 'Need a hand?'

'I'm good, thanks.'

Tyler opened the door to the café.

Buck laid a hand on his shoulder. 'Listen, thanks. Beating myself up for not being the right guy is dumb. I should blame the *town* for not being a big, dumb, attractive mess as well as me. That's what she was missing, and we both know Sunrise isn't like that.'

'No. But it serves the best coffee, right?'

Buck smiled. 'Sounds like, if you stayed, you'd have a shot at being a favourite customer. You know—seeing as I just lost my best two.' The smile faded.

'Lolita and Beckman love you *and* the town. And they live here. I don't think that bridge is burned.'

Chapter 20

Beckman had spent a few unusual nights with Lolita— in nine short months, circumstances had created expectation, angst and despair. Some days, their relationship was a catamaran, skimming across the waves. One big crest, and they might turn turtle.

Events were never anything less than left-field. Perhaps that was life's payback for the previous twelve years of routine and unadventurous plodding. Arguably, if they'd had the foresight to pack a tent for this road trip, the current situation wouldn't be so odd.

All the same, there's been no catfight, and I haven't received The Eyebrow—from either of them—so much as once. This whole thing has been crazy enough anyhow—why sweat this part?

The candles threw flickering shadows onto the dark walls of the den, only reinforcing the slightly creepy nature of the scene. Whilst he knew that a house couldn't collapse *below* floor level—especially an already collapsed house—his gaze occasionally darted towards the mass of crushed building above the ceiling.

'I thought you said it was safe.' Lolita pulled another slice of takeaway pizza out of the box.

'It is. Maybe it's the whole sleeping-with-your-girl-in-your-mother's-basement vibe. I feel like a teenager.'

'Weren't you just bragging how *few* girls you got to bunk down with in those days?'

'As opposed to this pull-out bed being probably very familiar to you.'

She slugged a beer. Across town, services were relatively intact—except accommodation. The place was overflowing with rescuers, visitors and displaced citizens.

As they couldn't consider driving home that evening, and the car seats were a recipe for minimal sleep, Beckman had joked that Ginetta's basement den looked pretty accessible and might be habitable. The alternative was to cram into the church shelter with mom, but that didn't seem appetising.

So here they were. It was one rung above the tent they didn't have.

Besides, how much sleep would they get, wondering about the revelation of the second mystery box?

He scoffed a pepperonied slice.

'Is this the kind of honeymoon you had in mind?' he asked. 'Pizza by candlelight, crammed into a cold room underneath a ruined house, hoping the cops don't kick us out for trespassing?'

She sidled over to him on the floor. 'It's peak romance, huh?'

'It's only missing a bubble bath and you in suspenders.'

She kissed him. 'I don't think either of those is *mandatory*. Local food, alcohol. Sightseeing unusual things. Plus a bed. That's plenty of honeymoon.'

He eyed Mrs Milan senior/Thornton's put-you-up. 'You can't be serious.'

She kissed him again. 'We could talk all night about those boxes. Or we could take our minds off them altogether. Just for a little while.'

At least we know her parents aren't going to stumble in and catch us at it…

Without running water at the property, they weren't entirely refreshed when they met Ginetta at the shelter the following morning.

When we get to the Motel tonight, we'll probably run them out of soap and water.

They bypassed conversation about the boxes—besides, it wasn't Ginetta's concern anymore. She had more pressing matters to deal with, like finding somewhere to live and coming up with the money to do so.

Beckman wished she'd at least concede to taking some of their money, if not Jack's, but her pride wouldn't have it, nor would she accept the chance to move back to Sunrise. It wasn't spite anymore, though: if she'd historically been metaphorically flipping the bird at Jack, now she was merely standing with arms folded.

Ginetta came outside to converse. Either she didn't want to air her dirty laundry in front of her new slum buddies, or she didn't want them to think she'd softened in her attitude towards her estranged daughter and scumbag husband.

She was carrying something. Something which didn't require much guesswork to figure (at least, compared to a box with mystery provenance and alarming purpose).

'Is that what I think it is?' Lolita eyed the covered dome with curiosity.

'I know you swallowed a lot of pride,' Ginetta glanced at the Mustang, 'And burned a lot of gas coming up here, and I know you think I'm being stubborn not taking your offer of help with a new house, but if you could find a place for Flint, that would be sweet.'

Stay calm. Don't let on how cool this is.

Lolita gestured to the church. 'None of your friends want him?'

'I think he's blotted his copybook in public once too often.'

'And yet, you want us to have him?'

'Sunrise is not such a… judgemental community as here. Besides, like you said, I've got more important things to worry about.'

'You could let him go?'

'He'd be all alone. He likes company. Just do me this favour, honey? Okay?'

Lolita weighed this. Then she eased up the drape which covered the cage. A squawk emerged. Lolita's face broke into sober amusement.

'I guess he is kinda pretty.'

Beckman craned in. Lolita pulled the cloth back further.

'Great rack,' chirped the parrot, with alarming diction.

Lolita snickered and put a hand to her chest.

Ginetta laughed awkwardly. 'Yes, well, Flint does speak his mind at times.'

Beckman glanced at Lolita. 'Should fit in just fine,' he murmured.

Lolita socked him gently in the stomach.

'Who's this clown?' Flint cocked his green-crested head at Beckman.

'Mom, it's… adorable.'

'He has his moments,' Ginetta replied.

'That's the spot, Jo. That's the spot,' Flint intoned.

Ginetta gritted her teeth and her cheeks coloured. 'Anyway…'

'Go, baby. Jo, baby.'

'You shut your beak, Flint.'

'Shut your beak. Shut your beak.'

Ginetta rudely tugged the cover down over the cage. 'Infuriating creature.'

Lolita's mouth was bursting with the laugh she was holding in.

'Flint's… going to be… fun,' Beckman suggested.

'Keep him covered—that's my advice.'

'If he's so annoying, why do you keep him?' Lolita wondered.

'It's company, it's easy to look after, and it doesn't have affairs. That makes Flint a veritable saint.' Ginetta patted her hair. 'Now, you take it easy on the way home.'

'Mom, I'm thirty-six. *You* take it easy.'

'I just went through a tornado, a break-up, a death, and having to make nice with a daughter I thought I despised. I'll be fine.'

'Despised?'

'*Thought*. Now, will you stay in touch?'

'Mom, we both said that last time, and look what happened.'

'People change. For some people, the only way is up.'

'Meaning you, or me?' Lolita asked.

'Yes,' Ginetta replied obliquely. 'Now, thanks for looking out for me, and thanks for the letter—which I don't promise I'll open, and sorry about Sandy. Just… maybe don't march into the library with that attitude of yours.'

'Attitude, is it?'

'And, for the record, I do approve of the man you married.' Ginetta's face creased into reflective affection. 'In fact, I think you did better than me.'

Better than a dead, sexist jerk. Wow, Mrs M/T, easy on the compliments, okay? Not sure my swollen head will fit in the car, what with having to carry home additional bulky, loquacious luggage.

He watched, the atmosphere crackling with tension, as the women came to within touching distance of each other.

Ten bucks says they don't hug.

'Promise me one thing, mom? Keep your cellphone charged, okay?'

'I will. And you have my permission—no, my insistence—to take my box back from Sandy. It was only ever a loan, a person in Sunrise I felt would do me a favour. She was the only bridge I didn't burn to dust. Now you and I are… talking, at least, it's rightfully yours. It will be when I die, and while I don't want that to happen any time soon—certainly not before you ring me to tell me which Maternity Ward you're on—I bequeath that box to you now. It seems you're the kind of honest, caring person who should have it.'

Lolita gave a happy sigh. 'Thanks, mom. I'll try and do the right thing.'

Ginetta tentatively reached out and stroked Lolita's shoulder. 'Now, run along. I'm having coffee with Elena. She *was* insured. And she has a great ass.'

Lolita's mouth opened and closed like a fish, then she shook her head in good humour and walked towards Beckman and the car.

'You can take a girl out of a crazy town, but you can't take crazy out of the girl.'

Ten bucks. Boom.

Chapter 21

Nine hundred miles, one passable Motel, two lengthy showers and zero breakdowns later, Beckman eased the Mustang off Infinity Highway and onto the hidden road into Sunrise.

Lolita had fallen quiet in the last hour, and he wondered whether she was thinking the same as he.

Wish I could get the coffee and root beer I desperately need, but one reconciliation is probably the limit for this week. All the same, I'd pay folding money to see Buck standing on the sidewalk, arms wide in an apologetic invitation, when we slide past.

It wasn't to be. Instead, they went to Jen & Berry's, where two familiar faces were a good enough welcome.

'So, you made it back in one piece.' Reba raised her milkshake in a toast. 'No bruises, no blown head gaskets?'

Beckman and Lolita sank into their chairs.

She'll rejoice in spilling the beans on the breakdown.

She did. Plus the skinny on the softening of mother-daughter tensions, a night underneath a house, and Mrs M/T's sexual… journey.

The subject of the boxes was left alone. They'd kept Flint in the car for that very reason. Whilst he'd stayed under wraps for most of the trip, they weren't naive enough to believe that the blanket stopped the bird from hearing as well as talking. It had demonstrated a regurgitative capacity a mother gull would be proud of, and the last thing they wanted was for Flint to cheerily pipe up, "These bozos have got two secret boxes" in the middle of a crowded diner. After all, Beckman and Lolita had been pondering the subject for most of the last day or so.

Plus, you wondered whether you'd be similarly enamoured of Lolita's fifty-something ass when she reached that age.

'So, what did we miss?' Lolita asked, when the tales were told.

'We had a crime.'

'Other than the murder Buck committed last week?' she growled. 'Sorry. Go on.'

'A domestic break-in. You know Romeo True?'

'They broke into a cop's house?'

'Some balls, huh?'

'Did they catch the asshole? Did Romeo tear him a new one?'

Reba shook her head. 'Still a mystery. Nothing was taken except a family heirloom, apparently.'

Lolita snorted. 'More trouble than they're worth, sometimes.'

Careful where you tread, darling.

'So…,' Beckman interjected, to change the subject, 'Dixon didn't come crawling back, I suppose?'

'No,' Randall said. 'But on the plus side, Buck didn't offer me a contract to go to the big city and put a bullet in her head.'

'He's taking it pretty well, then.'

Lolita gestured for calm. 'Please. Red flag subject. I made up with mom, and I did a damn good job not being a bitch, so I'm feeling pretty good and don't need a downer. We're back, and I did what Jack expected of me.'

Now we just need to do what Ginetta asked… and hope Sandy doesn't have her own request too, or we'll be chasing our tails forever.

How about that? You're actually keen to get back to being a salesman.

Yeah—because that means ordinary. Predictable. Safe.

Oh well. Old habits die hard.

They worked together in the kitchen to make dinner.

'Jack gets a box, and Ginetta gets a box. Two in the same family? What are the chances?'

Lolita set down the chopping knife. 'It's a small town. If enough families stay, you'll get coincidences.'

'What do you think old Spodge would say? Two emergency override switches in the same house?'

'He has to know already. He didn't stand in the way, so it must be okay.'

'That puts us in charge of the whole deal.' Beckman sighed heavily. 'Serious pressure.'

'To do the right thing or to ensure continuity?'

'Both. Besides, you do realise that if this crazy bad thing happens, we won't need "continuity", as you put it. We'll be the ones opening the box. Boxes.'

'Which is it? Dad's, or mom's?' she wondered aloud.

'Both. Has to be.'

'Why does it have to be? Maybe it's a failsafe. One could be lost. Two—you have safety.'

'So why do the boxes look different?'

Lolita resumed chopping the carrots. 'Search me. Maybe the box maker was a real craftsman, didn't like two pieces the same.' She shook her head. 'Anyway. It's not important.'

Beckman came close. 'No, but one thing is. God willing, we *don't* have to open the box—or boxes—we need to work out who to hand them on to. If giving that letter to mom got you all riled up with obligations of duty, this tradition knocks it into a cocked hat.'

Lolita bit her lip, set down the knife, and cupped his cheek. 'Is this code for what I think it's code for?'

'Not smut or insinuation—cross my heart. Practicalities.'

'Having a child.'

'Or two,' he chirped. 'One box each!'

I hope you called that levity right, dude. The knife is pretty close by.

'What have our families brought to the party? Sandra—spinster. Me—only child. You—the same. Think it's a sign?'

'Clearly, Jack and Ginetta couldn't pop out anything better than you afterwards, so they didn't bother.'

She smiled. 'And you?'

'They didn't want to burden the world with two Beckmans. One was more than enough.'

'You're telling me.' Her smile faded. 'This is serious—boxes or no boxes.'

He embraced her. 'I know. It's your decision. Yours is the life that'll be changed the most.'

'Hmm. And there's the rub. How can I spend years railing against Jack for being an absent parent, then step into his shoes at work and do the same? For all my desire to show the asshole that I—or any woman—could do a damn fine job running the business, I never wanted to be a workaholic with no time for being a wife… or a mom.'

'And I would have been a damn sight more absent a father if I was still a road warrior—seeing the family at weekends only.'

'I think the universe is sending us a sign, don't you?'

He pulled her close. 'Don't feel you have to make a snap decision. But I'm up for some practice if you are.'

Chapter 22

Over breakfast, Beckman's thoughts were sucked back into the gravity well that was The Mysterious Boxes.

Judging that it wasn't as taboo as, for example, mentioning the words "Buck Travis", he subtly took charge of preparing the bagels how she liked them, to bank some goodwill… just in case.

'I've been thinking—what kind of existential threat would be relevant a hundred years ago *and* today? Unless whoever created these boxes had the foresight for things like nuclear war or asteroid strikes, what kind of thing are we talking about here?'

'Maybe it's something to do with The Portal?'

Beckman set down his mug. 'And there was me thinking *I* was suggesting crazy things.' He waved it away. 'We got rid of The Portal anyhow. Well, Dixon did.'

'Her first act in disrupting the equilibrium of Sunrise.'

Beckman frowned. 'Don't tell me you wish she'd left the door open for Carlton to maybe come back?'

She shook her head vehemently. 'No way. But maybe the original settlers knew about The Portal? Even experienced something which scared them into creating this… emergency escape clause?'

'It's moot. The thing is gone now. Surely Spodge & Sons would know, and stop making the boxes such a big deal? No—it must be something else. Question is, what could threaten the livelihood of a one-horse desert town, and the same place decades later? It doesn't make sense.'

Lolita chewed pensively. 'Its secrecy? Isn't that what we hold dear the most? We're off the beaten track, tucked away—an island in the sea of crime, violence, chain stores, fear... you name it. Sunrise is an oasis. It must have always been that way. Maybe that's it? After all, how can two little boxes protect against bombs or armies? If you think they contain an all-powerful crystal that we can hold aloft to repel borders, I'd worry you were getting fantastical about it all.'

She took her plate to the sink. 'Anyway—it's moot. I've no desire to open it. All we have to do is get Sandy's box back, work out where to keep it safe, and then move on. Finally.'

'If she'll talk to you.'

'I was tact personified with mom. This time I'm turning it up to eleven. Besides, she's a librarian, for heaven's sake. It's hardly like going into war against Genghis Khan.'

The library wasn't as old as the Spodge premises, but it had certainly been around since the days of black and white (television, not vison, as Beckman reminded himself).

There were two staff; one male, one female. The latter was of the right age to be Sandra, but there was no helpful name badge. She was helping another customer, so Beckman and Lolita toured the space, winding up at the Local History section.

On the wall was a current town plan; beside it was similar from 1880. Beckman spied a few landmarks, but as expected, it had basically been a one-horse town.

He scoured the shelves for something obvious like a potted history of Sunrise, but to no avail.

'What are you looking for?' Lolita whispered.

'Just curious.'

'Let it go, honey.'

'I'm not allowed to find out a little about my new home?'

'There's hardly likely to be a book called, "How To Care For Your Curious Old Box".' She shot him The Eyebrow (Perspicacious version).

'Maybe we'll find out that Jack's ancestors used to be Mayor of this place or something.'

He thumbed through various thin tomes.

'More likely discharged from the Confederate Army for dereliction of duty,' she scowled.

'What happened to all that forgiveness?' he hissed.

She sighed. 'You're right. I need to be in a good mood to meet—'

There was a cough nearby. They turned.

Up close, the shape of the woman's nose gave it away. *Sandra Almost-Certainly-Thornton.*

Unless she took her mom's maiden name. Or her father's name. Either way, the nose is a Thornton nose, and it carried on into the Milan clan.

Lolita's nose runs in the family.

Ba-dum tss.

'Can I help you?' Sandra (Surname TBC) asked.

Lolita put on her sweetest smile. 'Sandra?'

'Yes?' she replied warily.

'I'm Lolita. Ginetta's daughter.'

Sandra wrinkled her nose. 'I know very well who *you* are.'

'And now I know who you are,' Lolita said brightly. 'It's always nice to meet new folks in town. Even, you know, ones I could have bumped into—even been introduced to—years ago.' She coughed. 'But, families, huh?'

'What do you want?' Sandra sniped.

'I saw Ginetta.'

'Hence the big reveal about the sister she never wanted.'

Beckman was impressed: Sandra held the tone of a librarian's quiet but time-poor helpfulness, edged with utter distaste.

'Her husband just died. She's probably not that interested in venting hatred right now.'

'And you?'

'I don't know you, Sandra. I'm only here on an errand.'

Sandra glanced at the shelves. 'Local history research?'

'Only to kill time. I'm here because you have something belonging to my mother, and she would like it back.'

'I don't have anything of hers. Certainly not the dumb gall she had to walk out on her family.' Sandra flashed her own sweet smile.

Lolita looked around. Beckman did likewise. Prying ears were not welcome now: a squabble was one thing to air; secret heirlooms were different.

'She gave you temporary custody of a wooden box. She'd like me to take it off your hands.'

Sandra shrank back. 'Would she now?'

'She asked me very nicely to ask you very nicely. It's in her estate, and in her gift to let me have. It must be a weight on your mind to look after it, not to mention that you'd have to get involved later in a messy legal tug of war with someone you despise. So, the polite thing is to pass it over now.'

'How do I know she wants me to let you have it?'

'Because, Sandra, how else would we know it even exists?'

'How did the topic come up? All part of a sudden air of detente? Is she dying?'

'No. You'll be pleased to hear she's right as rain. She simply wants the chain to continue to a *rightful heir*, as I'm sure she made plain when she *loaned* the box to you for safekeeping.'

'You're aware that a very similar box was *stolen* this week? In my position, I'd be very nervous about handing my box over to just anyone.'

Lolita frowned. 'Stolen?'

Reba said, honey. That cop's house.

'The criminal is still at large. Where did you say you were over the last few days?'

Lolita's eyes flared.

Beckman grabbed her hand to impart some calm.

'Firstly, in Kansas. Secondly, it's not *your* box. Thirdly, what do you mean—"In my position"? Since when is a damn librarian judge and jury round here?'

Without warning, Sandra clutched Lolita's arm and tugged her into an alcove. Beckman, attached at the hand, had to follow.

Jeez, I wonder how Spiteful Sandy treats people who return their books late? Cat o' nine tails?

'My position, Lolita, is more important than you can know. Ginny didn't say more than a sentence about that box, but I already knew plenty. I know they exist. I also know people shouldn't be poking around trying to find out what they're for. If one has gone missing now, things are at risk.'

Lolita was open-mouthed. 'What crazy nonsense are you on?'

Sandra looked around. Beckman was bemused: yes, there was reason to be cautious, but there were nerves in the woman's face. Something else, too. He sensed her mind running at full tilt.

'If the existence of that box—those boxes—and who has them is not for the ears of anyone in town besides their owners, this is not either. I only tell you because,' she looked Lolita up and down with a sneer, 'You're almost a relative.'

'Wow. I feel *so* blessed.'

'The reason those boxes stay hidden, and they have remained closed for generations, is not only because people do the right thing. It's because someone watches to make sure things don't get out of hand.'

'Spodge?' Lolita asked.

'No. Me. There's always one person with oversight. Like… a guardian angel.'

'You—an *angel*?'

'Metaphorically, honey,' Sandra said with disdain. 'The point is, if anyone tries to mess with a box, I have the right to take it from them. Even you.'

Lolita smiled knowingly. 'But we don't have a box. Only you do.'

Technically untrue.

But I like your moxie, baby.

After all, you're a hotshot CEO who gobbles up other companies for breakfast.

She's a librarian.

You can out-logic her with two hands tied.

'That's true.'

'And surely you couldn't strip *yourself* of a box?'

'No. Probably only the executor could do that. Not that he'd need to.'

'And how do you think he'd take the news that this "guardian angel" is in possession of a box in the first place? Doesn't that strike you as a lapse in this whole ancient web of… whatever? I mean, who polices the police?'

'I'm sure things will work themselves out.'

'Yes. By you handing over the box. If you're so damn invested in making sure people do the right thing, mom's box belongs with me, not you.'

'I'll certainly… consider it.'

'Well, I'll assume you know where I live. And I don't close at five.' Lolita brushed past Sandy and into the main open-plan area. 'Thanks for your help,' she announced. 'I knew the staff here would be able to provide me *exactly* what I was looking for.'

Chapter 23

Tyler necked another painkiller and gazed through the windshield. The main doors of Milan Lighting remained closed.

Still, it was not yet one o'clock, and Amaryllis was reliably punctual, so he should wait.

He was pleased that she'd embraced the remote working, utilising the small space they sub-let from Lolita. For Amaryllis—so used to a nine-to-five in the same location for years at The Pegasus Corporation—the jump to something relatively loose and peripatetic was a significant change. Yet, in comparison to the change in her demeanour, dress code, hair length and relationship status, a few days a week away from home base was not such a stretch.

After all, Sunrise had much to offer. Spending time here was pleasant, and it provided a bridge from his previous existence of constant travel towards something more manageable. Something which allowed time for things besides work. Things like having a picnic with his girlfriend.

A picnic wasn't the most original romantic gesture, but it was pretty painless.

He rubbed his arm. He'd debated the other, painful, gesture for a few days, then taken stock. Recent events had shown that words were easy to come by; gestures harder. Dixon had told Buck in words that she loved him and that she liked it in Sunrise. The following act had been to leave.

Tyler knew he was falling short when it came to words for Amaryllis, but hoped the gesture would have more impact. Besides, if he wanted to generate rapport with Buck, he needed to show the man that he was a grown-up now, not a one-night stand practitioner.

Getting on Buck's good side might, with luck, soften the big man's heart and cause him to accept Beckman and Lolita back into his café, and then into his life. That would make them all happier. Tyler wanted them to be happier, because they had made *him* happier.

His future looked different nowadays. It was in his control. Up until last year, it he'd been living with mom and putting in the daily miles to feed Mr Malvolio's black-hearted greed.

He'd never planned to leave that town, settle down, change jobs—certainly not until he'd snagged the Number One Salesman position. Mercifully, he'd avoided that fate.

Control meant responsibility and decisions. The CEO part was easy. Everything else needed direction—who to love, where to live, how to create a dream to aspire to. A *real* goal—not the desert island mirage Malvolio had peddled.

What did he *want* from life now? What was the goal?

Much as he worked his mind to it, he still didn't know—not for certain. He could only take baby steps which felt like being in the right direction.

Dixon walking out on Buck had shown Tyler that he didn't want Amaryllis walking out on him. Amaryllis might have plenty of reasons to leave: she'd had enough of Tyler as a boyfriend; she'd had enough of him as a boss; she wasn't thrilled with some aspect of Sunrise or the shuttling between her city apartment and the Sunset Hotel.

At least one of those reasons needed to be quashed.

As the Porsche's dashboard clock ticked over to 13:00, Amaryllis exited the building, replete in a navy pantsuit. She slid into the passenger seat.

'Is this a special occasion?' she asked.

A small, slightly fearful part of him wondered if this was code for "Is today the day you propose?". Arguably, however, the mere existence of the thought meant he acknowledged that it was a possibility—at least from her perspective.

'No, it's just lunch.'

He left that obliquely in the air, trundled the car out of the Milan parking lot, and took a left turn out of town towards the low hills.

Fifteen minutes later, they parked up on a rough track, walked a hundred yards to a view overlooking Sunrise, spread out the picnic and blanket he'd brought, and settled down.

Years ago, the Old Tyler would have tried to hurtle through the lunch part, aiming to get quickly to the outdoor shenanigans part. Not now; she'd made him better than that. All the same, her predilection for more upmarket, businesslike attire—replacing the somewhat boho wardrobe of previous years—only served to stir his desires.

'I could get used to this.' She gazed out over the view.

'Maybe not every lunch hour.' He winked.

'You're the boss, boss.'

'You do have a say in how much time we spend here. We're here as… partners too.'

'"Partners"?'

'You mocked me for saying "girlfriend" before,' he pointed out. '"Lovers" makes me sound one-dimensional.'

'You aren't that. You are pretty fine when it comes to romantic gestures, Tyler.'

'I want you to know—that's all.'

'You could just… say it.' She arched her brow.

'I thought about that. Then I thought, "Words are easy. Gestures are better".'

She raised her bagel in mock salute. 'Lunch is sweet, but if you want a free relationship tip, honey, maybe up your game.'

'I already did. Hang onto your hat, baby, because this is something you'll never expect.'

He pulled off his jacket, unbuttoned his shirt sleeve and rolled it up.

Her eyes widened in surprise and delight. 'It's… it's a… .'

He nodded. 'Amaryllis flower.'

'I can't believe you got tattooed for me.'

'First time for everything. And I have to say, it hurts *way* more than making lunch. You wouldn't believe it.'

She laughed. 'You know what's funny? I do believe it. What you won't believe… is this.'

She reached down, pulled up her trouser leg, and turned her ankle over so he could see.

There, in a small floral script, was the word "Tyler".

Chapter 24

After the meeting at the library—which Beckman ruled as an honourable draw—they went to the Milan Lighting office for a much-needed catch-up on work.

Jack will turn in his grave if we let the company tank now, especially if it's because our attention has wandered to a small wooden box—one whose existence was precipitated by the fact that Jack was in that grave.

Over afternoon coffee, Beckman was leafing through the pages of the Sunrise Beacon when something stopped him dead in his tracks and pushed aside the mere travails of Director Of Sales.

He went to Lolita's expansive cubicle and tossed the folded newspaper on her desk.

She shot him The Eyebrow (Unwanted Work Interruption version). He pointed. She read.

'Well, Sandra's going to have something to say about this.'

'How do you figure?'

'Her "position".'

He shook his head. 'I don't believe her.'

'Which part?'

'The guardian angel part.'

She tapped the paper. 'Maybe this will be the proof.'

'You think she'll have to break cover?'

'Old Spodge will. Sure, we're no experts on this, but what the hell is Romeo True doing? He's a cop. Surely upholding the law also means doing the right thing, obeying the rules.'

Beckman pulled up a chair and glanced at the article again. 'Maybe it's… a sting operation.'

'Stings are supposed to be carefully planned, keeping under the radar. Taking out a full-page ad spot saying, "Do you have a box like this? If so, bring it to the Sheriff's Office", isn't exactly subtle. I'll bet Spodge is apoplectic. One person announcing to the town that there's a casket? That's bad enough, but expecting other people to break the code of silence too?'

She shook her head. 'I mean, Romeo's not the sharpest cookie, but this is dumb as hell.'

'Or brilliant as hell.'

She sank against the backrest. 'One thing's for sure. I'm not going public about Jack's box—our box—unless it's on the compulsion of jail time. Unless everything Spodge said is some kind of scare story, this whole heirloom business has stayed *within families* for who knows how long. People have kept their damn mouths shut. I was going to say, "What if this hits the papers" but look!' She shook the Beacon. 'It's crazy.'

He gently took the paper from her and smoothed it out.

'What if it's a bluff? What if they're not expecting *many* boxes, only the stolen one. Look—there's even a reward. If a burglar broke in, grabbed an armful of stuff, and realised he'd wound up with nothing much of value—just a dumb old box—he'd find a way to drop the box somewhere in exchange for the cash.'

'And if the thief's already opened the box?'

'If it has any consequences, which I'll bet Spodge is keeping a beady eye open for, then it leads Romeo and the cops straight to the culprit's door.'

She sighed heavily. 'I know I shouldn't care about this. I know I need to focus on work. Jack spent decades building this. We had enough stress last year buying out EVI and fending off that runaway rat Dixon.'

'I hear you.'

'All the same, if we have a box, Sandra has a box, and Romeo has—or had—one, I can't help wondering how many others are out there.'

'If there's only those three, then the cops are out of luck. I'm keeping quiet, and I'll bet a million bucks Sandra won't speak up. Hopefully, it's bait for the thief; they return it, everyone forgets about it.'

He pointed at the newspaper. 'After all, it doesn't *really* give much away. It reads like a lost antique— something Romeo thinks may be part of a set. It doesn't scream "Deep Mystery", "Deadly Secret". We only know that ownership is special and private *because* we have a box too. Everyone else won't care less. They can't assume information they don't have.'

'And if there's more than three?'

'If the cops *do* get any handed in—not the stolen one—then providing they keep the names out of the papers, and don't open the box, I'd say it wasn't the end of the world. At least, not the end of Sunrise. Which would be a hell of a result, because the end of Sunrise is what the box is designed to prevent.'

'I don't like it, Beckman, that's all. I've got a feeling in my bones. This is a town that talks—you know that.'

'It's also a town that can keep secrets.'

Carlton's affair. Except, don't mention it. Not specifically.

'I love you to the moon and back, but you have to remember this has always been my town, not yours.'

She laid a mollifying hand on his. 'I don't mean anything by that, but burglaries around here are rarer than… honest travelling salesmen with a history of monochromacy. Now there's a break-in, and it concerns one of those boxes? There's a lie somewhere, and I think we need to be careful as hell, because I've lost enough this week already.'

Chapter 25

Tyler walked down Main Street like the cat that got the cream.

Amaryllis *cared* about him. It was an unusual feeling.

He clasped her hand tighter.

A familiar figure hove into view on the sidewalk ahead. He waved.

Lolita slowed to a halt. They were within spitting distance of Our Buck's.

'I'd ask if you wanted to come in for a coffee, but….'

'Thanks but no thanks, Tyler. The man can get by without my custom, and I can get by with other people giving a shit about me instead.'

Amaryllis laid a hand on Lolita's shoulder. 'You really should smooth this over.'

'I'll talk to the guy. I don't get the sense that this is *over*,' Tyler said.

Lolita shook her head. 'No, really. I don't need you playing mediator.'

'He's really in a funk—you know that?'

'And I lost my dad. He only lost a girlfriend. He could have taken a few hours out of his disappointment for the *one day* I was *really* in a funk.' She glowered in the direction of Buck's neon-lit frontage. 'I'm going to Wilson's. I've got more important problems to worry about.'

'Where's Beckman?' Amaryllis asked.

'Working. Trying to get our lives back to normal. I'll see you around.'

'I'll come,' Amaryllis blurted.

'It's fine, really.'

'You just said you needed *other* people to give a shit about you. I'm other people. I was your Maid of Honour. Does that count?'

Tyler barely heard the second half of the sentence. "Shit" was a new high for Amaryllis. Had all this cussing been pent up over fifteen years of prim subservience at Pegasus?

'I won't be as good company as Tyler,' Lolita replied.

Amaryllis leant in. 'Maybe I need a shoulder too?'

'Pumpkin pie for two, it is.'

Lolita watched Amaryllis pensively stir her coffee. 'Sorry. I should have accepted graciously. I don't have too many… shoulders anymore.'

'You have Reba. And Beckman, of course. That's two more than I have.'

'I think you'll find either of them delighted to lend an ear. You and Tyler almost feel part of the Sunrise family now.'

'Do we?'

'Do you not feel that?'

Amaryllis sipped. 'The back and forth to home—it feels like tourism. Don't get me wrong—a great kind, but it's like being… in limbo.'

'Why not move here?' Lolita clipped off a piece of pie.

'Alone, it would mean leaving Pegasus—realistically. I'm not sure I've the guts to do that.'

'Why alone? Are you and Tyler having problems?'

Amaryllis shook her head. 'The opposite. We wound up getting mutual tattoos.'

Lolita sat back. 'Wow. I mean, out of you and me, I'm the crazy one, and I'd never think about something like that. So—it's clearly love—what are these "problems"?'

'Is it love, though?'

'You mean because Tyler hasn't cut his ties and abandoned his old life like Beckman did for me?'

'No. Because he's never actually said "I love you".' Amaryllis offered a pointed look.

'And that worries you? Even after six months, tattoos, and I'll bet a whole lot of proximity.'

'Honestly, Lolita, a part of me still nags that a leopard never changes his spots. You heard what he used to be like. You were a lynchpin in the… "handover" from Mr Malvolio. Who's to say Tyler isn't still riding the wave? Salesman to rich CEO overnight? It would be easy to think he's only with me for appearances—to continue a sham which he only started to get my buy-in, to get the combination to the safe. To avoid me crying foul.'

Lolita savoured the mouthful of pie.

'I heard that Tyler was a lowlife before, but that would take the biscuit. Here's another thing: Beckman and I, we like you, and my own doting man is nothing if not a true student of behaviours and motivations. He'd see through Tyler in a second. If this was all a ruse, and Beckman spotted it, he'd find a way to tell you—or me, at least. From what I've seen, your man is on the level. Maybe he's still getting used to the idea of commitment.'

'I suppose.'

'Answer this—why did you get the tattoo? Pressure?'

'Not a bit of it. I think I got mine first.'

'Because you want this.'

Amaryllis bit her lip. 'I think I do. I'm not getting any younger, and if I thought Tyler wasn't right for… long term, then I should bail pretty quickly, huh? Find the forever guy somewhere else.'

'When's too late to make a decision? Yeah.' Lolita examined her coffee.

Amaryllis squeezed her hand. 'What decision?' she asked quietly. 'And I mean *yours*.'

Lolita gazed around the sparsely-populated coffee bar and had a brief internal debate.

'Long story short, we're thinking about having a baby. There's… pressure.'

'From Beckman?'

'No. From… obligation.' Lolita held up her hand. 'Not a topic for now. And I know my clock is ticking—much as I warned him off joking about it.' She smiled. 'But, there's lots to juggle, you know?'

'You'd rather wait. Until this… new life settles down.'

'I don't want to be too late and miss the boat.'

'Not a problem in my case. I hope Tyler understands that.'

'Forty-three is not impossible.'

Amaryllis looked sober. 'It is for me. Complications when I was younger. Isn't going to happen. But you—you're fine.'

'I hope I am. I'm not the most *regular* girl. Had a scare just last week. I'd hate to think Beckman bought into the perfect nuclear family life, and I couldn't… deliver. And mom was making insinuations about grandkids. And Jack's Will had *expectations* inside it. So, you know—pressure.'

'Do you want my advice? It's okay if you don't.'

'I think you're in pole position for independent advice. Beckman's invested, Buck's out of the picture, and Reba….' Lolita cocked her head, 'We've always got along, and she's dependable as all hell. But you've got, I don't know, a wise head—let's say that.'

'Six months in town, and I'm your new go-to girlfriend? That's a switch-up. Back in high school, you and I would have been poles apart.'

'Circumstances change people. Look at Tyler, for starters. So—what's the advice?'

'Take a fertility test. Make sure that a little Lolita or a baby Beckman is an option, when the time comes. It'll save a lot of anguish.'

'Sure?'

'What were you just saying about knowing where *I* stand?'

Chapter 26

Tyler sat at a corner table and watched Buck go about his business.

Selling for Pegasus for over a decade had honed his people-watching skills. It had done similar for Beckman and many of the sales force.

It used to be about seeking customers. Nowadays, it helped assess motivations, demeanour and mood.

The chunky proprietor was undoubtedly less in the dumps than before.

Was that Tyler's doing? Sure, Lolita had warned him off trying to engineer any reconciliation, but she hadn't said he couldn't discuss the Dixon situation.

After all, if Buck felt more upbeat about that aspect of life—or at least accepted it and moved on—perhaps it would alter his humours towards Lolita and Beckman?

Tyler purposely remained at the table until all the other customers had left, and Buck switched the flashing neon "OPEN" in the window for a permanently lit "CLOSED".

Buck wiped down the tables and then homed in on his last, stubborn patron.

He leant on the back of the chair opposite. 'I'm fine, Tyler.'

'Who said it was about you?'

'You think just because you gave me your two cents, I should offer you mine?'

Tyler stood and dropped a few notes on the table.

'You're right. I don't care what you think. We have nothing in common. Hell—I'm not even a proper citizen here. I'll ask Beckman. He may have hated my guts for twelve years, but he'll give me the time of day.'

He was halfway to the door when Buck spoke up. 'Thanks for asking.'

'I never asked.'

'Then, thanks for... staying.'

'You mean just now, or in town, period?'

'Both, I guess. But in town—it's a life choice. It's not for... city types, it seems.'

'Based on two people you dated? Sweeping statement, huh? Amaryllis and I are city people. Beckman was. Randall was. We love it here.' Tyler moved towards the table. 'Maybe Dixon said the issue was about Sunrise to save your blushes? Maybe she wasn't cold—only trying to save hurting you.'

'It works out the same. She's not here.'

'Let me ask you this. When your ex, Dena, left for Phoenix, do you regret not following her?'

'At the time, no.'

'Now?'

'What is this, the Spanish Inquisition?'

'What I'm saying is, if you wished you'd conceded to her way of life but didn't, why not concede now? If you care for Dixon as much as you did for Dena? Why not right that wrong?'

Buck sighed, pulled out the chair and slumped into it. Tyler sat.

'You are pretty sharp, Tyler.'

'It's why I made CEO.'

Buck frowned, then smiled. 'You made CEO because you left your predecessor to die, then took all his money.'

'You make it sound like a *bad* thing.'

'And you don't regret it?'

'Not for a second. I wound up here, and with Amaryllis. Nothing's forever, and Malvolio had his time in the sun.'

'And maybe I had mine with Dixon.'

'If you ask me, you gave in too easily. What's stopping you at least *trying* to make it work?'

Buck gestured around. 'This.'

'Bricks and mortar above love?'

'I thought we agreed you don't know a hell of a lot about love.'

'No, but I know about taking a risk and taking a shot.'

'I took a shot with Dixon. More than that—I tried so damn hard.'

'Maybe if you needed to try hard, it wasn't meant to be.'

Buck was taken aback. 'Are you saying *you* didn't need to try hard with Amaryllis? Beckman told me plenty about you. You were an A1 asshole, and now you're on the arm of what I have to say is a fine upstanding woman? You must have had to fight even the basic urge not to treat her like shit.'

'No. Not for a second. When I nearly went under that roadsweeper last year, I had plenty of days in a hospital bed examining my life. I had nobody except my own mom to miss me if I never made it through. I'd never built any bridges. It's corny, but I had an epiphany. There was another way. Maybe two women both wanting you *and* city life is your sign.'

'It's pretty easy to preach when you've had your own lightbulb moment. My roots go deep here.'

Tyler shrugged. 'I guess it's harder for you—if, by "roots", you mean "café", like you said.'

Buck's head drooped. 'There's more than that.'

'*People* you'd leave behind.'

Buck's nostrils flared. 'You got me, okay? The first day, I wanted to drive right up to the city and try and find a compromise—but I knew if she put her foot down, I'd cave. Why? Yeah—people. Person. Lolita, okay? No, we're not in *love*, but she's like the daughter I never had. A rock. That would have been too much. Six months with Dixon and I take a punt at quitting Sunrise forever and *hoping* we work out together? Lolita would have felt pretty betrayed.'

'Or she'd have been over the moon you got your *real* love.'

Buck waved a paw. 'Doesn't matter anymore. I wouldn't lose her by going now. I lost her already.'

'So—why not go? At least have it out with Dixon?'

'It makes me look desperate. She walked into this with her eyes open. She's smart. If hustle and bustle beats hugs and kisses, so be it.'

'You didn't give up on her before—when she was about to drive into The Portal and be gone forever. What changed?'

'I thought I could have a girl *and* a best friend—here. Now I can't have both here.'

'You could still have a best friend.'

Buck's gaze was penetrating. 'No offence, Tyler, but you'll never be the same as Lolita. What we had….' He sighed.

'Was a misunderstanding, which can be rectified much easier than a lifestyle choice.'

'I'm not running back to either of them, and that's final.'

'You'll wait here and hope?'

'You waited in the same job for ten years on the basis of hope,' Buck pointed out.

'Yeah—and in the end, I had to grab life by the balls to sort out the mess. Do something, Buck, please. You've got nothing to lose. What I did was pretty crazy, but it worked. Now I have everything I need.'

'Last throw of the dice?'

'Just don't burn bridges.'

Chapter 27

Reba and Randall stared at the slim white cassette on her kitchen table.

'I guess I've got a decision to make, and you have too,' she said.

He frowned. 'Isn't it the same one?'

'No. What I do about this is one thing, and you have to decide if it affects your position regarding… us.'

He bodily turned her around on the chair to face him: it was easy because he was eight inches taller and fifty pounds heavier.

He looked into her one good eye. 'Whatever you decide, I'm staying. I know you think this would give some guys a get-out clause, a sign to high-tail it out of town, but that's not me. I love you, and I'm staying.'

She stroked his cheek. 'And if I decide "Yes", does that make you happier, or regretful that we weren't… more careful?'

'I never saw myself as a settling-down guy. Matter of fact, I reckoned I'd be dead long before now, or no woman would be so dumb to date a guy like me. I won't deny this is kinda a shock, and I need to get used to the idea, but hanging out with April has got me thinking, now and again, maybe… what if?'

'Well, I need to sleep on it too, but I think we have something pretty damn good, and I'm not getting any younger, so…' She shrugged.

'I won't be bragging. I already snagged the best-looking, pint-sized, pistol-packing gumshoe in town. Crowing about knocking you up seems like showing off.'

'You have a way with words, Randall Ickey.'

'I'm a straight-shooter, that's for sure.'

A smile played on her lips. 'I think that's just been proven.'

He made coffee in her small, functional kitchen, and they went out to the back porch. Pop music drifted down from April's bedroom.

Reba toyed with the mug. 'I ask you something?'

'Sure.'

'How do you feel about meeting my parents?'

He did a double-take. 'But you aren't speaking to them.'

'Yeah. I was thinking about that. What I said to Lolita at the wake. She made up with Jack—just in time. Now she reached out to her mom. Hell—I even helped Beckman track down his dad. Feels pretty lame to play holier-than-thou about this. So… what do you say?'

'Let's say we did. What would you tell them about… today's development?'

She sipped. 'I don't know. Depends how it goes, I guess. They may not even open the door to me.'

'Long way to Tucson for a knock-back.'

'Yeah, but maybe they'll be feeling good about themselves—being right about what happened. Who knows, they might even be happy that I struck gold the second time around.'

Randall glowed inside at the idea of being referred to as 'gold' in the relationship department. 'It's your decision, honey.'

'I also thought—with my work hat on—that since we're in the neighbourhood, we might take a peek at how

Dixon is getting on.' She gave him a querying, how-can-it-hurt look.

'Dixon?'

'Buck said she left for a better life—her old life, and we both know—hell, the whole damn town knows—he's not taken it well. I've known Lolita fifteen years, and she and Buck never had a bust-up once. I'm not aiming to drag Dixon kicking and screaming back into Buck's arms if that's not what she wants. Still, if there's a chance of something—even a palatable explanation—making Buck sober up about the whole thing, it might allow him to make up with Lolita.'

'You're a P.I., not a matchmaker,' he pointed out.

'Sure, but if Dixon's moping around, regretting her decision, but trying to save face by *not* coming back here, who's to say our friendly concern won't sway her a little.'

'I'm not sure. She seemed like a pretty cold fish. You know—mergers, buyouts—the day job—maybe she sees the whole Buck episode as just another deal that fell through. No… *synergy*.'

'That's a hell of a word for you, Randall honey,' she said with her typically curious wink. 'Look, it can't hurt—like seeing mom and dad. We'd be pretty unlucky to come back zero for two.'

They arranged for April to spend the night at a friend's, gathered together a suitcase, and headed off for the impromptu trip.

En route, Reba regaled him with more background on her parents—it wasn't a subject she'd touched on before. Mom was a retired teacher, and dad was a skilled carpenter who had no intention of putting down his chisel.

Randall felt sad that they'd shown scant happiness for Reba's success as a P.I. and a parent. They'd even dismissed April's Asperger's as a 'phase'. He wondered how they'd feel about *his* previous, deadlier, 'phase', if the topic arose. All the same, he couldn't hide his past and hoped his love for their daughter would be readily apparent.

After three hours in the car, they pulled up outside a typical suburban house. The garage was expansive, and workmanlike sounds emerged from it. A sprinkler hissed on the lawn.

Reba killed the engine.

'So, what's your approach, my little detective? Stay low and guarded, or go in with all guns blazing?'

She took his hand. 'I'm going to admit that they were right about Elmer, that he was an unreliable douche, and I shouldn't have married him. Then I'll introduce you, say I'm older and wiser now, and I know what I'm doing. I'll tell them I'm pregnant, not married; and that I don't care if you don't propose to me, because you're a good man, you look after me, and I love you.'

'What about the fact that I used to be a hitman and unloaded most of a clip at you not so long ago?'

She met his gaze. 'Let's maybe leave that out for now, okay?'

Chapter 28

Beckman pored over the records in the Sunrise Library.

The place held town plans dating back generations, every copy of the Sunrise Beacon ever printed, a few books on local history (plus one on local flora, one on the background to the lightbulb-manufacturing industry, and a thin tome entitled 101 Things You Didn't Know About Sunrise).

Lolita had insisted—

No, not insisted. Suggested. But a wife's suggestion is seldom that.

—that they research the Milan and Thornton lineages to see how far back these mystery boxes went. Perhaps they would tie-up with an ancestor of Romeo True— maybe even Jeremiah Spodge—and shed light on the origin story.

Beckman half-hoped it pointed to a visiting circus clown in the 1900s, or a discredited snake oil salesman in the 1850s, and they could put the whole thing down to a joke whose punchline was way past its sell-by date.

Lolita was showing him an edition of the Beacon from 1894, in which the marriage of Franklin Milan to Bessie Crudge was announced, when a figure loomed beside them.

'Finding out about your new hometown, Mr Spiers?'

Ah. I see we've catapulted from withering glances to using surnames now. I expect we'll be invited round for tea within the decade.

'Just trying to get the lie of the land, *Ms Thornton.*'

He didn't know for sure that Sandra wasn't married, but all the signs were there.

'These records are very closely controlled, I should mention.'

'Because of your *position*?' Lolita said sweetly through gritted teeth.

'One can't be too careful.' Sandra glanced around. 'Those boxes are designed as a failsafe. A locked cupboard which is not to be opened, except by the right person at the right time. For certain, they have a provenance, and that must be as closely guarded as the boxes themselves.'

'Did you have words with Romeo True for going public?'

'He's a policeman. I'm sure he had motives. He's succeeded in getting one box handed in—but it's not the stolen one.'

'Really?' Beckman asked. 'So, will you take Lolita's box to the police station? I mean, if you'd already given it to us, we'd be sure to do the right thing, wouldn't we, honey?'

'Absolutely,' Lolita replied.

'I'm not sure that's a good idea. It all feels... fishy to me.'

'Surely the police position outweighs your own?'

'Lolita.' Sandra leant in. Beckman could smell her perfume—not the kind of scent which would attract a husband/wife/lover, even if its wearer intended. 'Romeo True, like us all, is a person first and a professional second. Nobody is above sating their curiosity about the box or boxes.'

'Even though the town's collective curiosity seems to have remained unsated for generations?'

'Every chain has a weak link. As someone who is keen for others not to break that chain, I'm not revealing my possession of your mother's box to anyone.'

Ha-ha! You said it was Ginetta's box! There's a crack in your armour, Ms Holier-Than-Thou.

'Well, Sandra,' Lolita said. 'When you do *deign* to pass over *my* property, I'll try to uphold your laudable attitude. Now, if you don't mind, my *husband* and I are tracing our family tree. I don't think there are any rules against *that*.'

Sandra's eyes flared. She pursed her thin lips but let the matter lie.

After she'd left, Lolita pushed her chair closer to Beckman. 'We should have got the name of whoever handed that box in.'

'Why?'

'Because I'll bet that if we follow that surname back, it'll intersect with dad's, mom's, or Romeo's before long.'

'You do realise, baby, that you own a lighting supplies company. Egypt and artefacts and provenances and that kind of stuff is not you anymore.'

'I get that. But—and much as I have no time for Sandra or her attitude—I have to agree that what Romeo True did, and what happened to his box, feels fishy to me too.'

They went for lunch at Ray's but kept the talk mundane.

Lolita was driving them home in her Miata when she pulled over to the kerb on Candela Avenue. She tugged on the handbrake but let the engine idle.

Did she leave her phone in the diner? Engine warning light?

'Reba said the only thing stolen from the Trues was that box. Right?'

'The only thing they put an ad out for, definitely.'

She shook her head. 'Reba knows Romeo, on and off. He said everything else was left alone. So my question is this: If these boxes—and who owns them—is the absolutely closest guarded secret around here, who the hell knew where to find one to steal?'

That was followed by The Eyebrow (What Do You Think Of Them Apples? version).

Beckman searched her eyes, then his mind, then the roof headlining, and came up empty. 'Nobody. Theoretically.'

'One person. Jeremiah Spodge.'

'Huh? A *lawyer* did the break-in? But they're such likeable, upstanding people.'

'There's only one way to find out. You switch on that Beckman Scrutinization Mode, and we'll go see if he's hiding something.'

They had to wait twenty minutes at Spodge & Sons. The coffee was mediocre. The air-conditioner rattled.

Finally, the secretary—barely five feet tall, unnecessarily blue shoes—said they could go in.

Approaching the door marked "J. Spodge Esq.", the strains of Metallica were unmistakable.

Beckman and Lolita shared a look of amused intrigue, then he knocked.

Silence fell.

Spodge, demure and sombre as ever, opened the door.

Well, Horatio, what about this lark, huh?'

They took the same two past-their-best seats in front of Jeremiah's still-undiminished In Tray. Beckman scoured the room for a music player.

Probably disguised as an old book, the crafty old sod.

'How may one assist thee?'

Lolita smoothed her skirt and cleared her throat. 'Forgive me for asking, Mr Spodge, but is it the case that there is more than one box like the specimen in my father's estate?'

Spodge's nose hair bristled in an extra-heavy exhale. 'It would be foolish for myself to deny such an apparent factitude, as events in this municipality attest to the existence of such additional items.'

'Yes. That's clear, I guess. Mr True and the unwanted publicity.'

'Very much so, Mrs Milan.'

'Am I correct in thinking that you were aware that Mr True owned a box, and that his parent's estate was lodged here? I'm only extrapolating, of course, from what you said—'

Jeremiah leant forwards and steepled his fingers. Reflexively, Beckman leant backwards. The chair creaked.

'Spodge & Sons have been executors for the estates of all box owners since time immemorial. We are entrusted with that grave duty.'

'So… you know *everyone* who has a box.'

'That logic proceeds, Mrs Milan. Thee are not the first to discern such a state of affairs.'

'Forgive me, Mr Spodge—I don't mean to cast aspersions or imply bad character—but isn't it feasible that you, as the one person in Sunrise who knows the holders of *all* these boxes, would be able to obtain them for whatever means you deemed necessary.'

A faint smile played on the man's grey lips.

I think the crusty metalhead is ahead of you, honey.

'Notwithstanding the impact on one's reputation by even considering such an act of desecration to the duty one has been foresworn to undertake, it would not be possible without attracting the attentions of… an individual whose role exists to prevent such subterfuge.'

'You mean like... a guardian angel,' Beckman inferred.

Spodge's grey retina swivelled to Beckman's position. 'That term is sufficiently explanatory.'

'Someone in town makes sure nobody—not even you—gathers all the boxes together for reasonable, or more likely unreasonable, ends?'

'Thee have adroitly understood the situation.'

'How many boxes are there? I mean, we know of at least four.'

Spodge sat back sharply. 'That information is *most* confidential.'

'Do you find it concerning—what Mr True did with that advert? Or even the burglary?' Lolita asked.

'Any breaking of the bonds of secrecy is looked upon most gravely by myself and the... overseer. Yet, until the thief involved in this misdemeanour is brought to task, no action can be taken. Nevertheless, it is the opening of the boxes—not the possession of same—which is the item of most import. The making public of the contents would be unconscionable. One has seen no evidence of such action. Hence, while one is disturbed, one entrusts that Mr True, as an agent of the law, will uphold the directives he swore to abide by.'

Spodge eyed them both, moved some papers on his desk by a centimetre, and asked. 'Will that be all?'

'Yes.' Beckman rose. 'Thank thee... one... you.'

As the door closed behind them, Beckman took Lolita's hand and held her there momentarily.

A guitar riff erupted.

Chapter 29

They slid into the car seats.

'So, Spodge doing a spot of burglary is pretty unlikely.'

Lolita bit her lip. 'I don't think that's the big news. My obnoxious aunt being some kind of Sheriff at the centre of the whole rigmarole is what I can't figure.'

Beckman shrugged. 'It fits with her job; brushing shoulders with public records, keeps abreast of the news.'

'I doubt Spodge would confirm or deny whether Sandra is the guardian angel.'

'For my money, he wouldn't know or be allowed to know. If he was some kind of evil box-collecting genius on the side, if he knew who the Box Police were, he could... I don't know... headbang that person to death, then get on with finding a perfect combination of tedious legal clauses to bore the box-holders into submission.'

She frowned. 'Hmm. I guess she was kinda nervous about us digging over town history. Bitchy, though.'

'She's only being difficult because it's you. She's got a chip on her shoulder a mile wide because you're the offspring of the sister she hates and a man she wanted for herself.'

'Yeah. She probably wanted to own that box by rightful lineage.' Lolita rolled her eyes.

'Beats me why she cares two hoots. It's just babysitting, except for forty years, not four hours. Like mom said, it's a weight of responsibility, not a damn free ice cream or the key to the pot of gold at the end of the rainbow.'

Lolita fiddled with the key fob. 'I wish I'd never gone to see mom. Then I wouldn't know about Sandra.'

'You don't mean that. Besides, if she is the guardian angel, she's on the side of protecting the town—and we all want that.'

She dropped him at the office and then went on an unspecified errand. Late afternoon, she picked him up, they stopped into Oskar's Pet Store to grab food for Flint, then had a cosy evening at home.

As he lay in bed, the box beneath the bed frame nearby, he set his mind to what kind of safe they should buy to keep the box… safe.

I wonder if they do them with fingerprint security? That would be cool. Ooh! How about a retina scan?

In the morning, he set off for a few sales calls around the district. The biggest deal was closed in the Town Of Six Sales. The folk there might not have been crying out for headache cures in the past, but there was a new mall going up, and Beckman wanted the supply contract for all the lighting. There was also a Coffee Planet branch, and he felt a familiar pull.

Just once, for old times' sake? Can't hurt.

The barista remembered him. Beckman declined the offer of a loyalty card. He paid, drank, and left.

A year ago, I would have felt odd to consider anywhere but here.

A week ago, I would have felt a heel to drink anywhere other than Buck's.

He sighed. Either Lolita or Buck needed to come to their senses and get the friendship back on track. Someone needed to wake up and smell the coffee.

At three o'clock, he stopped in at the Sunrise Library to indulge in research. He traced the Milan line—unbroken through male heirs—back to 1870. It was easy to follow the ownership of Jack's box back down the generations.

The Thornton line was more complex, disappearing into female heirs, marital name changes and large families. Still, with the aid of pencil and paper—plus logic and supposition—he arrived back in the 1880s again.

All the while, Sandra ignored him. Perhaps he was 'safe'? After all, he'd no axe to grind with her. Neither did Lolita—it seemed the animosity was all one-way. It was easy to see why Ginetta had left town: not only was Jack's misogyny too much, Sandra's presence must have been like a dark cloud.

It occurred to him that if Sandra's disdain for both her half-sister and her niece were as strong as it appeared, she might not relinquish Ginetta's box until the woman passed away. Then, she would *have* to comply with the demands of Spodge (or more likely Spodge's son at Spodge & Sons) and execute the executor's will when he executed the Will.

Perhaps this sleeping dog should be left to lie. After all, Sandra was The Guardian. She'd do the right thing in the meantime.

He headed home.

Lolita was on the couch with a significant glass of wine. The lights were low.

Romantic evening? Baby production practice?

Play it cool.

'Hey, honey.'

'Hey,' she replied quietly.

'I found some more stuff about the boxes.'

She sprang up. 'Will you shut up about the damn boxes!'

'Damn boxes,' Flint squawked.

'Shut your beak!'

'Shut your beak. Shut your beak.'

'Hey, calm down,' Beckman said. 'I was just tracing the ancestors, okay, and—'

'I don't care. I don't care!' Her eyes were creased in despair.

'Jeez, what did I do? I thought we *cared* about the box. It was your father's—'

'I know what it was. A millstone. An obligation from beyond the grave. Well, tough shit, Jack, because there's gonna be no damn heir in this house.'

'Not yet, sure, but I said I'll wait—'

Her eyes were wet now, her muscles tense. 'We'll be waiting forever. There'll be no baby. There's not gonna be an heir.' She threw her hands down like she was smashing dishes. 'Because I'm infertile!'

She barrelled past him, burst into tears, and slammed the bedroom door behind her.

Chapter 30

Beckman clutched the back of the sofa, steadied himself, manoeuvred around and sank into its embrace.

On the side table stood a picture from their wedding. Nothing about the whole day had been fancy, and a photographer was on the long list of things that hadn't been organised. Luckily, Reba was a dab hand with an SLR and had grabbed some nice shots. It was probably one of the few times she'd snapped evidence of a man in the arms of a woman who actually *was* his wife.

Beckman didn't know how long he stared at it, or near it, or through it.

Eventually, he tiptoed to the bedroom door, listened for sounds of anguish, but heard none.

He played the percentages and left her alone for a while.

He tidied. He couldn't remember the last time he'd tidied. He watched the ball game. He couldn't remember the last time he'd watched the ball game. He drank coffee. Those episodes were so frequent, his brain didn't bother memorising them.

He wondered what to do.

Darkness fell.

He had an idea.

He went to the bedroom and gingerly opened the door. Lolita was on her back, gazing vacantly at the ceiling.

He skirted the bed. She silently watched him like a hawk. He took that as a good sign—or maybe she was merely refraining from casting disappointment / ire / disbelief at someone who didn't deserve to be the target.

He pulled open the extensive wardrobe and moved slowly along the line of clothes. He plucked out one hanger, took the dress to the bed and carefully laid it down. Then he pulled out a matching pair of shoes and put them beside the dress.

He eyed her.

In for a penny...

'Put that on, then come with me.'

Her eyes flared, then danced. She frowned, went to speak, took a deep breath and gave the smallest of nods.

He held her hand as they walked down the quiet road towards town. The moon glowed a crescent, clouds drifting, the night warm. He glanced at her face now and again. Neither spoke: he still didn't know how to broach the subject; she was probably working out what the hell this trip was for.

The mosaic of lights crystallised out of indeterminate visual chaos of colour.

They reached Main Street.

There was scarlet and imperial and crimson and cherry and orange and mustard and lemon and burgundy and jade and magenta and olive and maroon and navy and salmon and candy and violet and indigo and sky and brick and chocolate and turquoise and lime and taupe and tomato and emerald and cyan and gold and tangerine and fuchsia and plum and heather and cobalt and sage and mint and caramel and wine and teal and lilac and coral and rose and fawn and oyster and ...

As she gazed around, he looked at her and at the symphony of colours that lensed through the tears running down her face.

Soon, they arrived at Our Buck's. Her body was alert, as if an enemy lay within.

'This is where we met.' He pointed at the corner table.

'Yes, Beckman, this is where we met.' She wiped her tears away. There was incomprehension, a flicker of memory, amusement, then query.

'We have us. We'll always have us. That will never change, whatever fates befall us.'

Neither had eaten, so they picked up tacos at Artie Villik's perennially open, perennially quiet sidewalk stand (how did the guy make any money?) and walked home.

They cracked open two beers and snuggled on the sofa. He hoped she'd have the good sense to raise the subject because, despite five hours of consideration, he still didn't have a clue how to say, "I'm so sorry. Please don't worry."

'We've got through worse,' she said, eventually, into her beer.

'We've got through… stuff, that's for sure. Worse? I can't make that call.'

'Before, we lost—or almost lost—things we had. Now we lost something we only *hoped* we'd have. Expected we'd have.'

'The box doesn't matter. It wasn't about the box.'

She looked him in the eye, then hung her head. 'No,' she breathed.

'We'll sort out the box. Sooner it's gone, the better. Jack would understand. Spodge will. They can't be angry at you for something that's not your fault.'

'All the same….' Her face creased. She took a deep breath.

'Yes. All the same.'

The conversation ran dry there. He went to the kitchen and poured them a JD on the rocks.

Later, at bedtime, he felt the box burning a hole underneath him, so he hopped out of bed, pulled the box out, and took it to the study, where he pushed it onto a shelf.

Out of sight, out of mind.

He slipped back under the covers. She lay an arm across his chest and pushed her head onto his shoulder.

Breaths rose and fell.

'April's a pretty grown-up girl. Sensible. Smart.'

'Hmm,' he replied, sensing where this was going. 'Detail-oriented. Honest. Reba says it's the Asperger's.'

'She's from the next generation.'

'That's true.'

'Reba and I go way back.'

'Yeah.'

'Hmm.' She squeezed him. 'Maybe I'll ask her.'

'Okay.'

She let loose and turned over. 'Spoon me, please.'

He willingly complied.

'I'm sad.'

'I'm sad, too,' he replied.

'But we have us.'

Chapter 31

In the morning, Beckman found Lolita to be subdued but not mournful. It was Saturday, so they had nowhere to be.

She put on some loud music, did some chores, and they didn't discuss the box, Sandra, or the test results. They let Flint watch them work.

'Great rack,' it squawked.

It may be annoying, but it has taste. And it's a pleasant diversion from… more curious or awkward matters.

'Who's this clown?'

'It's me, you dumb bird.' Beckman shook his head. 'You think it'd realise who its new parents—or whatever—are.'

'Bird brain,' Lolita chirped.

'Bird brain,' Flint replied.

'You try running a seven-figure business then, beaky.'

'Up yours.'

Lolita gave Flint The Eyebrow (Alarmed Amusement version).

'I don't know whether to throttle it or make a mixtape of its witty comments.'

'Kinda like me, then?'

She embraced him. 'Your idiocy is heavily outweighed by your adorableness.'

'Plus, I don't take a dump right beside my food bowl.'

'You know they live a long time—parrots?'

'So?'

'When it stops telling me I have a great rack, I'll know it's time for plastic surgery.'

The doorbell rang. They went to see who was disturbing their downtime.

Reba and Randall stood on the step.

'Are we disturbing your downtime?' Reba asked.

'Absolutely not,' Beckman said.

'Coffee's on.' Lolita waved them through.

'Bumped into the mailman.' Reba held up some envelopes.

'Chuck it in the study, hon. Probably stuff about Jack's estate.'

Beckman poured out the coffees, Reba joined them, and they sat in the living room.

Beckman eyed Flint.

What—no comments about Reba's chest? Clowns? Bird brains?

'Take a hike, pal. That's the spot, Jo, that's the spot.'

Lolita sprang up, threw the cover over Flint's cage, and retook her seat.

Randall and Reba exchanged an amused look.

Lolita waved it away. 'Don't go there.'

Reba drank. 'Jack left you a business and a huge house. Ginetta palmed you off with a bird that, frankly, has better conversation skills than Delmar. And is probably a better detective.'

'Not much gets by Flint, I gotta say.'

'I'm not too shabby myself.' Reba glanced towards the office. 'If you catch my drift.'

'You opened the *envelopes*?' Lolita said in disbelief.

Reba laughed. 'Hell no. We're buddies, Lol. I wouldn't do something like that.' She fell serious. 'But if there's something you want to tell me *in confidence*, you know I'm here.'

Beckman looked at the study, then Reba, then Lolita, and shrugged.

She can't know about the fertility test?

'You lost me there,' Lolita said.

Reba glanced at Randall, who was equally unaware of the matter at hand, then sighed. 'I saw the box. On the shelf.'

Oh, snap. That's right, dummy—under the bed wasn't good enough for you. Why didn't you just leave it out on the front lawn, or make up a billboard about it?

Who's the bird brain now?

'Ah, shoot.' Lolita clanked the mug down on the table.

'Now, I'm not saying anything here, but that looks a lot like the one Romeo True had taken.'

Lolita's palms snapped up in defence. 'Whoa! That is a whole line we are not going down. Really? You think I'd *steal* some damn box? From a cop?'

'Lol, I never said that. What I meant was he put that page in the paper to get those boxes notified to him.'

'And that is *so* not happening. Burglary? If you want to get all P.I. about this, I have two names off the bat already.'

Randall stood. 'Let's all take five here. We didn't mean nothing by it, and I'm sorry we ever came round, and we'll be quiet as church mice, right, honey?'

Reba nodded firmly. 'Absolutely. This whole box thing—whatever it is—is none of our beeswax. Romeo knows what he's doing.'

'Well, I'm glad you think so because it's all pretty fishy to me,' Lolita said.

'Because nobody with any sense would break into a cop's house? Because break-ins don't really happen around here?'

'No. Because Romeo says the only thing taken was that box. *That's* what stinks. Hardly anyone in town knows about those damn things.'

'You mean if it was stolen to order, by who? Not you, obviously.'

'Sheesh, no. Do we care that you got some box? No. Do we care you didn't hand it in? No.' Randall waved his mug. 'Subject closed. Can I get a refill?'

'Knock yourself out,' Beckman said.

Randall went to the kitchen.

'Between us, I never liked Romeo True. He's not a bad guy. He's just power-crazy. Looks down on me and Zebedee's guys—"amateurs".' Reba rolled her eye.

'Fastest way to stick it to him would be to solve his case. Fat use that newspaper ad was—he hasn't got his box back—or at least he hasn't said so.'

'So... if it was a targeted robbery, who in town *does* know Romeo owned that box? Assuming you can tell me—if us poor people without boxes are allowed to know.'

Lolita smiled. 'It's not like a secret club, honey. And if there's anyone I'd be happy to open up to, it's you. Hell, if there's something odd going on, there's no better person.'

'Clearly, most of the town knows *now* that Romeo had the box—but who knew beforehand?'

'We're not experts at this. The box came to us in Jack's estate, but there are certainly two people who know the boxes exist.'

'Who?'

'Jeremiah Spodge.'

'That old curio? Breaking and entering?' Reba smirked and drained her mug.

'I know. And Sandra Thornton.'

'*Librarian* Sandy? Jeez. She's a cold fish and everything, but a swag bag in the dead of night? I'm not convinced.'

'I thought you weren't supposed to get prejudiced in your line of work,' Beckman said.

'I'm not. Sometimes it's better to expect the unexpected. Anyway, why the curiosity?' Reba asked. 'Are you worried about the security of your box? Your home?'

Lolita shook her head. 'Not really. Just… a feeling. Like the robbery has opened a can of worms, and… we're not really allowed to say, but… the boxes are kind of an insurance policy against bad acts. It's a secret weapon that needs to stay secret—and it's not anymore. The point about keeping something secret is you don't want the wrong people finding out. Do you get my drift?'

Randall retook his seat. 'Sure. People hide affairs. Countries hide bioweapons because they'd only use them in emergencies, *and* they don't want any crazy idiots to steal them in the meantime.'

'Like I say, we're not experts, but you nailed it.'

Randall beamed. Reba patted him on the leg. 'Good sidekick. You may stay.'

'I'd hope so, after….' He clapped a hand over his mouth.

Reba looked daggers.

Lolita held up a placating hand. 'So, you have your own "box". We won't pry. A secret is best kept hidden.'

'Lol, look—I just went into the damn study, okay?'

'I didn't mean anything by it, truly.' Lolita looked at Beckman. 'Our dear men seem to have a habit of letting—or nearly letting—the cat out of the bag.'

Beckman died a little inside.

Reba bit her lip. 'This is no Government secret. Hell, this is good news. In a few weeks, you'll be getting intrigued anyway.'

Lolita held up her hand. 'Honey, honestly, we've enough crap to be worrying about.'

Reba frowned. 'Great, thanks. I thought you'd at least be a *little* bit happy that I got pregnant.'

Lolita's face hardened, her lip quivered, and she sprang up. 'Yeah, I'm delighted. Bully for you.'

Then she strode out.

Chapter 32

Beckman's heart sank.

It never rains.

He explained the situation to Reba and Randall, then they updated him on Dixon's status. He was surprised and heartened that they'd attempted to catalyse the woman's return, all with the best intentions. It was a blessing that Lolita wasn't in the room, as the mention of Buck was unlikely to do her mood any favours.

Reba and Randall left, and Beckman set his mind to the appropriate words to drag his belle from this latest funk.

He sat on the bed beside her.

'God, she can be insensitive sometimes. No way we're leaving the box to April after this.' Lolita shook her head in disbelief.

He squeezed her hand and offered the most direct, uncompromising look he could remember.

'I'm done with this pitiful, put-upon crap. She was *not* insensitive—she was *unaware*. Stop with the overreactions. You lost your father—we get it. You're sad—we get it. Your friend wasn't there—we get it. Stop the emotional tidal wave washing away everything you had left. You lost Buck because you couldn't see perspective. Don't do it again!' He pointed to the living room. 'Reba didn't do a damn thing wrong. Don't lash out at her. I married a strong woman. A beautiful, resilient force of nature. A sexy, kooky ball of sass. I'll support you 'til the end of the Earth, but I'm calling you out on this. You're on a slippery slope, and if you're going to take a rain check on kicking my ass, I have another remedy from Dr Beckman's Book Of Emotional Pick-Me-Ups... if you're game.'

She gazed at him forever. 'Okay.'

He led her to the hallway, grabbed the car keys, and they went out to the Mustang.

He dropped the hood, reversed out of the drive, and piloted them at not-fifty-five to a familiar location. The wind tugged her chocolate curls, sunshine reflected off the rims of her shades, and with every mile, her mood lifted.

He pulled off the road onto the rutted ground and swung behind the disused gas station in the middle of nowhere.

She didn't need to ask what came next. She hopped out, found a good spot, and drew in a deep breath.

Beckman clapped his hands over his ears.

When she was done bellowing out the days of accumulated anguish, he joined her on the scrub ground, checked her cheeks for tears—absent, her hands for fists—absent, and her eyes for love—present.

He drew her close.

'You're amazing,' she said.

'Takes one to know one.'

'Kiss me.'

He obliged. It quickly escalated in intensity.

She broke off, a glint in her eye. 'Do you want to park?'

He shrugged. 'Have to christen the pony sometime.'

She took his hand. 'Let's go and not make a baby.'

Chapter 33

'I'm sorry, honey,' Randall said.

Reba waved it away. 'We weren't to know. But, let's keep a lid on this, okay? The baby, the no-baby, and the box. Are we clear?'

'Crystal.'

'I should have watched my step. I thought Lol was pretty low after the fire and the Carlton thing last year, but this seems worse. Business is business, but friends are something else.'

'It's not like we weren't trying to help her out.'

Reba stopped the car. They were halfway home. 'Maybe we need to try some more.'

'Dixon seemed pretty fixed on her decision. Not sure what we can say to Buck—about her or Lolita.'

Reba shook her head. 'No. The box thing. The Romeo True thing. I get the feeling she wanted some bright ideas—even to set her mind at rest—but was too proud or distracted to ask for help.'

Randall squeezed her thigh. 'She couldn't ask anyone better.'

'Yeah.' She leaned her head against the backrest and closed her eyes.

Randall knew this was Reba's zoning-in stance. He waited for inspiration to strike.

'Who polices the police?' she murmured.

That was rhetorical, so he kept his trap shut.

Her eyes snapped open. 'Here's the thing. If someone broke into our place, I'd move Heaven and Earth to find the scumbag. From what I know of Romeo, he'd be the same. But he's got no leads other than an ad in the paper. I don't get it.'

'Absolutely. He's not narrowed suspects at all. Just trawled the whole damn town.'

'And Lol has a point. If this thing is so damn secret, who would know he had it? Besides Spodge and Sandra Thornton?'

Randall shrugged. 'Only people he told—even if he wasn't supposed to. Family? A friend on a drunken night out?'

'Sure. Answer's the same—it wasn't a lucky strike break-in; it was planned.'

'Well, unless we have access to security cameras in the bars where he goes drinking, we're S.O.L..'

She puffed a sober breath. 'Yeah.'

Then she sat upright, looked across at him, eyes wide. 'Honey, you're a genius.' She landed a huge wet kiss on his cheek.

'I am, aren't I?' He winked. 'Exactly *how* am I?'

She slotted Drive. 'Let's go see.'

Five minutes later, they stopped outside 444 Fresnel Drive.

Randall knew the house; April's best friend lived here. 'You suspect Mrs Fyx?'

Reba chuckled. 'No. But Romeo lives across the street, and Verna has security cameras on the front of her property there. She's a nervous soul, and the security system is high-end.'

Randall looked across the street. 'You think...?'

'It's a long shot, but I'll bet Romeo hasn't tried it. It'll show the triangle-shaped douche that you don't need two good eyes to spot a criminal if you know how and where to look for them.'

She led him up the path. Verna Fyx answered the door and let them in. Val wandered in from the kitchen and held out a four-fingered hand. (Reba had told Randall that Val lost his little pinkie in an accident at a Civil War re-enactment years ago). They shook.

Val offered them both a beer. It was only just past noon. But it was Saturday, so Randall accepted. Reba declined, citing "being on an active case".

Reba loosely explained why they were there, Verna led her into the living room to watch the security footage on the TV, and Val escorted Randall into the kitchen, where they discussed Corvettes (Randall's passion) and Civil War muskets (Val's hobby).

Randall felt sure the finger-losing episode would enter the conversation.

An hour later—having proven that Corvettes don't kill people, muskets do—they were joined by Reba, who announced that her work was done. Verna, an old school friend, swore not to breathe a word of what the tapes *appeared* to show. Reba offered to take the four of them out for dinner (and probably a repeat outing for the finger-losing story, Randall reckoned), then they took their leave.

They sank into the squishy seats of her fifteen-year-old Jeep.

'So?' he asked.

She pulled a memory stick from her pocket. '"Bang to rights" might be pushing it, but we have a very hot lead.'

'That's pretty fast work.'

'Let's remember whose idea this was.'

'Mine? All I said was….'

'Honey, if I were you, I'd take the credit. You just made me look good.' She leant across and pecked him on the cheek. 'So you'll be *getting some* tonight.'

Randall glowed inside.

She winked that very individual wink, slotted the key, and they headed off for a very late lunch.

Chapter 34

Beckman saw Reba's car pull onto the drive and wondered what could have happened in the last few hours to merit a second visit. Then he hoped Lolita wouldn't curtail the conversation again.

He fetched her from the garden, and they went to the door.

'Look, Lol,' Reba began.

Lolita stepped forwards. 'I was a bitch, and I'm sorry. You didn't put a foot out of line. Buddies?'

Reba eyed them. 'Yeah. Timing sucked, that's all.'

The women embraced.

'Right on target, as usual, Randall.' Beckman cocked his finger and winked.

That received The Eyebrow (Grow Up version).

'So, what gives?' Lolita asked.

'I've been sleuthing,' Reba replied.

'About what?'

'Missing… *items*. Wooden… *items*.'

'Ah.' Lolita glanced around—although nobody would have heard. 'Come in.' She slapped Beckman on the shoulder. 'Coffee on the terrace, I think, Jeeves.'

Reba held up the memory stick and recounted her visit to the Fyxs.

Beckman was glued to the story like it was flypaper.

'It doesn't make any sense,' Lolita said.

'Not on face value,' Reba replied. 'That's why we came here.'

'You're the detective, honey.'

'And you know more about the boxes.'

'What's there to know? It's handed down from generation to generation; you keep it safe, don't open it, and you hand it down again. Plus, you know, you keep it a secret.'

'I'd ask what it all means, what it's all for, but that feels pretty redundant.'

'Redundant seems to be the theme here,' Randall suggested. 'Why break into your own house, *not* steal anything, and then claim you were robbed?'

'Are you sure he didn't just move the box somewhere?' Lolita asked.

'We watched the footage twice,' Reba said. 'The Trues go out for a dinner date, he sneaks home after dark, breaks his own window, then goes back to the car empty-handed. If he moved it, it's real sleight-of-hand, but he didn't seem to even go *into* the property.'

'An insurance job?' Beckman wondered.

'Possibly. But who cares?'

'Unless he'd insured the box for a million bucks, then put out the Beacon ad as evidence of his desperation to get it back—to make it look genuine for the insurance people.'

'But why the *box*?' Lolita asked. 'The one thing he's supposed to hold secret above everything else. Why not claim his mother's genuine pearl earrings were stolen? Why go public about the box?' She shook her head in disbelief. 'And why ask for other people to admit having their own? It's like he's lost the plot.'

'One thing is for sure,' Reba said. 'It answers the theft question perfectly: who knew he had the box? Only he did. It puts Spodge and Sandra in the clear.'

'In the clear, sure, but they'll be hopping mad when they find out.'

'We should go tell them,' Beckman said.

Lolita flashed him a glower. 'Spodge—yes; Sandra—no way. Guardian or not, I'm not butting heads with her. At the very least, hearing about the burglary from us only raises suspicions about why we *care*, and I don't want her to get the slightest clue that we have our own box.'

'What happens when anyone confronts Romeo?' Randall put his arm around Reba. 'I don't want any comeback, just because we were doing our civic duty.'

Reba eased his arm down. 'First, we'll ask Spodge to be circumspect about revealing our evidence. Second, much as I love you, honey, I can fight my own battles. If Romeo lays so much as a finger on me, I'll have him arrested for assault, he'll be stripped of his uniform, and have to find a new way to make the repayments on that nice new home of his.'

'What I want to know is—why the ad?' Lolita stroked her lip. 'If the box *had* been stolen, sure, it might be a legitimate way to get it back. But he knew it *wasn't* stolen, so why do it?'

Beckman shrugged. 'To get hold of other people's boxes.'

'The whole thing was a smokescreen?' Reba wondered.

'If this was about gathering all the boxes together—for the first time in generations—then if Spodge catches on to that, he'll probably have a coronary.' Lolita shook her head, dumbstruck. 'This whole thing is like an intricate machine of duty and honesty, and one guy wants to bust that all down because he can't keep his curiosity at bay.'

'I'm amazed *you* can, Lol. Maybe it's being a P.I., but I'm curious as all hell about what's in that box.'

'You think we're not? I'm goddamn fascinated, but like we said, it's emergency use only. One asshole bucking the system isn't going to bring the town down around our ears.'

As it was Saturday afternoon, no self-respecting legal person would be in the office. However, Reba being Reba Garrity P.I., they knew where Jeremiah Spodge lived, and decided that waiting until 0900 Monday was time they didn't have if they were to nip this subterfuge in the bud.

Spodge's house was the antithesis of his office: immaculately maintained. Beckman had expected to wield a hatchet to cut through undergrowth, or don CDC suits to cross the mountain of discarded rubbish on the driveway.

Instead, they slid past the jet black Mercedes and went to the door.

Before Reba's finger reached the doorbell, Beckman intercepted it and motioned for the four of them to listen.

Huh? Vivaldi? What happened to some squealing axe torture or pounding bass?

Maybe he takes the weekend off from that too.

She rang the bell.

The music ceased.

I wonder if Spodge swears? How Spodge swears? "Diabolical deceptitude"? "Gadzooks"? "Thunderation"?

So long as he only takes issue with the Trues and not us.

After all, we're the good guys. Right?

The door opened.

Chapter 35

Reba and Randall led Spodge in convoy to the True household.

She'd only had to use gentle insistence to get them invited along, and was happy to sacrifice Lolita and Beckman's presence to achieve it. Spodge was already going out on a limb by allowing two non-box holders to be party to this dressing-down visit; the man had done well to temper his disapproval that the secret had passed Lolita's lips.

Reba had been at pains to point out that her discovery of Lolita's box was an accident, but Spodge had countered by saying that obtaining security footage of Romeo's deed was *far* from accidental.

'We're on your side,' she'd protested.

'Thy motives seem good,' he'd replied, 'Though one despairs that this regrettable incident seems to be developing into a significant incursion vis-a-vis the breaking of confidences.'

The clincher had been that she and Randall would be there to protect Spodge if Romeo—a well-built guy— took issue with the older man's accusations. As her job as a P.I. basically *traded* in secrets—and keeping them close to her chest when they were uncovered—surely she would remain tight-lipped about the whole affair?

Spodge's dark eyes had scoured her face for many moments, then he'd conceded.

When Romeo True answered the door in weekend attire (torn denims, check shirt with rolled sleeves), Reba couldn't discern who he was more disturbed by seeing—her or Spodge.

She smiled sweetly, Randall nodded, but they let Spodge do the talking.

Momentarily, they were inside, and after not offering refreshments, Romeo led them to the sitting room.

Spodge outlined the reason for their visit, and Reba watched the colour drain from Romeo's face. To his credit, the accused didn't ask to see the evidence.

'This matter is most serious and regrettable, Mr True. Do thee appreciate such?'

'Look, it's like this. I'm a cop, right? I gotta protect the town. So when it turns out both Julie *and* I got one of these crazy boxes, I reckon it's a sign. What's so wrong with that? I've a duty to do here. I'm not saying people can't have their own boxes if they want, but there's a reason for Sunrise Police to be ahead of the game. If something bad happens, it's our job to be front and centre, right?'

Spodge extended a bony finger and jabbed it uncompromisingly in his other palm. 'It is not thy duty to add rules and conditions beyond those set out by the weight of history. The matter of these boxes has proceeded without incident for decades. One is naturally aware that marital circumstances have precipitated two boxes residing in this household, and whilst that is regrettable, one does not believe it warrants action. However, one will convene with one's colleagues to ascertain whether thy two boxes should be parted forthwith. Redistribution of the assets is within our purview, should we deem that risk exists with the status quo.'

Romeo growled. 'Yeah. I guess.'

'If the Guardian was made aware of thine actions, one feels sure they would look most harshly on the situation.'

'I'll take my licks.'

'One will remember what curiosity did to the feline, Mr True.'

'Yeah. I do. I was curious—sure, but I only want to keep the town safe. We all do.'

'This would be thy reason for seeking to obtain—and obtaining—further boxes by deceit?'

'Look, Mr Spodge, I know a cop is not above the law, alright? But there's no law here, just some ancient baloney.'

Spodge's eyes flared. 'Baloney is the last thing this mechanism is, Mr True. It was carefully conceived by those who knew that their discovery could either provide succour to the town, or destroy its very essence.' He pointed. 'Subverting the scheme, and the rules one laid down at thy father's reading, will not lead to benefit, only chaos. Consider thyself warned.'

'Fair. I'll give you back that other box.'

Romeo True led them down to the basement.

A large flat-screen TV hung on the wall. A cabinet was full of sporting trophies.

Reba curled her lip.

On the table stood three boxes.

Spodge grunted and reached for the sofa to steady himself. His eyes were on stalks.

'Thee... thee *opened* the boxes! How... how...' He coughed, spluttered, and began to hack.

Reba feared for the man's life. 'Randall!'

Randall grabbed Spodge and held him up.

'Get him some water, Romeo, dammit!' she barked.

Romeo glowered at her, puffed a sharp sigh, then darted up the stairs.

She pointed at the huge glass doors which opened onto the terrace. A garden set stood outside.

'Give him some air, honey.'

Spodge, still sputtering in shock, raised a hand in thanks as Randall led him out

She wanted to give Romeo True a piece of her mind. She looked again at the boxes. They were set out in line, their lids closed, but in front of each was another element. The three slivers of wood were sharp rectangles like filo pastry, something more durable and carefully crafted than mere paper.

On each folio was carved just a few words.

On the top of each box was a different symbol.

She glanced around.

Spodge was seated, taking deep breaths, gazing into the garden.

Romeo's feet weren't yet on the steps.

Reba tugged out her phone.

Chapter 36

Beckman checked that the fridge was fully stocked.

Fridge Stocking, Room Beautifying and Forensic Ingredient Checking were three things he'd had to learn to do over the last nine months.

Before, during aeons of bachelorhood, Saturday night was most often marked by Idle TV Scrolling, Beer Bottle Label Peeling, and sometimes Hoping Dad Won't Call.

One puncture, a blur of crazy, and now you're the doting husband.

He gazed across the kitchen at Lolita and had a quick dote.

Pretty good timing, Amaryllis.

We need a night like this… or Mrs Milan does.

Way to get born on this day in history.

Lolita had said that the fertility test was Amaryllis' idea, so they'd be open about the situation, and he knew that their guests would be understanding.

Food, alcohol, company. No talk about babies, boxes or bequests.

A night off from life.

He opened the door to his ex-colleague and his ex-boss's ex-secretary.

Whoah.

That neckline certainly plunges.

Surely that's not The PA Formerly Known As Miss Broomhead.

Yes, she's evolved, softened, loosened in the past months, but...

Tyler flashed a knowing smirk.

We both did well, huh?

Beckman led them through, offering birthday felicitations and accepting the gifted booze.

In the living room, he spied Flint, alert in his uncovered cage.

He made a beeline for the bird.

Too late.

'Great rack,' it squawked.

He wheeled around, ready to offer Amaryllis a fulsome apology. Then, a picosecond before a word left his throat, he snapped his mouth shut, recognising that a misdirected apology would imply he'd made a causal link between the bird's words and Amaryllis' couture and *figure*, thus telegraphing that he'd noticed those things, which might cause a Bad Start To The Evening.

He looked at Lolita, then Tyler, and finally Amaryllis. Her *face*.

She laughed.

Lolita smiled. 'Sorry. He does say that.'

'Ah. So not just us,' Tyler replied.

'He's got a thing about it with me.'

'Yes. Flint's... observant,' Beckman said, feeling his cheeks colour.

'So he was talking about Lolita?' Tyler asked.

'Absolutely.'

'Great rack,' Flint repeated. 'Who's this clown?'

'He's adorable.' Amaryllis moved closer to the loquacious, multi-coloured conversation starter.

'You say that *now*....' Lolita murmured.

'Great rack. Who's this clown?'

'Are you sure he's not looking at us?' Tyler asked.

'No. Lolita.'

'Why, might he not think my girlfriend has a great rack?'

Beckman wanted the floor to open up and swallow him whole. 'I... I can't speak for Flint.'

Amaryllis was making cooing sounds towards the parrot. 'I don't mind.'

'Take a hike, pal. Grab me a beer. Grab me a beer. Great rack. Shut your beak. Shut your beak.'

Tyler reached out. 'Honey, you might want to....'

'Great rack.'

Tyler flashed a smile that was fifty percent awkwardness and fifty percent pride. 'I don't think it's about Lolita right now.'

Beckman wanted to point out that (1) Lolita's neckline was noticeable, but in a more restrained way, (2) Flint is always engaged by new people, and (3) Amaryllis bending forwards like that wasn't doing her chances any favours.

'Tyler, she's my old company secretary, so I don't think....'

Amaryllis stood sharply up. 'Old?'

Oh, snap.

Her face broke into a smile. 'It's my birthday, and a handsome young thing has just complimented this forty-four year old's bosom. Relax, Beckman.'

He exhaled heavily. 'Looks can be deceptive. Flint's going to shoot his mouth off one day and—'

'Secret boxes, secret boxes,' the bird chirped cheerily.

Oh, double snap.

'I think we'll say goodnight now.' Lolita bolted for the cage cover.

'Romeo stole the box. Secret box. Shut your beak.'

Beckman coughed awkwardly. 'Like I said, Flint's a real character and—'

'Romeo stole his own box?' Tyler asked in disbelief.

'That's the spot, Jo. That's it. Good night. Good night.'

Lolita hurled the cover over the cage and yanked it down. She held both hands to her head and grimaced in Beckman's direction. 'I'll throttle the damn thing.'

Amaryllis patted Lolita's arm. 'Don't do that. I think he's sweet.'

She rolled her eyes. 'He's all yours,' she joked.

Huh?

Beckman waved it away. 'Never mind. Now—drinks. Lots of them. Enough so we'll *all* forget what just happened.'

'You sure throw a party,' Amaryllis said.

'And I don't want to spoil it, but… the Romeo thing?' Tyler said.

'He says a lot of stuff,' Beckman blustered.

Lolita took his hand, eyed everyone, and her shoulders sank. 'Well, I was going to ask you three… *bosom* buddies not to spend the whole evening reminiscing about the good ol' days at Pegasus—'

'Those would be the *bad* ol' days,' Beckman corrected.

'—but I guess we now have another topic of conversation.'

Amaryllis laid a hand on Lolita's shoulder. 'I think we're all close enough that secrets are a *bad* idea?'

'This is kind of a *Sunrise* thing.'

'I know we may not live here, but we have an office here—which you provide—so I suppose that makes us part of the family?'

'Plus the whole multi-million dollar business investment, standing up front on your wedding day, helping you get rid of Carlton stuff,' Tyler pointed out. 'Oh, and it's my girlfriend's birthday party tonight—and would you look at the dress she went and bought!' His eyes widened, then creased as he laughed.

They all giggled.

Nope, not me. I wasn't looking at the dress. Not for a second.

Chapter 37

Romeo True was in the doghouse, and he knew it.

He'd gotten in trouble with Jeremiah Spodge—and was lucky not to have killed the guy through apoplexy. Then, Julie had reminded him what a dumb idea it had been all along. She made it abundantly clear that if they had to relinquish one box, it would damn well be his. The True line would be the one that became broken; she wouldn't give up the Lonnikan's box. She'd inherited that fair and square. It was his idea to fake the robbery, place the ad, and open the boxes. Whilst she'd seen his motives and been happy enough to go along with them, she'd turned on him pretty quickly when it all went south.

Still, he knew she loved him despite his faults and error of judgement, and he volunteered to take a night in the spare room as penance.

After all, some dumb old box wasn't worth breaking a marriage over. If they stayed together, he'd still be there if and when she needed to use her box in Spodge's "extraordinary circumstances", and he'd still be a cop at heart on that day, even if it came during his retirement.

He *did* want Sunrise to be safe. Only his curiosity had caused him to make a dumb move.

Besides, he'd still *seen* three boxes. He had at least *part* of the clues to the big puzzle. It was a masterstroke to make a record of all the boxes and their contents before

Spodge confiscated the one box that wasn't rightfully theirs.

It was an insurance policy, he told himself, which was a decent second prize. If a box owner didn't come forward on Sunrise's Armageddon Day—or whatever it would be called—he'd be able to proudly step in and help.

After a lazy Sunday breakfast, Julie left the house to meet some girlfriends in town. Romeo busied himself, hacking back overgrown parts of the garden.

He was taking a breather in the kitchen when there was a rap on the front screen door.

Would this be Spodge, back for a follow-up? Another neighbour introducing themselves?

'Ms Thornton.'

'Mr True.' Her face was familiarly free of makeup, her smart casual attire unchanged from the workday staple. Her tone remained direct—matter-of-fact without being threatening.

'Is this a library matter, a police matter... or a *social* call?' She didn't live nearby, and he struggled to think of reasons why she might merely 'Stop by'.

'It's an... administrative visit.' She gestured inside. 'May we?'

Sandra Thornton had an assertive quality that made refusal difficult. He wondered whether she would have made a good cop—able to say to a miscreant, "You'll put that weapon down now" without shouting or drawing her own firearm.

Romeo quickly got a sense of déjà vu.

'I'm led to believe you are in possession of two wooden box heirlooms, Mr True.'

'That's a private matter, and I couldn't say.'

'I'll put it this way: I know you are. I also know that as a result of your misguided newspaper bulletin, you've gained possession of another box.'

'How do you know—if it *is* true?'

'It's my job to know.'

Romeo's heart sank. Spodge's words echoed back. 'I guess the old guy did warn me that someone like you might be pissed off.'

She jolted slightly, as if spooked, unnerved. Was it his language?

'Did he?' she asked.

'Yeah. He said there was a… guardian?… who kept things in order.'

Her eyes darted. She smiled thinly. 'So you see, Mr True, there are fail-safes in place to stop unwanted congregation of the boxes.'

'I was doing it to help protect the town,' he protested… again.

'Well, I'm alarmed by the coincidence of all this. First, that Lolita Milan woman comes into the library and demands my own box from me—who knows *what* her agenda is. She's digging into the history of this box network, but I have my eye on her. And now I have it on you, Mr True.' She gave him a concomitant stare of authority.

He held up his hands. 'I gave my apology to Spodge. What more do you want?'

'I need to take your boxes. I'm empowered to do so.'

Romeo stepped back. This sounded fishy. 'I'll… have to clear it with him. Surely he would have taken them himself?'

The thin smile returned. 'And why do you think he didn't? Because he can't—isn't that logical deductive reasoning, *Officer*?'

He sense-checked. 'I guess so.'

'You did say that Mr Spodge indicated that it was the Guardian… myself… who was the ultimate arbiter?'

'Yeah.'

'So, I'll confiscate your boxes pending my consideration. At worst, they'll be returned as part of your inheritance, when your children may be deemed more trustworthy.' She shook her head. 'A policeman subverting such a pillar of the town's essence.'

'I get it, okay? Bad plan. Now, come get the damn boxes.'

He led her down to the den.

Her reaction was less injurious than Spodge's, yet she was filled with surprise and curiosity.

'You opened the boxes, Mr True?'

'Yeah, I did. Worse plan—I get it.'

'Where is the third box?'

'Spodge took it. To return to Mrs Klepp.'

'You opened that box too?' Sandra's eyes widened.

'Yeah.'

'Did it contain… directions, like these two?'

He put his hands on his hips. 'Hey—what is this? You're the damn Guardian, don't you know this stuff?'

Her tone morphed into a matronly, almost condescending lilt. 'Mr True. What is the point of a network of boxes, allocated to unconnected individuals, if one person—namely myself—knows the sum contents of all of them?'

His brain whirred. 'I guess not.'

'The contents are a mystery to me as much as they were to you and to Mr Spodge. My role is to ensure the information *remains* dissipated and to be one step ahead of anyone attempting to shortcut the system.'

'But Spodge knows who all the holders are,' he pointed out.

'And all the holders know—or should have worked out—that fact. They'd stop him from breaking his own code. So would I. I'll bet he's never revealed the *identity* of the Guardian.'

'No, sure.'

She nodded. 'Because the Guardian... I... police him too. Surely the enemy who is hardest to avoid is one whose identity is unknown. Someone who could be next to you at any point, and you wouldn't know.'

'Absolutely. Catching a criminal is damn hard until you know who they are.'

She carefully replaced the two slivers of wood in their own boxes.

'Now for one last truth, Mr True. Have you made a facsimile... a photograph possibly... of this and the third box?' Her eyebrows slid up.

The angel on his shoulder forced him to come clean. 'Yeah. We made a note and a drawing.'

He truculently opened a drawer, tugged out a sheet of paper, and passed it across.

'This is everything?'

'You're a real ball-buster, you know that, lady?'

'I only do what my nature compels me to. I have obligations to set things right, and neither you nor anyone will stand in my way. History will judge what I do to serve Sunrise and make it the town it needs to be.'

Chapter 38

Beckman's head throbbed. Gently. Like the distant pulse of a small ferry's engines.

The bedside clock read 09:11.

The taste in his mouth was stale.

Mercifully, the person in the bed was familiar, and someone he was married to.

You never woke up with a stranger, did you? No—that was Tyler's job.

Did you ever have to wake up and take a mental inventory of the evening's events—to ensure nothing untoward had happened?

Don't think so.

But nothing did happen this time, did it? It was only friends over for dinner. And talking. And wine. And beer. And JD. Although…

He twitched.

A grunt issued from the prone, soft, adorable shape beside him. It opened an eye. It groaned.

His mind, functioning on maybe five of its eight cylinders, sought to penetrate the fog.

'Honey?' His mouth was dry.

It lolled over, chocolate curls sliding across the face. Both eyes opened. They were rimmed in smudges.

'You didn't take your makeup off,' he said redundantly.

'Meh.'

'Honey?'

'Shhh.'

'Did we…? Did you…? Did we let slip about Tyler's *accident*?'

Lolita's face snapped to attention. She pursed her lips. Hard. She pulled herself closer and lay her head on his chest. Breath tickled his hairs.

'I think he forgave us,' she mumbled.

'Well, it looks a lot like he didn't literally kill us in our bed, so either he took it well, or he's out of bed already, secretly cutting your brakes.'

'Or your brakes.'

'You hired the hitman,' he pointed out.

'Wouldn't have needed to if you'd been a half-decent salesman.'

'Wouldn't have mattered if I hadn't wandered into this dumb town.'

'Wouldn't have happened if you'd stayed on the freeway.'

'Are you *still* drunk?'

'Only on love, B.'

'If I wasn't going to throw up before, I am now.'

He caressed her head.

'They did stay, right?' she asked.

'Why don't you wander downstairs in your underwear and find out?'

'How can you be hungover *and* mischievous? I can barely manage hungover and lucid.'

He gently kissed the top of her head. 'I'll go and get *all* our coffee, and a drip.'

Eventually, painkillers, coffee and a shower later, they were ready to face breakfast. Tyler was already there, looking barely the worse for wear.

I think I hate you a little bit. Obviously not as much as I hated you before. Maybe only enough to have you pushed under a snail.

Amaryllis' makeup was somewhat heavier than the night before.

Wow. Miss Broomhead loose was one thing. Taking a drink was another. Taking many drinks? How the mighty are fallen. Kudos to you, Tyler. You might have a keeper there.

As the nourishment seeped into their bodies, the conversation moved from blissfully spartan to pleasant reminisces.

He and Tyler found themselves out on the terrace.

Tyler checked they were alone. 'I didn't want to say before, but I'm working on Buck to make it up to you guys.'

'Tread carefully, okay? I was warned off fighting her battles.'

'Loud and clear. Anyhow, I told him to either get over the Dixon thing or do something about it. Not mope around causing collateral damage.'

'What do you care either way?'

'I don't. But if we're going to be spending more time around here, it'd be good if it wasn't under a cloud—especially one which affects you two.'

Beckman winced. 'Even after… what we almost did to you?'

'You put me on the road to Damascus, buddy. The outcome of that is I'm richer, happier, and I get to date a hot woman and drink a shit ton of your booze. So, bygones, okay?'

'Okay. And *will* you be spending more time around here?'

Tyler smiled. 'You mean so we can invite *you* over next time to drink *our* booze?'

'"Our"?'

'What—does that surprise you? That I might be serious about this?'

'No. You two seem pretty hooked up. Make sure it's right, that's all. You saw what happened when Dixon tried to make a snap life change.'

'Says the guy who moved here inside a week.' Tyler raised a knowing brow.

'Point taken. Just… if you do take the plunge, let's please agree to go easier next time.' Beckman rubbed his thudding forehead. 'I'm too rusty at this.'

Soon afterwards, Tyler and Amaryllis loaded Flint and its accoutrements into the cramped back seats of the Porsche, Beckman encouraged Lolita to at least *try* to look sad at the parrot's departure, and then they were alone again.

Only for an hour.

What happened to the quiet life?

Romeo True was at the door.

Oh, snap. Tyler was bluffing all along: he's squealed on Lolita for the hit last year, and now this triangular-physiqued small-town wannabe big-shot is going to slap us in irons for trying to kill a total swine but instead cause the victim's life to take a startlingly huge upswing. I mean, how fair would—

'Mr Spiers. Mrs Milan.'

He'd never spoken to Romeo before; only seen him cruising around, looking for non-existent crime, or heard his character being dissected by Reba or Lolita.

So, was the formality a police thing, an unfamiliarity thing, or a mood thing?

'Officer True,' Lolita said.

'Is this a bad time?'

No, but please don't use too many multi-syllable words or ask us to compute the cube root of pi. It's Sunday morning, and we've had That Kind Of A Saturday Night.

'No,' Lolita replied. 'Something wrong?'

Romeo glanced around. 'I'm not here in an official capacity. More a matter of *secrecy*... if you catch my drift.'

Laudably, pennies dropped through the sludge in Beckman's head. 'Sure, come in.'

Lolita offered Romeo coffee, and they all stood in the kitchen.

'Is this related to what I think it's related to?' she asked.

'Yeah. And before we get into it, I know what I did was dumb. I told Spodge it was well-intended, and I got ahead of myself, and I look like an ass putting out that ad.'

'We'll leave the words in your mouth, I think.'

Romeo's face flashed with disapproval, then he shook it away.

'So, what's the issue,' Beckman asked.

'We need to be frank. The issue of the boxes—and their ownership—is no longer the total secret it was.' He held up a defensive hand. 'The thing's not blown wide open, and I still have no clue what the whole baloney is about, but ears are pricking up, and I wanted you to know.'

Lolita canted her head. 'Why us?'

After all, we never said a peep about having a box.

'Sandra Thornton was just over at my place. She said the two of you had asked her about a box. Also, you'd been... researching the possible origin of the things.'

Lolita's nose wrinkled. 'Why would she tell you that?'

'Because she came to chew my ass out for what I did and—get this—she confiscated my boxes.'

'She what?!'

Romeo set his mug down. 'When Spodge came over with Miss Garrity, he nearly had a fit.' He sighed. ''Cos, I opened the boxes, didn't I? I'm sure Garrity told you.'

'She gave us the rundown, yes.'

'And Spodge said there might be sanctions from someone called The Guardian—Jeez, this whole thing sounds like something out of Marvel. Anyhow, next thing is Thornton turns up, and she's not happy.'

Lolita shrugged. 'I doubt she ever smiled in her life.'

'Right. So, Thornton took my boxes, 'cause she reckoned I'd subverted the whole process or whatever.'

'Arguably, you did.'

Romeo puffed out another sigh. 'Anyhow, a heads-up, that's all. If you're trying to solve the mystery, I'd say that's a bad idea. She'll be on you like a shot.'

'Due respect to her and you, looking up family history is not the same as opening a box we were told not to open.'

'It was done with the public good in mind, okay? Being ready for whatever disaster, or event, threat, civil unrest, whatever.'

Lolita swilled the last of her coffee in the mug. 'Feels like what's happened so far has caused enough ruckus around here.'

'And that's what she's trying to stop, I guess,' Romeo said.

Beckman's head, which already hurt, hurt more. 'You mean, she's trying to prevent a crisis which has been *caused* by the boxes? Sheesh. That messes with my poor brain cells.'

'I don't know, okay?' People having disagreements and maybe overstepping bounds—that's not serious. That's not the kind of thing Spodge talked about at my dad's Will reading. That doesn't compromise the town's existence or essence.'

'I've got to agree with you,' Lolita said. 'Besides, how does opening the boxes stop that? Or anything, come to think of it?'

'I think Officer True is in the ideal place to say.' Beckman eyed the man. 'You want to tell us what's in the boxes?'

Romeo laid his hand on Beckman's shoulder. 'We both know that's not going to happen. I have to draw the line somewhere.'

You know he's right. That knowledge is designed to be left scattered. No one person can know the whole story; not Spodge, not Sandra, not us.

Unless this rocking boat hits a tidal wave.

Chapter 39

After a sizeable and deliberately unhealthy lunch, Beckman and Lolita went for a walk on the hills. Without meaning to, they wound up on the crest overlooking Walter Whack's property, and took a rest.

Beckman knew that the discovery of a bullet nearby had caused some pretty serious dominoes to fall. He pondered, gazing out across the tapestry of roads, buildings and green spaces below them.

It's not quite a butterfly flapping its wings, but still…

'What're you thinking about?' Lolita asked.

'I wonder if they knew—back in the day—what they were setting out to protect? If they knew what kind of place Sunrise would be? Or was it always this… kooky?'

She smiled. 'I'm sure a lot fewer neon lights back in 1850.'

'Something brought the first Milan here.'

'Easy place to defend—with the ring of hills? Raise herds of cattle? Dig for gold?'

'No. I know this place like the back of my hand. If there was an old mine, I'd know about it. The kind of place I'd have sneaked off to when I was a kid. To sit and be angry about Jack never taking us anywhere.' She chuckled reflectively.

'Or to sneak off to with one of the first twenty-two who didn't make the grade?'

'Probably.' She plucked a blade of grass and toyed with it. 'I wonder if the Milans were always asses?'

'If they were, you broke the mould.'

'Hmm. And we'll break the line too, looks like.'

He squeezed her hand. 'A lack of tiny feet is not the end of the world.'

She met his gaze. 'No. But if opening our box could turn that particular crisis around, I'd do it in a heartbeat.'

'You're very… *pro* the baby thing all of a sudden.'

'Maybe losing Buck has left a hole in my life. Outside of you, there's love to give to someone.'

'Spread it around our friends,' he suggested. 'You see how they rally to the cause. Offer shoulders, support. Keep secrets.'

She smiled. 'Get us drunk.'

'Which is all a hell of a lot better than family, am I right? You can choose your friends.'

'Let's go easy on them, okay? Jack didn't know what a can of worms he was opening up by passing down that box. Neither did mom by telling me about Sandra.'

'It only feels like a can of worms because Romeo True thinks he knows better than decades of sensible people who kept their heads down and their curiosities to themselves. Plus, getting within ten feet of your aunt seems to trigger her authority complex.'

She stroked his leg. 'At least it's not personal. She's doing her highfaluting protector role to everyone. I'll bet there's been someone like her every generation too. We *can't* be the first set of people to dig around for what this is all about. We just can't. People want what they can't have.'

'Maybe we shouldn't feel so bad.'

'I don't feel bad, B. Just… intrigued. I don't mean open-the-box intrigued. Only… interested. You know what—I just thought of something else. We're not the only one in a pickle about not having children. Sandra's a spinster, so if the Box Watchdog is hereditary, what the hell happens next? Are they going to draw lots for who wields the shield of justice?'

'Who draws lots? Can't be Spodge—he doesn't know Sandra's the Guardian. And before you say, no, we are not telling him and breaking even more damn rules.'

'Maybe there's a secret committee, too?'

He laughed. 'The way we're going, half the town is involved. Not much of a secret, then, is it?'

She sighed. 'I don't know. All I want is to get mom's box off Sandra—which is all legal and above board—then get that fancy safe you wanted, put our two boxes away, and forget the whole thing.'

'Will you forgive me if I remain interested on your behalf?'

She peered over the top of her sunglasses. 'Is this going to get obsessive, like The Portal was? That thing did get a bit out of hand.'

He smirked. 'In a good way. We did *improve* the town. That's even better than keeping it safe the way it is.'

'For an honest man, honey, you sure find a way to bend the rules sometimes.'

'I won't remind you of your complicity in a whole bunch of things that weren't *entirely* selfless.'

'Wise, husband.'

'I've got bitten by the bug, that's all. The whole frontier town, cowboys and horses, saloons and guns thing. Maybe I watched too many movies.'

He scanned the scene, picturing a ramshackle place, in black and white, with an old moustachioed Spodge, possibly a fully-bearded Milan and others, plying their trades. Perhaps Romeo's ancestor was the town Sheriff?

He felt her hand on his arm. 'What?' she asked.

'Reminiscing.'

Amusement bloomed on her face. 'For a past life in a place you never lived? Only you could do that.'

'I never had much of a life beyond Pegasus and Coffee Planet—you know that.' He laughed. 'Actually, boxes with interesting properties was pretty much my trade before I met you. Do you think that's a sign?'

She smiled. 'I never thought of it like that.'

'So, if I have some spare time, I'll indulge a spot of research. I already started on your ancestry. I don't need to go anywhere near your box, Sandra's box, anyone's box. But what if the male Milans *were* always assholes? Wouldn't you feel better that it was fate that Jack behaved like that?'

'You know what, if you can find a Wanted poster with Ol' Mad Duke Milan, we'll have something to laugh about, and hell knows I could use a lift.'

He kissed her. 'Okay. I may have sneaked a look at the library's staff rota. Sandra Dee doesn't work Mondays, so I'll get along quicker without her laser eyes singeing my neck hair.'

Chapter 40

Beckman went through proper channels and took the first eight hours of the working week as a vacation day. There was no mileage in attracting snide looks from other team members who might have thought he could swan in and out as he pleased because he was, in a genuine and extremely pleasant sense, *sleeping with the boss*.

After a coffee at Jen & Berry's (he was beginning to *not* miss Buck's brews, and wasn't sure he liked that feeling), he went to the library. The duty librarian was Allie Kuck, a very different proposition from Sandra Thornton because she was young, helpful and the corners of her mouth went up as well as down.

He picked up where he'd left off last time, tracing Jack's ancestry back to 1847. The town was founded in 1842, so Jesse Milan was one of the first settlers.

Next, he looked through period photographs and found the whiskered man listed amongst a set of portraits doubtless taken using flash powder.

"Just stand there, sir, while I set off a small explosion not far from our heads."

For good order, he investigated the history of Spodge & Sons, and found it was indeed located in the same building and, oddly, founded by a Jeremiah Spodge.

Either it's a coincidence, or the guy is immortal. Now THAT would out-box the mystery boxes. Out-Portal The Portal.

Probably a coincidence. Let's hope. Not sure I could cope otherwise.

He was examining the photographs for evidence of a True ancestor (logically, as a box owner, Romeo must have Sunrise lineage) when a familiar figure appeared.

'Didn't take you for a bookworm, Beckman.'

'Just… doing some research.'

Reba glanced around and whispered, 'Related to you-know-what?'

'Loosely. You?'

'I may have gotten curious about it.'

'Sandra'll kick your ass if she finds you meddling.'

'I'm a detective. *Not* being found meddling is my job. Anyway, I'm not *meddling*. I'm doing research on a subject.'

'Would this subject wear a badge?'

'He might.'

Beckman coaxed Reba into a corner, but they kept voices hushed.

'Did you get a bad read off Romeo when you were there?'

'No more than I did already. Maybe I have a thing against jocks, but I was intrigued that he had his own two boxes. He basically conned one more out of someone—who's to say the two he had weren't rightfully his?'

Beckman shook his head. 'He can't have started with zero—otherwise, how would he know they were a thing? One is certainly his—or it was Julie's. The other—who knows?'

'Fine, sure. Well, I was looking into him anyhow.'

'So was I.'

He eyed her suspiciously. 'Do you not have other cases to work on?'

She clasped his arm. 'Beckman, you guys are my friends. This town is my home. We already had Carlton

Cooper try to screw things up, and we made a pretty good team on that. You have a nose for bad eggs; I have a job that involves proving who did what to who, and why. If we're both looking at Romeo, what does that say?'

'Honestly? I have no argument with the guy. I believe what he did came from a good place—plus sharing everybody's curiosity.'

'He opened the boxes, buddy,' she reminded him.

Aw. She called me 'buddy'. That's a first.

'I know. And he got what was coming. Wait—did you know that Sandra confiscated his two boxes?'

Reba was startled. 'Shoot. No. Why?'

'Turns out she really is a guardian of some kind. Watches out that people don't go round pinching boxes, opening them, turning over rocks about this whole web of Who Knows.'

'Well—librarian—that's a pretty good spot to keep tabs on people.'

'Yeah. Makes sense. Just wish she wasn't such an ass at the same time.'

'Looks like it runs in that whole clan.'

'Clans is what I was looking at. I want to trace all the box holders we know, check they're legitimate.'

'I was on the same trail.'

'Then let's divide and conquer.'

By mid-afternoon, things were proceeding apace, and they hadn't attracted any flak from Allie.

There were five boxes that they knew of: Jack's was traced, Romeo True's came from Barratt True, and a photograph existed of that guy. Julie True's ancestor—although her lineage was complex—was most likely Denver Falz. The woman who'd responded to the newspaper advert, Mrs Klepp, had another early Sunrise settler, Kalvin Klepp, in her family tree.

Lucky that we're doing this in a small town that has grown slowly, had little emigration, and wasn't populated by endless Smiths and Browns.

It was all too easy. Why hadn't anyone done this before? He assumed that the twenty-first-century digitisation of records made things a whole lot easier. Maybe people had stayed in their silos before, kept their mouths shut like they were told, left the entire thing alone? Or else, on any other day, Sandra Thornton or her predecessor would have rapped their knuckles when they surmised what he and Reba were up to.

Again, he reaffirmed that they weren't breaking Spodge's rules: tracing the original box owners didn't amount to revealing anything that wasn't in the public domain. It was merely a jigsaw puzzle, albeit one where the completed image was a surprise.

Plus, Spodge knew *every* box holder. He's the one who needed to be watched. Beckman didn't know if there were no more boxes in town, five more, or fifty more.

There was only one more box to trace—Ginetta's, which she'd told them her father Calvin Thornton had bequeathed. Reba had spent hours on this one box.

She wheeled her chair over and tapped Beckman on the shoulder. 'You wanna get some air?'

'Are we done here?'

'If we're getting air, we should pack away the… evidence, just in case.'

'So, let's call it a day. I could kill for a soda.'

They logged out of the computers, put back the files and headed out into the warm sunshine. She pointed at a bench on the green space out front of the library.

They sat.

'Five bucks says you didn't want air,' he said.

'Look, we're on the same page about this. There are no certainties. It's much easier when I have a photograph of Mr X in a clinch with Miss Y when he should be at home with Mrs X. This is… joining dots.'

'Absolutely. So what dots have you got?'

'I found Calvin Thornton's settler, William Thornton. Short, mean eyes—not that it matters. The point is—assuming we're looking for boxes in the early days of the town—the Thornton line—Ginetta's line, is as genuine as Jack's or the other three.'

'Both Lolita's grandfathers had history.'

'Absolutely. Romeo and Julie—two boxes ending up in the same family— that's just a quirk of statistics. Same with Jack and Ginetta.'

'A long shot.'

Reba nodded. 'Sure. But if you had a box, and you fell in love with a woman, you wouldn't stop marrying them on the small chance it later turned out they had a box too. Or even if you knew they already did.'

'Depends how many boxes there are. If there are like a hundred, the odds of pairing up with someone are much higher than if there's just these five.'

'Beckman, being honest, the math part I could care less about. If Spodge isn't bothered, why would we be? We're not doing this to stick a spanner in the works. We're doing it to check on Romeo—and you said he's clean.'

'Everybody is, so where's the fire? Why are we out here?'

'You told me you found Spodge's ancestor.'

'I did. But I never believed his story *wouldn't* check out. The Wills of all these people need executing. It's as immutable as needing undertakers or doctors. Sunrise of 1842 would have a legal guy. If the boxes were conceived back then, and Spodge's firm has kept the wheels of inheritance moving—telling people what they can't do and must do—then the system created by... whoever... works.'

Reba recrossed her legs. 'And I like it. In fact, I'm a sucker for it, like the beauty of a pistol. All the parts, well-oiled, simple yet very effective.'

'Why do I hear a "but"?'

'Let's say there are just these five boxes—for argument's sake. We have five settlers with proven lineage. We have Spodge with proven lineage. What's missing?'

'Reba, buddy, you're a private investigator. I'm a lighting supplies salesman who enjoys figuring out why people do stuff, who might have a headache, and trying to protect the woman I love. You're the brains of this outfit. I'm just here learning about a new home I gave up that old life for.' He faced her, sheepish. 'I'm also getting distracted by the idea of Stetsons and spurs and guns, and horses up and down this road. I was never in one place long enough to give a rats ass about it. Not until now.' He smiled. 'Maybe this whole sudden interest is me over-compensating.'

She laid a hand on his knee. 'Honestly, if you're trying to do the right thing by Sunrise, that's all that matters. You're probably Spodge's ideal box-keeper.'

'Except obviously, I'm not—Lolita is. I'm a keeper by proxy.'

'It washes out the same. Anyhow, you want the benefit of my razor-sharp sleuthing brain?'

'Absolutely.'

'The way I see it, the other lineage we need is the Guardian. That person must have been conceived at the start, too, or the whole thing falls apart. Someone needs to keep all box-holders in line—be ready to lock horns with whiskered desperados who might want to break the code.'

'Sure. Damn certain Sandra would be happy to take on shooters and fighters. Bare-handed. One look could kill.'

'The Guardian needs to be able to hold their own— you can't deny that. Just one problem.'

'What?'

'Sandra is not Calvin Thornton's daughter. We know that. She's only Ginetta's *half*-sister. That's the reason she didn't get given Ginetta's box originally. She couldn't have. She would never have been in Calvin's Will.'

His brow furrowed. 'I get that. That's not news.'

'No, it isn't. Sandra is the daughter of Beth—Ginetta's mom—and a guy called Sully Lively—the guy Beth had the affair with. If Sandra is a Guardian, one of her ancestors must have had that role too.'

'Your logic's watertight so far.'

'Beth, maiden name Scribb, has no ancestors in Sunrise before 1945. They arrived after the War. And Sully Lively? He moved here in 1953 as part of the labour force building the old bottling plant. He and Beth must have hooked up in a bar or a dancehall or whatever.'

'Am I reading this right?'

'We know we're only joining dots, yeah? There are holes in this thing you could drive a Hummer through. But if this whole enterprise was conceived in the 1840s, then the only missing piece is the Guardian. Either there is no such person, they invented the role later—maybe after something went wrong, or if there *has* been a Guardian since day one, Sandra Thornton has no blood connection to anyone from that time.'

Chapter 41

Beckman watched Lolita during dinner. Her eyes were in constant motion, the pace of her eating ebbed and flowed, frowns came and went.

It's like a machine in there. A giant, beautiful machine. As graceful and valuable as Buck's faithful coffee machine Bessie, only wrapped up in an exterior much less function and much more form.

He'd fed all the data into the computer, and now it was processing. The problem was, this computer had baggage; it had a stake. It had emotion.

Yet, all three computers did. Reba was biased against Romeo True, Lolita was biased against Sandra, and he…? He was prejudiced by past events. Taking things at face value was tough. Letting go of gnawing doubt was tough. The obvious answer—the simple answer—wasn't good enough.

When he'd seen Carlton Cooper kiss Wanda Whack at the gas station, knowing Carlton was dating Lolita, he could have assumed that Wanda was Carlton's sister or cousin or some such.

When he'd found Miss Broomhead's handwriting matched Charlie's, he could have put it down to coincidence.

When the Milan warehouse had burned down, he could have dismissed it as an accident.

Every time, even if things didn't smell overtly fishy, he jemmied a whole school of marlin into the circumstance anyway. Why? Damned if he knew.

The problem was, things turned out decidedly piscatorial in any case.

Do you have a nose for this—is that it? Trying to muscle in on Reba's territory?

No. It's that damn curiosity of yours. The people-watching. The figuring out. Looking for an angle, a way to make a sale—a legitimate sale. To find a solution that's truly there—not peddle or flim-flam. To fix things. To make people better. Make things better.

Or else it's to make up for twelve years of drudgery, mega-mileages, solitude and non-event.

To live a little. To dare.

He gazed at Lolita.

You (not you personally, of course) changed Tyler by nearly killing him. The guy is mostly unrecognisable. Much less the rebel, the ass, the chancer.

You nearly died that week, too. You also woke up with new eyes. A new outlook. Confidence—that's what it is. Maybe a pair of balls. Courage of your convictions.

And every rock you've turned over has produced a slug. You're batting three for three.

If you hadn't told Lolita that Carlton was cheating, she'd be in an unhappy marriage.

If you hadn't high-tailed it from Pegasus and tried to hide out in Sunrise, you'd be dead.

If we both hadn't gone up against Carlton, we'd have lost Milan Lighting.

This?

It's probably nothing.

He sipped his beer. 'It's probably nothing.'

'I agree.' She looked him square. 'Like you said, history is a mess of lost information, word of mouth, affairs, forgery, illegitimacy, scandal, unspoken secrets, dishonesty and power struggles. There are a million ways in which this is *not* what it seems like. So what if Sandra is a guardian? So what? She's not mom's favourite person, and maybe she's not ours. Maybe she pulls the legs off spiders in her free time. Who gives a crap? If history has given her that job, we let it lie. We keep Jack's box. We stay in our lane.'

'And mom's box?'

'We have to get that back, sure. Even the Guardian must see that the lineage has to be followed. Them above everyone. If I was being a bitch about it, maybe it got her hackles up, and she did it to spite me—to spite mom.' She snorted. 'I have a history of people doing things to spite me. To get revenge.'

'But like you say, *Guardian* Sandra outweighs *person* Sandra. Duty trumps family.'

He cleared their plates into the kitchen, then reconvened on the sofa.

'And the one in a million?' he asked. 'She's lying?'

'She knows a lot about it all. Too much for coincidence.'

'She's a librarian. Look how far Reba and I got today. She's had Ginetta's box for years. Why has she not had a head start on this, cooking up this persona so she can throw a cloak over the whole thing?'

She took his hand and lovingly stroked one finger. 'There's always a conspiracy with you, isn't there?'

'That's the exact problem. There always *is*.'

'Maybe this is fourth time lucky. Maybe this is a storm in a teacup.'

'I hope like hell it is. I hope I'm being an idiot. I want a clincher, that's all. Don't you? If she can wave some credentials in my face, I may feel like a heel for a while, but at least we'll know the whole thing is under control.'

'You think she can *prove* her status?' Lolita asked.

'Anyone can *say* they are the Guardian. You could. Reba could. Spodge, I trust one hundred percent to be who he is. The box holders are a matter of family trees and logic. Sandra? I don't trust her, and she fails the lineage test.'

'And what if it isn't her? Getting back mom's box might be a petty family squabble, but if we told Spodge, I'll bet he'd come down on our side. When that's done, what do we care? If someone—whoever—is doing what they've been instructed, keeping this safety net intact, *that's* what's important. We all like Sunrise the way it is. We want everyone pulling in the same direction to keep it like that.' She smiled. 'Even you, you little outsider you.'

'I get it—I've come in and upset the delicate ecosystem. Rocked the boat. *Created* those storms in teacups.'

She tousled his hair. 'No. Not at all. You want to do the right thing. You always do. It's one of the reasons I married you. You don't like dishonesty. Here's the news—neither do I.'

'Problem is, I don't know how she *would* prove her status. I doubt they give out badges.'

'Plus, she'd be unlikely to help *us*. We're the enemy.' She laughed. 'Ironically, I might be the daughter *she'd* produced if she'd managed to steal Jack away from mom.'

Beckman shuddered. 'I'd hate to think what you'd be like. Not the ray of sunshine you are in *this* universe, that's for sure.'

She kissed him. 'So, how will we rest our conscience if we can't get proof she is the Guardian?'

He toyed with her brown curls. 'We could try to prove someone else is.'

Chapter 42

Tuesday. Lolita told her PA that she and Beckman were taking an 'offsite meeting' that morning.

They sat in the car, sipping from takeaway cups, waiting for the library to open, and working out a plan for conducting more research without alerting Sandra.

Finally, a solution arrived: Lolita would swallow her pride, present her sweetest face, and engage Sandra in a wholly unconnected topic. Possibly feign interest in the history of lightbulb manufacture in Sunrise. Ask Sandra how her weekend was. Subtly indicate that Milan Lighting might sponsor a refresh of the bulbs in the building.

Meanwhile, Beckman would scour the digital archives of the Sunrise Beacon for clues as to the identity of the original Guardian.

If challenged, he'd legitimately be able to say that he wasn't trying to track down other box owners, discover the origin of the boxes, or anything else which might upset Ms Difficult.

A knock on the Mustang's window made them jump.

Rumbled already?

No.

He rolled the window down.

'I thought stakeouts was my line of work,' Reba said.

'If that's what we were doing, clearly we're about as inconspicuous as a six-foot yellow neon spyglass.'

He noticed that her takeout cup sported the Our Buck's logo.

She noticed that he'd noticed. 'He and I are still talking. I hope that's okay. I didn't take sides about the whole thing.'

Lolita waved it away. 'I don't want the guy losing custom because we had a… falling out.'

Yeah, like falling out of a plane at 37,000 feet, plus associated hard landing.

'He's still not himself,' Reba replied.

'That makes two.' Lolita sighed. 'So—were you going in?' She pointed at the library.

'I figured I was more… under the radar than you two. Actually, my dumb brain kept me awake, chewing it all over.'

'That makes three of us,' Beckman said.

'From what you said, Sandra getting sniffy with you two *could* be personal, like she doesn't want you in her… sphere, making her jealous or whatever. Ordinarily, I'd be billing you two-fifty a day for doing my job, but let's call this one a busman's holiday, okay?' She winked.

One day, I'll pluck up the courage to ask what happened to her eye.

Or I could ask Lolita; if these two have been tight for years, I'll bet that story has come out.

Lolita touched his arm. 'How about you stay clear of the newspaper records. Look through old pictures or something. Town plans. It might come in useful. But if my house was built on an old Native American burial ground, keep it to yourself, okay? I don't need anything else filling my head. I'm already worrying about where mom's going to find to live, whether Buck will do something dumb to drown his sorrows, or if Amaryllis will have a U-turn on animal sympathy, try to throttle that bird and wind up getting pecked in the jugular.'

'Let's all try not to get pecked in the jugular by the old bird in there.' He pointed at the library.

As they headed across to the building, he wondered whether this was what Ethan Hunt felt like before a mission.

Almost certainly not.

He kept his head down, and each stuck to their tasks without communicating.

Lolita strung out her diversionary role as long as she could, but wound up sitting opposite Beckman, using her laptop to catch up on trivial things like management reports for the head of a multi-million dollar company.

Around noon, Reba breezed past, murmured 'Okay', and exited the building.

He and Lolita soon packed up and followed. He'd probably had the most interesting morning of the three of them, lazily becoming immersed in the Sunrise of the Old West, getting familiar with the look and feel of the place, reading stories of brawlers and bad sorts, a fire in the old stables, and a blacksmith who was buried with his favourite anvil.

They met up at home. Lolita scrabbled together lunch, and they gathered around the table.

'Don't keep us in suspense, honey,' Lolita said.

'I didn't find anything concrete, that's for sure,' Reba replied. 'On the other side, I didn't make any links between Sandra's line and the early settlement.'

'So, her case is weak,' Beckman said.

'Verging on non-existent. Nor did I find anything glaring which points to the identity of a Guardian back then—although, being fair, I have no clue what I'm looking for.'

'But you did find *something*,' Lolita assumed.

'Some of the names we know—Milan, True, Klepp—they do come up in the papers. Seems they may have hung out together.'

'I found a photograph from the dedication of the town water well. There were a bunch of guys with tools. Milan was one, Thornton, a guy called William Wott.'

'Maybe they were labourers, construction workers,' Reba suggested. 'They could have been part of the first bunch who decided to build a place here.'

'Something about the water well?' Lolita wondered.

'You mean like they found an alien artefact down there?' Beckman laughed.

She flashed The Eyebrow (Watch Your Step version).

'I thought we weren't after the point of the boxes, or even who has them?' Reba said. 'Come on, guys, you can't ball Romeo out for trying to discover the answer and then go right ahead yourselves.'

Beckman hung his head. 'I guess not.'

'This is about Sandra, and whether she's a threat, an innocent, or a lynchpin.'

'So why did you wrap up and call time?' Lolita supped her coffee.

Reba tapped the table with an index finger. 'Here's the thing. The library has a digital copy of every edition of the Beacon back to Issue 1. It was only weekly back then, but that's still a lot of column inches about rustled steers, new businesses opening up, and fights about land ownership.'

'You gave up because you were starting to see double?'

'No. There's one Issue missing. These are not things you can check out like a book. The library is short by one file.'

Lolita entwined her fingers. 'Which I'll bet the Guardian has deleted, because it's very sensitive and important.'

'And who better to do that than the librarian?'

Chapter 43

Lolita got up and paced.

Reba leant across the table. 'Does she have these Sherlock Holmes moments?' she murmured.

'It's a blessing. I'd rather she did that than tear strips off people or rush in where angels fear to tread.'

Reba nodded. 'She did work out that hologram thing at your offices. Pulled a fast one on a certain hitman of our acquaintance.'

'Came up with the scheme to trick Carlton too.' Beckman watched Lolita chomp on an apple. 'I'm not knocking your detective chops, buddy, but my gal's got a cerebellum as beautiful as the rest of her—which we both know is pretty damn beautiful.'

Reba put on an impish expression. 'Let's just say that if I ever… swayed in the direction you told me Ginetta has, I'd give you a run for your money. Buddy.'

She patted his hand.

I think that's classified as Too Much Information.

I hope Randall keeps her on the straight and narrow. Particularly the straight part.

Lolita eased into the adjacent seat.

'Here's the problem.' She set the apple core on the table. 'Sandra, as the Guardian, could absolutely legitimately delete that file—to protect dark forces from joining one too many dots. Equally, Sandra—and I'll skip over our emotional issues—as a mere townsperson but with *access* to delete that file, could have done it out of spite for any number of reasons. And that's the problem. If that one piece of history has been surgically removed, it's either because she's telling the truth, or she isn't.'

'Do you want to flip a coin?' he joked.

The Eyebrow (Are You Sure You Wanted To Say That? version).

'In other words, Reba said, 'We're back where we started. We need evidence—maybe not conclusive proof, but at least reasonable doubt—to sway things either way.'

'Maybe the answer's in that edition of the Beacon,' he said.

'You mean she removed it because it casts doubt on her claims?' Lolita asked.

'Yes. Or, if she is the Guardian, she did it for the right reasons.'

'Either way, we need to see that file,' Reba said.

'Do you have a piece of magic un-delete software in the Private Eye tool bag of yours?' he snarked.

Her face fell. 'No. I don't.'

He and Lolita sighed.

'But,' Reba continued, 'As Lol knows, I worked at the Beacon when I started out. I'm still pretty tight with Finlay McMackery, and I'm almost sure they keep a physical copy of every Issue in their archives.'

Lolita's eyes widened, then she bit her lip. 'The only problem is we risk opening Pandora's Box. If Sandra's masquerading, that newspaper might prove it. Alternatively, it might expose this whole enterprise. That's pretty scary.'

'It's Schrödinger's Cat,' Beckman said with a shrug.

'Whatnow?' Reba asked.

'We don't know what the truth is unless we look for it. If we do nothing because we're afraid of seeing something we shouldn't, we risk letting a rogue element perpetuate. Either we get proof she's not the Guardian—and nothing more, or we *don't* get proof, but we *do* get a clue—big or small—into what these boxes are all about.'

'We know we're honest—that's the difference,' Lolita said. 'I'd hope any of us three would disown the other two if they blabbed about the secret.'

'We're the Three Musketeers, bound by loyalty to each other and the town,' Beckman proclaimed proudly.

Lolita coughed. 'That's one way of putting it. It's a matter of conscience. There's a piece in that newspaper that answers something about all of this. I'd put money on it. I absolutely don't want to find out anything more than we need. I don't *care* what the boxes mean. They exist to protect this town. Logically, we as box holders have that duty too.'

'It's what Romeo said he was doing,' Reba reminded them.

'Whether we believe him or not. He was finding a way to gather all the boxes. That's a no-no where Spodge is concerned. Now Sandra has three boxes, Spodge has one, and we have one. The balance of power is with her. The question is, is what she's doing legitimate, or another misguided crusade like Romeo's?'

'So, let's vote,' Reba said. 'We'll only go to the Beacon offices if it's unanimous.'

Chapter 44

Beckman was walking around Sunrise with an old street map in his head. Occasionally he'd superimpose a mental image—in sepia, with tatty edges and blown highlights—over what his retina saw in the here and now. It was the closest he'd ever come to time travel.

Unless The Portal had done that? Taken us back at least two hundred years to before civilisation existed on this spot? We'd always considered it a parallel universe on the same timeline. Either way, it was nonsensical, unbelievable and pure hypothesis.

All the same, it had happened.

It only serves to make this small collection of old, carved wooden boxes look positively normal.

Curious—yes. A sense of walking a tightrope between right and wrong—yes. A test of bonds between friends (and lovers)—yes.

Let's hope that Issue 109, March 1848, gives us an 'Aha!' moment and not an 'Oh, snap!' one.

Fortune favours the brave. Best foot forward. You miss 100% of the shots you don't take.

And other clichés.

The offices of the Sunrise Beacon were a twentieth-century rendition of a nineteenth-century construction: horizontal white boards broken up by modest windows displaying the antiquated logo of the newspaper. It was a place proud of its roots, and had remained on the same lot—220 Candela Avenue. (Although it was named Winter Avenue in the 1840s, after one of the settlers,

Alden Winter. Most streets had lost their original names when the lighting business came to town).

Finlay McMackery was a stout guy of about fifty, with jet black hair, round glasses and a neckerchief. He and Reba shared a hug, passed a few moments in reminisce, then she introduced Beckman and Lolita, which was wholly unnecessary: Lolita Milan had been The Woman Who Wears Swing Dresses for years—and hence hardly went unnoticed by anyone. Beckman had briefly been That New Guy Who Cures Headaches, later The Guy Who's Dating Lolita, and finally plain ol' Beckman, because when your name's Beckman, other monikers are usually redundant.

(He'd once Googled "Beckman". There were four others in the US. He'd also looked up monochromacy. That was less rare. Still, even with his vision now normal, the chances of anyone confusing him with someone else were small. Either way, he'd be happy to be The Guy Who Married Lolita. So long as, after this stunt, they didn't become The Couple Who Ruined Sunrise And Got Banished).

As Finlay was a busy guy, with this week's Issue to prepare, he waved them down to the basement to pore over yellowing paper, for reasons Reba had heavily glossed over.

The vault was fitted with rows of huge cabinets, which were pressed together until you wanted to create a walk space, whereupon you'd turn a huge wheel on the end of the cabinet, and the whole MacGuffin would move sideways on rails. There were a dozen of these, and eight needed to be moved.

After the fourth one, Beckman really got into the role.

After the fifth one, he went "Wheeeee!" as the contraption clanked across.

Before the sixth one, he got The Eyebrow.

'I always thought whoever married Lolita would need the patience of a saint,' Reba said. 'Actually, it's the other way around.'

Beckman pouted theatrically and wheeled the last two rows across.

They walked down the newly-created space, checking the dates on the metallic columns, until they reached the desired point in history. Reba danced her fingers through the large suspension files and landed them on the holder marked "109".

It wasn't empty.

'The game's afoot,' she murmured.

She levered out the two-foot-high publication, which was wrapped in protective plastic, and carefully carried it back down the row. At the other side of the room was a large table. She laid the paper down.

Beckman drank in the snapshot of past times. It was like living in a movie or a dream.

'Don't miss a single column inch, okay?' Reba said.

They huddled together, under the weak light of two overhead lamps whose bulbs seemed to be older than any of them, and pored over the typeface.

'No?' Reba said after a couple of minutes.

They shook their heads.

She turned the wrapped page, opening up a double spread of pages two and three.

He tried to read meticulously, looking at the words and names but got distracted imagining the images behind the stories, the atmosphere.

'Anything?'

'No,' Lolita said.

Pages four and five—the middle spread.

Nothing. Well, nothing relevant.

'No,' he said at the end.

Six and seven.

He read about the arrival of the Mollick family. An advert for Rollo's General Store (which he knew was on the site of what was now Jen & Berry's). A stagecoach robbery.

Lolita leant in. Her finger hovered.

He looked closer.

A barroom brawl. Six men taken to the cell to cool off. Milan, Thornton, True, Klepp, Falz, Wott.

Lolita's gaze met his. He eyed Reba.

They all took a step back. His forehead tweaked with introspection. Lolita bit her lip.

Reba tapped her finger gently on the table. 'I'm relieved. This tells us very little.'

'Very little that's confidential,' Lolita said.

'The question is, was the argument *about* the boxes, or did it precipitate the boxes?' he wondered.

Lolita touched his arm. 'So you're not perfect, Mr Observant. Read again.'

He wanted to say that he'd never claimed to be perfect. Only… sufficiently good—as a salesman, friend, and husband. Instead, he re-read.

'Well, hello…' he whispered.

'It's not everything, but it's not nothing,' Lolita said.

Reba pulled out her phone and took a snapshot of the article. 'We shouldn't outstay our welcome.'

'Agreed.'

Reba closed up the old document, replaced it in its slot, then Beckman *maturely* returned the archive carriages to their original positions.

The sunshine was a shock after the cool, dim storage bunker.

'This is an *outside* conversation,' he suggested.

'It's a milkshakes-and-root-beers-in-Filament Gardens conversation,' Reba agreed.

'I'll buy,' Lolita said.

He was getting used to Jen & Berry's root beer, and that made him sad. He wanted Buck's root beer back again. He wanted Buck back again. The man's knowledge, wisdom and counsel would be ideal at this point.

Oddly, there was now a glimmer of that prospect.

The second best soft drink in town slid down nicely.

'It could have all started that night,' Reba said.

'Ree, let's focus, okay? It's not about what they did, what they know, why they argued—hell, it may just be a huge coincidence, but—'

'It was a small town. Three hundred people. All five of the names we know were in those Sheriff's cells at the same time.'

'Plus William Wott,' Beckman said.

'Then I'd argue he's the person most likely to have been the original Guardian,' Reba said.

'Absolutely. Until we trace his descendants. But we're all thinking the same thing, aren't we?' There was pleading in Lolita's tone, yet it was edged with disappointment. 'We *know* the Sheriff has a descendant in town.'

He couldn't argue with her logic, chiefly because he'd come to the same conclusion, and he was sure Reba had too.

'The Guardian is an authority figure. Who better to keep order, to stop squabbles again? To protect the town?' Lolita sucked hard on her straw. 'A cop. Like Romeo.'

'Romeo is *not* the Guardian,' Reba scowled.

'I agree. I mean, the old Sheriff is the most logical first Guardian. He might have protected with more brawn and bullets than warnings and observation, but still. Maybe 1840s Spodge didn't tell the five guys that the Sheriff was going to watch over them, but the two legal big shots might have worked out the whole deal.'

'One thing's for sure—there won't be anything written down about it anywhere,' Beckman said. 'This is word-is-bond stuff. If they created the secret, the box network, around that time, we won't find it in the papers, the books, Wills or photographs. We're lucky as hell that we got what we got.'

'And what we got is a signpost at best. We can't *prove* the Sheriff's line is the one which carries the Guardian.' Lolita shrugged.

Reba's tone was placating. 'We don't need to dig up anything to prove it. We can just ask the man.'

Lolita's head dipped. 'He'd deny it, wouldn't he? Or at least say "no comment".'

'Sandra didn't,' Beckman pointed out.

'Except, *honey*, she was lying.'

'Lol, I know you don't want to admit it, but the only way to be sure she *is* lying—and doing something I don't like the look of—is to ask the *real* Guardian.' Reba put a hand on Lolita's shoulder.

'We don't know if he really *is*.'

Reba leant against the bench's backrest. 'Well, we're out of other options. We could stop everyone on the street and ask them if they're the chosen one, but it's a damn sight easier to go to our first best lead.'

Lolita sighed. 'I know.'

'I'll do it if you don't want to.'

Lolita gazed at her friend's face for a long time. 'No. You're not… in the middle of this thing. Yours is not the relative who put me in this position. We couldn't have got this far without you, Ree, but I need to grow some balls and put this thing to rest.'

'And if he won't speak to you? Or Beckman?'

'Sure, you're Plan B.'

Reba smiled. 'Thanks.'

Something had been worming around Beckman's skull since they'd left the Beacon offices. Now it burrowed out into his throat.

'I know we all want this to be one big coincidence, but there's another nail in the coffin for happenstance. You know what the old Sheriff's building is now? It's a café.'

Chapter 45

Tyler accelerated away from the junction, leaving the desert road behind. Soon, the town sign for Sunrise slid past.

'Sunrise. Sunrise,' Flint squawked from the bijou back seats where his cage was wedged.

'You know, I'm not sure how kind it is to treat the bird like this. Shuttling back and forth twice a week?' He looked across at Amaryllis. 'It's not the most practical idea—having a pet.'

'So which do we give up—the parrot or the two-centre living?'

Tyler lowered his voice. 'We know which is *easier* to ditch.'

She smiled. 'I'm sure Flint won't be offended by having three new owners in as many weeks.'

'Flint. Shut your beak. Great rack,' the bird replied.

'It's your call, honey,' Tyler said. 'You took him off Lolita's hands. I can't think he'd be happy to be left alone at your place half the week, or stuck in a hotel room here. Besides, it's kinda overkill to rent out a room every day of the year just to keep the bird in it alone when we're up at Pegasus.'

'If we had a proper *place* here, it might be different.'

He recognised the inference in both the words and her expression. A tremor of fear took him. He shook it away.

Why was it so alien to consider getting an apartment—even a house—together in Sunrise? They had a place in the city.

But that was *Amaryllis'* place. He'd merely moved in. It wasn't a jointly chosen house. It wasn't the next step on the commitment ladder of abandoning their previous sole-occupancy properties and getting a new home *together.*

If they decided to get a second bolt-hole in Sunrise— the "home in the country" for the newly well-heeled twosome—it would undoubtedly be a rubber stamp for their relationship.

She might think: he's serious about me. It's true love. It's marriage. It's forever.

The problem was, his heart and head hadn't made peace about it. She was as likely to be right as wrong.

'I know we have a few bucks to our name, but I don't want to look like city slickers waltzing into Sunrise and splashing out on property like the new money we are. People might get sniffy.'

'Is that the real reason?' she asked softly.

'What do you want me to say? That I'm having second thoughts?' He put his hand on her knee. 'I am one hundred percent not. I'm a one-woman man now, and that woman is you.'

'There are shorter ways of saying that, Tyler. Three little words, in fact.'

He checked the mirror, eased in the brake and brought them to a halt on the outskirts of town.

He cupped her cheek. 'Every day, I know I'm lucky. But every day, I wonder when you'll wise up and see through all this.'

'Is there anything to see through? Either this is the best and longest sales pitch of your life—and I don't know what you'd be aiming for, except to break my heart one day by throwing off the cloak in an explosion of utter misogynistic cruelty—or you're actually a decent human being to your very core.'

He lowered his hand and took hers. 'That's the problem. I'm still figuring that out. I don't want to break your heart, so I don't want to do anything—or especially say anything—which puts it in a position to be broken.'

She pondered that.

'Alright. But know this. First, I love *you*. Second, I may be forty-four and unable to have a family, but I have as much of a shot at a happy ever after as anyone. If you are that decent human being, at least let me know in good time, okay? I think I'm a pretty good catch for someone, even if it's not you. After all, I know Flint speaks highly of me.'

'Flint speaks. Decent catch. Great rack.'

They laughed. Tyler stroked the gear lever pensively. The flat-six idled.

'There's a holiday home out past Saul's place. Let's get it for two weeks, let Flint stay there, you and I see how we go, then we'll decide if something more permanent is… desirable. Okay?'

She nodded. 'Just one condition.'

'Name it.'

'*One* week.'

They checked into the Sunset Hotel, covered Flint while they tested the bed, then walked down to Our Buck's for an afternoon snack.

While they waited at their table, Tyler observed Buck. The man worked earnestly—taking orders, making food and drinks—but without the customary bonhomie.

'He's still hurting.'

'Think about if you lost Beckman and me in the same week,' Amaryllis replied. 'I'd hope to hell that you weren't over it in a few days.'

'Because you're such a good catch?' he replied impishly.

'I'm a helluva catch, Tyler Quittle. Matter of fact, I think Buck is too—as a friend, as a rock. And Lolita.'

'Things come, things go.'

'Easy to say when you never had what Buck had, with either Lolita or Dixon. You can't identify with that loss.'

He was momentarily hurt. He felt seen, then he realised it was on point. 'Did you ever have that?'

'No. Girlfriends back home, but never soulmates. Certainly nobody through Pegasus—I doubt Malvolio would have allowed fraternisation. And never... a significant physical thing.' She took his hand. 'A bond characterised by those three words.'

He smiled. 'And I thought we were so different.'

'The playboy and the spinster?'

Those words felt harsh, a caricature, yet that's how he'd viewed them both for twelve long years.

He shrugged. 'Two different skins over the same need.'

'I suppose,' she reflected.

He checked the clock. Buck still hadn't come to take their order. Were they suddenly in the enemy camp?

He rose. 'I'll order at the bar.'

At the long wooden counter, Tyler waited behind an old lady who was settling her bill.

Buck held a crisp note up to the light.

'Have you been printing money again, Mrs Finkel?' Buck flashed the lady a cheeky grin.

'Mr Buck, you're a cruel man.'

'Well—I see a crisp hundred and an eligible lady, and I wonder either why she's not married or whether she's up to no good.'

Mrs Finkel patted a wrinkly hand on the countertop. 'Now, give over. I came into a little money, that's all, and my favourite coffee man should have some.'

Buck opened the register. 'Let me see if I can break this down.'

He rifled in the drawer. 'So, did you lose someone? I'm sorry if you did. I know my frie… I know *someone* in town lost her father recently.'

'No,' the lady said sombrely. 'I don't have any family left. I suppose that's why Ms Thornton was so kind to me.'

Buck gathered some bills together. He caught Tyler's eye but looked away and huddled towards his customer.

Tyler turned to the side, offering privacy, although the lady must have been a mite deaf as her voice didn't quieten.

'So kind—how?' Buck asked.

'I'm not supposed to say, but I guess now that thing appeared in the paper, it's not the secret it was. I had my own box, so I did, and heaven knows I don't have any children to pass it to, so Ms Thornton—she's such a kind soul—said she'd mind it for me.' The woman sighed. 'At my age, I know I won't be around too long, and it's been a weight on my mind, so it has, that old box.'

The register drawer closed. 'And Ms Thornton gave you a hundred dollars for the privilege?'

'Two hundred, actually.' Her voice lowered a decibel or two. 'She said I wasn't to mention the money. It's a matter of the town's security, don't you know. Well, heaven knows I'm not right for that kind of duty anymore, so Ms Thornton took it under her wing, and she'll find the best thing to do with it. She said it was one of her… goals, in her job.'

Buck coughed. 'She certainly tries to help people. Well—here's your change, and I'm glad to hear you weren't burdened with loss or taken in by a confidence trickster.'

'Heaven no, Mr Buck. Just a few dollars for peace of mind, and glad to spend them here, helping your lovely business. Oh, and how is that good lady of yours? I haven't seen her about for a while?'

Tyler heard the sigh from ten feet away. 'That… didn't work out, Mrs Finkel. Difference of… opinions about Sunrise.'

'Oh. Aw. That's sad. You should be happy, Mr Buck, not alone.'

'If I had a dollar for every person in town who told me that, I'd be a rich man.' The chuckle was cheerless.

She shook her head. 'What is there not to like about our little town?'

'The "little" part, it seems.'

'It was once even smaller, I'll tell you that.'

'It was indeed.'

'Well, I see this young man is waiting for me to quit yapping,' she flashed a toothy grin at Tyler, 'So I'll be on my way. Look after yourself.'

'I will, Mrs Finkel. Thank you.'

The lady shuffled to the door.

Tyler offered Buck a nod of greeting.

'I hear you got a parrot,' the proprietor said.

'It has zero social graces.'

'Do me a favour; don't bring it here. When even the birds start telling me to chase down Dixon, there'll be bird soup on the menu pretty damn quick.' He snorted. 'What can I get you?'

'Two coffees, pie, and a side order of the courage to do the right thing.'

Buck eyed Tyler, then leant heavily on the counter. 'The right thing for who? Her, or you?'

'Both.'

'Ain't that always the conundrum.'

Chapter 46

Beckman and Lolita sat in the Miata, parked a hundred yards from the café.

He checked his watch.

It was a new watch. Relatively. The previous one had taken issue with their trip through The Portal, so she'd bought him something fancier, something less mall.

Maybe it had been time travel. Time travel probably doesn't take too kindly to watches, doing their pesky trying-to-keep-time thing.

Maybe that's what Dixon took issue with; the reason she left; Sunrise is just too… not quite the same as other places. Still, every town has secrets. History. Assholes. Saints. Disagreements. Politics. Death. Birth. Arrivals. Departures. Agendas. Crime. Love. Hate. Revenge. Friendships.

'I feel like Ree,' Lolita said.

'You mean a stakeout?'

'Hmm. Makes him sound like the enemy, huh? The suspect.'

'He's not that, and you know it. Who knows—maybe he's been sitting in there for days, hoping you'll walk back in.'

'Yeah, well, this isn't an apology visit. It's… more important than that. And I'm not walking back in—like we said.'

He held her hand. 'Which proves you're looking out for him, on some small level. Not wanting to create a scene in there.'

'Don't get me wrong, I want this to be really civil, but if he gets assy about me or this whole business, I don't want swears in the air. Kids go in there. Plus, this is supposed to be private, although the boxes are now about as under the radar as Delmar's pursuit technique.'

The neons in the window of Our Buck's flicked to Closed, Buck locked up, went to his Ranger and pootled away.

Beckman glanced across at Lolita. She reached behind her glasses and wiped away what looked like a drop of moisture.

'You okay?'

'I do love that man,' she breathed. 'I wish we hadn't…' Her head fell.

'I know,' he said.

She gazed down the street, trance-like.

Eventually, she said, 'It makes sense for it to be him. He's always at the hub of everything that goes on. He sees. He hears.' She chuckled. 'He's hard to argue against. He was my big bear. All I ever got were hugs, but he's got claws when he needs, so if it is him, he'll stop Sandra in her tracks.'

'And if it isn't him?'

She looked across. 'Then I guess we have to hope it works itself out. Because this… normal life we'd expected is getting shorter by the day. I want off the ride now.'

'Actually, I was kinda enjoying it. It beats peddling boxes forty hours a week.'

'One thing's for certain; it's easier with you here. Dad would still have died. I would still have fallen out with Buck, visited mom, met Sandra. Romeo would have done what he did. Makes a change, huh? Last year you were bleating on about how everything was your fault, banging your head on my shoulder, and boy did that get tiring.'

'Now it's your turn to do the leaning,' he said.

She shook her head. 'I'd rather put the box in the attic and get back to both standing upright.'

'Apart from when we're laying down.' He jiggled his eyebrows.

'I really do think a piece of the ghost of Old Tyler is inside you, reprobate.'

'Well, a chunk of you has definitely rubbed off on Amaryllis.'

'Maybe so.'

'And aren't we all better people for it?' he asked with deliberately forced gravity.

She nudged him in the ribs. 'You're still an idiot, though.'

Chapter 47

Lolita's finger hovered over the doorbell for a second, then she gave it a good shove.

Beckman wished he'd been an octopus, so he could cross even more fingers, then realised octopi don't have fingers.

"Still an idiot, though."

Buck opened the door. His gaze fixed on Lolita, switched to Beckman for a while, then went back.

'Yeah?' His tone was guarded.

'Does the name Sheriff Colt Travis mean anything to you?'

His eyes narrowed. 'Maybe. Who's asking?'

She partially extended her hand. 'Hi. I'm Lolita. I *think* we've met.'

Buck didn't rise to that—whether it was sweetness, humour, or barb. 'I meant "Why?"'

'Because that man took an oath to do good around here. Did you?'

Buck took a step back. 'What's this about?'

'If you know, maybe it would be better if we came in. If you don't know, maybe invite us in anyway? I hear you're a decent sort. You know—from other people.'

Beckman saw the tension in her jawline: she was holding herself together. The town was bigger than two people's squabbles. So was its future.

'I don't like your tone.' Buck's was muted and even.

'I don't want to fight. We've done enough of that. We just have to ask about something. It's *important*.' She gave him her best uncompromising stare.

Buck's barrel chest inflated slowly, held for an eternity, then released. He stood aside and jerked his head.

They filed in like naughty schoolchildren.

Beckman sat gingerly on the edge of the sofa, as if ready to jump up and… do… he didn't know what.

Lolita sat beside him. Buck sat opposite.

Frost/Nixon, anyone?

'Shoot,' the big man said.

'You get that this is *very* hard for me—being here,' she replied.

'Because of what you said.'

'Because of what *you* said.'

Beckman forced a laugh. 'Let's go out and come in again, shall we?'

Lolita ignored it. 'Do you know Sandra Thornton?'

'She's not a regular, but… yeah.'

'And you know about Romeo True, the robbery, the ad, the….'

'Yeah, yeah. Why would I not? Your point?'

'Is it… Is that… all *right* by you?'

Buck cocked his head. 'I don't follow.'

They'd discussed this beforehand: whether to reveal their box ownership to Buck. Ordinarily, she'd disclose pretty much anything to Buck—although these were not ordinary times for their relationship. On the other hand, they shouldn't reveal their box ownership to anyone. It would have been interesting to have conducted this experiment in control conditions, i.e. which took priority—Spodge's directive or her need for allies if something untoward was going on.

They'd decided that if Reba, Randall, Tyler and Amaryllis knew that Jack had left them a box, Buck was only one more. What was the worst that could happen? Besides, if he *was* the Guardian, he might know anyway.

She took a deep breath. 'God, I hope I'm doing the right thing,' she murmured.

Me too.

'When Jack died, I got everything in his estate.' She closed her eyes and paused. 'Including a small wooden box.'

'Okay,' Buck replied, more neutrally than Switzerland.

'So we're *interested* in what's going on with these boxes. Sandra, Romeo. Etcetera.'

'Okay.'

'Are you worried?' she asked.

'The future's not certain.'

'Sandra's been telling people she's some kind of... guardian, where the boxes are concerned.'

Buck stroked his five o'clock shadow. 'Is that so?'

'And how does *that* sit with you?'

'A lot of questions here, Lolita.'

'Look, Buck, I think we've wound up getting mixed into something wrong here, and we thought you of all people might be able to... shed some light on it.'

'Me of all people?'

'You're not making this easy.'

Understatement of the year.

She gathered herself again. 'Are you the Guardian?'

Buck shifted in his seat. 'The Guardian does not make their identity known. Except in extraordinary circumstances.'

'How would you know that?' Beckman interjected.

Buck shot him an evil eye. 'No comment.'

'Sandra made her identity known,' Lolita pointed out.

'Then that proves she's not the Guardian, doesn't it?'

'Does it?'

'I think so.'

'But do you *know* so?'

'How would I know?'

'If you were the Guardian,' Lolita said. 'After all, only one person can have that role.'

'Absolutely.'

'So, is it you?'

'No comment.'

'Then it's her. Or it could be her,' Lolita inferred.

'No, it isn't.'

'Definitely?' She leant forward. 'It's important. For the good of the town. For my sanity. For my family. At least have the civility to help me out with that.'

Buck massaged his forehead. 'No. It's not her.'

'Yet, you're okay with what she's doing? Masquerading, obtaining boxes by stealth. Circumventing the… system.'

'Why would I not be?'

'Because you're the damn Guardian! It's your job.'

'Says who?'

She threw her hands up. 'Jeez, it's like getting blood out of a stone. We're doing the right thing here—do you not get that?'

'I get that you're getting riled up over something that should ordinarily be left alone.'

'So you *do* know about the network of boxes.'

'Why would I not? The café's busy. People talk. Word gets around. You *know* that, Lolita. You both know that.'

'Fine.' She stood, sharply. 'I just thought we could count on you. As a… as… as a person of authority. As the Guardian, dammit, to do something about this woman. She owes me a box from my mother, and she won't hand it over. She's hoarding information. She's lying to people.'

'She's a librarian,' Buck said redundantly.

'I know that! And you trump that. Your job is to stop things getting out of hand—which is exactly what's happening.'

'*If* I'm the Guardian, which you're so keen on proving.'

'Come off it, Buck, we all know you are. What do you gain by being an ass about it? So we're not friends anymore—I could give a shit. This is *Sunrise* we're talking about.'

Buck rose slowly. Beckman didn't like his body language. He stood too.

Buck's voice was low and even. 'Did you ever think that what Sandra is doing might not be a catastrophe? Did you ever think it might have an upside?'

'Spodge said that the opening of boxes was for existential emergency only. And I don't see one. I see a hidden agenda—and I don't like it. This is my town. This is *our* town.'

Buck's gaze searched their faces. 'You need to know this. What's behind all this can save the town, save the people, in an emergency—that's right. In unscrupulous hands, it can turn this place into a breeding ground for greed and strife. In the right hands, it could be a shot in the arm this place needs.'

'This place needs nothing.'

'Debatable.'

She moved closer. 'You know what it's about, don't you? You're not just the Guardian—you've crossed another line. You've opened a box, or broken a rule, or—'

'I've done nothing. Nothing beyond circumstance. If I knew the whole picture, and I was this… conniving, self-serving asshole you paint me as, don't you think I'd already have blown this thing wide open?'

'I don't know. But you *are* the Guardian, and you're letting Sandra on her own merry way to blowing this thing wide open for whatever her own ends are.'

'And who are you to say that's such a bad thing?'

Lolita recoiled. 'You're screwing with history. With something that decent people have left alone for decades.'

'If I thought people would suffer, I would absolutely stop this.'

'How do you know people won't?'

'Because this could make Sunrise a better place. Bigger, happier.'

She jabbed him in the chest. 'I don't *want* it bigger and happier, dammit. And who are you to allow it?'

'I'm the Guardian, Lolita. What I say goes.' He shoved her away.

Beckman got a horrible feeling in the pit of his stomach. He wanted to have a towel in his pocket, so he could throw it into the ring.

Her eyes flared. Her fists balled. 'Why? Why now? Why are you letting someone screw with this place?'

'Because everyone benefits. More friends, more customers, more money. Tell me you don't want that.'

'Of course I damn well don't want it! I love this town how it is.'

'Well, not everyone does.' Buck turned away.

Beckman watched her face cycle through disbelief, anger, query, and land on realisation.

'You're doing this to get Dixon back,' she said through gritted teeth.

'I'm not *doing* anything.'

'You're *allowing* it.'

'We don't know what will happen.'

'You selfish son of a bitch.'

Buck span. 'Go to hell, Lolita.'

'I can't believe this.' Her mouth hung open.

'That figures. Miss Holier-than-thou can't even give two shits about a friend's one last shot at happiness.'

'*Friend?* Not in a million years.'

'You used to care. Hell—you helped me win her over.' He jabbed his finger at her. 'You got your happy ever after, but to hell with mine, huh? Screw Buck, and any chance he's got for love? Well, I don't care what you think, and if I want to throw the dice to get Dixon back, I damn well will.'

'Over the good of the town?!'

'It will be good. For everyone.'

'You can't know that.'

'You don't know what I know.'

She drew herself up to him. 'I don't want to. I don't want anything to do with this. You disgust me. You may be a big man, but your heart is small and shrivelled and only cares about itself. I'm glad she left you. I wouldn't want any woman to have to put up with such a thoughtless, weak asshole. Your ancestor may have been a Sheriff, but this Travis is a two-bit con man who'll sell his friends down the river for his own ends.'

Beckman saw the colour bloom in Buck's cheeks.

He saw the tic in the man's neck. The hand move.

He saw the future a second before it happened, and he hated it. His soul girded itself.

Still, he couldn't move fast enough.

Buck's hand cut across Lolita's face, and she crashed to the floor.

Chapter 48

Beckman sat on the kerb, head in his hands. He wanted to cry but felt too empty, even of tears.

His mind was a tornado, whirling over everything—what had happened, what had caused it, what might come next, how he might have acted differently, how it could have been prevented.

Things were more straightforward when you had nobody. Just you and Bogie and the apartment and the drudgery of Pegasus and Coffee Planet. Sure, Malvolio was a cruel swine, and Tyler was a boastful ass, but they were just… colour. Colour in a monochrome world. Things you could deal with. No surprises, no mysteries, no break-ups, no fisticuffs. The biggest challenge was Salesman of the Year; the biggest jeopardy too.

Life in an anonymous big town where nods and howdys were the staple. Yes—all the services and choices you could want, but no personality.

You'd trade Sunrise now for a fat helping of drudgery.

Would you?

No.

So the place isn't perfect. It has… humanity—warts and all. Ups and downs.

She was right before. Sitting your ass on a cold kerbstone is not what she needs. A problem shared is a problem halved, and you need to work that ol' Beckman magic to gee her up. You did it once, twice, more—you can do it again.

She was the butterfly that flapped its wings and gave you this life, this wife, this town. These friends.

So one friend is lost? Big deal.

Think of the good news. Because there is good news. A silver lining in this seemingly vantablack cloud. We know where we stand now. We know who is on our side. We weren't imagining things. A problem can only be tackled when it's been identified.

We could only beat Randall when Randall appeared. Before that, he was just in your mind.

We could only turn the tables on Malvolio when we knew he was guilty.

Carlton only became a target when we had proof of his misdeeds.

Now, we're more confident than ever that this town faces an existential threat to the status quo. We know the potential aggressors.

Lolita needs to see that. She needs to see the upsides. Sure, they suck, but they are there.

And the good news is that, like she said, she isn't alone now. She has friends. We have friends. Allies. The town may have one Guardian, but it has a least six Super Guardians, self-empowered to out-Guard the Guardian and anyone else pretending to be the Guardian.

Hmm. Super Guardians. That's good.

Maybe not share it, though. Not yet. Could get filed under 'idiot'.

First order of business: get off the kerb.

He stood.

Second order of business: find Lolita.

He pulled out his phone and dialled.

He dropped into the immaculately stitched leather bucket seat and thunked the perfectly engineered German door shut.

He gave Tyler a précis of the contretemps with Buck, to a stunned audience. He revealed chapter and verse on all the box-related shenanigans. He said that Lolita had blustered out and, despite having no quarrel with Beckman, jumped in her car and redlined it up the road.

He told Tyler that he was a buddy, and that Porsche's perches were a much better resting place for his backside than Arizona's sidewalks.

Tyler passed on some new information regarding Mrs Finkel and her innocent but misguided bequest of a box to Sandra. Beckman did the maths. Beckman didn't like the maths. He also didn't enjoy not knowing where his wife was.

'Where to?' Tyler asked.

'Try the house.'

They went to 1002 Edison Avenue, but she wasn't there.

He pondered.

Where would a distraught girl go?

Tyler drove them to the abandoned gas station, site of Pegasus parlay, back seat liaison, and multiple anguished screams.

She wasn't there.

Ordinarily, she'd run to Buck for solace. Possibly Reba?

They tried Reba and Randall's place.

No joy.

They called in at the office.

Her chair was empty.

Think, Beckman, think.

She won't do anything dumb; she never has, even when more was at stake than a friendship.

He asked Tyler to take them to the former site of The Portal, site of navel-gazing, rock hocking and ex-fiancé banishing.

She wasn't there.

She's gone to confront Sandra? Lay a punch on the woman or make a citizen's arrest?

The Miata wasn't at the library.

'I'll take any suggestions you have, buddy. For a small town, it's big enough when you want to find a person.'

'She has no other bolt-hole?'

He sighed. 'Not that I know. It's not like we were childhood sweethearts. I'm as new round here as you are.'

'I dunno.' Tyler shrugged. 'I was never with a woman long enough to know where she might go for a spot of waterworks.' He chuckled. 'And I was probably the cause of enough waterworks too. I never had anyone—not that I cried, you understand.' He winced.

'But you would now, right? It's allowed, when shit hits the fan. It's okay—you're reputation's safe with me.'

'Losing Amaryllis, losing the company—I might get pretty down about that. I guess you'd be front and centre for company if that was the case. Funny, huh?'

'Quid pro quo. You're here now—for Lolita and me.'

'And the town,' Tyler pointed out.

'Yeah. Thanks.'

'For what? I gave you zero suggestions. The last time I got cut up about something, I ran to mom. Lame, huh?'

'Like I said, your secret's safe.' Inspiration crackled through his skull. 'Wait a second. Mom.'

'But her mom's like a day's drive away.'

'True. But she had another parent too.'

Tyler killed the engine.

Beckman scanned the pockmarked compound until he saw the lone figure.

Tyler laid a hand on his shoulder. 'At least she can't get into a fight with him.'

'She was done fighting with Jack. Maybe Buck had to catch all her broadsides now.'

'Do me a favour? Eggshells, okay? You two are like my role models for a happy ever after. You can't break up.'

Beckman looked across at Tyler. 'I do "idiot" pretty well, but if I avoid that, I know she's not pissed at me. I might get caught in the blast, but that's the risk when you go to defuse a bomb. You okay waiting?'

'Actually, I thought I'd go defuse that other bomb— or try to.'

'I think he'd hit you harder.'

Tyler waved it away. 'I've been hit before. Husbands, mostly. Sometimes wives. I survived a roadsweeper—I can survive a barista. You'll get a ride home?'

Beckman climbed out. 'I guarantee it. One hundred percent.' He thunked the car door closed. 'But keep your phone on anyway.'

Chapter 49

Beckman approached Lolita without stealth or fear: the plaster needed to be ripped right off. Besides, if she had any sense, she wouldn't do anything to antagonise the best friend she had in the world—not right now.

He stopped six feet away, to be on the safe side.

She was gazing down at Jack's headstone.

'Sorry I drove off.'

That's probably meant for you, buddy. Doubtful that she's apologising to a dead man for a minor misdemeanour years ago.

'No problem.'

She turned her head and reached out. He took her hand. She squeezed it like a vice.

She'd been crying. You didn't need the patented Beckman Observational Skills to work that out.

'I didn't need Buck here. I have *you*. I loved him like a father, brother, uncle, but I'm not a *child*. I called him weak and selfish back there.' She hung her head. 'What a joke. What a bitch. *I'd* lay me out for that.'

'You're not a bitch,' he said softly. 'You were at the lowest of lows, and you needed your posse around. You needed the Sheriff to ride in and scoop you from the gutter of loss, and he wasn't there.'

'I had *you*.'

'You had Buck *first*. I don't want—didn't want—to take that away from you. Marrying me is not about switching off all your existing bonds. I'm extra. I'm not a *replacement* for what you had with him. I'm… a bonus.' He smiled deliberately. 'Like the best possible bonus. Winning the lottery, basically.'

The Eyebrow flickered into life, then died.

'Sorry. What I mean is there was nothing wrong in wanting him at the wake. Hell, I'd take a bear hug from the guy on a bad day. It's a hell of a lot different to your hugs, your emotional medicine. Doesn't mean both wouldn't be nice.'

'But he wasn't there. He had his own issues, his own life. I should have seen that. He gave me so much for so long, and then I threw a guilt trip on him and blew it all in a minute. And that put him even more in a funk. Maybe it's caused this crazy logic he's on. Definitely, it made that conversation back there a hell of a lot harder than it needed to be.' She gingerly touched her cheek. 'And I got my just deserts.'

He tenderly lifted her chin, examined her face and looked into her blue eyes. 'A decent man doesn't hit a lady.'

'Maybe I wasn't much of a lady.'

'Does it hurt?'

'Might bruise. But that fades. The stuff that's going on? That's more serious. It's got momentum now.'

'Tyler told me that Sandra has got hold of box six. Some old lady handed it over because she thinks Sandra is some angelic twin-set-and-pearls with only the town's best interests at heart.'

Lolita pinched her forehead. 'This is way beyond personal now—what she's doing is not about mom and me. And Buck? Lord knows. If he thinks the boxes will somehow magically bring Dixon crawling back, then not only is he deluded, he's trading the whole town for his love life. Even if he was still my friend, my best friend in the world, I would absolutely not let him pull a stunt like that. And now, now that we're not even speaking? I've nothing to lose by not hitting back like an express train.'

'Yeah. I get you.'

She peered at the headstone. 'We've still got an ace card, Beckman. Neither Sandra nor Buck have got access to our box. They can't do anything without it.' She pointed. 'The old ass didn't give me a burden. He gave the town a lifeline. Same as ever—I always cursed him, yet he rescued things at the last minute.'

'If he was alive, I think he'd be turning in his grave when he saw what was going on.'

'I think that if he was alive, what he'd want right now is to be dug up.'

Then she flashed the cheekiest smile, and Beckman knew he would be getting that ride home.

Chapter 50

Tyler knocked on Buck's screen door.

The sky's blue was deepening towards dusk, and there were lights on in the house. Still, there was no answer.

He skirted the house on the right side, across the grass which needed cutting, down the side, and onto the back deck.

He stopped.

Buck was in an easy chair, a bottle in his hand. Not a small bottle. Not a beer bottle.

Tyler sighed. He'd seen Buck take a drink or two, but not this. He hoped the man was only an inch or two into the liquid, and that his mind would still be open to sense and logic.

Buck sat up a little. 'I don't want any sanctimonious crap,' he called.

Tyler took that as a good sign, because it hadn't included a demand to get the hell off the property. Was Buck sad drinking or angry drinking?

'She could get most people's hackles up, that one, huh?' He moved closer.

Buck eyed him warily. 'Yeah.'

'Gives as good as she gets, too, I guess.'

'Always.'

Tyler dragged a chair around. It scratched loudly on the decking. 'She had me pushed under a roadsweeper. I mean, she didn't do it herself, but I'll bet she would if circumstance were right.'

'I reckon so.'

'To my mind, a woman's got a right to hit a guy. If he's crossed a line.'

There was a glass on the table, unused—Buck had been swigging from the bottle. Tyler pulled the glass over and reached out towards Buck's hand. The bear's eyes narrowed, then he gingerly passed across the JD. Tyler poured a measure, then, subtly avoiding encouragement by not returning the bottle Buck, set it on the table.

He took the glass, held the whiskey up to the low evening sun, and took a sip.

Tyler wasn't a whiskey drinker, so it smarted. It showed too, which wasn't ideal: the veneer of comradeship might be broken already.

Buck frowned but said nothing.

'I've been hit a few times. I always deserved it.' Tyler took another sip. 'Almost had my nose broken once. She liked to work out.' He forced a chuckle. 'I crossed the line so many times, my boot damn near erased it.'

Buck grabbed the bottle, sat up, drank, and fixed Tyler in a gaze. 'What's this about?'

Tyler shrugged. 'Checking in on you. I know we're not actual *friends*, but seeing as Lolita can—probably—hit a guy, I wanted to make sure you hadn't cracked your head open on a corner or something. Lying unconscious, whatever. People need their coffee tomorrow morning, right?'

Buck looked away. 'She didn't hit me.'

'Oh. Right. Good.' He drank.

Silence fell.

'Did you ever hit a woman?'

Tyler deliberately looked away. 'No. I was an ass, but I was never that low.'

'Lord Almighty,' Buck breathed.

'But shit happens, I guess.'

'What have I done?' Buck murmured.

Tyler summoned bravery, drained his glass and reached for the bottle. It was time to get properly into the game, to make the man feel he had at least some kind of shoulder to lean on.

Buck swigged, filled Tyler's glass, and slumped back into the chair.

'We all make mistakes.' Tyler consciously kept his voice reflective, non-threatening. This was just another sale, only he wasn't selling a headache cure; he was selling salvation and reconciliation.

'What a heel. What an ass. I've lost the only real friend I had. For sure this time.'

'That may be so.'

'We were like mac and cheese. It has to be the world's best platonic friendship. Had. Had to be.' A sad smile broke on Buck's face. 'We know each other's life story. ATM pin. I even have keys to her house.'

He looked down at his hand and made a fist. 'She and I are as dead as Jack is. As dead as Dixon and I are.' He opened his fingers, wrapped them around the bottle and drank. 'You know what the irony is? She'd be the person I'd be talking to about stuff like this. Life. Love. Decisions.'

'I'm a rank second best, I know.'

'But you came. You're alright, Tyler.'

'There's stuff to figure out, so I guessed if you wanted an ear, you should have one. You know—help you do the right thing.'

'Is this about Dixon again?'

'I dunno. Seems like her leaving started all this. If you'd gotten her back, maybe you wouldn't have been so low, maybe you wouldn't have hit your friend.'

Buck leant sharply forwards and held the bottle out straight. 'You give out a lot of advice for a guy who never fought for a girl. Only ever slept with desperate, unavailable or vacuous women. Hell, you don't even have the balls to tell this real, decent woman you love her. I *told* Dixon I loved her, and she still left.'

'So, telling a woman you love her doesn't stop her leaving—that's what I'm hearing.'

Buck sighed. 'If you want to make your own excuses for not doing it, be my guest. Your life, your relationship.'

Tyler waved it away and took another draw on his whiskey. 'I'm not here for me.'

'No, but if you don't tell Amaryllis you love her, that may be *her* reason to leave you.'

'She thinks I'm stalling for time; that's what it is.'

'Are you?'

'Yeah—but I *know* I am.' Tyler laid his head against the chair back and gazed at the heavens, where pinpricks were appearing in the clear deep blue. 'I don't know what it's supposed to feel like—real *love*. So how do I know whether this is it or not?'

'Maybe you only know when the other person leaves and your heart breaks. It shows that you didn't want it to be broken, which means you must have been in love.'

'Kinda too late by then, huh?' he snorted.

'Seems so.'

'Is that how you feel—felt—about Dixon?'

Buck looked into the neck of the bottle. 'Yeah.'

'And you just broke your heart again, didn't you?'

Buck scowled at Tyler, then fell sober. 'Yeah.'

'Hard to fix it if it's broken twice.'

'Lolita will never forgive me. Hell, *I* won't ever forgive me.'

'So, before, you said you stayed here on account of her. Now what? Why not go? Dixon hasn't got to forgive you—you did nothing wrong there. Maybe that's a bridge you *can* build. If she was serious about the… love thing. And if you were.'

'I'm working on it. I think I have a ways to go now.' Something bloomed on Buck's face. Was it the drink colouring him up, or a mental breakthrough? A light at the end of the tunnel? 'Actually, Lolita could have just shown me the way.'

'Every cloud has a silver lining, huh?'

'Maybe not silver, but worth taking a shot at, sure.'

Chapter 51

The box lay on the dining room table. Lolita and Beckman sat on either side, like chess players.

Two other pieces were on the board. Beer bottle-shaped pieces. Beckman hadn't decided whether they were drinking out of relief, or for courage. Partly it was medicinal, as Lolita kept holding the cold glass to her cheek to reduce the swelling.

'How can I still feel bad when others have done worse?'

'Because we've held the moral high ground,' he replied. 'Now we have to ride down into the valley.'

She frowned. 'Do we?'

'We can only fight back if we're on the same pitch. I can't believe we can fight knowledge with ignorance.'

'Dad would be disappointed in me. For reneging on his wishes, on Spodge's directive.'

He put his hand on hers. 'He'd be proud that you were trying to stop… whatever… crisis looms over this town. Your town. His town. The town where he worked so hard to build a business that employs so many people and—literally—lights up so many lives.'

'Would he?' She cocked her head.

'Honestly, I don't know. But if it'll help, the Lolita Milan I met—nine months ago in that establishment—did her darndest every day to rebel against her father's wishes. So, take your pick—you're right either way.' He gave a sober smile.

She fingered the raised emblem on the box's lid. 'What are we afraid of?' she murmured rhetorically.

'Honestly? The unknown. Unexpected consequences. These boxes have remained shut—and scattered—for a reason. First, because they're only for emergency use, and we can't be sure this is that emergency. But, worse case, it means we've jumped the gun, we find out it's a false alarm, and we close the box, and wait for the real deal— obviously hoping it doesn't happen in our lifetime.'

'And second? I think the second is the one I don't like.'

'Second, they're to remain shut because opening them prematurely does have consequences. Unknown, worrying consequences.'

'The release of a curse?' Her expression showed disbelief in her own fantastical words.

'The release of information. Reba said there's information inside. Collect all that information together, and you have power. Who knows what kind of power, but information is always power, isn't it?'

'Well, Sandra's been hiding information, so I'd put money on it being a power… thing.'

Beckman slugged his beer. 'Look, this is your box by rights, and technically it's your decision, but I'll support you either way. I know you're worried. I am. But listen, at least three other boxes have been opened, and I haven't noticed a curse, or plagues, or cracks appearing in the earth, or zombies walking the land, or an alien spaceship firing up, a beacon, a sudden influx of armed troops, loss of power to the town, an invisible force shield appearing—'

'How would you know it had appeared if it was invisible?' The Eyebrow (Gotcha! version).

He smiled. "Levity. Levity is good. It balances…."

'Dread.'

'This is the right thing. I feel it in my water. Like the bad vibe I got from Carlton and Wanda. The feeling that someone like Randall was on my tail. The lurking threat of Dixon's takeover plan. I have form.'

'Well, if I open the box on your say-so and all hell breaks loose, I can at least blame you and point the finger when Spodge comes calling with his red hot poker, or a flock of ravens to pluck your eyes out.'

'You know what I love about you?'

She cocked her head. 'What?'

'Some days, you can be almost as much of an idiot as me.'

She patted his hand. 'Now, let's not get carried away, darling.'

He poked his tongue out. Then she did.

I'll miss this banter when the ravens come.

'So, you want me to do it, or will you?' He reached for the box.

She pulled it towards her. 'Finders keepers, losers weepers.'

She fingered the old catch.

He took a deep breath.

Well, it's been fun.

The doorbell rang.

Chapter 52

He opened the door.

'Reba. Randall. It's… well, it's *night*.'

'Sorry, is this too late for old married couples to have visitors?' she snarked.

Beckman felt a hand on his shoulder. 'No. Absolutely not. I'll get the old ball and chain to get her Zimmer frame into overdrive for you, and we'll put on some soup.'

Now he was pretty sure he *heard* The Eyebrow.

'I apologise,' Lolita said. 'As ever. In fact, I'll issue a standing apology for about half of what comes out of his mouth.'

'Half? I'm doing pretty well, then.'

Reba shook her head, and she and Randall brushed past.

What? It's gallows humour. You watch—they're bound to be here to tell us about the locusts.

As Beckman followed the guests through the dining room towards the living room, both slowed up.

Lolita stopped and put hands on hips. 'What? Okay—busted. We were going to open it.'

Reba exhaled hard. 'Finally.'

'Finally?'

'I mean, it's your call and all, but… you know. Sandra. Romeo.'

'Plus, we heard about you and Buck,' Randall said.

'The hitting part or the Guardian part?' Beckman asked.

'The hitting part. Tyler called in.' Reba inspected Lolita's cheek. 'You okay?'

'Cheek fine, heart—not so much.'

'The Guardian part?' Randall said.

'Yeah. He admitted to it.'

'And he'll do what?' Reba said.

'Sit on his fat ass, it seems like. He's so down he couldn't give a shit if the whole town goes to hell in a handbasket.'

'Who says it will? Don't those boxes *save* the town as well?'

'It doesn't need saving, Ree. It's fine. Sunrise is fine. It's more than fine. Dammit, it's perfect, isn't it?' Lolita threw up her hands. 'It tempts marvellous, beautiful people like Beckman, Randall, Tyler and Amaryllis to want to *stay* here. This place is a goddamn gold mine of life-affirming joy!'

Beckman looked at her. Then at Reba, then Randall. Reba looked at Lolita, then Beckman, then Randall.

Randall shrugged. 'What?'

'Tyler and Amaryllis want to stay here?' Reba asked.

Lolita closed her eyes. 'I'm paraphrasing. Point is, we don't want the town to change. We like it how it is—right?'

'Right,' the three chorused.

'So why would Sandra or Romeo—even Buck—want to do anything to change that?'

Again, glances were exchanged.

Reba tapped her fingers gently on the table. 'Hmm. Maybe because they've seen what's in the boxes, and they think it makes life here *even* better?'

'Then if it does, why the hell has nobody opened the boxes before?' Lolita asked. 'What's Spodge trying to do—suppress happiness by making the whole thing seem like an impenetrable conspiracy? Tell all the box holders that the boogie man will come get them if they try to achieve nirvana? Come *on*, people, there must be a downside.'

She eyed them all in turn, heaved a sigh and sank into the nearest chair. 'This is exhausting,' she mumbled. 'Trying to save the world is hard work.'

Reba laid a hand on her shoulder. 'That's why we're here.'

'Yeah. Thanks.'

The fridge hummed. The box stared at them.

'So,' Beckman said, 'Soup? Or beer?'

The box lay on the dining room table. The four sat on either side, like bridge players.

Four other pieces were on the board. Beer bottle-shaped pieces.

'I know you, Lol,' Reba said. 'You're a good person. This is tough. I get that. But by your own admission, Sunrise is in danger. The box is there to stop that.'

Lolita's finger stroked the table adjacent to the box. 'We'd be no better than the others who opened the box and tried to discover the secret.'

'Sorry, you're wrong. They didn't do what they did selflessly. They have an agenda.'

'Which you said could be to *improve* the town.'

'And you said we're happy as we are.'

Lolita shook her head disconsolately. 'So either we're trying to prevent something bad, or we're standing in the way of something good. And we don't know which.'

'But if it's good, we'll go along with it—yeah?' Randall asked.

'I think Spodge will have something to say about that.'

'It's a fifty-fifty call,' Reba said. 'The fact is, we know we'll do the decent thing. We can't vouch for the others.'

'You mean we're the good guys?'

Reba nodded. 'Yeah. I think if anyone heard this whole story, that's what they'd say about us.'

'Well, someone is going down in history. If it's us, I hope we're on the side of the winners.'

Lolita fingered the catch again.

Beckman held his breath.

Reba and Randall leant forwards.

'Can we take a vote on this?' Lolita asked.

'Open the damn box,' Reba said.

Lolita looked at Beckman for guidance.

Conundrum: you can only tell her what she wants to hear if you know what she wants to hear. Problem: you don't know what that is.

Backstop: try to be the Voice Of Reason, as opposed to Voice Of Idiot.

'We can't stop this if we don't know what it is. We're empowered to save the town. That's what the box is for. Open it, honey. Nothing bad can happen.' He clutched her hand. 'You're with me.'

Lolita scanned the three faces again.

Took a deep breath.

Flipped the catch.

Opened the box.

Chapter 53

Beckman craned over.

No beam of light emerged from the box. No skeletal hand. No troupe of clowns, swarm of bees, deadly gas or demonic voice.

He checked the faces: Randall—nervous anticipation, Reba—nonchalance, Lolita—The Eyebrow (as yet uncatalogued version).

She pulled the box closer, peered inside, then reached in with reticent pinched fingers and pulled out the contents. She laid the item on the table.

It was a sliver of wood about six inches by four. It appeared as old as the box—over 150 years—but not fragile.

He reviewed the faces: varying degrees of curiosity. Any dread had passed. He was reminded of the few seconds either side of The Portal, when What Awful Fate Will Befall Me? morphed into Oh, Here We Are; Interesting.

Nonetheless, Reba was the most relaxed. Why? His brain whirred. Perhaps she was used to facing danger, the unknown. Solving mysteries. Expecting the unexpected.

Or was it something else?

Come on, brain.

While short-term memory was being accessed, he set his optic nerves to their task.

The wooden leaf was carved with three words. Not written (probably too susceptible to damage or loss).

"From The Library".

Whāt from the library? Borrowed from the library? Run away from the library? Angry spinster from the library?

Lolita pulled her hair forward and played with it. 'Hmmm.'

Hmmm is right. Definitely hmmm.

'Coincidence? Reba asked.

'I'm gonna say yes,' Lolita replied. 'If this box has remained closed for decades, plus the fact that Sandra doesn't *really* have a damn thing to do with this whole legacy, then I'm not getting wrapped up in even more conspiracy theories. Besides, there are more important things to work out. Like what it actually *means*.'

Randall pulled the box towards him and eased the lid down. He fingered the raised pentagon on the top.

'Ree, did the others have this?'

That's it! Reba saw the boxes Romeo had. She said he'd opened them. That's why she wasn't worried about bolts of lightning or the undead or SWAT Team raids.

'No,' she replied. 'They had numerals.'

'You saw the other three boxes,' Lolita said, warily, irked.

'Hold on, Lol. I didn't give you chapter and verse on that because if Spodge had wanted you to know what went on, he would have let you come along. I held my end up—I kept quiet about what I saw. Information to stay scattered—isn't that the rule?'

Lolita pressed her lips tight, constraining harsh words and disappointment at her friend's actions.

Beckman decided that intervening would be a good plan. 'Okay, buddy. I get it. You told us Romeo had three boxes—we knew that. You didn't say Spodge had let you *see* them.'

'It all happened fast. Besides, the boxes aren't the issue. It's what's inside them.'

Lolita fixed Reba in a familiar interrogative stare. 'You said Spodge nearly had a coronary because Romeo had opened the boxes too. That's not second-hand information either, is it? You've *seen* what's inside them.'

Reba gave as direct a look as she received, stood brusquely, downed her beer and went to the fridge. She pried the top off another bottle and leant on the kitchen island.

All three looked at her.

'I'm a detective, okay? It's what I do. I keep my mouth shut when I think it's best. So I was wrong this time? Sue me. I'm not *against* you, Lol. You've just spent half this evening debating whether to open the box. You think I *like* carrying information like this around in my head? Being exposed to eyes-only stuff? I feel... dirty. Well, at first, I did. Then I realised that if Romeo was happy to break the bond of trust for his own ends, what's a little collateral damage?' She swigged. 'Besides, I'm a good guy. If I didn't tell you—my best friend—what I saw, I think that's a damn good indicator that I can keep my mouth shut.'

'If it's any consolation,' Randall said. 'She hasn't told me either—about what was inside.'

'Or the carvings on the outside,' Reba added.

Lolita considered this. She went to Reba. 'Okay. Sorry. I'm not the boss of you. Not the Guardian, not Miss Morally Perfect. I suppose I should be pleased you can keep a secret.'

'I kept quiet about Carlton and Wanda—for your protection, and damn, that was hard. This? We don't know who's in the right and who's in the wrong. Best option is to tell nobody. It's not personal. I don't *suspect* you, any more than I would Randall or April. Remember—word gets around. All it takes is for Buck to be drinking like he was and to let a word slip out, and suddenly someone like Sandra has information that seals the deal.' She put a hand on Lolita's shoulder. 'I'm on your side. I would always have told you about those three boxes when the time was right. When the chips were down.'

'They are *right* down. So—do you remember what was in Romeo's boxes?'

'I can do better than that.' Reba pulled out her phone. 'I took a picture.'

Chapter 54

They huddled around Reba's phone, which lay on the dining table. It was crowded, and the image had to be zoomed in and moved to see everything.

Lolita sat back. 'We're being dumb. Let's be detectives about this. Send me the image, Ree, and I'll print it off.'

They huddled around an A3 colour image, which was much more accommodating. In the interim, Beckman had rustled up nachos and coffee. It was past ten p.m.

Score one for Reba's businesslike instincts to pap anything suspicious.

She brings the investigative skills.

Randall can handle a gun if that becomes necessary.

Lolita brings grit and logic.

And you? What do you bring to this posse of do-gooders, this team of heroes?

Ah. You brought the nachos and coffee.

Now, where were we?

Lolita's box bore a pentagon and the "From The Library" message.

One of Romeo's was carved with "II" and "Nine hundred paces West".

Romeo's other said "IV" and "At the striped boulder".

The last box had "V" and "Six hundred forty paces South".

Hmmm.

He wanted to say it. He desperately wanted to say it, but it was bound to be Peak Idiot. Wasn't it?

'This is a treasure trail,' Lolita whispered. She looked up. 'That is the dumbest, lamest, least original idea those cowboys could have come up with. But it feels… right. Right?' She gave a querying look.

'It's a *something* trail,' Reba said. 'It's a route to a spot, a landmark, a thing. Probably not an X, but even so.'

'But I know this place like the back of my hand.'

'There are millions of acres out there, beyond the town boundary. If you've explored all those, then you did a lot more with your teenage years than date boys and drink Buck's sodas.'

'Why a pentagon, and not an "I"?' Randall asked.

Lolita stared into space for a moment. 'Mom said her box had an "I".'

'We're missing "three",' Reba said.

'And more, if there are more than six total.'

'I think six is the number,' Beckman said. 'Six people in the cell that night. We know we're missing two boxes—one and three.' He pulled over Lolita's box. 'Five sides on the pentagon. Five more pieces to go with this… master box.'

'Master?' Randall said.

Beckman pointed at the note. '"From The Library" must be the start. The first instruction. The rest follow in numerical order. One origin and then five steps.'

'To where? To what?' Reba murmured.

'To something which can save the town or kill the town,' Lolita said.

'A forcefield? An energy source, something related to The Portal?' Beckman said.

Five eyes stared back at him.

'Let's try less science fiction, shall we, honey?' Lolita said.

'And there was me thinking there were no dumb ideas at this point.'

'The only dumb thing is trying to save the town when it doesn't need saving, or wanting to ruin it, improve it, change it when it's fine how it is. Let's assume there is— and yes, this is crazy—an X out there,' she gazed through the window into the night, 'Finding it doesn't mean we have to take a shovel to it. In the same way that opening these boxes is not the critical step. It's only the first step. If we get a break, maybe that's the only step Sandra wants to take.'

'Or Buck,' Beckman pointed out.

'Same. And Romeo—he only wanted to know what it all *meant*. He wasn't about to press the button on anything.'

'Or so he says,' Reba said.

'I'd like to believe that Sandra and Buck are decent enough people at heart that satisfying their curiosity was sufficient. To be the person who broke the code, the only person in Sunrise who knows the *whole* secret.'

'Only, not the secret—just where to find it.'

Lolita nodded. 'Ideally, yeah. Because it would mean the status quo remains.'

Beckman pulled the box towards him and closed the catch. 'The thing is that nobody does know everything. We're missing two boxes—Ginetta's and the one Sandra conned Mrs Finkel out of. And Sandra? She doesn't have this one.'

'Don't forget Buck.'

'He's the least of our problems. He hasn't seen a single one.'

'It seemed like he was hoping Sandra would do his dirty work for him—whatever that is.'

'You think they're in cahoots?' Reba was stunned.

'I doubt it. But then, I doubted a middle-aged woman would go around deleting archive files and bribing townsfolk. And I definitely never thought my lifelong friend would lay me out with a right hook.' Lolita sighed heavily.

'Looks like there are no dumb ideas after all,' Beckman said.

'So, it's a stalemate,' Reba concluded. 'We can't get Sandra's boxes, and she won't get ours.'

'She doesn't even know we have one,' Lolita said. 'Unless one of you has squealed. Or Spodge.'

'Or Buck,' Beckman said. 'We told him, remember? If they are in cahoots, maybe he's already passed that little gem along.'

Reba pulled a face. 'Actually, I'd put money that she already knows. She's seen that missing newspaper article—and long before we did. I'll bet she absolutely knows Jack had a box, and that you have it now.'

Lolita thumped the table. 'Damn. Damn her and her... librarian life.'

Beckman sniggered.

Worst. Insult. Ever.

'She wouldn't... break into this house? Would she?' Randall looked around.

'If the alternative is trying to con us, she's smart enough to know that I'm smart enough that it'll never happen.'

'So—stalemate,' Reba said again. 'Nuclear standoff.'

Lolita slowly shook her head. Her eyes darted in time with her brain patterns. 'No. She's gone so far, taken so many risks. Sure—we've seen through them all, but she doesn't know that. I don't know what her endgame is, but she won't stop now. She'll find a way. Who knows what other information she's got access to? Something that should be in the library but isn't?' She looked at the ceiling. 'A secret camera she's already installed, listening to us even as we speak.'

'I thought there were no dumb ideas,' Beckman said.

The Eyebrow (Pardon Me? version) appeared, then disappeared as quickly.

She shrugged. 'I guess. She's hardly a criminal mastermind.' Worry flitted on her face. 'Is she?'

'Recent evidence suggests that people we know can do pretty crazy, warped, clever stuff,' Reba said.

'Carlton,' Lolita murmured.

'If memory serves, outmanoeuvring was our winning strategy.'

'Yeah, but that was because I knew how to press his buttons. Sandra—no clue.'

'I don't think we need a clue,' Randall suggested. 'It's a simple race for the line. First one to get—or see—all the boxes has control.'

'Control over what?' Lolita asked.

'Information,' Reba said. 'The six clues to the X. Remove a clue—burn it, bury it, whatever—the trail disappears. Forever.'

'Except we can't let that happen. Don't you get that, Ree? This jigsaw was put in place to give future generations access to a lifeline. We can't *remove* that lifeline. We can't destroy evidence to stop it from getting into the wrong hands. What happens when the *real* existential threat comes along? This is just a middle-aged woman with misplaced logic or a personal crusade. Jesse Milan and his buddies didn't create their boxes for *that*—surely? If we have the temerity to think this is Doomsday, and we're wrong, then in years to come—even after we're dead—we're condemning the town to a worse fate than anything that could possibly be happening now.'

Beckman scanned the visitors. They conceded to Lolita's logic.

'You mean, we do nothing?' Reba asked.

'Until we can come up with a better idea.'

'And if I have a better idea?'

'Is it dumb?' Beckman asked, then wished he hadn't.

'It's… sneaky.'

'We wouldn't be the first people in all this to be sneaky,' Randall said.

'Sneaky how?' Lolita asked.

Reba winced. 'We get into Sandra's house and look at the other boxes.'

Chapter 55

At ten the next morning, Randall called to confirm he was at the library and Sandra was there, at work as if it was a regular day.

Reba collected Beckman and Lolita in her Jeep, and they went to the destination.

Sandra's house was helpfully the last property on a dead-end road, a small but tidy house whose rear garden pointed towards the low hills which circled the town.

Reba had done her research: the neighbour was a single guy who worked at the shoe store, so he was out.

If they needed luck to smile on them, it seemed to be, yet even an old hand like Reba was nervous about accessing a property in broad daylight. There was no solid cover story for breaking in: the best grounds were evidence of obtaining property—Mrs Finkel's box—by deception.

They all hoped nobody would happen to call by.

Beckman's heart thudded as he screened Reba with his body and watched her pick the lock.

Still, actually seeing someone pick a lock was very cool.

Keep that to yourself.

Travelling salesman to housebreaker inside twelve months. Jeez.

At least Randall's going in the other direction: hitman to credit controller in the same period.

Let's say the universe has evened out.

The handle turned.

He glanced around at the quiet outer residential street, then followed the ladies inside.

Reba's brief had been… brief: in and out as fast as possible. No admiring the drapes, wincing at the knick-knacks or checking the contents of the fridge. They only needed to find boxes I and III, get a photo, and leave.

He hoped there'd be no false panels to find, safe combinations to trawl, cameras to evade, dog to mollify, or pesky parrot who might repeat back to Sandra anything it heard in the next five minutes.

They split up.

The living room, kitchen, dining room and WC were a bust.

They went upstairs.

The two bedrooms, WC, and junk room yielded nada.

They rendezvoused in the hallway.

The garage, accessed by an adjoining door, was empty.

Beckman pointed at the remaining door, which logically led to the basement.

Reba pulled the handle. The door was locked. 'Shoot.'

'Looks like it's "find the key", ladies and gentlemen,' Lolita said.

Beckman took the kitchen and carefully scoured cupboards and drawers.

Zip.

He found Lolita in the lounge, doing a detailed search by eye.

'What if she's got it with her?' he asked.

'Then Reba picks it, I guess.'

'Can't pick that,' Reba replied from behind them. 'Sorry.'

'Too much youth misspent on journalism and photography, not enough on criminal techniques—that's your problem, Ree.'

Reba beamed. 'I'm the total model of a reluctant burglar.'

Lolita was staring at a framed photograph. Beckman followed her over to it.

'You got it bad, didn't you?' she murmured.

She picked it up. The image was from a newspaper, but it wasn't a news story so much as a piece from the social pages. In Sunrise in the Eighties, a small-town publication had space to stretch to wedding pictures. Perhaps it was because Jack Milan was something of an upcoming businessman even then.

Undeniably, the photo had been scissored out with careful vandalism: Ginetta wasn't in the frame—only her arm around Jack's waist.

'Looks like she kept on pining, even when she lost her man,' Beckman said.

'The woman's got a screw loose.'

'If this stunt has anything to do with it, I hope she knows Jack's absolutely out of the picture now.' She pulled a sad smile. Then a frown.

She lifted the frame. Turned it over. Attached to a magnetic strip on the back was a key.

'Saves me shooting the lock out, I guess.'

Beckman and Lolita spun.

Reba held her hand up. 'Kidding. I didn't bring my gun. What—I'm going to shoot your aunt?'

Lolita gritted her teeth. 'Any blood relationship between Sandra and me is an accident. Like a Three Mile Island type.'

'Okay. Sorry.'

Lolita took a breath. 'Sure. Now let's hope she hid this for a reason.'

They went to the basement door, the key fitted, she flicked on the light, and they descended the stairs.

The room had nothing in common with Ginetta's den (or what it would have looked like if it hadn't been partially decorated with other shards of the house).

It was functional, sparsely appointed—washer dryer, chest freezer, old armchair, aged table—but the headline wasn't on the floor but on the walls.

A giant corkboard covered one wall. On it was a huge spider diagram.

Beckman ran his gaze over it. It contained the complete lineage of all the six box holders. At the top were photographs of the bewhiskered sextet. At the bottom were images of the current holders, culled from various sources. Lolita was shown on the day she shook hands with Walter Whack to takeover EVI Lighting—a newsworthy story that day.

To one side was pinned images of the boxes and their respective instructions.

On the opposite side were old and new town plans.

'I feel like the FBI at Lecter's house.'

She gave him The Eyebrow (Unnecessary Hyperbole, Darling version). 'Let's just say she was a little ahead of us.'

Reba patted Lolita's shoulder. 'At least she hasn't been throwing darts at your picture. Which is something.'

He shrugged. 'So she was ahead of us—we kinda knew that. What's missing is anything that tells us what the goal is. What the X is. Logically, we have to assume she doesn't know.'

'No, Beckman, sorry. Assuming is dangerous. People assumed she was the Guardian just because she said so. The lack of physical evidence of… a pot of gold, missile silo, whatever, doesn't mean the information's *not* in her head.'

'But it doesn't mean it *is*,' Lolita countered.

'Agreed.' Reba gestured to the wall. 'She has all the information—except your box and its contents—but there's no indication she plans to *do* anything with it. There's no action plan.'

'Come on, Ree. I know all this is pretty… drastic. Pretty subversive. I think pinning a diarised agenda of when she's planning to wreak havoc is just too… serial killer. Besides, she still only has a six-step map without the key piece. She can't do a damn thing without my box.'

'But we know she'll get it,' Beckman said. 'Somehow. Will she sit on the whole thing? Really? A hundred-yard dash and then stop in front of the tape?'

Reba clasped Lolita's arm. 'If we don't assume the worst, and the worst happens, how will you feel then?'

Lolita's head fell. 'Appalling. I mean, I feel bad enough opening boxes, opening doors, breaking promises.'

'What if she uses this information and takes it to its ultimate end?'

'We don't know what the end is.'

'Let's assume it's detrimental. Even if it isn't, or she doesn't pursue the full six-step trail, what's to stop her hiding the information like she deleted the newspaper file? Or destroying it? Or holding the town to ransom over it?'

Lolita frowned. 'Ransom. Like, money?'

'I'm just spitballing,' Reba said. 'Looking for any angle that makes sense, because of who she is, what she wants, her life, her job, her enemies.'

'You mean, besides flat out greed?' Beckman asked.

'We all have that, a little, don't we? But would we do all this?' Reba tapped the corkboard.

Lolita drifted off, a thousand-yard stare. Then she fingered the picture of Jack on the wall. 'She always wanted Jack. If she'd won him, instead of mom, she'd be a millionaire by now. Maybe that's what she wants—a spot of financial payback because her life didn't go the way she wanted.'

'That's twisted,' Reba said.

'That's a big leap,' Beckman said. 'Due respect, honey.'

Lolita sighed. 'I know. But I'm not sure we care about motive. Just information. Ree—pap some pictures of those missing boxes, and let's get the hell out.'

Chapter 56

They met Randall back at Lolita & Beckman's and filled him in on their discovery.

Randall's eyebrows crept further and further up his forehead, then disappeared under his hairline, tumbled down the back of his collar and plopped out from the hem of his jeans.

Reba held up a warning finger. 'Don't you dare say you'll "take care of her".'

'Thought never crossed my mind.'

'Shouldn't we take all this to Romeo True?' Beckman asked. 'If he was serious about being a good cop with the town's interests at heart?'

'And if he isn't?' Reba said. 'If he's part of what Sandra's cooking up? Hire a trustworthy public citizen to do some of the box collecting for you?'

She has a point. Nobody is proven innocent yet.

'I guess.'

'Take it to Captain Bosman?' Randall suggested.

'He sat on his ass after my warehouse burned down. Why is a couple of missing boxes and a wall full of genealogy going to give him motivation?' Lolita slugged her coffee.

'We can't just sit here and let her work out a way to get sight of this box.' Beckman tapped the offending article. 'She's resourceful.'

'You could get it offsite,' Randall suggested.

'I can't believe she wouldn't tear the place apart—or find someone to do it. Hell—maybe she'd tell Spodge we'd done something unconscionable, get him to commandeer my box, then find a way to sneak it out of his office.'

'There's a lot of "ifs" there,' Reba said.

'I'll take any better ideas if you have them. We're the last target in her sights—the final piece she needs to do... whatever.'

'The "whatever" is the problem,' Beckman said. 'No proof of motive. Even if we did get a fair hearing from the cops, Sandra could bluster it out, saying she's not done anything illegal, nothing to *actually* jeopardise the town.'

'You're saying we *let* her get the box—just to catch her in the act?' Lolita's mouth hung open.

He ran out of intellectual steam. 'I didn't mean that. I... I don't know what I meant.'

Sheesh, this is hard.

Reba laid a palm on the table. 'Hold on. What if she only *thought* she'd got your box—a decoy of some kind— so she went ahead and executed her "whatever" plan?'

'You have a lovely butt, honey,' Randall said, 'So if you plan to magically pull a replica centuries-old box out of it, I hope it won't damage the delightful petite, peachy quality.'

Lolita feigned gagging. 'Get a room.'

'Ignore him,' Reba said. 'The same way he seems to have cheerfully forgotten that, despite meeting my father for the first time just days ago, the man is a master carpenter.'

Beckman's brain cells held hands in a perfect circle and began to hokey-cokey. 'Are you going all Colonel Hannibal Smith on us?'

Reba nodded. 'If you're prepared to let this box out of your sight for a few days, and if I bribe the old man by saying I'll name this bundle,' she patted her abdomen, 'After him or mom, he might knock together a facsimile of your curio.'

Lolita gritted her teeth. 'I'm not sure.'

Randall laid his palm on top of Reba's. 'Sandra wouldn't *steal* the box—would she? It's too... underhanded. Obvious. Discoverable. Besides, the box is not the thing. The *message* is the thing.'

'By the same logic, she wouldn't steal the message. I'd see it was missing and raise hell.'

Reba drummed her fingers. 'Okay, so I'll ask dad to forge the wooden filo. Put different words on it.'

'What words?' Beckman wondered.

Lolita waved a hand. 'Details. What do we *do* with the forgery, Ree? Take it to the library in my handbag and accidentally leave it there?' She scoffed. 'Anyone might find it.'

Reba glanced at them all. 'Actually, you remember what happened here, in the study? And especially at Romeo's, when all the boxes were laid out? I think you leave the box unattended on this table and invite Sandra over for a kiss-and-make-up. If she's half the brains we think, she'll take a look at the forgery—maybe even a photo, consider her work done, the battle won, then run off to cackle inanely and rub her hands together with glee. Or whatever town-wrecking nutjob librarians do when they think they've hit the jackpot.'

Lolita wrinkled her nose. 'Invite her over?'

'"Come into my parlour," said the fly to the spider. To paraphrase.'

'And then we follow her?'

'Something like that. Catch her red-handed. I have a photo of the... mission control room in her basement. Romeo can give evidence that she sequestered his boxes. We can ask Buck to make a statement that he's the Guardian. I'll even rig up a spy camera so we can prove she opened your box.'

Lolita set her elbow on the table and held her forehead.

Beckman pushed closer and put his arm around her

shoulder.

'Why us? Why me? Why can't we get a break?' she said. She whacked the table. 'Why the hell couldn't mom have held onto her box. If Sandra hadn't got her hands on it, all this could have been prevented.'

'She was doing what she thought best for Sunrise,' Beckman said. 'Which is what we're all doing.'

'Six against one, Lol. You're not alone.' Reba reached across the table and squeezed Lolita's arm.

'Six?'

'Tyler and Amaryllis. They're going to try to talk some sense into Dixon, so she can maybe set Buck back on the straight and narrow. This whole thing is a damn sight harder with the Guardian—the one who's supposed to stop people like Sandra—being asleep at the wheel. If we can get him on our side, and back in your life, I'll bet the world will look a whole lot rosier.'

'I dunno.' Lolita shook her head. 'I can't believe Dixon is the kind of person you can talk round. It took nearly dying to make her see sense last time.'

'I could always—,' Randall began.

'No warning shots across anyone's bows, mister,' Reba said. 'We're treading a fine line as it is. Let's focus on our checklist. You and I need to get to mom and dad's, fix up that fake message.' She rose and scooped up the box.

'It'll be a weight off, having the thing out of the house,' Lolita said. 'But... go careful, okay?'

Reba patted her belly. 'Going careful with precious cargo is our mantra at the moment anyhow.'

Chapter 57

Tyler's car thack-thacked over the expansion joints in the freeway.

'I feel bad,' he said.

'That's good,' Amaryllis replied.

'Huh?'

'Feeling bad means you have a moral compass. You can't tell me that was the case a year ago?'

He knew she was right. 'I don't know how the hell anyone put up with me.'

She patted his thigh. 'It was a struggle, that's for sure.'

'I can't believe you and Malvolio cared much either way. As long as we made the sales, that was fine.'

'Don't equate him and me, please. Besides, there was something of the reprobate about you that I liked.'

'You had a crush on me all that time? Sure.'

Her eyes smiled. 'Crush, no. Intrigue, yes. Maybe dreaming you'd whisk me away from drudgery and servitude, and shake me into discovering... life.'

'Didn't I?'

'I suppose you did. And in return, I made you give a shit about friends, women... parrots.'

He sighed. 'Not so much to want to keep him, though. And guilty as hell about what Lolita will say.'

'I don't think she'll care two bits. Besides, Flint was too much of a chatterbox. If he repeated what he said this morning, then… well, I'd want the world to swallow me up.'

His cheeks coloured. 'Me too.'

'My fault. I shouldn't have been so… direct in my amorous language. So descriptive and… wanton.'

'No, the directness was damn fine.' He smirked. 'We should have kept the cage covered, huh?'

'I do feel a little bad too. But I justify it by knowing that birds like to fly free. I'm sure Flint will… discover life too.' She gazed out of the window at the passing countryside. 'Out there.'

'We didn't throttle the bird, at least there's that. Lolita threatened to.'

'True. But we have a problem now, mister, the way I see it.'

'How so?'

'Flint gave us pressure to find a place in Sunrise that was more… accommodating and permanent than a hotel. Fine by me—not so much by you. Because it feels like rushing into commitment, and I know that scares the hell out of you.'

His mouth opened and closed. She had him, not on a technicality but on a gigantic, obvious clause. 'Yeah,' he murmured. 'It does.'

'And if I said it scared me too, even a little?'

'Really?'

'You may not have had love, but you've had relationships—'

'Short ones.'

'All the same, it beats my record. Plus, I have to believe that you're a reformed character. Plus, you're the boss. Plus, it could be the thin end of the wedge. What if we like it here so much that we want to sell up in the city and move? Do you really want that commute?'

'No. But neither do I want to ship the whole operation—warehouse, Wilbur and the rest—here. It's selfish. The kind of thing Malvolio would have done.'

'We could easily establish a satellite office. Something beyond renting desks off Lolita. Stay in a hotel in the city, instead of here. That place has no *soul*, Tyler. Not like here.'

He narrowed his eyes. 'You've thought about this whole thing, haven't you?'

'I'm a PA. Organising is what I do. Maybe this time it's about the life I want. With you. So—busted.'

'I should be flattered, I guess.'

She smiled. 'I think you should. I'm a helluva catch.'

'You are.' He fell serious. 'Let's see if we can't help make the atmosphere in town a little less... toxic... if we're thinking about making that big leap.'

'If?'

'You gave me a week, remember?'

'You're a devil, Tyler.'

'A leopard with changed spots is still a leopard.'

They sat in the parking lot at GigantiCorp, and Tyler put a call into Dixon's PA, claiming to be the accountant for the Adelaide Foundation—the charity Dixon set up after her sister died. He said that there was an urgent private financial matter and asked for a meeting. The PA told him that Dixon was out of the office at another meeting. He pushed her for the location, then hung up.

Then he drove to Hoko, a fancy eatery on the edge of town, and found a spot on the street nearby. They took seats in a café opposite and drank coffee while waiting for Dixon to finish her working lunch.

When she parted company with the anonymous suit, he grabbed Amaryllis' hand, and they dashed across to intercept their quarry.

Dixon's eyes flared. 'Not you as well.'

'Come on, Dixon,' Amaryllis said, 'I'll bet this is your favourite spot for smooching prospects. Don't get yourself barred by making a scene.'

Dixon scowled and jerked her head. 'Walk.'

They walked.

'We're not your enemy,' Tyler said. 'In fact, we're on a mission of mercy.'

Dixon motioned them to a bench, and they sat.

'Why is everyone coming here, trying to persuade me I've made a huge mistake? Any why everyone *except* Buck?'

'Why, would that be a clincher?'

'Don't put words in my mouth, Tyler.'

'Buck's on the rocks. He's talking about never loving again. He and Lolita are at loggerheads. He's even threatening to….' Tyler wondered how to raise the stakes without disclosing the secret boxes. '…rampage through town like Godzilla.'

Dixon scoffed. 'Nice try.'

Amaryllis laid a hand on her shoulder. 'No hyperbole. You walking out on him has made big waves. Tidal.'

'I didn't walk out on *him*. I'm in… I'm very fond of him. It's Sunrise. It's too small. And much as Lolita tried to help, she can't pay me what I'm worth.'

'So they save you from walking into The Portal, out of existence, and that's not worth some gratitude and a pay cut?' Tyler asked.

'You expect me to crawl back out of *gratitude*?' She shook her head. 'This is Arizona, not Hollywood. Sometimes things don't work out.'

'So, you're happy here? Among the suits and high rises, expense accounts, air kisses and chain stores?'

'What are you—converts? You two are city people too.'

'Were,' Amaryllis said. 'Things change. We both sold our souls to a corporate overlord, and saw a better way. Honesty, friendships, the comfort of Sunrise.'

'You forget one important thing,' Dixon said. 'My corporate overlord pays handsomely, and a lot of that goes to the Foundation. Leaving the city and taking a pay cut means fewer funds for research. Plus, I do a lot of awareness work here. I met another person who has the same thing that killed Adelaide. The hospital here is considering a piece of diagnostic equipment that could be a game-changer. But it needs funds.' She jabbed a finger on her knee. 'That's my duty to my sister, and to all the others out there suffering. I have to finance that machine. I like my job, and it suits me to put my wages into a good cause. You two don't know me that well. Buck and I... we were *good*. But if I leave here....'

She trailed off, looked around. 'I'm not sure my conscience could stand it. Maybe in a year or two, when things are fixed, I'll look him up. If he's still single, and he'll forgive me, we might have a chance again. I like Sunrise. I do.' She sighed. 'I like all of you. But I have to do what I set out to do—make a difference to this disease. You can see that, can't you?'

Amaryllis hung her head. 'Yes. Well, we tried. I just hope Sunrise is still in one piece. Buck too.'

'How much is the machine?' Tyler asked.

Dixon frowned. 'I don't know. A million, at least. The Foundation has raised two hundred grand.'

Tyler dug into his inside jacket pocket.

'Honey,' Amaryllis cautioned.

'You're not the one who's seen Buck this last week. I never thought you could put a price on a broken heart. I also know that Sunrise is priceless just the way it is.'

He pulled out his check book and drew a pen from the breast pocket of his tailored suit.

Dixon's eyes were wide. 'This is not about you, or money. This is about me, and Buck, and Adelaide.'

He wrote the cheque, tore it out and handed it over. 'It's about all of those and more.'

'Take it,' Amaryllis murmured.

'You can't *buy* love,' Dixon insisted.

'We don't need to. We're pretty sure you already have it,' Amaryllis replied. 'I know what I want, with who, and where. You couldn't buy that either. You just *know*. Lolita reckoned you didn't have a conscience, that you were a cold shell. Doing what you do for the Foundation proves you do have a heart. A big, laudable one.' She took the check from Tyler's fingers and pressed it into the woman's palm. 'Now, there are no compromises to make. No conscience to fight.'

'And we know we did what *we* could to help the people we care about.' Tyler stood. He took Amaryllis' hand. 'Making a decision to change your life forever is damn hard; take it from me. When you have everything else you need for the future, the only remaining question is whether to embrace true love.'

Chapter 58

Kelvin Dawson peered warily at the box. 'Is this on the level?'

'It's… need to know. Will you do it?' Reba asked.

Randall saw apprehension in the man's face.

'It's really important,' she continued. 'And I hear there's nobody better qualified than you.'

Kelvin eyed them both. 'I'm not keen on meddling.' He sighed. 'Not again,' he added quietly.

'Again?' Reba asked.

Kelvin shook his head. 'Need to know, Reba. Need to know.'

She swallowed down an instinct to pry, realising that the matter at hand was too important to risk.

'I know we're not bosom buddies anymore, but this isn't about me.'

'It's about your town,' Kelvin said.

'It was your town once too. It's still just as wonderful. Unless someone ruins it.'

Kelvin opened the catch on the box and carefully removed the sliver of wood. 'I remember Jack and Ginetta. Sad he went so soon.'

'So, help Lolita, huh, dad?'

'I guess you'd stop speaking to mom and me again otherwise?'

Reba shrugged. 'I dunno. But the baby needs grandparents, right?'

Kelvin turned the artefact over in his hands.

'I'll see what I can do.'

Randall pulled Reba to him under the covers.

The motel wasn't fancy, but it was preferable to crashing in Kelvin and Ella's spare room, having to watch what they said and keep *amour* to a minimum. Although her parents seemed to have accepted him as the new person in Reba's life, it was guarded, tainted by the behaviour of her ex.

He stroked her shoulder. 'Why didn't you retake your maiden name?'

'Dunno. There were more important things at the time. Raising April. Kicking Elmer's stuff out of the house. Rowing with mom and dad.'

'I'd have thought you'd drop any association with Elmer like a hot brick.'

'Sure. But I kinda got a reputation in town, working with that name. Plus, all the admin's a bitch.'

'I'd help,' Randall said.

'Might be redundant, though.' She tickled his chest hair. 'You know, if someone wanted to change it to a brand new name in the not too distant. To go through all that paperwork twice feels like a big waste of time.' She gave him a pointed look.

He cupped her head and kissed her. 'Would you change it? Hypothetically?'

'Almost certainly. Like you said, I should really ditch that sonofabitch's legacy.'

'So... do you want me... us to change it? Officially?'

She pushed away a few inches, making focus easier, and sought veracity in his eyes. 'Don't do it for that.'

'I'll do it 'cos I want to.'

'Okay. But don't rush in and make a mistake. Lot of fast hook-ups happening in town recently. Not all work out. Look at Buck.'

'I know my ground. Before, I didn't think it mattered to you.' He caressed her bare ring finger. 'Certainly not to do it because it was... expected. I wouldn't do it just to stop your mom and dad treating me like… like I'm on the outside looking in.'

'No. Do it because it's what you want. You know— small town, single mom, one eye, knocked up, has a habit of bending the rules to do the right thing.'

'Gives great snuggles,' he added.

'I'll do my best, but I won't be *quite* so close in a few months.'

He rubbed the bridge of his nose.

'You say *you* bend the rules? Think about what I used to do. Nothing decent or honourable in that.'

She cupped his cheek. 'That was before.'

'So now I need to do the decent thing. No—scratch that. I *want* to.'

Her gaze explored his face. 'Are you sure? Remember, I said no rush. The right answer will wait, because it absolutely has to be right.'

He pondered. 'Okay. I'll wait. How about… your birthday, later in the year? That means I'll never forget the date.' He smiled.

'Or if you do, I get *two* reasons to kick the shit out of you every year.'

'I'm not perfect—you may know that about me.'

She bopped his nose. 'No. But you'll do.'

'I'll take that as a Yes.'

'Sure. But we're keeping it quiet. No ring, no big fuss.'

'Keep a secret in Sunrise?' he asked. 'I think we've found out that's pretty much impossible.'

'Except that was just a bunch of old boxes. What's at stake here is more important.'

'I hope you mean snuggles,' he snarked.

Chapter 59

Beckman set his fork down and watched Lolita roll the last tomato around her plate with a finger.

'What?' he asked.

She looked up, and her shoulders fell. 'What if Sandra doesn't take the bait?'

'I think it's more important that we know the plan for if—when—she does. We can't have Reba tail her—it won't work. If the clues take Sandra on a winding trip across open ground, it's for sure that Reba would be spotted. She's a good PI, but even with desert camo, she'd find it tough. Plus, when Sandra reaches her destination, it might take more than one pint-sized sleuth to stop her doing whatever it is that gets done when the X is found. Someone else needs to be there: us, maybe Romeo.'

'I get that. But what if she *doesn't?*'

'Then we lose nothing, and she gains nothing. Back to stalemate. She's still one clue short.'

'You're forgetting something. We *do* have all the clues now. Doesn't that weigh on you?'

'You mean my conscience? No. It would only bother me if we'd done something about it.'

'And your curiosity? The thing that's written through you like a seam of gold? How do you not go stir crazy with excitement and desire to see what this is all about?'

He clasped her hand. 'Because everything we've done is to *prevent* the secret being discovered. To try like hell to hold the ancient network together. We're the real Guardians now. Stitching the trail together and going out there ourselves is not only unnecessary, but it's also wrong, and it's weak. And weak is what you said Buck was, for even considering letting the secret free.'

She nodded. 'I guess. What about the plan for tailing Sandra?'

He lifted her hand and guided her away from the table and onto the sofa. 'I thought about that. Obviously, we already know the trail she'll follow—we can simply lay the six steps out. Because she's starting from the wrong place—the place Kelvin is forging—she'll wind up at a false X. We can either walk the route tomorrow and make a note of the GPS final coordinates, or we can make a pretty good guess using a ruler and a detailed map. Then we can scope out a safe place nearby, somewhere we can lie in wait until she turns up. Reba can tail her in town, twenty-four-seven, until she goes to the start point and begins the trek. Then Reba calls us, and maybe Romeo, and we go directly there—which is bound to be faster than her pacing across the landscape. We'll have her bang to rights for a deliberate attempt to subvert the box system.'

'Bang to rights on what charges? Answer me that, Holmes.'

He stroked her cheek. 'I don't have to. If we want to know what charges to press, the best person is an actual detective. Or an actual cop. Relax—we've got this.'

'I can't believe we're talking about trying to get my own aunt incarcerated.'

'Like you said before—blame your mom. In fact, she'll probably be delighted at the outcome. Might complete the healing process.'

'Let's not go crazy here. I'm pleased we didn't stay enemies. I think Jack'd be happy too.' Her expression sobered. 'I'd sure have to tell her—whatever Sandra winds up doing. And I guess I need to tell her not to hold her breath for the patter of tiny feet.'

She laid her head on his shoulder.

He stroked her hair. 'Don't get sad. Not again. It's a waste of a good life on bad thoughts. When this is all over, let's sit down with Reba and see what she says about leaving the box to April or the baby. She's run this race with us. It's the next best thing to asking her to be a godmother—which I know you would have done.'

'I would so.' She took his hand. 'You're the best.'

'I have my moments.'

In the morning, while Beckman was reviewing the company's recent sales figures (Lolita had reminded him that amateur sleuthing was fun but didn't pay a cent), Reba and Randall arrived with the forged wooden sheet.

Lolita laid the original and the copy on the table and inspected them.

'Besides producing stand-out daughters, your old man's pretty good with his hands too.'

'It's not indistinguishable, but Sandra's not coming for an antiques inspection. If it looks like the missing piece in her puzzle, she won't think twice.'

Reba patted Lolita's shoulder. 'I hope it works, hon.'

'The forgery is the easy part. Now I have to go make nice with the woman.'

At the library, Beckman watched as Lolita engaged full Eyelash Flutter Mode and asked Sandra if she'd like to come over to the house for a coffee after work. There was, she said, no point in them coexisting in town and trying to avoid each other for the rest of their lives. She even promised not to badger Sandra to hand over Ginetta's box.

Beckman held his breath.

Sandra eyed Lolita with bemusement, then apprehension.

She's probably wondering whether this is a trap.

Big news, lady—it is!

But not that kind of trap. A different one.

Oh, snap.

Your face better not be betraying that this is a trap. Don't hold your lips like that. Move them. No, not like that! Just relax. Don't act like anything's up. Act natural. Be loose. Look over there, like something's caught your eye. Act distracted by a book on the shelf. What's that one there?

"TRAPS AND HOW TO MAKE THEM".

Curse you, world!

'That'd be… nice, I suppose, Lolita.'

Boom.

As six o'clock approached, his stomach jittered.

Now, let's try to act more natural than you did earlier, okay?

And stop looking up at where Reba's hidden the camera.

If you do that when Not The Guardian is here, she might catch on, and you'll scupper this whole enterprise. Plus, be on the receiving end of a whole new world of The Eyebrow.

Sandra was right on time.

They had left the box, closed but unlatched, on the side in the living room—visible but not prominent. Lolita had reasoned that Sandra knew there was a box on the premises and would take any opportunity to take a peek inside, providing she didn't get caught. Sandra probably thought she had Lolita right where she wanted her: after all, they hadn't done her level of research, nor seen the missing Beacon article, had they?

Beckman hoped that Sandra's pride would be immediately followed by a fall.

He didn't recall seeing Lolita "put on" a persona like this. Yes, she was different at work than at home, and morphed—like many people—to fit circumstance and company, but this degree of steel-lined sweetness was unusual.

As they sat on the sofa, sipping coffee, he watched Sandra's eyes like a hawk.

It became clear that she'd spied what she was meant to spy. At an appropriate moment, he casually, and deliberately by accident, slopped coffee onto the table.

'Oh, snap!'

Lolita shot him a fake scowl.

He sprang up and dashed to the kitchen to fetch a paper towel. There weren't any (because he'd put them away earlier). He called for Lolita to help him find some.

She called him an idiot, left Sandra alone in the room, and came to 'assist'.

They blustered for a full minute, raised their voices in an apparent marital squabble, then he trotted back to the spillage to mop it up.

Sandra was not sitting precisely how she had been.

He summoned the mental will to avoid glancing at the box. He saw Lolita not peek either.

They continued their three-way conversation until Sandra excused herself, citing a dinner appointment with a friend.

You have friends? Wow.

Ooh—catty. The woman's fine. Just not your cup of coffee, that's all.

Or perhaps she's merely put on a veneer for the last hour, like Lolita? Who's to say she's not rotten to the core.

So long as she took the bait, that's the thing.

Lolita showed Sandra out.

The door closed.
'Well?' she said.
'Let's check the tape.'

Chapter 60

To Sandra's credit, she'd waited at least fifteen seconds before stepping briskly to the box, flipping up the lid, memorising the contents, and returning to her seat as if butter wouldn't melt.

Beckman held up a palm.

'You want a high five?' Lolita asked. 'It was Reba's idea.'

'I'll take a high three?'

'Here, have this.' She kissed him.

'Now what?' he asked when the much-better-than-a-high-three-or-even-a-high-five was finished.

'We let Ree do what she does best.' Lolita scooped up her cellphone and dialled.

Throughout dinner, he couldn't help glancing out the terrace doors, watching the light level diminish towards dusk.

'Relax,' Lolita said.

'I'm trying to. Feel like a firefighter, waiting for the alarm.'

'I doubt she'd go at night.'

'We doubted pretty much all of this,' he reminded her. 'She'd have to take time off work if she went tomorrow.'

Lolita shrugged. 'Maybe she'll wait until Sunday.'

He gave her a lame impression of The Eyebrow. 'You think?'

She sighed. 'No.'

'Early tomorrow, I reckon. If Sandy has any sense, she'll use tonight to map it out.'

'If she maps it out, we won't get a head start. We need her to follow it methodically.'

'What we need, and what we get, are not the same. So long as Ree calls us the second Sandra leaves home, then calls Romeo, we'll get there about the same time.'

'So I should relax.'

'Yeah. Not that I'm not jumpy too.'

'I should run you a long hot bath.'

'And then climb in halfway through?' The Eyebrow (I See Your Game, Mister version).

'My motives are about as transparent as hers, huh?'

She winked. 'Yeah. But less despicable.'

Beckman's bedside clock read 07:22 when Reba rang, startling them both awake.

Maybe setting an earlier alarm would have been an idea? Idiot.

They quickly showered together

—see, this could have been languid and fun instead of brief and practical—

bypassed breakfast

—which should have been carby and caffeinated—

and hopped into the Miata.

(No way I'm taking the Mustang over rough ground. Sure, this is an important matter, but there are limits).

The direct route to the GPS coordinates took them West to the outskirts of town, down the nearest dirt track, which led to an abandoned ranch house, then out over rutted grassland. The low sports car flounced around, and Beckman winced with every thud, but Lolita pressed on regardless.

Soon they spied Reba's Jeep and, nearby, Sandra's station wagon.

The two women stood apart, like high noon under the low morning sun.

Lolita brought the car to a smart halt in a cloud of

dust.

'Easy, okay?' he said. 'Remember, Ree is recording all this.'

'I was nice before. I can be nice again.' Lolita climbed out.

Beckman followed, spying a police car scooting towards them at pace.

'What is this?' Sandra demanded.

'We were just meeting Reba here for a morning walk,' Lolita chirped. 'What about you?'

Beckman noted the tension in Sandra's body, the spade visible through the rear window of her car, and her very un-librarian sneakers.

'None of your damn business.'

Romeo True parked up.

'Morning, Lol,' Reba said.

'Hi, hon. She say anything?'

'No. Just more "none of your damn business" kinda stuff.'

'And what the hell is he here for?' Sandra arrowed an arm at Romeo—who looked like the early alarm call had caught him similarly unawares.

'The game's up, Sandra,' Romeo said.

'What *game*?'

'We know you're not the Guardian,' Lolita said. 'We have it on authority from the *actual* Guardian.'

'Horseshit.'

Wow. You sure don't curse like a bookworm.

'I know you looked inside my wooden box. We know you deleted the digital file of the Beacon Issue 109. Romeo told us you stole his two boxes. Tyler heard Mrs Finkel say you paid her off. We know you've put two and two and a few more together—and broken every rule Spodge told everyone not to. Look around,' Lolita spread her arms wide. 'Why this spot in the whole neighbourhood? This one spot?'

'I have no idea.' Sandra folded her arms.

'You didn't even pace it out,' Beckman said. 'It was forensic—the same way you've been operating for weeks. Unpicking the stitches that hold this crucial old puzzle together.'

'Then how the hell do *you* know this is the spot?'

Lolita laughed. 'Because we know it isn't. There's nothing here. Go ahead,' she waved. 'Go your life. Take a walk. Use the shovel. Use a theodolite, a compass, a sextant. Heck, we'll send Romeo out for coffee and muffins to keep you going. You've been had, Sandy.'

'Bullcrap.'

'I'm afraid so, Ms Thornton. You've been out-thought. Hoaxed.' Romeo pulled cuffs from his pocket. 'The charge sheet is waiting for you at the station.'

'Charge sheet?'

'Extortion, impersonating a public figure, destruction of records. There's more. I got... creative.'

'You damn well started this!'

'Luckily, I'm in a position to finish this. I did what I did for the good of Sunrise. And now I'm going to do it again. We'll be passing on the details of your actions to Jeremiah Spodge. There may be provisions in their records for further sanctions against you.' He stepped to her. 'Why did you do it?'

'Eat shit, Romeo.'

Sheesh. We have a list of Issues here longer than your charge sheet, Ms.

'Take her in, Officer.'

Always wanted to say that.

Romeo flashed him an Okaaaay, then, with her glower burning holes in first Lolita's skull, then Beckman's, Reba's and finally Romeo's, he carefully cuffed Sandra and led her to the car.

As the blue and white sedan lolled across the deserted landscape, the threesome let loose a simultaneous sigh of relief.

Yet, Reba shook her head. 'I don't like it.'

'What's not to like? Great plan, well-executed, suspect detained. Isn't that a dream result for P.I. Garrity?' Lolita asked.

'She went too quietly. After all this, to fail at the last? Even worse, to be duped by you?' Reba stroked her chin. 'It's not right.'

'What, you think Sandra and Romeo are in it together now? He started it, and she finished it? He wouldn't have come out here. He'd have called it all hogwash, so they could fly under the radar.'

'Maybe this was all for appearances? To give you two—all of us—the impression we got our woman, that the matter is over.'

'Sorry, Ree,' Beckman said. 'I don't buy it. Besides, what can they do now? She'll work out that our box was forged, but it's a dead end. She can't know where the real origin folio is. She certainly can't tear our house apart looking for it—that would definitely put her, or both of them, in line for *non*-creative criminal charges.' He put an arm around her shoulder. 'Case closed, okay? Armageddon prevented.'

Reba eyed them both and shrugged. 'I guess. I'd still love to know what she was going to do.'

'I'm not sure she knew. After all, we don't know what's at the X—the real one. Nobody does. Not in the Beacon, nothing in the library, no clues on the boxes. It's a treasure map to unknown treasure.'

'If it even is treasure,' Lolita said. 'It could be something deadly or unfathomable. Who knows—after all these years, maybe it doesn't work anymore, or it's gone.'

'If it has, then Sunrise is in trouble. It's supposed to be a lifeline. What if we're all relying on a get-out that's died, or been stolen, withered, broken, rusted, evaporated, or even—to keep Beckman happy—been reclaimed by its alien masters?'

'Ree. It's either Sandra and Romeo are the new

Bonnie and Clyde, or E.T.'s gone home and taken his box of tricks back. Really?' Lolita patted Reba's back. 'Are you sure it's not the lack of caffeine in your blood system?'

She nodded. 'Probably. Come on—let's fix that.'

Chapter 61

Beckman took the wheel and piloted them, in convoy, to Jen & Berry's, where they inhaled a significant breakfast. Randall arrived halfway through, and they recounted the story in hushed tones.

It's probably moot: word gets around. The story will start to leak as soon as people can't find the book they want and demand to know why a superficially wholesome woman is behind bars and unable to recommend a standout non-fiction on mindfulness.

As they paid the check, Beckman noticed Randall unusually quiet and pensive.

On the sidewalk, he drew the man to one side. 'What's up?'

'What happens now? We give the boxes back to the right people?'

'I guess we should ask Spodge for advice.'

'You'd have to tell him the whole thing. And we've not all been… *entirely* above board.'

Good point.

'I don't know. Maybe… maybe you and Reba take Mrs Finkel's box, as she sure didn't want it.'

'Still have to tell Spodge, so he can update his records.'

Beckman put his head back and gazed at the sky. 'This is a mess.'

'Sure. But we didn't make it. We only tried to fix it.'

Lolita and Reba came over. 'What's up?'

Beckman was still picking out wisps of cloud. 'What do we do now? Let Romeo go to her place and confiscate the evidence? Let him tell Spodge? Do we put in a request to get Ginetta's box back from Sandra? I mean, it's probably the only legitimate act in this whole sideshow.'

'How about we don't stand on the street?' Reba suggested. 'Next, you'll be using a bullhorn.'

'Come over to the house,' Lolita said. 'Thinking caps on again. One last time, hopefully.'

They gathered around the dining table.

'Here's the thing,' Beckman said. 'We dug a great big hole, and now we have to fill it in and make it look like the hole was never there.'

Reba shook her head. 'You can't. You can't put things back how they were. Can't erase memories. Not even Spodge can do that. We can get the boxes back to the two other folks in town, the two back to Romeo, and two under this roof. We could even get a new scan of Issue 109 and add it to the library archive, although maybe future generations shouldn't have a quick signpost like Sandra did.'

'Where do you stop?' Lolita asked. 'We could start scratching out other pieces here and there to make it even harder for the trail to be followed. We're talking about messing with history here.'

'For the greater good,' Randall said. 'All that's important—which was ever the case—is that all the box holders come together at the time of crisis. Nobody needs to know or do anything more than that. That was the legacy, the design.'

'Assuming the design still works,' Reba muttered.

Randall touched her shoulder. 'What?'

'Nothing.'

'Of course it still *works*. Why would it not?'

'It's easy to *say*, honey. To assume.'

Randall tapped Lolita's box. 'A box is a box. The instructions are intact. It's survived generations.'

'Not the trail—whatever's at the *end* of the trail. No one person knows what it is or where it is, so nobody— not even the Guardian—can do any… I don't know… random status checks. What if it needs power? Or running water? What if it's in the hills and a rockfall has crushed it?'

'Crushed what?'

She patted the table insistently. 'That's the point. Don't you see? For the first time, there's a chance to see this thing—whatever it is—and make sure it's still intact, ready, available, suitable—pick an adjective—for our children and those after.' She glanced around. 'Am I being crazy here?' She stood and paced. 'Yeah. I guess I am. Being protective. Selfish. Feeling beholding to April and… the new one. Wanting them to have the security and specialness of this place.'

'Nothing wrong with that,' Lolita said.

'You're talking like we're some kind of maintenance crew.' Beckman pinched his forehead. 'Feels a lot like creating an excuse. Going beyond even Sandra.'

Lolita took his hand and squeezed it. 'Mr Honesty again, huh? We're not talking about *doing* anything. Certainly not acting on what we find. Hell—if it's a thing for saving the town, there's no call for using it. Not now, when the danger we all feared—Sandra—is out of the picture.'

'And if we get to the X and it's something that… improves the town, like Buck said, would we not yield to temptation?'

Lolita retracted her hand. 'Not in a million years.' She folded her arms. 'And I can't believe you'd even think that about me, or our friends.'

He folded forwards and laid his head on the table. 'Shoot. I'm sorry.'

Reba ruffled his hair. 'No offence taken. This has all... screwed us up a bit. Bent our consciences, perspectives. But we did good, remember? We used the secret—and our heads—*against* a threat. So it has value. Even if we didn't go the whole nine yards.'

'But now you want to,' he murmured.

'We should check it out. That's my vote. Oil it, blow cobwebs off it, tuck it up in bed again—whatever. This is a *good* deed, Beckman. We're preserving the legacy, not taking it away. Definitely not getting on the bullhorn about it.'

Lolita rubbed his shoulder. 'She's right. We'll all go, one car, take a look, then get back to selling lights and drinking coffee and not making babies.'

He sat up. 'Those are three of my favourite things.'

'Get your map, then, Holmes, because I'm sure as hell not pacing this one out.'

They gathered the five images together with the authentic origin instruction—"From The Library", Beckman used the pencil, ruler, compass and calculator, and they plotted out the new course to the X.

Even though Reba's father Kelvin had only changed the origin to "From The Bank", it still made a significant difference to the path.

At the fifth instruction, however, he paused, bemused, and retraced his work. The answer came out the same.

His finger tapped the map.

'What's up?' Lolita asked.

'It doesn't work,' he whispered, afraid to believe it.

'What doesn't work?' Reba said.

'Check it over,' Randall suggested.

He was about to protest, but there was no harm in a do-over—this was no boy scout orienteering trip. This was A Big Deal.

His finger landed on the same spot. 'The box says "At The Striped Boulder".'

'I've seen one or two besides the one we used before. Lightning strikes. Permanent. Good marker for a secret designed for longevity,' Reba said.

'Yeah. Sure. Problem is, there can't be any here. This is the middle of the river.'

Randall shrugged. 'Washed away?'

'No,' Lolita said. 'You'd need a virtual tidal wave. And it's not exactly the Colorado. I've been out that way, too. Picnics with Carlton. The river's wide and flat. Grass is green. Good for... romance,' she smiled sadly, 'But not boulders.'

'So what's gone wrong?' Reba asked. 'Are we missing a box? Are we using the wrong scale? Did the bank move since the days of Jesse and the gang?'

'No.' Lolita put her elbows on the table and cupped her chin. 'I think we all need to accept something pretty crappy. The whole thing is probably a hoax.'

Chapter 62

The following morning, dispirited and no closer to ideas for tying up loose ends (without making themselves seem culpable), Beckman and Lolita went to the office, attempting to distract themselves by pretending it was a regular day.

He caught up with emails and calls, declined a meeting with a client who would only harangue for a price cut, and went double on the mid-morning order from Mabel the Bagel.

His mouth was full of bready goodness when his desk phone chirped with a call from his favourite line.

'Hey.'

'You wanna come in here?' Lolita said.

There was a curious tone there, like something was afoot. His nerves jangled. 'What is it?'

'Just come.'

He just went.

Standing in Lolita's spacious office, large as life, and as unexpected as, say, an interdimensional portal, was Ginetta Milan or Thornton.

He bypassed a double-take and went directly to a triple.

Lolita flashed him a How About This For An Encore? version.

'Mrs... Ginet... mom,' he stuttered.

'So, mom's here,' Lolita said with excessive cheer.

'That's… that's… *apparent.*'

'Hi. Son.' Ginetta said.

Son? What is this, Candid Camera?

Did they invent robot lookalikes designed to short-circuit the brains of innocent lighting salesmen by pretending to be pleasant and familial?

'I… guess,' he guessed.

'Horatio, huh?' Lolita said knowingly.

'Pardon me?' Ginetta said.

'Private joke.'

'Ah.'

'So, should I recap for Beckman, or…?'

'Go ahead, Li.'

She calls you "Li"? Not keen. Still, priorities.

'Mom decided to call by because… she opened Jack's letter.'

'Don't tell me,' he said, 'Jack wrote "Ha-ha, it's all a hoax".'

'Pardon me?' Ginetta said.

'Oh. Er. Private joke.'

'Ah.'

'Sorry about him, mom, he can be….'

'An idiot,' Beckman clarified. 'But a pretty decent, loving one at times. Anyhoo. This letter?'

Lolita scooped the paper from her expansive desk and passed it across.

Beckman read: "Don't be angry at Lolita". He looked at Mrs Milan junior and, probably, Mrs Milan senior (not Thornton).

'I think what dad meant was, "It's all on me. Don't hold a grudge".' Lolita took the letter and carefully folded it. 'He finally had an epiphany. He wanted us to live like… civilised mother and daughter.'

'So I came,' Ginetta added. 'Although, being honest, a small part of me was tired of living in those

circumstances. You know—before you suspect
alternative motives.' She chuckled reflectively. 'Don't
worry, I didn't do a U-turn on wanting the old house. It
would be easy to refuse that out of principle and spite.
No—simply too many ghosts.'

'Your choice, mom. I'd be churlish not to offer you
the guest room.'

Ginetta did a so-so of the head. 'Let's see. Maybe the
hotel tonight. Did you get your box back from Sandy?'

Lolita scoffed. 'Now that is a *whole* other adventure.
Makes a little tornado look like a sneeze.'

'How so?'

'Not here, mom. Walls have ears.'

'Okay. You know best.'

'Come to the house. Changed a lot in fifteen years.'

'Haven't we all.'

Ginetta followed them back to 1002 Edison Avenue
in her old Mercedes, and Beckman gave her a tour of the
place while Lolita put together some lunch.

It was oddly… normal.

He felt simultaneously sad that Lolita had been
deprived of this relationship for so long, and equally keen
to invite Marlon over for a visit. Mom might be more of
a stretch—he didn't know if her new sheep-farming life
in Australia would provide the means for a plane ticket.

Perhaps he and Lolita should fly out there instead?
Have a proper honeymoon?

Conversation over lunch was equally convivial.
Beckman noted the earlier tension evaporate from
Lolita's frame.

Ginetta finished and set down her cutlery. 'So let me
guess, Sandy was a holdout.'

Lolita leant back and blew out a gust of air. 'Oh God,
where to start?'

'Was I right? Was this all an albatross around the neck?'

'Look, mom, I don't want to fall out—not again, but hell yeah. What's worse is you caused it.'

'Not fall out? With that tone?'

Lolita stood smartly and cleared the dishes into the kitchen. It was her signature move to defuse the confrontation.

'What?' Ginetta asked quietly.

'You did kinda light the touchpaper,' he replied.

'How did I?' she called.

Lolita clattered cutlery into the dishwasher. 'Tell her, honey.'

Being the lesser of two evils, Beckman did as requested and gave Ginetta the whole nine yards. It was pointless not to: she knew about the boxes, and the story was likely to blow up anyhow, for better or worse.

Ginetta sat calmly, sipped her soda water, and listened.

Lolita eventually retook her seat opposite.

Beckman reached the denouement of the tale, wherein the feisty heroine, her adorable sidekick and their two friends defeated the evil witch in a standoff in the wilds of the Arizona landscape.

This would make a good movie.

'Sandra's in jail?'

'Holding pen, mom. And does that mean we fall out again?'

Ginetta smiled. 'No, it means Jack and I inadvertently created a "don't take things lying down" ethic in you, honey.'

'It wasn't personal, honestly. It's about the town. But you have to admit, if you'd hung onto your box, it would never have alerted Sandra to the whole scheme. So you're kinda the one who's responsible for her position.'

Ginetta patted the table. 'Excellent.'

'Hold on. Let's not wheel out the schadenfreude.'

'It's not that. It proves I was right all along.'

'That it's all an elaborate hoax? A century and a half joke by a bunch of cowboys with nothing better to do than screw with the minds and lives of future generations?' Beckman swept up his mug, hoping that the coffee had miraculously changed into whiskey while he wasn't looking.

It hadn't.

It hadn't even morphed into Buck's coffee, which was still an improvement over not-Buck's brew.

And how quickly we forget that whole mess when a bigger mess comes along.

Hopefully, Spodge'll chew Buck out for not being a decent Guardian—take him down a peg or two.

Maybe we'll end up in the same doghouse together. That'll be an interesting coexistence.

'No, Beckman,' Ginetta said. 'I was right about the box being more trouble than it was worth. A magnet for mischief and mayhem.'

'Easy to say after the fact,' Lolita snarked.

'Except I did something *before* the fact. Let me get my bag.'

Ginetta went to her roller case, which she'd left in the hall, and returned with a slim Tupperware container. She removed the lid and laid the contents on the table.

'You are kidding me,' Lolita breathed.

'No fights, okay?'

'What have you *done*, mom?'

'Look, when I got my box after your grandpa passed, I damaged it, like I said.' She puffed a breath. 'Thing is, the box opened that time. I saw the wood-paper thing. I was curious, who wouldn't be? More than that, I was worried. Sandra was always buzzing around. She was trying to steal my makeup, my boyfriends; I was worried she'd sneak into my bedroom one day and try to get some kind of revenge by messing with my stuff too. She was a nosy bitch. If she found that box—that note—, who knows what crazy stunt she would have pulled.'

'I think that's just been very much proven,' Lolita scoffed.

'Exactly.'

'So why did you give it to her when you left?'

'Because the town, dad's wishes, and whatever the box was about—that trumps any sisterly ill-will or suspicions. Anyway, the point is, I got my revenge in early.'

She fingered the sliver. 'I went to Reba's father, Kelvin—he was the best in town—and paid him to make a copy, a decoy. Then I put that copy in the box, so that if Sandra did something dumb and opened the box deliberately—not like my accident—she couldn't... do any damage.'

'You *forged* a lynchpin of this whole puzzle?' Lolita was stunned.

'Like daughter, like mother—right?'

Lolita's mouth snapped shut.

She has a point.

'Kelvin put a different message on it?' Beckman asked.

'You can see—south for north. It was bound to screw everything up. Take someone to the wrong place.'

Lolita snorted. 'Good try, mom. Except you screwed up. The puzzle doesn't work at all with your piece. You wind up in the middle of the river.'

'Well, how was I to know?! The point is, I stopped her. How about some gratitude, darling?'

'Oh mom, don't get me wrong, I'm grateful—or I would have been if we hadn't done our own forgery. The question is, when were you planning to tell me this? What if the crisis—a real one—happened right now, and you were still up in Kansas, oblivious?'

Ginetta shrugged. 'I don't know. I left it in my Will. I reckoned nobody would need it until after I was gone.'

'Technically, the boxes weren't needed *this* time.' Beckman turned the new piece over in his fingers. 'It was the boxes that caused the problem. That and greed or stupidity or whatever. If this clue had been in our box, and Sandra had gotten hold of it before we smelled a rat, she'd have all the clues now. The right ones.'

'Instead, she's been outsmarted twice. That'll teach her to try and swindle me out of men, out of Jack.'

'You know, you may be alright, mom.' Lolita took the shard and replaced it in the box. 'I'll put this in the study, with the other… evidence, until we work out how to wrap this up.'

'Then how about we all go out for ice cream and bask in the glory of the female Milans saving the town.'

'Sure. Just not to Our Buck's. That's something else I need to work out how to save.'

'Talking of saving,' Ginetta glanced around. 'Where's Flint?'

Beckman and Lolita shared a look of dread.

'Um, he…' Lolita began.

'The thing is. Ginetta. Mom…' he said.

'Flint is, well, was—'

'Fun and everything but—'

'He just—it didn't—'

'He died.'

What?

'Yes,' Lolita blurted. 'It was very quick. Painless. We woke up, and he was… gone.'

'Very sad,' Beckman added. 'He made us laugh. But now… well, there you go.'

'Oh,' Ginetta said, downcast.

'But you know what cures sadness like this?' Beckman said. 'Root beer ice cream.'

Chapter 63

As he drove the three of them to Jen & Berry's, he felt Lolita's eyes burning into the side of his head.

What? It's the perfect solution. It avoids any searching questions. Birds die. So long as we don't bump into Tyler and Amaryllis, and they don't spill the beans—in Flint-esque fashion—we'll be fine. She'll never know.

Well done on that, by the way. Known your mother-in-law for three days, and already you lied to her.

She kind of lied to us, though, about the faked note.

Let's call it a draw.

He slid the Mustang into a spot outside the diner.

As he reached for the door handle, he paused to let a car pass. Buck's Ranger. It visibly slowed, the driver surveyed the scene, then the V8 picked up, and the car scooted away.

What did we do now?

Probably surprised to see Ginetta back in town.

They went inside the cool air of the diner and took a booth.

'So, I'm bound to ask—how long are you staying?' Lolita studied the menu. 'Which is worse—Tornado Alley or your sister?'

'Half-sister. And… I don't know. I just wanted to repay the debt. Show you I could hold out my own olive branch. And, by the looks of things, you could do with someone else on your side.'

Lolita clasped Beckman's hand. 'I have this idiot, plus Reba and Randall.'

'I meant Buck.'

'I know. But sometimes things end, mom.'

'And sometimes things can be repaired.' Ginetta flashed a knowing look.

'*Mr Travis* has not exactly covered himself in glory since we saw you. He made the collapse of the box network seem like a good thing. Like it would do the town a favour. He's broken in pieces by Dixon leaving, and we all know love makes us do dumb things.' She sighed. 'I thought he was better than that. Smarter. More loyal.'

'There's always a price to loyalty, honey.'

'Timeout, okay? We're not here to bitch. We're here to celebrate. You may have kicked off this whole shitshow, mom, but at least you were here to wrap it up.'

Berry wheeled over on her skates. 'Well, isn't this a surprise?'

'I'm pleased to see you and Jen really made a go of this place', Ginetta replied.

'You look well, Mrs M. Visiting?'

'Just making sure the town is surviving without me,' Ginetta joked. 'And getting acquainted with my son-in-law.'

'Beckman's been a real addition to the town,' Berry said.

Vini, vidi, vici.

'Addition of what, that's the question,' Lolita smirked.

The diner's door rapped open. Beckman glanced round.

Romeo True saw them and made a beeline for the table. Beckman got a sinking feeling in his stomach: it was unlikely that the man was joining them for an impromptu toast.

Berry reversed. 'What's up?'

Romeo scanned their faces, caught a faint memory of a previous inhabitant, gave Ginetta an awkward smile, then looked around furtively. He crouched down beside Lolita.

'Look, this is awkward as all hell,' he said, voice low, 'but Ms Thornton… well… she kinda… escaped.'

Lolita snorted. 'That's very good, Romeo. You got any others?'

'Serious as a heart attack,' he hissed, eyes darting nervously.

Oh, snap.

Lolita leant over. 'Sandra has *broken out of* prison?'

'Not broken out. But… got away. Yeah.'

Lolita's jaw set hard. 'I knew it. We gave you enough rope, we took your apology at face value, we believed your crap about doing things for the best of Sunrise, and now—'

Romeo clasped her arm. 'I didn't let her out. This is no inside job, I swear.'

'And we should believe you, why?'

Romeo turned his head and pulled down his collar. There was a red welt there.

Lolita shook her head. 'Anyone can hit themselves or tell their accomplice to make it look like there was a fight.'

'If I was her accomplice, wouldn't I be out there, helping her?'

'Helping her do what?'

'How in the hell do I know? Why do you think I came to you?' He jerked his head towards the corner of the room, rose and walked away.

Lolita sighed. 'Sorry, mom. You order. Gotta speak to the Keystone Cop.' She thumbed for Beckman to follow, then went over for the pow-wow.

Romeo put his hands on his hips, exaggerating his physique.

'So, you want our help catching a suspect *you* lost?' Lolita cocked her head. 'What happened—did you forget to search her for the file or the lock picking kit?'

'My balls are on the line—I get that. And it would be a damn sight easier to cook up a story, to avoid that look in your eye, but here it is. I heard a cry, then a loud noise in the cell. I go in; she's on the floor, eyes fixed. I think maybe she had a seizure or something.' He sighed, massaged his forehead. 'I check her over, go to help her up, suddenly she's moving, grabs my weapon, threatens me with it. Asked for the cuffs, I go to hand them over, she gives me this,' he pointed at his neck. 'I woke up, cell is locked. I hollered for Karl; he let me out, I came straight over. So, yeah—I fell for a stunt.'

'She's lost the plot,' Beckman mused.

'Oh no. I think the plot's the last thing she's lost.' Lolita held her head. 'But where would she go? Home?'

'I sent Karl over there,' Romeo said. 'I figured maybe she went to your place—have it out with you.'

'Well, she's SOL because we're here. And I think breaking and entering is beyond even her.'

'I'm not so sure,' Beckman said.

'If she wants her revenge, she'd see the car wasn't there—why break in?'

'To get a look at the boxes?'

Lolita's face paled. 'Oh shit.' She grabbed his hand. 'Romeo—you check our office, library, anywhere else you can think of.'

'And if she's cut and run?' Romeo asked.

'I doubt it. She's had this thing—whatever it is—within her grasp. I can't believe she'd quit now. You may want to check her basement. Alone. There's... sensitive stuff in there. If you *really* want to help bury this secret, put it back where it belongs, you'll not want some of these details on any police reports. It's stuff that Sandras of the future would dig up and use to pull the deck of cards down again. This may not be *the* crisis, but it's *a* crisis, and you're either on the right side,' she thumbed her chest, 'Or the wrong one. Come on, Beckman.'

They turned for the door.

'Honey?'

Oh yeah—Ginetta.

'Sorry, mom. Ice cream later. Get something if you want, then get a cab home. Assuming my psychotic aunt hasn't torched the place.'

'I knew that box was no good.'

'The box is fine. It's the caretaker that's the problem.'

Leaving two strips of rubber on the asphalt was something Beckman had longed to do since he'd first become smitten with Mustangs as a teenager. He'd even had the opportunity in the last six months, sometimes thinking about rising early and heading out to a remote spot like Latrop Road to do a standing start burnout (and hoping the fifty-year-old mechanicals would survive), but always reined himself in.

Now, however, the chips were firmly down.

He eased out of the kerbside spot and pinned the throttle. Small amounts of Pirelli were vapourised.

'Don't let me hit her,' Lolita said when the screeching had abated. 'I don't need a counter-charge of assault.'

'I'm sure Romeo would thank you for the payback by proxy.'

'I hope he'll rip up your speeding ticket, at least.' She glanced at the speedo, which passed 55 as they gunned down Main Street.

Halfway down Edison Avenue towards the house, they passed a certain Ford Ranger moving apace in the opposite direction. Beckman caught the driver's gaze for a fraction of a second.

What're the chances he was coming over to apologise?

Miniscule.

The seatbelts tugged at their chest as he stopped the car on, if not a dime, then at least a quarter.

Sandra's Merc was not on the street or the drive.

Nevertheless, Lolita bolted from the car, and he jogged up the steep drive in pursuit. She paused at the door, pushed it to see if it would swing open with an ominous creak, as per so many TV clichés.

It was shut fast. There was no sign of forced entry.

'Maybe she went round the back?' Lolita said. 'Broke in there.'

'Or Buck did?'

'Unless he was just passing by.'

'You think?'

She swallowed. 'No.' She put her key in the lock, then froze. 'He has a key.'

'Maybe he popped in to leave flowers and a note.'

She gave him The Eyebrow (Now Is Not The Time For Jokes version), tugged the key round and burst inside.

All was quiet.

'Sandra?' she bellowed.

Guess we're not going with the surprise option.

No response.

She moved quickly through the hall, kitchen, dining room and living room. Not a thing had been touched, as far as Beckman could see.

As they entered the study, she came to a halt. Their box and the photographs of the other five were still there, in a line.

'Still here,' she breathed with relief.

He went closer. Inspected the collection. Pulled up a recent memory.

'Yeah. But in a different order.'

Her eyes widened. Hand came to her mouth. 'You don't think…?'

'I do think.'

Chapter 64

Two new black lines appeared on Edison Avenue.

I'm billing either Buck or Sandra for at least two new tyres. And probably counselling.

'You have the moves in your head?' he asked.

'Yeah. But I wish we'd mapped it out now. Have to do it the old-fashioned, Old West way. Paces and patience.'

'So will Buck.'

She frowned. 'It's like four miles in total.'

'Then I guess we'll have earned a double-scoop by the time we get back,' he beamed.

He leaned on the brake pedal and brought them to a stop outside Vinny's Conveniences, left the engine running, dashed out and returned a minute later with a litre of water and a pack of twinkies. He lobbed them into her lap, forewent his seatbelt, and drove them the last half-mile to the library, where he brazenly slotted the car into a Disabled bay—the only available space.

Buck's Ranger was nearby.

'Romeo can rip up the parking ticket too,' he said.

They went to the front entrance of the library, Beckman took out his phone, called up the GPS, jabbed a finger out in the direction of North, and they set off.

She clasped his hand. 'You do get me into some spots.'

'I thought we'd done enough cause-and-effect to last a lifetime. Besides, I'll bet I have a comeback for any suggestion you come up with. I'm only here in the first place because Saul picked me up—you want to blame him for toppling the first domino?'

'But then we wouldn't be together. Swings and roundabouts. Or swing dresses and roundabouts.'

'Are you going to talk hooey all the way to... to wherever?' she asked.

'Just trying to take my mind off what'll happen when we get there.'

'I hear you. At least Buck's a more reasonable person at heart than Sandy T.' She sighed. 'Or was.'

The sun burned their heads, the Twinkies disappeared, and the water bottle was half empty by the time they arrived, dust-ridden, at a striped boulder the size of a pickup truck.

Only 640 paces to go.

They turned South.

'If this last part's wrong, I will scream. And cry. And curse like you never heard. And wish I'd worn sneakers this morning. And punch Romeo's lights out.'

'Agreed. On which note—where *is* Sandra?'

Lolita shrugged. 'She'd already been and left? Maybe she's who moved the photos—not Buck. In fact, maybe he *was* just passing by. Maybe we have him wrong.'

'Yet he parked at the library?'

'Fair point. I guess we'll find out soon.' She scanned the way ahead as they picked their way up the slightly inclined rocky ground. There was little to see in any direction, and nothing to hear.

He checked his phone: 500 paces gone. They should be able to see something now: a barista, an aunt, or a Something Unknown.

The landscape yielded nothing.

His stomach growled, and mouth felt dry. He took another slug of water, passed it to Lolita, and she did likewise.

Guess I put the "travelling" back into "travelling salesman" for a day.

Would rather do it behind the wheel.

Still, this is more important than winning a Pegasus sale. Or even a Milan Lighting sale. It may even be what keeps Milan Lighting—and Sunrise—on the map.

Although clearly it isn't, and never was, on the actual map.

Could this be what the X is? The secret behind why Sunrise is a need-to-know kinda town?

Whoa.

If those are the stakes, I hope little old us are built to handle the situation.

600 paces.

He surveyed the immediate vicinity, which remained devoid of landmarks. He scoured the ground. Their pace slowed.

620 paces.

'Six twenty,' he announced.

'Maybe it's another Portal?'

'And he already went in? Why? No guarantee it works the same. He's too smart for that. Or she.'

The phone showed they'd walked 640 paces south, as per the last instruction.

They stopped.

'Now you got me worried. What if we do stumble through another Portal?'

'You really think?' she asked.

'Baby, this whole exercise has been the world's longest game of straw-grab. There's no pot of gold anywhere here. No building. No sign. No box. No big red button. But there has to be *something*.'

'*Has* to be?'

'Okay, maybe that's too black-and-white. Ought to be. If here's any damn justice in the world.'

'Split up?' she suggested.

'Hell no. Not if your Portal idea is on the money. Not having you go in there alone.' He took her hand. 'Come, walk with me.'

He stepped to the nearest chunky rock, hefted it up and placed it atop another. A landmark. Then he found a third, smaller one and added it on top. Then he retook her hand and began walking a spiral, round the rock tower, radiating outwards.

'Read this in a book once,' he said by way of clarification.

'Books are good. You know, if you have a librarian that'll let you borrow them.' She winked.

The radius of the path was about thirty paces when he saw it. His hand shot out. She looked. *Both* eyebrows went up.

She pecked him on the cheek. 'Who's my practical little idiot, huh?'

They walked over to it.

The hole was rectangular, about two feet by four, and definitely man-made.

'Permission to say "Bingo!".'

'Knock yourself out,' she replied.

'Bingo.'

'So, what do you think?'

'How's your spelunking?'

'Whatnow?'

'Your claustrophobia?'

'Not a problem. You?'

He shrugged. 'Fine. Conscience?'

'Fine.' She pointed. 'We go down, come back, use that iron cover over there, put some rocks and dirt back over it, job done.'

He looked into the dim aperture. 'And if Buck's down there? Or Sandy?'

'We'll have it out with them.'

'And if they won't see sense?'

She folded her arms and glanced around. She bit her lip. 'I don't know. But let's put the cavalry on standby.' She pulled out her phone.

Well done for not saying, "And what if there are aliens down there?"

He crouched down and clasped the first rung of an old metal ladder that led down into the gloom. He tested it for strength. It seemed fine, yet a shiver ran through his body.

He hoped if it was Buck down there, the man had brought a flask of coffee.

He wondered whether, if it was Sandra, she still had Romeo's gun.

Chapter 65

Ginetta bid farewell to Clint, watched the cab pull away—wondering if the man was a little too young for her—and walked up the drive to 1002.

Only the Miata was in the drive, so she assumed her daughter and Beckman were still out in the red car. She went into her handbag and pulled out the spare key Lolita had graciously left her with.

It was odd to be back in Sunrise. Butterflies still danced in her stomach. Why did she feel like an outsider in her home town? Perhaps it was nerves about how things would play out with Lolita: they didn't feel out of the woods yet.

As she reached the door, her pulse accelerated.

It had been jemmied open.

She clutched her handbag to her chest. She wished she'd brought her P238, rather than left it wrapped in underwear in the bottom of her suitcase inside the house, away from the prying eyes of a daughter who'd probably take umbrage at the thought of her mother packing a pistol.

She took three deep breaths, put her ear to the gap and listened for noise inside the house.

She heard nothing. The perpetrator could have left.

She would go directly to her suitcase and arm herself. Or should she walk away? Or call 911? Not the latter—the local law didn't seem to be too competent.

She scanned the porch for ideas. Something metallic poked out from under a bush. She went to investigate.

The jemmy.

She slid it quietly out, got the feel of it in her hand, and went to the door.

She listened. No voices. No footsteps.

She clutched the jemmy in her right hand, held it up, then eased the door open with her left hand.

The first footstep inside was tentative, the second surer, the third deliberate. She peered and listened, peered and listened. The jemmy was cold, heavy and evil. Footsteps on the wooden floor were quiet yet impossibly loud. Blood roared in her ears.

This is not what moms do, she told herself, not even for daughters they love.

In a few more steps, she had a clear line of sight to the suitcase.

Do moms switch a jemmy for a gun? Are they that cold to stalk an intruder with intent?

A noise erupted to her left side.

She swivelled, raising the jemmy.

There was only a split-second to see the figure, recognise her, be stunned and alarmed, before the heavy book thundered into her shoulder and sent her sprawling on the floor. The jemmy fell from her grasp and clattered across the wooden boards. She howled in pain.

Sandra loomed through the study door, reached down, grabbed Ginetta by her high-price lapels and hauled her up with startling ease.

Her eyes burned. 'You stupid bitch.'

She tugged harder on Ginetta's jacket, drawing her hunched, then dragged her into the sitting room and pushed her down onto the sofa.

Ginetta's head whacked onto the chair arm, sending reverberations through her skull. Something landed in her midriff.

There was a click.

'Put those on.' Sandra aimed the police-issue Glock 19 at Ginetta and waggled it instructively.

Ginetta's mind blazed, heart raced, palms bloomed with sweat. 'What the—?'

'Now.'

Ginetta complied.

Sandra's eyes darted, assessing the situation. 'You damn well stay put.'

'And if I don't? You'll shoot your own sister?'

'Half-sister, and even the half is a stupid state of affairs.'

'People break up,' Ginetta stated. 'It's life.'

'Like you and Jack—and there's another dumb mess.'

Ginetta shook her head. 'His fault, not mine.' Her nerves fizzed, her wrists hurt—she'd clamped the cuffs on too tightly.

'And I could have stopped that. It would never have happened to you in the first place. But, oh no, Ginny's the pretty one; Ginny always gets the boys.' Sandra sat on the arm of the sofa and levelled the gun.

Ginetta recoiled, sprawling onto her back against the cushions. 'You can't *steal* my boyfriends.'

'And look where that got you—trampled all over by Jack and then quitting because you couldn't handle being second best to the office. Well, here's the news, *sister*—we would have worked out, Jack and I. *I'd* have shown him who's boss at home. *We'd* have stood the years. *We'd* have been the talk of the town. I'd be wearing that string of pearls.'

Sandra pounced, clutched the necklace and ripped it from Ginetta's neck. Ginetta howled in shock and pain.

Sandra tossed the broken chain aside. Pearls skittered across the floor.

'*We'd* be Sunrise's millionaire couple. I had what it takes to be with a man like that, not you—Miss Pity Me, Miss Lonely At Home. This is *your* damn mistake. Your selfishness. I'd have it all now if you hadn't been such a bitch. And then you come in here, looking to crack me over the head for looking at those boxes.'

She strode purposefully into the dining room and returned with a napkin.

She glowered at Ginetta. 'Don't be dumb again. I'm not stopping now, not when I'm so close.'

Ginetta dug deep for some mental strength. 'I lived with the ass for years. Put up with his sexism and belittlement. My daughter spurned me. I quit town and lost all my friends. My last husband stole half my money. You can't hurt me.'

Sandra smacked the gun down on the coffee table, drew the napkin into a length, and threw it round Ginetta's face.

Ginetta, fighting sobs, knew what she had to do. She opened her mouth, accepted the gag, and winced as Sandra pulled it impossibly tight and tied it off. She gagged.

Sandra stood and levelled the gun. 'If there's any brains behind that hundred-dollar make-up, you'll stay there and let me do this. This isn't your town anymore, and you're not the big shot. I'm going to find this thing— whatever it is—and it'll put me on Page One.' She shook her head. 'Should have stayed away, Ginny. Should have kept that box. Should have quit trying to hold me down.'

Sandra grabbed Ginetta's handbag from the table, fished inside, drew out her mobile phone and stuffed it in her pocket. Then she went to the cordless house phone on the side cabinet, scooped up the handset and pocketed it too. 'I'm taking the keys to Lolita's car. If I were you, I'd lay there for a while and think about whether all the shit you did to me was really worth it.'

Ginetta offered the most brutal stare she could muster, but her eyes were blinking so much, on the verge of tears, that it was a lame effort.

Sandra merely sneered, turned and left.

Chapter 66

Beckman wondered whether his standard chivalrous "ladies first" applied to a perilous descent into an unknown cavern wherein a potential assailant lay.

'I'll go first,' he said.

'Yeah. You will.'

He took a deep breath. 'Love you.'

She rolled her eyes. 'That's dying talk. Get in the hole.'

Pulse rattling, he reversed up to the gaping maw, reached a foot over the edge, located the first rung, stepped tentatively, then harder, and put his weight on it.

It held.

Of course, it held. If Buck or Sandra had broken it, and fallen the rest of the way, it would be broken. Idiot.

By that logic, if a rung feels intact, it is, and it will hold you, so don't show yourself up. Get your ass down there.

After all, Sandra wouldn't shoot, would she? Not an innocent unarmed man on a ladder.

Nah.

He descended.

Above him, the sky darkened as Lolita followed.

As his eyes adjusted to the low light, he became aware of a faint glow from below. The air was clean, except for an edge of dankness peculiar to caves. The only sound was his and her soles on the metal rungs.

The light definitely had a bluish tinge now, as the rock shaft opened out, feeling less oppressive.

'How far?' she called.

He peered down, hands roughed by the harsh surface of the rungs he clutched. 'Hold on.'

He paused. A rocky floor was only a few feet below. He looked up towards the small square of light. The distance was probably seventy feet.

'Almost there.'

His foot reached for bottom, and tension left his frame as both shoes hit rock. He moved away from the ladder, and Lolita came down the last few rungs. He held her waist as she stepped away from the descent. Both were breathing hard from effort and nerves.

Her hand found his and squeezed.

At the risk of stating the blindingly obvious, he said, 'It's an abandoned mine.'

Her mouth fell ajar.

An ethereal glow permeated the space, a cavern disappearing at least two hundred feet in a wide arc away from their position. The ceiling was maybe forty feet above them, and the floor sloped down a few feet from the ladder's foot. The glow emanated from the walls, and there was something else running in a thick vein close to his left hand.

Gold.

'Oh heck, Beckman,' she breathed.

The beauty and even existence of it tore at his emotions.

'Why... Why is it abandoned?'

'I... I don't—'

Footsteps on rock. He almost jumped out of his skin. She shrieked. He gasped.

Please be friend, not foe.

Friend, not foe.

Not alien.

Not ghost.

A shape emerged from the half-darkness by the undulating wall.

A familiar shape. Not ghost, not alien.

Friend, or foe—that was the question?

'It was never dug out, because that would have turned Sunrise into a magnet for money-makers and ne'er-do-wells. A booming town, the talk of the country. Back in the day, things would have spiralled out of control. Same story every year since. But now, we're smarter, and we could all do with a financial shot in the arm. A boost. A chance to put Sunrise on the map.'

Beckman felt sweat bloom in Lolita's palm.

'We're in a pickle now, aren't we? On account of you and I aren't talking, and yet I really need to talk to you, Buck. You *really* need to see what an ass you're being.'

'The problem is, I don't care what you think, honey. I know *what* it is. I know *where* it is. Soon, I'll work out how to make that work for me. For us all. For Sunrise. For Dixon. Even as a tourist attraction,' he gestured around. 'Beautiful, isn't it?'

Beckman felt Lolita lunge, and tugged her back. 'Stop it,' he instructed.

She spun, and her eyes flared. 'Don't you tell me—.' She stopped. Her eyes clamped shut, jaw set hard. The breath from her nostrils was audible.

'I'm not fighting *you*,' he murmured.

Her eyes snapped open. 'I know. I'm sorry. We're fighting... *him*.'

'I don't want to fight, Lolita,' Buck said. 'I want you to see that this is the right thing.'

She shook her head vehemently. 'But it isn't. Ruining the town to win a *girl*? Did you stand too close to Bessie one day and get your head filled with steam instead of common sense and goddamn loyalty?'

'We did this already. I lost Dena the first time because she couldn't choose between me and the small-town life. I'm not letting that happen with Dixon. She's my last shot. Last chance at a life with someone. Inject some life, some buzz, some *commerce* into town. Dixon will have the career, the lifestyle and the man she needs. Wants. *Loves.*'

'When they say love is blind, you're goddamn textbook.'

'You tried to have Tyler killed to make Beckman stay in town!'

'This is not about me!' Her yell echoed throughout the cavern. 'Use the beautiful brain in that fat head of yours. What's the first thing that'll happen if you tell the world there's gold under Sunrise? Huh?'

'Easy. Number one, Dixon comes back. Number two, people flock here, businesses thrive, houses get built, everyone in town gets richer. Everyone needs coffee, food. *Lightbulbs.*'

She snorted. 'You're a stupid ass. You don't know the first thing about market forces. What happens when there's a sniff that this is the hottest town in the State? *Big* business comes. Little guys get bought up or squeezed out. Coffee Planet comes.' She stepped into his personal space. 'Selfish two-bit café owners go bust.' She looked him up and down with disdain. 'And it would serve you right.'

She spat on his shoes. Beckman recoiled, heart splintering.

'Hoisted by your own petard. I wanted to make up with you. With all my heart, I did. You were all I had, for so long. Now you're nothing. You're dead to me. I don't *want* to get richer. Neither does Reba, Berry, Saul, Clint or anyone. We want our town. You take that away, you may get Dixon, but she'll be the only person in Sunrise who'll even look at you.'

Buck's eyes boiled with rage.

Lolita's brow arched. 'What—you going to hit a woman again? I'll be sure to tell Dixon. She might reevaluate what kind of person you are.' She wrinkled her nose. 'You stay here and fondle your precious treasure. We're leaving. Word starts getting around, right damn now. Not about all this—about you. Judas.'

She grappled for Beckman's hand, found it, and drew him back to the ladder.

Beckman listened, nerves jangling, but the barista remained mute.

They climbed.

Chapter 67

With every step on the rusted miners' ladder, the rectangle of light above widened, the light became whiter. Yet, the next steps in their lives—in this whole affair—didn't become any clearer.

How do you stop Buck blabbing? Not with force, and words don't work. What's to do?

Thirty feet to go.

Twenty.

Ten.

'That'll do!' A woman's voice rang down upon them.

Lolita stopped smartly, and Beckman almost headbutted her feet.

'Out of the way, Sandra,' Lolita called wearily.

'Not a chance. What'd you find? An old mine? Buried treasure?'

'No dice. Let's talk about this.'

'No dice. Stay put.'

'Or what?'

Beckman heard a familiar click.

So, she does still have Romeo's gun. Glad that issue's cleared up.

'You'll shoot people for climbing out of a secret mineshaft now? Gone right off the deep end, haven't you?'

'So it is a mineshaft.'

'Yes!' Lolita bellowed. Beckman winced at the cacophony in the narrow passage. 'There's gold and emeralds and rubies and priceless old books and the secret of eternal life and some douchebag who thinks Sunrise needs to be the next Las Vegas, just so he can get laid. Alright? Let us up, and you can come get a look for yourself. Hell—why not go into business with the dumb fool. Go the whole hog and sleep with him for all I care. You two deserve each other.'

A laugh drifted down. 'No. Thanks, but I'll stay up here. Someone has to get the word out, and I'm afraid it won't be Buck.'

'You're too smart for this, Sandra. I know we're not friends, but you're too good of a person to ruin the town.'

'I don't want to *ruin* it. I want to enlighten it. What people do—I don't care. What I care about is not being just some woman who works in the library. I want what I would have had if I'd married Jack. If he'd chosen me, we'd have been solid, and I'd have had a good life and then some of his inheritance.'

'You can't screw with the future to change the past,' Lolita called.

Beckman shifted his handhold. His palms ached. He strained to see past Lolita's frame, towards their nemesis.

'I can give it a damn good try. I'm telling everyone about this place—not everything, only enough to create interest. About the settlers. All my research, the miners' pact. There's be interviews, talks. Hell—I'll even write a book. Advances. Royalties. I won't be Mrs Jack Milan— I'll be better than that. I'll be the woman who holds the key to the town.'

Lolita laughed. 'Great plan. But you can't stand there forever. And if I make one call, smarter people than you will be around to confirm that you've lost your mind.'

'You are absolutely right.'

Ha-ha! Well done, honey, we've got her on the ropes now.

Thunder and lightning—as if they were standing beside its source on Mount Olympus—detonated in the space above their heads.

Lolita screamed.

He feared she'd lose her grip and send them crashing to the rocky floor below.

Sandra fired again, into the wall below the shaft mouth.

Lolita squealed. 'Down! Down!'

His feet wobbled into motion, and quickly they were ten feet further from the existential threat.

'You be good and stay down there, you hear?' Sandra called.

Then came an awful grinding, screeching sound— metal moving against rock.

'Lord, no!' Lolita yelled. Her feet retreated from his view as she began to climb. He followed.

Darkness closed in. He leant to one side, looking past Lolita, as the heavy metal cover was slid back in place.

Where does she get the strength?

Lolita stopped. Fragments of rock rained down on them, scraped from the hole's edges.

With the sound of a million nails on a million blackboards, the rectangle of light narrowed to a sliver, then disappeared.

Lolita bawled anguish.

'Calm down!' he rapped. 'Take it easy. Breathe.'

'How can I breathe when—'

'Because if she can lift it, so can I. We'll go down, swap places, come back up, and I'll shoulder it out the way. Worse case, Buck will. He may hate our guts, but I'm sure he'd like to get out as much as we do.'

Her breathing came hard. 'Okay,' she replied eventually.

Silence fell.

He strained his ears. What was that sound?

Oh, snap. Oh no.

'Climb. Go up, honey,' he said calmly.

'Why?'

'Go up. Please, now.'

She ascended, he followed. Quickly, in the gloom, he sensed their position at the shaft's summit.

'What now?'

'Shh,' he cautioned.

He listened, fear clenching ever tighter, as the unmistakable sound of a car engine burred. Then the metal cover groaned in protest. The engine died.

'I needed the walk anyway,' came Sandra's distant, disembodied voice. 'See you around.'

In a moment, the only sound was the blood roaring in his ears.

'Baby?' Lolita asked, voice faltering.

'Yeah,' he said. 'Not sure either of us can shoulder charge a Mercedes.'

Chapter 68

Beckman took charge of his nerves, brain and breathing, and brought them within normal parameters—admirable in such abnormal circumstances.

Still, his head swam, either through blood rush, stress, or the depletion of energy.

Pretty sure Buck didn't have a flask with him. Doubt there's much to eat or drink down here.

Unless that's the real secret—an infinite bounty of life-preserving, even immortal elixir?

About as likely as aliens.

He continued, step over step, downwards into the brightening aura of the cave.

At the bottom, the feel of rock underfoot was nirvana. He stretched his scratched, aching hands. Lolita stepped off the last rung and flopped into his arms.

He kissed the top of her head. 'Be strong.'

'I'm trying.'

'She can't leave her car in the middle of nowhere forever. Someone will come.'

She clutched tight. 'I know someone will come. The question is when.'

He stroked her upper arm. 'Yeah.' He was lost for anything more insightful or supportive.

Footsteps.

'What happened?' Buck kept a safe distance.

'Sandra's closed the door and parked two tons of metal on top,' Beckman replied. 'So I guess Esme'll be earning a lot of overtime covering for you today. And tomorrow. And next week.'

'Excellent Guardian work,' Lolita added. 'You prick.' She clutched Beckman's waist and drew them away.

The dusty, mineral smell suffused Beckman's lungs. He spied a blue-gold tinged boulder and eased their backsides onto it. It was dry, uneven, and not a patch on the booths at Jen & Berry's. Or even the chairs at Our Buck's.

'Reba might come,' Lolita said sadly. 'If she puts two and two together.'

'Let's hope.'

'I wish there was another set of boxes other people could open if *we* were in mortal danger.' She chuckled, but it was hollow.

'We'll get out,' he said—although it was a bluff.

'So will the secret. That's definite. She'll go to the Beacon, make tomorrow's edition.'

'Assuming she finds someone who doesn't think she's lost her marbles. Which she clearly has.'

'Honestly, Beckman, I'm out of fight about it now. The odds are too great. Besides, I don't like the alternative.'

'What alternative?'

She looked him in the eye. 'If she's only keeping us here until the secret is out, then we needn't worry about going hungry for a day. I hope she's that impatient. Otherwise, if she wants to build herself up, hold the town to ransom for a few million until she spills her guts, she'll sit on the details for a few weeks. By then, we won't be around to offer any resistance.'

His gut began to eat itself.

At least in The Portal, we could have got a tan while we died.

Footsteps.

'Why will Reba come?'

'Get lost, Judas,' she yapped.

'Why will Reba come?' Buck repeated.

She sprang up. 'Because I called her and told her to tail Sandra.' She snorted. 'Should have told her to tail you. Should have seen you'd sell the town down the river to expose a secret you and your family have sworn to protect. Then she'd be here already. I called it wrong because I didn't truly believe you'd do anything worse than what you already had.'

'I wish I hadn't.'

'Too late. You loved Dixon—I get that. You deserve to be happy—I get that. But being so damn selfish and putting one person over many? Over friendships and livelihoods? Now you're going to die in a hole in the ground with two people you hate.'

Buck's face creased into anguish. 'I don't *hate* you.'

'What—you have a habit of hitting people you *like*?'

Buck took a step back, found an outcrop of rock and sat heavily. He bowed his head. 'Every hour since then, I've wanted the world to swallow me up. Now it has. I got what I deserve.'

'Problem is, we got it too. No good deed goes unpunished.' Lolita laid her head on Beckman's shoulder. 'Why can't I just leave the hell alone?' she mumbled.

'Because you're a good person. You both are. And I was dumb to throw that away.'

'Yeah,' Beckman sniped. 'You make old Tyler look like Mother Teresa.'

Unearthly silence descended.

Beckman gazed around, pupils wide in the dim light. The outer wall curved away to his left. In front of them, the ground fell into a shallow bowl. He couldn't see the other side.

He ran his hand over the yellowish seam on the wall behind.

'Is this really gold? he wondered aloud.

'Apparently,' Buck replied.

'And how would you know?' Lolita sniped. 'Geologist now, as well as a horseman of the apocalypse?'

Buck stood. 'I'm sorry—okay? I'm sorry a million times over, every second of every minute of every hour. I'll collect every thesaurus of every language in the world and text you a new word for 'sorry' in every spare moment I have. You can have a free tab at the café for the rest of your life. Hell, you can punch me in the gut. Right now.' He stepped close and thrust his ample midriff in their direction. 'Come on, I've seen you punch. You're no stranger to it. Take your best shot. I deserve it. Only forgive me, okay? Please, for the love of God, let's cut this mauling and bitching and hate and a waste of life. Of *love*.'

'Don't you get it? You did this *for* love. Not of me. Of her.'

'I had to try *something*,' he protested.

'Driving up to the city would have done it. Ever think of that? Reba did. Tyler did. Trying to dig you out of your...' she chuckled forlornly, '...hole.'

'Actions speak louder than words.'

'Come on, buddy,' Beckman said. 'How about a sense of perspective? Turning the whole town over to excavators, miners, scientists, opportunists?'

'This secret is the key to prosperity. There's always a place for that. More rides—better for Clint. More intrigue—better for Reba. More demand for neons— better for you two. Bigger business—ideal for Dixon to get her pant-suit kicks and big paycheck for the Adelaide Foundation. Win-win.'

Lolita rose slowly. 'Not overnight. Don't you get that? The vultures, the press, the metaphorical gold-diggers— yeah, they might come quickly, but Sunrise wouldn't be transformed into a stable, bustling place for years. It's not a quick fix. And what if it didn't become the kind of place you were still a fan of? What if you got romantic love but lost the feeling of belonging? And lost the café? And your friends, whose town you screwed? All on the chance— not certainty—that Dixon would come back. And stay. And love. And make a life with you, fitting around all the crap and upheaval you'd caused? What if she saw that you'd damaged your friends and turned people against you? You think she'd still consider you a warm, caring human being?' Lolita shook her head. 'You're playing fast and loose, with terrible odds. If hitting me was dumb, this is next level idiocy.'

Beckman nodded. 'Definitely. Take it from a sometime idiot. We'd probably make you a crown out of all this gold and proclaim you Travis, Sunrise's King of Assholes.'

'So, if you're doing this, or going to let Sandra get away with blabbing about this place, don't bother trying to apologise in endless tomes. Don't try to make up with me, with us.' Lolita shook her head. 'Because it will be war. And you will lose us. Absolutely and permanently.'

'The offer of a punch is still there.' Buck gave a supplicating half-smile.

'No. A punch is what killed Houdini, and I don't want you dead. I just want you to wake up and smell the....' She sighed. 'Well, you know.' She took Beckman's hand. 'Come on. I need a walk. I'm feeling woozy.'

They paced away.

Chapter 69

They only walked far enough for Buck to be a dark blob against the blue glow, which seemed to have no source—not in the air, nor the rock, nor tiny creatures which flitted around.

They stopped, and he held her, their heads in the crook of the other's neck, hands in the small of backs.

His head experienced a pervading lightness, though this was balanced by steadier nerves and abdominal butterflies which were now at rest.

'Shouldn't we explore, look for another way out?' he asked.

'If we do, and someone comes back there, we might miss our chance.'

'We should ask him to stay put. Divide and conquer.'

'Except, if he decides to carry on his idiot scheme, who's to say he wouldn't take the rescue and leave us here—like Sandra has—to prevent us from stopping him squealing.'

He stroked her hair. 'I don't know. You appealed to his basic decency. Not much more to be done.'

'I'll bet he'd do anything to get out of this sarcophagus, same as us.' She drew back. 'Even as far as teaming up with us—or at least pretending to.'

'You want to gamble? When you told him not to?'

'I don't want to die here, baby. If he's serious about not wanting me to die as well, then I'll go with those odds. Honesty got us out of the Portal. I've been straight as an arrow with Buck about his part in this shitshow. Maybe lightning will strike twice.'

He chuckled, remembering that actual lightning striking Esmond Belcher had started this whole life-changing adventure. Maybe metaphorical lightning would allow the experience to continue.

He took her hand, and they went to see if the leopard had changed his spots or, ideally, returned to being the giant pussycat they'd grown to love.

They stood six feet from the big bear—much more than arm's reach.

Buck sighed and ruffled his hair. 'Look. Here's the thing. I've felt worse these last few days about losing you than I did about losing Dixon. She and I had six months. You and I have twenty years.'

'That's not news. And they're not the same… relationships.'

'No. But when you….' He tailed off, massaged his forehead. 'When you two hooked up, I had a feeling things would change between us. When you got wed, I was pretty sure of it. I'd be on the outside looking in. I can't compete with Beckman, and nor should I. So, having Dixon… filled that space. I'd lost you—to love— but I'd still lost you. And you'd lost me to love, I guess. And then the merger, and you getting busy—it showed we weren't what we were. And when Dixon left, that was it. A great big hole in my life—a space you would have filled before, but not now. Maybe I expected you to realise that, which was dumb.'

'Don't you think if you married Dixon, I'd "lose" you? Especially if this white knight hadn't ridden into town to fill my life? It cuts both ways. I'm no substitute for her. I can only ever be your friend. You need— deserve—someone more than that.'

'Yet, when I try, I fail, and I get balled out for trying to win her back.'

'When you try like this, yeah.'

He nodded. 'I know. I see that.' He sighed heavily. 'So this is what's up. You've been a rock for so long. You never walked out on me. Dixon left after six months. You're the reliable one. You're worth fighting for. I did nothing wrong to lose her, and I can't change myself to get her back. Only the town, and that's… risky. And you? I absolutely did something wrong to lose you, and I *can* change that. I can say a billion apologies, or take a sock in the mouth. Teach you how to use Bessie, get on my knees and beg, give you the deeds to my house. Just tell me what, and it's yours.'

He clasped his hands together and gazed around the cavern. 'If it's a fix that only lasts until our last breath here, or decades more if we get out, it's still worth it. I'm not good at winning women back—you know that. So tell me. Tell me what you need.'

Beckman's heart thudded. Lolita's face creased into sadness and concern, indecision and desire.

Come on—free coffee for life? Sure, this was a bad break-up, but get some perspective here, honey.

Oh, plus the whole getting-help-trying-to-escape-certain-doom angle—that too.

Lolita put her shoulders back and filled her lungs. 'A hug. I'll take a Buck Special with a side order of contrition.' She opened her arms.

Buck enveloped her, pulled her head to his chest and lay his chin on her head. 'I'm sorry. I love you, and I don't want us to ever do that again.'

She nodded faintly. 'Back at you.'

Is that a tear in your eye, buddy?

Beckman brushed his face.

'You wanna bring it in, Beckman?' Buck spread one arm.

'Why not? First time for everything.' He found a comfortable spot and slotted into the three-way clench.

'I'm sorry, friend. I'm not that guy.'

'No. You're an Okay Guy. More than that. Very Okay. The Best.'

Buck made a throaty noise. 'Is this about the offer of a free tab?'

'Am I that shallow?'

'Yeah, you are. But an Okay Guy too. Very Okay.'

'The Best?'

'Don't push it.' Buck kissed the top of Lolita's head. 'The Best is here. She loves me and the town just as they are, and that's all I need. Dixon? Didn't make the grade, I guess.'

Beckman reversed away, then Lolita.

'So you'll give up this baloney? This shot at having it all?' she asked.

'Yeah. Not worth the risk.' He looked around. 'We still have to get out of here, and I don't reckon I'll have much luck left over if that happens.'

Chapter 70

For good order, Buck climbed the 73 rungs, a few expletives tumbled down on top of Beckman and Lolita, then the man descended.

'Unless our ancestors left some dynamite down here, we're SOL for now.' Buck kicked a stray pebble, which skittered away into the shadows.

Beckman sank onto their new impromptu chair, Lolita followed.

'What even is this place?' she muttered.

Buck hefted a rock as big as his head and set it down beside them, then perched his padded posterior on its pointy periphery.

'Promise you won't get mad?'

Lolita sat up straight, then softened. 'I'm all out of mad. At you, anyhow.'

'I was at Dena's place one night… well, I was at Dena's place a lot of nights, but you know what I mean. She loved garage sales. Would pick up most any crap. Like an archaeologist, she was.'

'I remember.' Lolita smoothed her hair pensively. 'You two were good. Wish you… you know.'

Buck waved it away. 'Fate. So, she was going through some boxes she'd picked up. Old photographs of the town. Pictures of the café before it was mine. Trinkets. Bric-a-brac. Stuff that the old woman had collected. There was a notebook. Inside were some old papers—

like, ancient.' He winced, shifted his position. 'There was a letter—no, not a letter, a piece, like notes for a newspaper article. We read it. Dad had already passed, handed the baton—the poison chalice—of being Guardian, so I knew there was this whole shebang out there, or at least in the past there was.'

'An article from the Beacon?' Beckman asked. 'Issue 109.'

'No. A piece that never made any Issue. It would have been 110, I guess, but Finn Dodds—that was the reporter guy—never filed it. Or was told not to file it. The old woman—Mrs Dodds, whose garage sale it was— also had a ton of back issues. Seems Finn liked to keep a copy of anything he had a column in. Pride in his work as a young journo—maybe his mom kept them. Who knows? Anyway, the one article, you won't find it in any records. Not even Sandra. Reason? Finn overheard the posse arguing—this was before the bar brawl. They talked about the cave, the start of the mine. The gold. This blue… whatever. The argument was about whether to tell everyone or take the secret to their graves.'

'Holy crap,' Lolita breathed.

Buck's smile was thin. 'Seems they made the right decision. Sunrise wouldn't be Sunrise if it became a big city.'

'But they knew it could, if it needed to be. If the place withered and turned into a one-horse town, opening the boxes would bring people to the mine, and they could get back that bustle.'

'Is that what Spodge meant by existential?' Beckman asked. 'Plenty of frontier towns died.'

'Look around,' Buck said. 'This is more than a gold mine. Mines are small and dangerous. This is… nature's sanctuary. A hiding place. From enemy armies, from missiles. Hell, from nuclear fallout. Everyone in town could fit in here.'

Lolita whistled softly. 'You could literally save Sunrise.'

'Yeah.'

Beckman pinched the bridge of his nose. 'If you didn't mind a headache and,' he pulled out his phone, 'Zero bars.'

Lolita darted The Eyebrow (Man Up version). 'Next, you'll be complaining about the lack of decent coffee.'

'Well, I wasn't going to, but....' He smiled. 'It's the blue that has me worried. I never saw a cave, a mine, or anything like it.'

'Lol, did you ever meet Dr Sleck?'

'You introduced us, I think, but no.'

Buck looked at Beckman. 'In the dictionary under "crazy science guy", it says "see him". Smart, John Lennon glasses, terrible dress sense. Anyhow. He was convinced that this area was created by an asteroid strike—torus of hills, maybe some kind of radiation which blocks GPS.'

Beckman sat bolt upright. 'I moved to a radioactive town? You might have warned me! I mean,' he took Lolita's hand, 'She's worth it, but still.'

'Relax, honey. There's nothing.' She peered around the cave and winced. 'At least, not on the surface.'

'So by the time Reba turns up with a tow truck and a jemmy, the three of us could be primordial soup.'

Buck held up a hand. 'Like she said, Sleck said nothing had been found.'

'Nothing familiar to Earth science, you mean.'

She rolled her eyes. 'Here we go with the E.T. stuff again. Who cares? There's gold, there's a safe space—that's what's important. And did you never hear of phosphorescence?'

'An afterglow *after* radiation is removed,' Buck explained. 'So we're sitting on the debris of an alien rock? Look at the upsides. Billions of dollars in gold, and enough light for me to see you make an idiot of yourself again, Beckman. Better that than being stranded in pitch dark, huh?'

'Not sure I like the idiot part,' he muttered.

'Look at the downsides,' Lolita countered. 'Two reasons for Sandra to tell the world—to turn this place into a giant quarry, or the next Area 51.'

Her head dipped. 'Either way, she gets what she wanted—fame. Money. Maybe even a man whose morals are low enough to marry a woman like that.' She scoffed. 'Not even Jack was that low. He was a goddamn saint compared to her.'

Buck stood. 'So we have to stop her.'

'I'll take any bright ideas,' she said dismally.

'Give me your phones. I'll see if there's any signal just underneath the trapdoor.'

'Good luck,' she sniffed.

'Hey. Lighten up. Where's my ballsy, never-say-die best friend?'

She sighed. 'You're right. You go. Who knows? Might work.'

'Why don't you follow me up? Have a good holler, in case someone's passing by.'

'Now that *is* a stretch.'

Buck laid a paw on her shoulder. 'Humour me.'

'Remember our Screaming Place?' Beckman suggested. 'That's pretty good for the soul, right?'

She met his gaze. 'I guess. Come on.'

Buck went first, Beckman followed, and Lolita was last up the uneven rungs.

When Buck's head scraped their prison ceiling, they held station while he tried to get a signal on each of their cellphones in turn.

There were to be no miracles.

'Ree won't come,' Lolita said from beneath Beckman's shoes. 'She started her tail too late. If she'd been following the car already, she'd be here by now. She must have picked Sandra up when she got back to town on foot. Probably watching her right now—whatever she's doing.'

'So who else knows we're here?' Buck asked.

'Nobody.'

Maudlin silence fell.

'Hopefully, Reba will stop her going to the Beacon,' Lolita said. 'If that's Sandra's angle. How else will she get the word out?'

'Lol?' Buck said guardedly.

'Yeah.'

'You know she has a show on Radio Sunrise? Book Talk. Six o'clock Wednesdays.'

'You're kidding me.'

'Kid? Here? Now?' Buck replied. 'I'm all out of "dumb".'

Beckman heard her kick the stone wall and yelp in pain.

'Not a chance this place is a time tunnel too?' he murmured to Buck.

'No. It's Wednesday.'

His spirits fell through his chest, slipped out of his trouser legs and careered down the shaft. The horrible silence returned.

Lolita broke it with an ear-splitting, 'Help!'

Lost for better alternatives, Beckman joined in, then Buck. Over and over until Beckman's throat was sore and his head spun.

The quiet closed in.

'Let's go.' She began to descend.

'There'll be another way,' Buck added.

Beckman knew it was said with encouragement, yet devoid of belief. Still, he climbed down, hand over hand, checking below, so he didn't kick his wife in the head and make things even worse—if that were possible.

'Wait!' Buck called.

What now?

He stopped.

'No fooling,' Lolita said.

'Shhh!'

They fell mute. The subterranean lull reverted.

Except…

Beckman tipped his head and grimaced in the way people do when trying to hear a faint sound, even though it makes no difference whatsoever.

Holy cow.

A faint, indistinct rumble, dying away.

He strained, pointlessly, harder, trying to shut out the nothing in the hope of hearing a something.

The metallic screech was like the world ending. He went to clap both hands over his ears, then realised he needed them to hold onto the rungs, so he didn't.

His heart rate doubled.

A sliver of light appeared. Then a thin rectangle. More cacophony. A square. Then a fat rectangle.

Buck was already climbing, his frame growing more distinct in the blooming light. Sunlight.

Salvation?

He set off in, if not hot pursuit, at least warm pursuit. Below, Lolita urged him on.

'Hello?' Buck called towards the hole.

The big man slowed, Beckman likewise. He leant out and peered past the barista occupying half the width of the shaft.

A head appeared, silhouetted by the strong sun.

'Lolita?' came a voice.

'Mom?'

Chapter 71

The light was more beautiful, the air cleaner and sweeter, the colours more vibrant.

Lolita clutched Ginetta like a life raft. When she let go, Ginetta squeezed Beckman like he was a favourite nephew and planted a perfumed kiss on his cheek. She even hugged Buck.

Beyond raw emotion, it appeared that mom had brought powers of metamorphosis. The Miata was there, with a seriously crumpled front end, but Sandra's Mercedes was conspicuously absent.

'What did you do with the…?'

Ginetta pointed. At the bottom of the low incline, the offending doorstop was on its side.

'I broke the window, released the parking brake. Then I gave it a push—gentle as I could, honey—with your car.'

'I don't care,' Lolita replied.

'I also had to rip off the trim to hotwire it.'

Beckman peered inside to assess the veracity of a middle-aged woman's outrageous claim of grand theft auto.

'We do have keys,' Lolita pointed out.

'Sandy took them. And the phone.'

'How did you know where to come?' Buck wiped welcome sweat from his brow.

'What, you don't think I can read a map and use a ruler?'

Lolita hugged her again. 'You're incredible.'

'I know.'

Buck coughed. 'I hate to spoil this love-in, but it's after five. Sandy's on in under an hour.'

Beckman looked at the two-seater sports car, then did a double count of the number of people required to fit into it. One hundred percent overcapacity.

Make it one-twenty, allowing for Buck's... persona.

'What's happening?' Ginetta asked.

'Your... our... that woman is going to broadcast this century-old secret to the whole town. We have to stop her.'

'Why, what's down there?'

Lolita shook her head vehemently. 'No. I love you, but no. You gave away the box; you absolved yourself of responsibility. You don't need to know. Nobody does. That's the point. Don't make me tell you because I'm fresh out of energy for break-ups and make-ups.' She gave the hardest of stares.

'Really, Mrs M,' Buck added. 'It's for the best.'

After an eternity, Ginetta nodded. 'You two take the car. Buck and I will stay and... cover this up.'

Lolita squeezed her arm. 'Thanks.'

Beckman slid into the passenger seat, Lolita behind the wheel. She fumbled for the loose wires and completed the circuit. The starter whined, then ceased.

She tried again. Nothing.

'How hard did you hit that two-tonne car, mom?'

'Too hard?' Ginetta squeaked.

Beckman hopped out.

Buck tried to pry the bonnet open, but it was stoved too severely. 'We got out—that's the main thing.'

Lolita dejectedly joined them, then looked across the vista towards the distant buildings. 'At least the radio station's on this side of town.'

'What's the plan?' Beckman asked.

'I'll literally make it up as we go along.'

'If you need help, talk to Mona, she's the tech,' Buck said. 'We... get along.'

Lolita jabbed his chest. 'Not two-timing me, are you, big lug?'

He ruffled her hair. 'Not even in the same league. Now, run along. Or at least, walk along. Time's wasting.'

'And revenge is a dish best served... sweaty, probably.'

Buck tossed across her cellphone, then Beckman's, and they set off.

One foot in front of the other.

Again.

And again.

Many, many times.

'We won't make it in time,' he said breathlessly after twenty minutes of rough terrain and hot sun.

'I've had an idea.'

The radio station was an isolated, two-storey building on Ohm Street, dwarfed by its excessive transmitter tower.

Beckman had never tuned into WSUN 102.2, but might in future. As long as the music was fine and the DJ wasn't a crazy librarian with a penchant for live burials and excessive gunplay, it could be the station of choice chez Milan/Spiers.

They arrived at 18:04, after losing millimetres of shoe leather and about two pounds belly fat.

Reba's car was one of the four on the lot.

Randall opened the front door like a valet. 'Welcome back.'

They trotted inside, down a short corridor, and Lolita carefully opened the door to the engineer's room.

Reba sat there. Beside her in the second weathered leather chair was Mona. Mona had fiery red hair, a jade green sweatshirt and was studiously inspecting the bank of switches and dials in front of her.

'She locked the door as soon as I arrived.' Reba pulled headphones off and pointed at the heavy partition leading to the recording studio.

Beckman looked through the expansive glass window divide.

Sandra, headphones clamped to her head, chatted nonchalantly into the microphone. Then she caught sight of the two new arrivals, her eyes flared, her mouth froze for a second, then she very deliberately gave them the finger. She pointed at the door, beamed, winked, and returned attention to her show.

Beckman wanted to sock her.

'Did you get here in time?' Lolita asked.

Reba nodded. 'Five minutes before. She started the PSA right on six.'

'You heard it?'

'Yeah.'

'I didn't,' Mona said. 'Like Buck asked.'

Lolita laid a hand on her shoulder. 'I owe you. Name your price.'

Mona shrugged. 'You made up with Buck. So, he'll not be a grouchy ass anymore. That's plenty.'

'I'll credit Sandy this,' Reba said. 'She teases the story very well. Makes it compelling. Enchanting. Entrancing.'

'What's her normal audience?' Beckman asked.

'Nine hundred or so,' Mona replied.

'Oh well,' Lolita said. 'Shame.' She turned to Reba. 'She ask why you were here?'

'I said I was considering some voluntary work behind the desk.'

'She buys stories as easily as she sells them.'

Reba winked. 'Yeah. Great, huh?'

At 18:55, Rollo Brick arrived for his seven o'clock show. Lolita gave him a cockamamie excuse for their presence. He had a quick conflab with Mona, then as the red display above the window ticked to 18:59, Sandra wheeled herself across to the door, unlocked it, and Rollo went inside.

As he did so, Romeo True eased open the main door and waited by the wall.

At 19:00, Mona flicked a switch on the panel.

Sandra emerged at 19:01.

She sneered disappointment at Lolita. 'There was another way out, I suppose.'

'There's always a way out, *auntie.*'

'Think you're so clever. And what's Inspector Clouseau here for?' She thumbed at Romeo. 'Extra audience for today's little… message?'

'I didn't hear a thing,' Romeo said calmly.

'Never mind.'

'Nor me,' Mona said.

'Me either,' Beckman chorused.

Sandra shrugged. 'You know it all already.'

'I heard,' Reba said.

'Good. But you already knew, didn't you?'

'Yeah. So no harm, no foul.'

'Whatever.'

Lolita stepped close. 'Actually, no harm at all. Sixty minutes of dead air, right, Mona?'

'Not a word, not a hiss. Off-air for one glorious hour. Easiest shift of my life.'

Sandra stared, dumbfounded.

Beckman clocked the moment that the burners in her belly lit. Her face went from flesh to pink to orange to red to purple faster than the ignition of Saturn V.

He saw her fist ball, her body shape change, her eyes lock on Lolita.

And that was when he gave in to the temptation to sock her.

For chivalry, of course.

Chapter 72

With Sandra under double guard at the police station, cuffed and ankle-tagged, Reba, Randall, Beckman and Lolita went to Our Buck's, where the proprietor had laid on a special late-night opening for selected guests.

Beckman debated when would be a good time to check whether Buck was serious about the free tab.

It'd be taking advantage, though. We're far better off than he is, even before Jack's inheritance.

Best say nothing. Being back here is good enough.

The warm brown nectar slid down his grateful throat.

'We have to give Spodge chapter and verse,' Buck said.

'I know,' Lolita replied.

He squeezed her arm. 'I'll do it. I'll cop to dereliction of duty. We'll work out a way to distribute the boxes. For certain, you'll have to give up one of yours. And the Trues. Find some worthy, trustworthy people.' He chuckled, hollow. 'People better than me.'

She looked up at him and took his hand. 'There are plenty worse than you. And I wasn't perfect.'

Reba stepped over. 'Maybe it needs to be someone practised at keeping secrets. Someone who already knows what's at stake, and is more likely to do the right thing.'

Beckman and Lolita exchanged a glance.

'The thing is, Ree, we were... we'd need to find someone to inherit our boxes—box—seeing as….' Lolita's head dipped, 'You know.'

Reba's face brightened. She crouched down to where Lolita sat at the table. 'April? That's the sweetest thing, Lol. I know it can't make up for your situation, but if that's what you choose, I'm sure our girl will be honoured.'

'If Spodge approves, of course,' Buck said.

'What's not to like?' Lolita said. 'Gets the thing out of the hands of irresponsible adults.'

'Talking of—we have to decide how many charges we want to press against Sandra. How tough we want to make the rest of her life.'

Ginetta—who'd been chatting with Randall—came over. 'Personally, if she's out of the town, that's good enough for me. Might even make me, I don't know, consider staying.'

Lolita put an arm around her shoulder. 'Really, mom?'

'I know which of the two of us cares more about Sunrise. And… I suppose I'd gotten homesick.'

'If Sandra gets locked up far enough away—but somewhere a tornado can't rip the prison roof off and give her a chance to scale the walls—she'll be out of sight, out of mind. Back to before you dropped the bombshell about her, mom.'

Ginetta fell sober. 'Hmm.'

'What?'

'Pulling hair, stealing boyfriends, calling me names? Years behind bars for that? Makes me feel like the bitch.'

'Don't forget theft, breaking and entering, resisting arrest, false imprisonment….' Buck began.

Ginetta put a hand on his shoulder. 'All the same. I don't want to feel like Elliot Ness.'

'She's shown that she won't listen to reason.'

'She was never given an alternative.'

'You have a better idea, mom?' Lolita asked. 'Come live with us under house arrest? Have her committed? Shoot her into space? Why will she keep her mouth shut?'

'Who says she'll keep her mouth shut in prison?' Reba asked. 'If she tells enough people, one of them will finish their sentence and go in search of a newspaper.'

'She has to want to keep quiet—and know the consequences of not doing so.'

'And she needs out of this town,' Ginetta said. 'Minimum.'

'This is a big ask,' Buck said. 'I know from personal experience that people only leave Sunrise when there's a draw to somewhere better.'

Lolita patted his shoulder blades. 'Then I guess you're in the pow-wow for how we make this happen.'

Beckman had never talked to anyone behind bars before. Sandra was hardly Hannibal Lecter, yet it was odd to come face to face with the consequences of your actions—to see the hardship you were causing another person.

Still, Sandra deserved something, even if it wasn't a thin mattress and an hour's daylight a day for the next ten years or more—even if all the charges stuck, which wasn't guaranteed. She'd doubtless sink every last penny into the best lawyer she could find.

The carrot was better than the stick. Surely?

Sandra came to the bars and studied them all—Ginetta, Lolita, Reba and him. She looked dreary and somewhat beaten—but she tried to come out fighting.

She scoffed. 'Here for a gloat? Enjoying locking up your own kin? And you said *I* was the revengeful bitch.'

Lolita shook her head. 'We're turning the other cheek. Like you should have, instead of jeopardising the livelihoods and happiness of the inhabitants of the town where you were born.'

'Whatever's down that mineshaft, we all know it's instrumental to Sunrise's survival.'

'Absolutely. Or, like Spodge told us—and everyone who has a box—it's also the key to trashing this place. You may have gotten rich and famous, Sandra, but you would have been hated too. Ostracised. A suitcase of greenbacks and a few TV interviews isn't worth that.'

Beckman held a briefcase aloft. Reba stuck out her arms, and he laid the case on there like a shelf, clicked the locks and opened the lid.

Sandra's eyes widened, then narrowed in suspicion. 'You're buying my silence?'

'Plus, we're organising for that mineshaft to be filled with concrete, and another one sunk in a new place. By a contractor from out of town. We'll alter the messages in the boxes and redistribute them. Start over.'

Lolita's words were only partly true—but Sandra wouldn't know. Especially if she liked the look of the briefcase contents and took the offer she was about to receive.

Ginetta took a set of keys from her pocket and tossed them into the briefcase. Beckman shut the lid. Ginetta swiped through her phone and held it out for Sandra to see.

'Here's a picture of my house. Taken only a few weeks ago. Twice the size of your place here.' She swiped again. 'Here it is on a satellite map. We'll pay for a removal truck and a week in a hotel in Garden City until you get set up. Plus, you have the money.'

Sandra backed away, paced, then sat on her spartan bunk. 'What's the catch?'

If only you knew.

'You stay there, you escape jail time,' Lolita said. 'You come back here; Romeo will be waiting. You breathe a word about the boxes and the mineshaft—although the location will be wrong, and nobody will believe you anyway—the judge will be waiting. You put a foot wrong, Spodge will freeze your assets, and you'll wish you had the comfort of even a place like this.'

Ginetta pressed against the bars. 'You were entrusted with a secret. You blew it. You put yourself above Sunrise, and that's unforgivable. Take the money, take the keys, and get lost. Final offer, no negotiation, or you'll find out just how badly orange suits your skin tone. *Sister.*'

'And my car? The one you trashed, *sister*?'

'You can have my Jeep,' Reba said. 'I need something with better provision for… little ones.'

'And my house?'

Lolita went to the bars. 'You can sell that. Half price. We may have a buyer already.'

'Half price?'

'Or free. Your choice. You saw the briefcase. I'm being generous as hell with Jack's money—money you craved and almost killed us to get. If he knew what you'd done—in his name—he'd pay for the prosecuting attorney to get you twenty-to-life. I still might. You're book smart, Sandra. Now be life smart.'

Chapter 73

A week of everyday life was manna for Beckman: in the office for nine, meetings, sales calls, lunch at the desk, inconsequential gossip. Stolen kisses with the CEO.

Buck glossed over the details of his meeting with Jeremiah Spodge: things were on a need-to-know now. He called in at the house, took the box Sandra had been babysitting but left behind Jack's example.

Things were back as they should be—as they had been, weeks before.

With a difference: Lolita knew she had an aunt, but that aunt was no longer in town. Her house had been cleared the day before. It was now available to be offered to potentially interested buyers.

One of those buyers was having a birthday celebration at the best venue in town.

He watched as his Saturday night date pulled on a favourite swing dress. He zipped her up.

'You think they'll stay? Relocate?' she asked.

'Baby steps, I think—that's Tyler's style. He's not ready for all-in yet—with Amaryllis, with a home, with Pegasus.'

She embraced him. 'Maybe the Main Street sign will convince him that Sunrise wants him—them—here.'

'Well, if he's looking for a sign for what to do, you can't do better than a sign.'

She rolled her eyes. 'I love you. Idiot.'

'I love you. Mrs Idiot.'
They kissed.

He parked her showroom-sparkling Miata on Main Street, and they walked down to Our Buck's. The array of lights strung across the street read "HAPPY BIRTHDAY TYLER".

The hubbub in the café was upbeat. He didn't hear the words "Sandra", "box", or "mineshaft" at all, which was a blessing.

Romeo and Julie True were even talking freely with Reba and Randall. Saul and Buck were laughing about something. Clint and Ginetta seemed to be getting on famously.

Wonder if she's into men again now?

None of your damn business. So long as she finds a place to live, and quick. It was heartening at first to have her around at home—seeing mother and daughter make up. Now? It's a marital household, and some marital… undertakings go better without someone listening through the walls.

Would Reba and Randall take Jack's old place? More room for April to play, space for the little one when it arrives? Reba's house is fine enough for Ginetta—no mansion, but much less pancaked than her last place.

All in good time.

As the old iron wall clock struck seven, Buck led them all in a rendition of Happy Birthday. Tyler stood in the centre of the circle, lapping it up, then terminated the applause by scooping Amaryllis up, bending her over and kissing her with a flourish.

There were cheers.

Then he righted her, clasped her left hand in his, and sank to one knee.

The room fell quiet.

You never do anything by halves, do you, Tyler?

'Amaryllis Calliope Broomhead. You are the light of my life. You have rescued this wandering, wayward soul. You have opened the best chapter in my life. You are a knockout beauty and the stuff of dreams. And I am head over heels in love with you. Will you do me the huge honour of—'

'Yes!' she yelled.

Laughter and whoops went around the circle like a Mexican wave.

Lolita entwined her fingers with Beckman's.

He saw Randall whisper in Reba's ear. She studied his face, then nodded. She cast her gaze around the guests, grabbed Randall's hand and raised them both aloft, like victorious boxers.

'We're engaged too!'

Only the slightest surprise and delay preceded another chorus of joy. The place descended into hugs and kisses.

'Anyone else?' Ginetta joked, sipping on newly-supplied champagne.

Laughter, ranging from polite to appreciative.

Then chatter broke out. For three seconds.

The door swung open.

Chapter 74

Voices ceased as if with a chainsaw.

Dixon walked in.

This is getting silly. Did we fall asleep in the mine and are still dreaming? There was definitely something in the air down there.

Buck leant his weight against the counter.

Dixon's gaze alighted on them all in turn. She had encouraging smiles for Lolita and Beckman—but what did they mask? Another agenda?

Beckman didn't know what to do. His mind blazed with hope and conspiracy, disbelief and expectation.

She locomoted—tall and slim as ever, casual in the businesslike way that only she could—towards Buck. All eyes swivelled to follow her.

'Hi.'

Well, that's a pretty safe opening gambit. He's in a good mood too. You may have picked a decent day to give it a shot—if that's why you're here.

A slight noise of the door being carefully closed. Beckman looked around. A plainly dressed guy of about forty, spectacles and sensible shoes, tucked into a space between the wide window and a nearby table. He clasped hands in front of his belt and watched.

Not sure bringing your new beau is a good plan, though, lady. Playing with fire on a happy day like this.

He tuned in to the words which were not being kept low and private enough.

'Hi,' Buck replied.

'You didn't do anything wrong—you know that? I said that.'

Buck nodded. 'I know. But you broke me. Your leaving broke me, and I almost broke a ton of other things. Friendships. This whole town. For you. I was doing it for you.' He ruffled his hair. 'It was dumb. Like, beyond crazy dumb. Love makes a man do crazy things.'

She moved closer. 'I had to go. No—I *thought* I had to go. The job was too much. The Foundation was too much. You *know* how important it is to me.'

'I thought I was more important, that's all. Or at least in the ballpark.' He wiped the counter, which didn't need wiping.

'The Foundation is… sorted now.' The glance towards Tyler was brief, but Beckman still saw through it.

'So you came back. Hoping I'd forgive you.'

'I wasn't happy anymore. Boss pulled me up for losing focus. Your friends came, told me… some truths.'

'And you gambled—like you did before—that switching locations would work out. Second time lucky?'

'Yeah,' she said earnestly, reaching a hand to him. 'Because everything else was there, right?'

'But it wasn't enough, right?' he replied pointedly.

'I have my resignation letter ready to mail… if Lolita will have me back.' She glanced over.

Lolita gave a thumbs up.

Don't look a gift horse in the mouth: (1) it'll make Buck happy, and (2) she'll be a hell of an asset to the business.

'It's that easy, huh?' Buck asked.

'I heard you and Lolita fell out. Guess that got mended? And you and I didn't have half as much as that to heal. Plus—we didn't fall out. I left.' She smiled. 'It was dumb. Like, beyond crazy dumb. Life makes a woman do crazy things.'

'I take you back—just like that?' He stood closer, inspected her face. 'And why will it work this time? How do I know you'll stay? That you're serious? That you and I trump everything—work, career, the charity? Why, Dixon?'

'You want to know I'm serious?' She turned and gave a faint nod towards the person who clearly wasn't her new boyfriend/fiancé/husband.

The man walked over to them.

'This is Father Aldo. He's licensed. I know this venue is licensed. We have witnesses. The ring—we can do later.' She pushed up to Buck's chest. 'I chose wrong before. I made a mistake. You have the heart of a lion. Of a prince. I know it loves. I'm pretty sure it can forgive. So, if it can—I choose Sunrise. I choose you.'

Beckman was pretty sure nobody was breathing. Chests were filled to bursting, ready for the outcome. Lolita grabbed his fingers and squeezed them so hard they might break.

Be smart, dude. Choose well.

And soon, before we all pass out.

Buck cupped Dixon's cheek. 'Happy ever after, huh?'

'That was the idea.'

'This is Sunrise. Not Hollywood. You don't get to break my heart, walk back in and expect forgiveness and gratitude wrapped up in a convenient wedding. It doesn't work like that.'

Oh, snap.

She took his hand away and stepped back. Her shoulders collapsed. 'I had to try.'

'You showed you're serious; I'll give you that.'

'As a heart attack.'

Buck darted a look at Lolita. 'Bad choice of words.'

Dixon put a hand to her head. 'Not doing very well, am I?'

'Breaking up is hard. Making up is harder.'

'Making up is *better*.'

'Except we never fell out. Like you said, there was nothing wrong. Not with us, only… perspective.' He brightened. 'And bringing… Aldo was a much smarter, much less risky, much more *romantic* thing than what I was trying to do to win you back.'

She cocked her head. 'So… if you were trying to win me back, what changed? Why the "No"?'

He took her hands. 'For a smart woman, you have blind spots. Imperfections.'

'Huge ones.'

'I said I wouldn't snap like a twig and marry you on the spot. I said I wouldn't heal in two minutes flat. But take you back? Absolutely. No question.' He looked at the Father. 'Not tonight, friend. But maybe soon, okay?'

He pulled Dixon to him and kissed her.

The ensuing collective exhale nearly tripped the seismograph. In Tucson.

As the hugs and relief danced around the room, Beckman became aware of a tapping noise and sought out the source.

He darted three paces to Lolita and pivoted her towards the window.

Her eyes came out on stalks.

My thoughts exactly.

'How the hell…?' she began.

'Darling?' Ginetta was quickly at their shoulder. 'Is that…?'

Lolita pulled a face he'd never seen. Ginetta displayed The Eyebrow (Care To Explain? version).

'I lied, mom,' Beckman blustered. 'I thought losing him would make us—me—seem… untrustworthy. With having the box—your box—and everything. Death was… not *im*plausible.'

'He flew away,' Ginetta stated.

'Kinda, mom.'

'Oh, hell,' came Tyler's voice. 'How'd that damn parrot find his way back?'

The Eyebrow disappeared, Ginetta's face creased into a smile, then a smirk. 'Seems it's hard to stay away from this town of ours.'

Chapter 75

It took a week for the tension to entirely leave Beckman's body. It all felt too neat—he was awaiting the bolt from the blue, the resurfacing of a monster, the wheels to come off.

They couldn't have come out on top—no consequences, no paybacks—this time, could they?

Who or what would mess with their lives this time? What would break the cycle of sales calls, meetings, coffee breaks, time with friends, hours in Our Buck's watching the world go by?

What would put a spoke in the wheel of marital harmony—cooking together, lounging together, lying together? Walking, talking, loving, laughing?

There had been something in that alien cavern, hadn't there? An invisible force that was even now, day by day, hour by hour, messing with their bodies and pushing them towards some physical and emotional precipice?

Consequences.

A good deed being punished.

Sunrise getting revenge for the near-miss to its existence.

He stood at the kitchen island, drinking coffee, fingers tapping nervously.

She should be back from the doctor by now. An all-clear is quick. Problems need talking out.

Being off-colour is not serious, though? An inexplicable out-of-sorts?

Hurry back with the explanation, honey.

Or ideally, a clean bill of health.

Because if the alien Whatever got you, it must have got Buck, got me…

The sound of a key in the front door.

He dashed to meet her, heart frozen in fear and anticipation.

She closed the door.

He tried to read her body, her face, her eyes.

There was no pallor, no weight of the world. Instead, there was… contentment?

'What?' he asked. 'What?'

She gently took his face in both hands and kissed him.

Her eyes danced with the light and wonder of a billion stars, a million neons.

'We're going to have someone to leave that box to.'

THE END

Chris Towndrow has been a writer since 1991, and Tow Away Zone was his most well-received book to date.

He began writing science fiction, inspired by Asimov, Iain M Banks, and numerous film and TV canons. After a brief spell creating screenplays across several genres, he branched out into playwriting and has had several productions professionally performed.

Tow Away Zone was originally conceived as a screenplay with a visual, black comedic, offbeat style, and this translated into a unique book that transcends genre.
Writing this "Sunrise" trilogy supercharged his passion for writing, and he is already looking to develop a new project in the arena of quirky black comedy.
In the meantime, he continues to write sci-fi adventures and is also broadening his repertoire of genres into historical fiction and contemporary drama.

Chris lives on the outskirts of London with his family and works as a video editor and producer.